D0409177

COURTSHIP & CURSES

COURTSHIP & CURSES

Marissa Doyle

Henry Holt and Company
NEW YORK

Henry Holt and Company, LLC
Publishers since 1866
175 Fifth Avenue
New York, New York 10010
macteenbooks.com

Library of Congress Cataloging-in-Publication Data
Doyle, Marissa.
Courtship and curses / Marissa Doyle. — 1st ed.
p.   cm.
Summary: In 1815, Lady Sophie Rosier's first London season is marred not only
by her physical and emotional scars, but also by magical attacks on her
father and other members of the British War Cabinet, and while
Sophie's magical powers are unreliable, she and her new best friend
Parthenope decide to investigate — despite the distraction of
Parthenope's handsome cousin.
ISBN 978-0-8050-9187-8 (hc)
[1. Witches — Fiction.   2. Magic — Fiction.   3. People with disabilities —
Fiction.   4. Self-acceptance — Fiction.   5. Aristocracy (Social class) —
Fiction.   6. Great Britain — History — 1800–1837 — Fiction.   7. Brussels
(Belgium) — History — Fiction.   8. Belgium — History — 1814–1830 —
Fiction.]   I. Title.
PZ7.D7758Cou 2012
[Fic] — dc23
2011031999

First Edition — 2012/Designed by April Ward
Printed in the United States of America

1   3   5   7   9   10   8   6   4   2

For my three sisters,
all of whose names start with R

Courtship & Curses

Chapter 1

London, March 1815

Aunt Isabel was, as usual, exasperated. "Molly, I don't know why I brought you shopping with us. While that color will do for a creeping plant on a blasted heath somewhere, it will not do for poor Sophie." She motioned away the bolt of yellowish green satin proffered by the dressmaker's assistant.

"Ha!" Aunt Molly tilted her head and squinted at the rejected fabric. "I thought it reminded me of something. It's just the color of toadflax leaves, y'know. But toadflax doesn't grow on heaths. It's a meadow and hedge-side plant."

"I was not knowing that toads had the flax," Madame Carswell observed. "Do they make linen from it too? English toads must be terribly clever." She turned her head slightly and winked at the fourth member of the party seated in Mrs. James's exclusive Bruton Street shop.

The young woman her aunt had called "poor Sophie"

caught the wink and smiled down at her lap. Now Aunt Isabel would say something about not having time to examine what grew in the hedgerows and then probably go on to say something about Aunt Molly's botanical obsession destroying her fashion sense.

"Well, *really*, Molly. Some of us are far too occupied with *worthwhile* pursuits to spend our days poking about hedgerows. And I must say, your doing so might account for the shocking state of your hair."

Ah, well. She'd been half right. Sophie smoothed the wrinkles out of the buttery-soft kidskin gloves in her lap and felt her smile fade. She'd been scrunching up her gloves again. But glove scrunching was the only way she could relieve her feelings, at least here. Shrieking into a pillow would have to wait until she was home, alone in her bedchamber.

Every one of these shopping trips had followed the same course, like the farces at Covent Garden: The shopgirls would end up red-faced with suppressed giggles while Papa's sisters quarreled over nothing. Or else Aunt Isabel would examine fabric and designs and shake her head, murmuring how they would just not do for Sophie, what with the poor girl's *limitations*. Either way, they'd leave the shop empty-handed and move on to the next one, where the same thing would happen. At this rate, she'd never have any gowns made in time for the season's round of parties and balls. If there were any, now that Napoléon was back on the throne in France and all of Europe in an uproar.

Maybe that would be for the best, said a hateful little voice in her head. *Cripples don't dance at balls. Even if they're the daughters of marquises with substantial fortunes.*

Thus the scrunched gloves. Sophie wished she could scrunch them small enough to stuff in her ears and drown that voice out.

Thank goodness Madame Carswell—Amélie, as she just yesterday asked Sophie to call her—had been staying with her and Papa and Aunt Molly for the last few days. Her company had made today's shopping trip with the aunts much less odious. If only Mama . . . but she couldn't think about Mama now. Her nose turned red when she got the least bit teary, and sharp-eyed Aunt Isabel would notice at once.

Sharp-eyed Aunt Isabel was examining a bolt of cherry pink silk held by the other of Mrs. James's assistants. Sophie leaned forward, entranced. The color was beautiful, warm and vibrant, but Aunt Isabel's bushy eyebrows had shot up most of the way to her hairline. "That shade, for *Sophie*?" Her voice dropped. "Haven't you eyes to see with?" she hissed at the assistant. "She would stand out like a sore thumb in a color like that! Gray or snuff brown is much more appropriate."

Sophie sat back. Of course. A color like that would draw attention to her . . . and to her infirmity. At least to her external one.

"*I* think it would be perfect for Sophie." Amélie examined it, head to one side. "See how it would bring up the lovely color in her cheeks. I have a length of sari silk just that shade. It is still in my box, I am thinking."

"My *dear* Mrs. Carswell," Aunt Isabel began. Sophie braced herself. When Aunt Isabel my-deared someone, it was because she felt the person thus addressed anything but dear. "While India is doubtless full of very interesting things, I fear they are not quite, ah, *suitable* here, and certainly not suitable for poor,

3

dear Sophie. I know you lived there many years, but you are in England now. Surely Mr. Carswell explained—"

"Oh, they don't make linen from it. Wrong sort of flax," Aunt Molly said in her botanical lecturer voice. "It's very good for chickens and keeps them from getting chicken gall, I am led to understand, so why it's not called chickenflax instead of toadflax is beyond me. Culpeper says it cures the dropsy and pimples, at least when used as a face wash. For the pimples, that is. I don't think a face wash will do much for dropsy. Do y'suppose chicken gall is the same as dropsy? Unless it's pimples, and how would you tell if chickens got pimples under all those feathers, that's what I'd like to know."

Aunt Isabel had begun to turn a color remarkably similar to the rejected silk. She opened her reticule, pulled out a tiny silver box, flipped open its hinged lid, and sniffed at it. "My head—you've no idea how I suffer. Molly, will you *please* stop prattling about plants for at least a few moments and attend to the matter at hand?"

Aunt Molly's brow wrinkled. "I was. You were just saying that satin was the same color as toadflax, and I—"

"Sophie." Amélie Carswell's soft, French-inflected voice insinuated itself under Aunt Molly's protest. "Come and look at the ribbons with me. They are very fine, I think." She rose—gracefully for such a small, plump person—and held out her arm.

Sophie stared up at her arm. True, she limped like a drunken sailor on shore leave, but that didn't mean she couldn't rise from her chair by herself and walk a few paces across the shop to—

But no. Mrs. Carswell—er, Amélie—wasn't the aunts. Her gesture was meant to be a friendly one. It wasn't always

easy not to jump to conclusions. Besides, she was tired, and Amélie's arm *would* be a welcome support. Let her heavy, ugly, dull brown cane stay where it was, looped over the back of her chair.

She struggled to her feet and took Amélie's arm. The flow of the aunts' bickering didn't cease as she and Amélie made their way to the display of ribbons and laces on the wall.

"You looked as though you had had enough of that." Amélie ended her sentence with an expressive lift of her eyebrows. "Your *tantes*—they mean well, I think, but they are so busy being themselves that it is difficult for them to pay much attention to you."

"Oh, they pay me plenty of attention. It's just . . ." Sophie fell silent. Aunt Isabel frequently reminded her that a cripple should always show the world a patient, forbearing face. "Papa says they've always been that way, even when they were small. They mean well, and I'm . . . used to it."

"But that doesn't mean you must like it, eh?" Amélie said, running her finger over a length of pale blue ribbon and glancing sideways at Sophie. "Tell me, do they often remind you that you cannot walk as others do?"

Sophie felt her chin rise defensively and hated herself for it. "Well, I cannot."

"But that does not mean it must rule your life. Will you tell me how it happened? Or were you born with it?"

Amélie's voice was gentle but matter-of-fact, and it defused Sophie's defensiveness far more effectively than pity would have. "No. It happened two years ago this summer, at Lanselling— that's my family's seat. There was influenza in the neighborhood, and I came down with it. I nearly died, but my mother

brought me through it. Then one morning I woke up and found I couldn't turn over in bed because my legs ached and wouldn't work. The doctors said I would never walk again, but Mama was determined to prove them wrong. She wrapped my legs in hot towels and stretched them and massaged them, but one still stayed weak and began to shrivel." That wasn't the whole story; Mama had done considerably more than wrap her legs when the doctors weren't present. But she couldn't tell Amélie—or anyone—about *that*. Nor about what else she'd lost after her illness.

"Then my—my little sister . . ." She paused to steady her voice. "My little sister Harriet came down with it as well. Mama was nearly frantic caring for her, but she couldn't save her. And then Mama fell ill too and . . . and died. I think it was exhausting herself nursing us, and then losing Harry." Sweet little Harry, with her gold curls and soft, round baby face, had been only five.

"She died of grief as well as sickness," Amélie said softly. "And your leg?"

"It mostly works, but it is shorter than my left leg, and the foot turns in oddly. It makes me walk with a most noticeable limp. It always will," she couldn't help adding bitterly. Two years ago, she'd been looking forward to her come-out just as any girl of her age and birth did. She'd longed for the London season, for sweeping through minuets and country dances at balls . . . and maybe, if she were allowed, dancing the scandalous, delightful new waltz. Mama had seen to it that she learned well, even hiring a dancing master to stay at Lanselling for a month each summer to teach her and neighboring girls when she was fourteen and fifteen. She still dreamed of what it felt like to dance.

Amélie touched her arm. "Yes, you always will limp. But you *can* walk. It is better than not walking, *n'est-ce pas?*"

"Not if you listen to the aunts. I sometimes think Aunt Isabel would prefer it if I were a complete invalid. Bringing a cripple out into society is rather trying, though she assures me that we ought to be able to find a younger son, maybe, or a half-pay officer who might be willing to overlook my deformity in light of my family and marriage portion." Sophie glanced over her shoulder back toward the aunts. Behind Aunt Molly one of the shop assistants was hiding her face in her handkerchief, her shoulders shaking with laughter. That meant they'd probably be leaving soon. She turned back to Amélie and saw that she was frowning ferociously, as if angry. The frown vanished as Sophie met her eyes.

"Never mind. I will tell you what we shall do, you and I," she said briskly. "We will nod and smile and let your aunt not buy that cherry silk, and then I will make a present of my sari fabric to you for a dress."

Sophie stifled the exclamation of pleasure that rose to her lips. "Oh, I couldn't possibly—"

"Ah, *ma chère*, you gave yourself away when you looked at it, and I shall not permit you to say no. You and your papa have been so kind that it is the least I can do. Besides, it is not a color I shall ever wear again." She glanced at the mourning ring on her hand.

Sophie reached out and covered it with her own. Drat it, she should stop being so selfish and remember that she wasn't the only unhappy person in London. "I'm so sorry Mr. Carswell . . . never reached home. Papa was looking forward to seeing him after all these years. He said they were very close at school."

"Ah, I too regret it." Amélie sighed. "And my Jean was so looking forward to coming home to England again. Over twenty years in India he stayed, all for my sake."

Sophie nodded. Papa had been so pleased when he received a letter from his old Harrow friend last autumn. John Carswell had been the younger son of an earl and had gone into the East India Company because of his lack of prospects in England. Papa had sometimes spoken of him regretfully, though Sophie had never been sure if that regret was due to missing his friend or wishing that he, too, had been a younger son able to adventure in India instead of being ninth Marquis of Lansell.

Mr. Carswell had evidently surprised everyone by marrying in India instead of returning to England on leave to woo and wed a bride . . . and surprised them further by marrying the daughter of a French military adviser to the ruler of one of the Indian princely states. The long years of war between England and France had made him decide to remain in India and not visit home, lest his wife be snubbed or worse by her English in-laws because of her nationality. But last summer he had written to Papa that he was coming at long last to see his home and old friends and in hopes of regaining his health, worn down by the climate.

Then, just two weeks ago, another letter arrived from Portsmouth bearing sad news. It was from Mrs. Carswell, reporting that Mr. Carswell had died from a bleeding ulcer shortly after

setting sail from India. It enclosed a brief, shakily penned note from Mr. Carswell himself, saying that he knew death was imminent and asking Papa to help his widow on her arrival in England. Papa had at once sent his secretary to find Mrs. Carswell at Portsmouth and to accompany her to her husband's ancestral home to bury his heart there, as he had wished. That sad task accomplished, Mrs. Carswell had come to London to thank Papa. They'd all been charmed by the small, plump, bright-eyed woman in her soft gray pelisse and black gloves and hat, who was devastated by the loss of her beloved "Jean" but obviously interested in London and in them. It hadn't been hard to convince her to stay with them for a few weeks while she decided what to do.

"Well, I'm glad you are here," Sophie said staunchly. "If it weren't for you, I'd—" She glanced at the aunts.

"You need not explain, Sophie. Lady Isabel has no daughters, no? So she cannot resist busying herself with her only niece's *entrée* to society . . . but she is not sure how to present a niece who is out of the ordinary. And Lady Mary—or should I say Molly, as you do? She is a dear, but if you have not leaves or roots or stems, she doesn't quite see you, I think. And as for you"—Amélie tilted her head to one side—"you are excited for the season yet fearful because of your legs that do not walk gracefully."

"How do you know all that?" Sophie blinked back sudden tears.

"It is not hard to know things if your eyes are open and you use them. Remember that, Sophie. Your eyes are your best tool." She made a small humming sound under her breath as she fingered the ribbons. "How old are you, *ma petite*?"

"Eighteen. I might have come out last year, but I was not strong enough. And we—we did not have the heart for it." Not that she was sure Papa did, even now. After Mama had died, he had withdrawn into his work on the war like a hermit crab crawling inside a discarded shell. With Emperor Napoléon Bonaparte back in power, would he ever emerge?

"Eh, not a child at all. Then *les tantes* should not treat you as one. Come, let us choose the dresses you would like. No, do not look back. They are quite happy as they are, so we shall not disturb them." Amélie took her arm and led her across the shop, beckoning to Mrs. James, who hovered behind the aunts, looking anxious. "I shall give you my sari length. That would be lovely for a dinner dress, no? Ah, Madame James, as you see, the other ladies are busy, so we shall choose some pretty dresses for my friend here. What will the *jeunes filles* be wearing at your Almack's this spring?"

The dressmaker looked relieved that a sale seemed much more imminent. "Yes, madam." She studied Sophie a moment, then nodded. "Clear, true colors. White rather than ivory, too, for collars—high ruffs at the neck will be much seen again this year. Let me see. . . ."

In a few moments, the counter was piled with lengths of muslin and poplin and crepe. Amélie regarded them with satisfaction. "Now we are getting somewhere. If you will be so kind as to bring a chair for my friend here . . . yes, that will do." She unrolled a bolt of apple green sarcenet to hold up next to Sophie's face. "A walking dress in this, I think, with the skirt white and a spencer to match, and a snip of fabric we may take to the milliner." She handed the bolt to Mrs. James and selected another.

"You are so kind," Sophie said to her when a happy Mrs. James scuttled back into her storeroom for more fabric.

Amélie's cupid-bow mouth curved into a smile. "But it is not all kindness. By helping you, I help myself. We take each other's minds off our sadnesses for a little while, yes?"

"Oh, not a little while!" Sophie made up her mind to broach the idea that had been simmering in the back of her mind. "Won't you stay with us for at least part of the season? If you're going to direct my wardrobe, you must stay and see me wear it."

"But your family—your papa—he will not wish to keep a stranger at his table so long—"

"You are not a stranger," Sophie interrupted her. "You're his dear friend's wife . . . and you're my friend. If . . . if it would not be too disagreeable, I would very much like you to stay with me."

Amélie smiled again. Some of the melancholy had faded from her eyes. "Thank you, *chère* Sophie. When you say it thus, then I must say yes, if your good papa agrees."

The bell on the door jangled, announcing the arrival of another customer. Aunt Isabel and Molly ceased quarreling as the newcomer paused on the threshold to survey the room, then swooped toward them like a large predatory bird oddly attired in tropical plumage. "Lady Isabel! Lady Mary! What a delightful surprise!" The woman nearly skidded to a halt beside the aunts and rested a gloved hand on her ample breast, as if transported by joy.

Aunt Molly squinted at the woman in her shortsighted way and looked dubious. Aunt Isabel did too, but nodded pleasantly enough. "Umm . . . oh, yes. Lady Lumley—it *is* still Lady Lumley, isn't it? How do you do?"

The woman curtsied. She looked about the aunts' age, but her bonnet was in a much more youthful style than theirs. "Very well, thank you, and yes, still Lady Lumley. I've yet to meet anyone who might make me forget my dear Sir William, rest his soul. Is it not wonderful that spring is finally here? I have been quite pining to see old friends again. Are you here for the season?" Lady Lumley's tone remained effusive, but there was a questioning gleam in her eye.

Aunt Isabel bowed slightly in her chair. "We are. My niece Sophronia is making her come-out this year, and—"

Sophie winced, just as she always did when anyone used her full name.

"Your niece? Not"—Lady Lumley blinked rapidly—"not dear Lord Lansell's daughter? But I thought . . ." She leaned toward Aunt Isabel and muttered behind her hand—not that it muffled her words any. "Well, I had heard that she was feeble-minded and a hunchback. In fact, just the other day someone mentioned—"

Aunt Isabel drew herself up. "You heard wrong," she said coldly, and beckoned to Sophie. "Lady Lumley, my niece Lady Sophronia Rosier. Sophie, Lady Lumley."

"Good day, Lady Lumley." Sophie rose as gracefully as she could and curtsied. To her surprise, her voice was calm, unshaken by the anger that this woman's thoughtless babbling had roused. How had such a rumor started? And would she hear it at every event she attended this season? *How pleasant to meet you, Lady Sophie! Why, you hardly look half-witted at all!*

Lady Lumley examined her closely. "Oh . . . er . . . you're very like your mother, though I'm sure I can see your dear papa in you as well. Such a handsome man. . . . It will be a pleasure to see him—er, see you in society this year." Lady Lumley looked past Sophie to Amélie, who still stood at the counter piled with their chosen fabrics. "Another relation? How charming that all your aunts—"

"Oh, Madame Carswell is not a relation," Sophie corrected her.

Lady Lumley's smile dimmed. "Isn't she?"

"She is a dear friend of the family. In fact, she will be staying with Papa—er, my father and me for some weeks as the season begins. May I present her?"

Lady Lumley now looked distinctly dismayed. "Oh . . . ah, how-de-do." She barely bobbed her head in Amélie's direction, then turned back to Aunt Isabel, her smile widening. "I shall call soon. It will be delightful to resume our acquaintance. Are you both staying at Lansell House?"

"I am at my own home, thank you," Aunt Isabel replied, slightly testily. "Mary and Sophie are, of course, with my brother."

"Charming! He is quite the hero, is he not, with all the work he has done in the War Office defeating the wicked French? I must come and lay a laurel at his feet." Lady Lumley positively simpered—Sophie had read the word in a novel once without quite being able to picture the action, but now she could. Clearly. She curtsied again and went back to the counter and Amélie.

"That vulture," she whispered. "Not all the French are wicked just because of Napoléon! And the only reason she wants to call is so she can make eyes at Papa."

"Not everyone has the understanding to make the distinction between the emperor and his empire," Amélie said mildly. "And yes, I expect that is the reason for her wish to call. It is not surprising that the unmarried ladies will cluster round him like bees to the flower, hoping that they may catch him."

"Catch him! But . . ." Sophie fell silent. Amélie was right. Mama was gone, and Papa was a widower. What else should she expect?

"Sophie." Amélie patted her hand. "Your papa is a grown man and can take care of himself. You should be thinking instead about the young men who will be clustering around you after they see you in these dresses we have chosen."

What young men? Hadn't Amélie heard what the loathsome Lumley woman had just said? Hunchbacked . . . feeble-minded. . . . The hunchbacked part would be easily disproved; hopefully the feeble-minded part would as well. But there was no denying that she limped and resorted to using a cane when tired or forced to remain on her feet for long. Why would any young man want to woo such a young woman, apart from those drawn by the fact that she was a marquis's daughter with £35,000 to bring to her prospective husband?

And why would *she* want anyone who wanted her for those reasons?

"Well, *ma chère*." Amélie was putting her gloves back on. "Your *tantes* seem to be at loose ends, and we should—how does the expression go?—we should poke while the iron is hot. Go to them and suggest they order the carriage, and I shall speak with good Madame James here about these dresses."

"*Strike* while it's hot, I think you mean, but . . ." Sophie swallowed and watched Lady Lumley finally relinquish Aunt Isabel and turn to the shop assistant waiting patiently by her side. "But I'm not sure it's worth the trouble."

Amélie stopped tugging her glove over her wrist and looked

at her. "It is worth the trouble because I say it is. And you will see that I am right."

Sophie opened her mouth to disagree, then instead bent—Amélie was shorter than she—and kissed her cheek. "Yes, Amélie. Thank you."

"Ah." Amélie's eyes got that misty look again. "Go, and I shall strike that iron."

Sophie did her best to keep the aunts distracted as they collected gloves and made sure their pelisses were properly fastened, and she watched Lady Lumley glower at Amélie during the consultation with Mrs. James. As their footman opened the shop's door and Mrs. James came to bow them out to their carriage, Amélie took Sophie's arm. "We have stricken the iron. Your first fitting is tomorrow," she murmured.

"But how will we get away?"

Amélie pursed her lips. "Leave that to me, *ma chère.*"

"Oh, are you leaving?" Lady Lumley's penetrating voice followed after them. "Why, I am as well. Dear Lady Isabel, I hope I can prevail upon you to give me a place in your carriage as I fear it is coming on rain, which always gives me the headache. Surely your friend won't mind riding with the coachman just this once—"

Sophie turned. Lady Lumley was hurrying toward them past the shop's counter, her skirt fluttering in the breeze of her haste, her eyes narrow with determination above her wide smile. Loathsome indeed—and how *dare* she insult Amélie like that?

Before she could stop herself or even think, she inhaled deeply, drawing in her concentration with her breath, and focused on the edge of the wooden counter. The polished oak

split into splintery fingers and caught at the back of Lady Lumley's dress. A thin but satisfying ripping sound was heard, followed by an even more satisfying shriek from Lady Lumley.

Good heavens, she'd *done* it! She'd actually done it!

Aunt Isabel was already through the door, but Aunt Molly paused and looked over her shoulder. "Did you say something, Lady Lumley?"

The Loathsome Lumley had come to a halt, both hands behind her back. "Uhh-h-hhh . . . no . . . that is, yes, I . . . g-good day to you, Lady Mary. It was m-most pleasant to see you."

"Oh. Good day." For a moment, Aunt Molly looked as if she were going to return to shake hands. Sophie pressed her lips together, trying not to giggle: If Aunt Molly did, Lady Lumley would have to let go of her skirt, now torn down her backside. But Aunt Molly just bobbed her head and hurried after Aunt Isabel. Sophie nodded graciously at Lady Lumley and, still holding Amélie's arm, followed Aunt Molly through the door.

"Most singular, that Lumley woman," Aunt Molly said when they were safely ensconced in Papa's carriage. "Where do we know her from?"

"We were at Mrs. Harmon's school with her that year—I think it was '87. Mousy little thing then, always watching. Her father was a solicitor who did well with his investments, else she never would have gotten in. Mrs. Harmon was usually most particular about the social station of her students, but money often made up for breeding." Aunt Isabel sat ramrod straight as usual.

"She appeared more like the cat now than the mouse," Amélie observed, looking at Sophie.

"Except for her squeak," Sophie said under her breath. But her glee had faded. Why had she done that, right in front of the entire shop?

Maybe because she hadn't expected it would work.

Two years ago, she'd lost something besides Mama and the ability to walk freely. She'd also lost her magic.

She'd been very small when the magic lessons started. Between four and half-past five every afternoon, Mama had locked her sitting room door lest a footman wander in with more coal for the fire, and they had practiced together—the easier things like moving spells (her collection of Chinese snuffboxes dancing a precise minuet in midair) to more complicated changing spells (turning Mama's dozing Abyssinian cat from golden brown to purple to green) and spells harder still, like the windows Mama could cut in the air that let them look onto Polynesian islands and Icelandic volcanoes and herds of American bison on endless grassy plains.

Mama had told Sophie that she had been so thankful to have at least one daughter who also possessed her powers. Not that boys could not as well, but it was much less common; Sophie's younger brothers, Francis and Wrenford, had never shown the least magical aptitude. Then Harriet—Harry—had been born, the little sister she'd always wanted. She and Mama had been so happy when Harry had frightened her nursemaid into a faint by making the animals in her wooden Noah's ark march up the gangplank two by two—well, not happy about frightening the poor girl—and had planned how they would teach her together.

But Mama and Harry were gone, and so was Sophie's magic—vanished, as if she'd never had it. For the first year, there hadn't been a glimmer of it, and all her concentration and will couldn't move as much as a dead leaf. Life had been very black—at least, what she could remember of it. There had been no one she could ask about it, no one to explain why this had happened to her. Had her illness maimed her mind and spirit, just as it had maimed her body?

Over the last several months, though, she'd seen hints that perhaps she hadn't lost all of it. Very occasionally she would point at a dropped pencil and it would drift up into her hand just as it had before. It could happen after fifty tries or after one; there seemed to be no pattern or indication that practice was helping her regain her power.

So perhaps Lady Lumley was right after all. Maybe she was feeble-minded. Maybe she had lost more than just her magic—maybe she'd lost that spark that made her *her*. Some days she couldn't bring herself to care about anything . . . and on the days she did, someone like Aunt Isabel or Lady Lumley would happen along to remind her of what she was now.

Sophie sighed and stared out the carriage window at the passing London street. For years she'd looked forward to coming to London for her first season. Now that she was here—now that *it* was here—she understood that getting through it was going to be the hardest thing she'd ever done.

Chapter

2

Much to her surprise, Sophie had her fitting the following day and on several others, accompanied only by Amélie. When she asked Amélie how she'd managed to persuade Aunt Isabel to give up the shopping expeditions, Amélie shook her head.

"Do you need to know the 'how,' *ma chère* Sophie? We discussed it, and I was able to make her see that it was an unnecessary burden on her time that I could take instead."

Sophie wasn't quite sure she believed that, but she could well believe that Amélie could face even Aunt Isabel down. So she had the apple green sarcenet walking dress as well as four others in gray and rose and fawn and blue. She had the cherry pink dinner dress made from Amélie's sari fabric, with its elegant gold embroidery about the hem, and three others in pale pink and white and blue trimmed with lace flounces and roses and forget-me-nots formed of ribbon. Her new riding habit in deep sapphire blue, looking dashingly military, would be ready next week, along with three carriage dresses, two opera dresses, four promenade dresses, and four morning dresses suitable for shopping or receiving calls.

But the ball dresses! They made her ache with both longing and sadness. Amélie had insisted she have them, even when she protested that a cripple would hardly be attending balls.

"Are you so sure? I think it will be expected that you still must attend them and the Almack's *assemblées*, even if you do not choose to dance . . . and *eh, bien,* who knows that someday you won't?" she said.

"And call attention to myself quite spectacularly by falling on my face? No, thank you."

"Ah, but a partner who cared about you would never permit you to fall."

"What makes you think I shall ever find such a partner?" Sophie asked, rather tartly.

"What makes you think you shall not?" Amélie shrugged. "Whatever you say, *petite.*"

Of course, after that it seemed inevitable that their first invitation of the season was to a ball.

Sophie sat next to her father in the carriage, facing Aunt Molly and Amélie. Aunt Molly returned her regard smugly, Amélie less so.

Sophie's dress was . . . well, it was perfection. Amélie had chosen the pale gold crepe, with its delicately fluttering skirt and modestly rounded neckline. The color brought up gold highlights in her boring brown hair—

Her hair. Sophie closed her eyes and tried not to think about her hair.

Aunt Molly and her ancient maid, Bunty, had cornered Sophie after Amélie left to be dressed by her little Indian servant, Nalini, who had accompanied her from India and seemed to be perpetually round-eyed and shivering.

"Since you've no maid here yet"—Sophie's maid had not yet arrived from Lanselling due to a sprained knee—"we're here to help," Aunt Molly proclaimed, closing Sophie's bedroom door and leaning against it, concealing something behind her back. "You know what a genius my Bunty is with hair. Must come of all the pruning and training she does on the shrubbery walk at home."

Sophie, seated at her dressing table, involuntarily put protective hands to her head. Did she *look* like a shrub? Aunt Molly was the one who looked shrubby. She still wore her hair in the fashion of her youth in the 1790s, cut short and spiky in the style that had come from Revolutionary France called *la mode Titus*. "Thank you so much, Aunt. I know Bunty's a genius, but really, I'm nearly done."

"Nonsense! You young girls wear your hair so primly these days." Aunt Molly left the door and came to stand behind Sophie, squinting at her in the mirror over the dressing table. "None of the flair we had, eh, Bunty?"

Bunty made a grunting noise that sounded like assent. Sophie glanced at a bulge in her apron pocket that looked suspiciously like pruning shears. Oh, dear. "I know, Aunt, but really—I'm fine."

Aunt Molly's shoulders drooped. "Of course you are. I just thought . . . your mother should be here to help you get ready

for your first ball, but since she's not . . . I know I'm a poor second best, but . . ."

"Oh, Aunt." Sophie twisted on the stool to look at her. Aunt Molly was a plant-obsessed old maid who rarely stirred from the country—Mama had hinted that she had been Crossed in Love in her youth—but she *was* her aunt. "That's so sweet of you. But . . . um . . . no trimming, if you don't mind too frightfully much."

Aunt Molly beamed at her. "Gracious, there's no time for that. We can take care of it tomorrow. Now, let's see. We could manage cadogan ringlets, couldn't we, Bunty? There's nothing prettier than that, I think. And just look what I made for you to wear with 'em!" She whipped out the hand that was still behind her back and flourished something at Sophie. It was a very large wreath of yellow roses twined with ivy. "I thought it would go with your dress—y'know, the yellow and the gold."

Sophie hadn't dared to look herself full in the mirror when they'd finished, but the long curls of hair hanging over her shoulders were unavoidably in her view and would have been perfectly fashionable if this were twenty years ago. They contrasted almost ridiculously with her lovely, modish gown, and she didn't even want to think about what the wreath might look like, plopped atop her head so that she was sure she looked like a crazed Greek nymph. Flowers were a fashionable adornment for hair right now, but this looked more like the wreath worn by the winning horse at Goodwood.

She'd managed to scoop a handful of hairpins into her reticule before going out to the carriage. Now if she could only find the opportunity to slip away from Aunt Molly, she could disappear into the room set aside for ladies as soon as they arrived at Lady Whiston's house, deposit the wreath in a drawer somewhere, and pin the long curls into something less old-fashioned. Maybe Aunt's attention could be diverted to a potted palm. Yes, that might work.

"Your hair, Sophie," Amélie ventured after a few moments as they clattered around the square. "It is quite . . . how do you say it . . . ?"

Sophie could not meet her eyes. "Aunt Molly's Bunty kindly did it for me," she said. *Perpetrated* was perhaps a better word, but why hurt Aunt Molly's feelings now? A slight ache settled itself low on her forehead, as if her head were independently protesting the treatment it had received.

"Brings back memories, don't it?" Aunt Molly said, wiggling in her seat like a proprietorial puppy. "That's just how I wore my hair when I came out. Isn't she darling, Gil?"

"Hmm?" Lord Lansell turned away from the window and glanced at his sister. Light from one of the new gas streetlamps deepened the shadows etched by the lines in his face. There were a lot more of them than there used to be. "What was that?"

"I said, isn't Sophie adorable?"

Sophie watched her father try to force his attention from wherever it lived these days back to the present. He'd been buried in his work at the ministry now that Napoléon was back and further war looked inevitable. She knew how important his work was, how valued he was by both Lord Liverpool, the prime minister, and Lord Palmerston, the head of the War Office. Would he be able to unbury himself once the war was over . . . if it ever ended? Or would he find somewhere new to hide from Mama's memory?

"Oh. Yes, quite. Is that the style for ladies now? I can't keep up with them anymore, I confess," he said, trying to sound jovial.

Amélie coughed delicately. "Indeed, monsieur, one hears that in London the styles change sometimes over the course of an evening. Sophie may find it necessary to redo her hair at least twice tonight. It is fortunate that I brought a comb just in case."

Sophie met her eyes. Amélie's expression hadn't changed, but it didn't need to. Dear, *dear* Amélie.

They arrived at the Whistons' house shortly thereafter. Lady Whiston had been caught up in the craze for Egyptian antiquities that had followed Napoléon's conquests there, and her London house showed it: The classical Greek columns lining her entrance hall had been remodeled with plaster and paint into lotus-topped Egyptian ones.

Aunt Molly squinted up at them as they finished being welcomed by Lord and Lady Whiston. "Wrong number of petals for a lotus," she muttered.

"It's just a decoration, Molly," Papa replied patiently.

"Hmmph. That's no excuse."

"Perhaps it is a different species from what you know," Amélie suggested.

"Oh, I hadn't thought of that! Maybe I ought to have another look." Aunt Molly started to veer back toward the entrance hall.

"Later, my dear." Papa took her arm and guided her toward the grand staircase that led to the ballroom.

Sophie gazed up at the tall bank of stairs with dismay. She knew that ballrooms were generally on an upper floor—*knew*

it, as their ballroom at home was. So why had she made the idiotic decision to leave her cane at home tonight? Vanity, of course . . . but having to cling to the banister all the way up the stairs would look even less attractive. What an entrance to make to her first event of the season.

"Sophie." Amélie stood next to her. When Sophie looked at her, she held out her arm. "Will you go up with me? I dislike to go alone to a room full of strangers."

"Oh, Amélie . . . I was an idiot," Sophie whispered. "I should have brought my cane, but who brings a cane to a ball? And mine's so ugly—"

"Sssh. It is not important now. Besides"—her voice dropped—"we can look out for Lady Whiston's boudoir, in case the fashion for hair changes in the next few minutes. I have a presentiment it may already have."

The Whistons' ballroom was devoid of lotuses, adorned instead with botany-free copies of Greek and Roman statuary (apart from a stylized laurel wreath on an Apollo's head). They found seats under a bust of Zeus set on a very tall pedestal.

Aunt Molly plumped down onto one of the delicate chairs and started fanning herself violently. "Shockingly hot in here with all these people. I'd forgotten what balls were like. Don't stand there, Gil—you're blocking the air." She closed her fan and thwacked Papa's backside with it.

"Sorry, Molly." He stepped to the side, under Zeus.

Sophie chose a chair on the opposite side of the statue from Aunt Molly and slid it as far back against the wall as it would go. Once everyone's attention was occupied, perhaps she could at least take off the wreath and hide it under her chair. Or else she could do a quick transference spell and relocate it . . . except that any spell she tried probably wouldn't work, or would go awry and plop her wreath on top of the lobster patties in the supper room.

But this was an emergency. If she didn't do something about her hair soon, she'd shrivel up and die of embarrassment. She leaned close to Zeus, slightly behind Papa, who was standing in front of the statue's plinth, then bent over as if to examine one of her slippers and yanked the wreath off her head and under her chair in one motion. There! Now if only her head would stop hurting and she and Amélie could escape and fix her hair, then she could relax and at least enjoy watching the crowds at her first party of the season—

A flourish of music made her look up. A minuet was commencing its graceful ordered steps, and she watched the dancers keenly. Hmm, she could maybe consider dancing that if the orchestra could be convinced to play a little more slowly, but the turns could prove to be tricky if she used a cane, which she'd have to.

"Your dress is among the prettiest," Amélie murmured, sitting down next to her. "Did I not tell you it would be so? Over there—that young man has been gazing at you for the last several minutes."

Sophie sat up straight, very quickly. A young man? Looking at *her*? "Where? Which one?"

"There—*doucement*, Sophie, do not turn so sharply in your seat—that young man with the dark hair, not too far away. See?"

Sophie tried not to stare too conspicuously, but it wasn't easy. "I can't . . . oh—is he wearing a dark blue coat?"

"I think so. He looks very sincere, I think, as well as

handsome. Do you know who he is? No? We must find out. And see how those young women over there—to your right, by the statue of Venus—are looking at you."

"They're whispering behind their fans," Sophie muttered back. "It's probably my hair they're discussing, not my dress. I managed to—er, remove the wreath, but can't we slip away now and fix—"

"Lansell!" A burly, graying man in a maroon coat and limp cravat strode up and bowed to Papa. "A surprise to see you here, sir!"

"Sir William." Papa bowed as well.

"So they let you out of Whitehall occasionally, do they?" Sir William laughed and elbowed him. "A man's got to get a breath of air occasionally, I suppose . . . though I wouldn't take it amiss if old Boney stopped breathing. *À la lanterne*, wasn't that what the frogs used to say during their filthy Revolution? Hang him from the next lamppost! So when do we go to war?"

Sophie felt Amélie wince at the man's mangled pronunciation of the French phrase.

"That would not be my decision," Papa said. "My task is to ensure that we *can* go to war, if the government and Allies decide—"

"Allies, my foot! It'll be us who'll pull their chestnuts out of the fire once again, mark my words! I don't know why someone didn't do something about Boney back on Elba. A pillow over his face in the middle of the night would have done the trick in about two minutes—"

Papa bowed. "Quite possibly, but just now it is only two minutes before the ladies have my head for talking politics in a ballroom." He turned slightly and held out his hand. "May I present Sir William Branstead? Sir William, my sister Lady Mary Rosier, my daughter Lady Sophie, and our friend Madame Carswell, just arrived from India."

Perhaps Papa had hoped the reference to India would distract Sir William, but something else caught his attention first. *"Madame* Carswell?" he asked, almost accusingly.

"My husband was English, Sir William, but I myself am of French birth," Amélie replied politely.

"Hmmph." Sir William's eyes narrowed. "Not many Englishmen I know of go about marrying Frenchies. At least not loyal ones."

Sophie gasped aloud before she could stop herself. Amélie's expression did not change, but her shoulders stiffened.

"John Carswell was my best friend when we were boys," Papa said. His tone remained light and pleasant, but the temperature around him seemed to have plummeted. "And I am honored to have his widow as a guest in my home. I would also be most honored if she would give me this next dance. Madame?" He gestured to the center of the room where lines were forming for a country dance, bowed, and held his hand out to her.

Amélie hesitated. Sophie knew that she'd had no intention of dancing and had not even planned on attending any balls because of her recent bereavement—one simply did *not* dance in black gloves. Still, it was the perfect dismissal for this horrid man—Papa was making it clear he preferred dancing with Amélie to continuing the conversation.

Sir William knew it too; he flushed, and his bushy gray eyebrows lowered and bunched like aggressive caterpillars. He bowed shortly and turned away without another word.

Sophie quickly unbuttoned the tiny buttons at her wrist and

yanked off her gloves. "Wear mine," she said, handing them to Amélie. "They're not perfect, but they'll do."

Amélie's stiffly held shoulders relaxed. "Sophie, *ma petite*—"

"I don't need them while I sit here. Please?"

Amélie hesitated a moment longer, then without another word stripped off her black gloves and slipped Sophie's on. They were snug and too long, but would do for one dance. As Papa led her out to the lines, she glanced back at Sophie. Her eyes were suspiciously bright.

"There you are!" Aunt Isabel loomed out of the crowd like a warship emerging from the fog. She surveyed Sophie's dress keenly and said, "Hmmph." Sophie knew it was because she couldn't find anything to criticize about it and smiled to herself.

Deprived of that, Aunt Isabel turned to Aunt Molly. "Where is my brother?" she demanded.

"He's dancing with Madame Carswell. Isn't that lovely?" Aunt Molly replied cheerily. "I don't think he's danced since—"

"But she's in mourning!" Aunt Isabel looked happily scandalized and settled in the chair next to Aunt Molly to wait, no doubt, to deliver a lecture when the set was over. Sophie sighed and sat back to watch the dancing. Papa moved awkwardly, as if he had forgotten how to dance, but Amélie glided with smooth and lively grace through the figures, nodding encouragement to Papa whenever he hesitated. Look, he was actually smiling down at her now as he took her hand to lead her up the center of the rows of dancers. Maybe that dreadful Sir William had done them all a favor by being so unpleasant.

She let her gaze wander the ballroom. Where was that young man whom Amélie said had been watching her? She hadn't been able to catch more than a fleeting glimpse of him, enough to see that he had dark, almost black hair above a high forehead and very dark brows that appeared even darker above startlingly light eyes—blue, probably, though it would be, um, interesting to get another look and confirm the impression. But annoyingly, he was no longer there. Had he been looking at her, really? Or was he just an art enthusiast admiring the ballroom's statuary? He couldn't have been admiring her—at least, not with her hair in its present state. As soon as Amélie and Papa came back, they *had* to escape and find the ladies' withdrawing room—

"What lovely girl?" drawled a voice to her right. "There? Oh, that's Lansell's daughter, Lady Susan . . . no, Sophie. Just out, they say. Always helpful to get an early look at the year's crop of girls, don't you think?"

Sophie sat up and tried to look in the direction of the voice without turning her head, but another statue on a plinth hid her view. Another voice, much quieter, said something she couldn't hear. The drawling voice chuckled.

"Unexpected, en't it? I'd heard she was a sickly little scrap that drooled, but it looks like she's quite a taking chit, even with the outlandish hair. Of course, with the marriage portion she's sure to have, even a humpbacked simpleton would be worth a go, eh? I might cast a lure or two myself and see if the tasty little fish bites. Shame to let all that brass go to waste, and I'm sure she'd be grateful. I say, I'm dry as a desert. Care to find something to drink in this crush? No? Well, excuse me, then—"

Sophie was not sure how she did it, but she calmly and unhurriedly opened her fan and waved it gently in front of her face, hoping to conceal the angry flush and tears that the overheard words had raised. What horrible things to say about anyone! If she ever heard that voice again, she'd—she'd do something nasty to him. In the meanwhile, all she wanted to do was leave, or at least go up to Lady Whiston's room to do her hair. Or just hide.

Two long, final chords from the orchestra announced that the opportunity might occur soon. The dancers made their reverences to each other, bowing and curtsying, and the lines dissolved as the gentlemen escorted the ladies back to their seats. Papa was still smiling down at Amélie as he led her by the hand, weaving past other couples. Sophie noticed women casting speculative glances at them and remembered Lady Lumley. In another five minutes, they'd probably be inundated by ladies stopping to chat and bat their eyelashes at Papa. Yes, look— one was stopping him now, just a few paces away from where she sat. She'd never make it to Lady Whiston's room at this rate.

"Lord Lansell! What a delightful surprise!" the woman said, gazing up at him through her lashes as she dropped him a slight, graceful curtsy.

She was accompanied by two men, the taller of whom greeted Papa enthusiastically. Sophie tensed, wondering if this would be another Sir William, but his cordial tone was much more sincere. "A pleasure to see you outside of Whitehall, sir! You're just the man I was hoping to see tonight. May I present the Comte de Carmouche-Ponthieux? He's on a mission from Ghent," he added in a lower tone.

Sophie knew that the rightful king of France, Louis XVIII, had fled France when Napoléon returned and had settled in Ghent, just over the Belgian border . . . close enough to hurry back to England if necessary, where he'd lived in gloomy splendor all through the years of the Directoire and Empire. This comte, who must be working for him, was a compact, handsome man with a thick gray streak in his dark hair and soft, rather sad eyes.

As he moved forward gracefully to return Papa's bow, Sophie heard a clatter, and Aunt Molly gasped, "Auguste!" She turned and saw that Aunt Molly had jumped up from her chair, knocking it over in her haste, and was staring at the Comte de Carmouche-Ponthieux.

He turned too, and the blood drained from his face. "Marie!" he whispered, staring. *"Mon Dieu, Marie, est-ce vous?"*

"Yes!" she cried, holding her hands out to him. "Oh, Auguste, it's your *petite* Marie! I can't believe . . ." She trailed off, her mouth working and tears starting up in her blue eyes.

He stepped forward and took her hands, gazing down at her raptly. *"Mon ange,"* he said softly. "I thought I would go to my grave without seeing your face again. Have I died without knowing it, then, and gone to heaven?"

Sophie goggled at them as they stood with clasped hands, staring at each other. Good heavens, was he talking to *her* aunt Molly? Who was this comte, and how did he know her . . . unless . . . could this be the lost love of Aunt Molly's youth, the reason she'd remained an old maid?

Aunt Isabel had stood up too. "Who is this, Mary? What is going on?"

The tall man raised an eyebrow. "I think the comte is known to some of you, then, Lansell?"

Papa smiled, but his eyes were troubled. "I think so, Palmerston. Unless I'm wrong, I'd guess it's been more than twenty years, though."

Ah. So this was Lord Palmerston, the Secretary at War and Papa's superior at the War Office. Sophie spared him a quick glance, but she was more interested in Aunt Molly and her comte. Over twenty years—so this *must* be Aunt Molly's lost love. What had happened to separate them?

The comte lifted one of Aunt Molly's hands and kissed it, then turned to Papa and bowed. "You must forgive me, sir . . . the name Lansell, I did not remember it—only Rosier. We met once or twice, I recall, but you were not yet the marquis." He looked back at Aunt Molly, and a soft, incredulous smile touched his mouth. "It is a miracle, is it not? You have not changed a bit. I would know you anywhere, my Marie." Then he straightened, and a somber look crossed his face. "But I should not call you so. Surely you are a duchess now, or at least a countess, with a family and—"

"No, Auguste. I'm still just Mary Rosier," Aunt Molly said. A tear slipped down her cheek. "I was sure that you were dead," she whispered.

"I nearly was, *petite*—more than once. But God spared me. Now I know why." He smiled at her, then turned back to his companions. "Milady West—Lord Palmerston—Lord Lansell— I would ask your indulgence for a few minutes. This is a thing extraordinary—" He offered Aunt Molly his arm and drew her a few feet away from them.

"Upon my word!" Aunt Isabel said, staring after them. "Gilbert, do you know who that is? Are you just going to stand there and let them *talk*?"

Papa raised an eyebrow. "What would you like me to do, Isabel?" He turned away without waiting for an answer. "Lady West, it is a pleasure to see you. May I present my daughter,

Sophie, and our friend Madame Carswell? Sophie is making her come-out this year."

Sophie rose to her feet—not easy to do gracefully without her cane—and curtsied. As she did, a soft, grating sound from nearby startled her. Zeus's heavy marble pillar seemed to tremble, then tip away from the wall . . . and straight toward where Papa stood with Amélie and Lord Palmerston.

Chapter 3

Time seemed to slow to a horrible crawl as Zeus teetered, then tumbled through the air.

"Papa!" Sophie shrieked, or tried to—but her voice would only come out in a whisper. What could she do? A shielding spell would protect him . . . but a transference spell would cast the statue aside completely, if only she could get the words out in time.

Then a voice called, "Sir!"—a male one, she thought—and the urgency in it seemed to free her own frozen voice.

"*Transfe*—" she shouted and launched herself forward.

Or tried to. But her right leg would not hold her, and she fell heavily to the floor, her spell cut off midword.

As she fell, she saw a dark-haired man appear from nowhere and shove Papa and Amélie to the side, out of Zeus's path. It was the beautiful young man in the blue coat who had been watching her earlier—she was sure of it.

His momentum carried him toward her, and she saw his eyes widen in surprise just before he tripped over one of her sprawled limbs. A dull, booming *THUD!* punctuated his fall as Zeus struck the floor as well.

"Uhhf!" Sophie gasped, and tried to push herself up. Gracious, were her limbs showing? Could everyone see her twisted right leg? Oh, please, anything but that!

"Uhhf!" the young man grunted, and Sophie realized that he was practically half atop her, his legs tangled with hers. The same realization also seemed to strike him at that moment, for he all at once scrambled to his feet as if the floor were the surface of a griddle and stood over her, breathing hard.

"Good God—are you injured? I'm so sorry! Please, let me. . . ." He bent to grab her upper arms and hoisted her to her feet. Sophie stumbled, trying to find her balance, and winced because one of her long ringlets was caught somewhere. *Drat* them anyway.

"Did I hurt you? How could I be so cursedly clumsy to you, of all people. . . ." He pushed her tumbled hair out of her face, his other hand still firm on her shoulder, and she saw that his eyes weren't pale blue as she'd guessed but gray, gray like morning fog over the meadows at home, deep-set under dark brows drawn down in concern. . . .

And something else. She'd felt it on her ungloved hands just before she fell, a blast of cold, charged air. . . .

Magic.

There had been an unmistakable aura of magic in the air, tingling against her bare palms as if someone had just done a spell in the immediate vicinity, barely a few feet away.

"Lady Sophie?"

Sophie blinked. The young man was staring at her, and she realized that he still held her by the shoulder, absentmindedly smoothing her hair back from her face. "It wasn't you, was it?" she blurted.

"What?"

"The spe—um, nothing, sir. I beg your pardon—I'm a little overset—" She moved slightly. The young man started and dropped both his hands.

"You—Lansell—Lord Palmerston—I was afraid you—he—" His cheeks bloomed red above the points of his crisp collar. "Did—did I hurt you, falling over you like that? I'm sorry to have been such a clod."

"No, it was my fault entirely." Sophie tore her eyes from the young man's face, realizing as she did that the orchestra had stopped playing and that a jostling, murmuring crowd had gathered around them and Papa and the broken remains of Zeus on the floor. A deep gouge marred the herringbone parquet where the bust had struck, and its head had rolled some distance. Dear God—if Papa had not been shoved aside—

"Papa!" she cried, turning to search for him.

Her father stood a few feet away, white-faced and silent, his arms around an equally pale Amélie. Lord Palmerston stood staring at the floor, his jaw slack in shock, and Lady West was sobbing. Then Papa shook his head as if to clear it. "We're quite unharmed, thanks to this gentleman." He held his hand out to her. "It's all right, Sophie. Don't cry."

"It was so close—I felt the wind from it as it fell," Amélie murmured. She turned her face away from the chunks of white marble littering the floor and hid her face in Papa's shoulder. He bent his head and murmured something to her.

"I'm not surprised you did. It was *this* close." Aunt Molly, her eyes enormous, was there too. She held her hands up a few inches apart. The Comte de Carmouche-Ponthieux nodded his agreement.

"'Thank you' seems rather inadequate under the circumstances," Papa said, lifting his head and looking past Sophie to address the young man. "But it must do, at least for now." He looked into his face. "Do I know you, sir?"

Lord Palmerston raised his quizzing glass and cleared his throat. "It's young Woodbridge, isn't it? Rendlesham's son?"

The young man stepped toward him and bowed, looking pleased despite his pallor. "Yes, sir. I—"

"Good God, Lansell. Are you all right?" Lord Whiston had finished pushing his way through the crowd, closely followed by a white-faced Lady Whiston. "Palmerston, you too? I can't think how—those pedestals were *bolted* in place. Damme, stand back, everyone. Give them some room to breathe. Please, madam, won't you sit down?" He held his arm out to Lady West and led her to a chair. "Someone fetch some wine!"

Sophie tottered back to her chair while everyone fussed over Lady West and Amélie, which suited her quite well. She needed a moment to catch her breath and to puzzle out precisely what had happened.

Except that she already knew. Someone had just tried to make the bust of Zeus fall on Papa or one of the people standing with him. With magic. Though she'd tried, she'd fallen before she could get a spell out . . . if it would even have worked. If that young man hadn't been there—

But who could possibly want to kill them? Amélie was a complete stranger, and Lady West looked harmless enough.

Which left Papa and Lord Palmerston. *Why* would anyone want to hurt them? Who possessed magic—magic strong enough to move a marble column bolted to the floor?

"Here, my dear." Lady Whiston was before her, holding out a glass of hock. "No, don't stand up. Be still and drink this. It was a fright for you as well, wasn't it? Did you injure yourself when you fell?"

"I'm quite well, thank you, Lady Whiston." She took the glass and sipped cautiously. The wine was delightfully cool and sweet. "Your Zeus—we were right here next to it, and it seemed so solid and unmovable."

"So I thought too." Lady Whiston's forehead furrowed as she took the seat next to Sophie. "I shall certainly at the earliest possible moment speak to the workmen who put it there for us. I can't have statuary falling on my guests. Thank heavens for Woodbridge's being so observant and quick."

Sophie forced her face into an expression of what she hoped was only polite interest. "Woodbridge? Is that who pushed Papa and Madame Carswell out of the way?"

"Hmm? Oh, yes—Peregrine Hollesley—the Earl of Woodbridge. He's Lord Rendlesham's eldest. Their estates are up in Suffolk, on the coast. Fine boy. We know him well—has an interest in government, like your papa—Foreign Office I believe, since the War Office will—one hopes—not require much help any longer. He has two younger brothers in the navy and cousins in the army, and felt it quite keenly that they saw action and he could not, as his father's heir." She smiled. "Do you wish me to make him known to you?"

"Oh, I . . ." Sophie knew that her cheeks were glowing pink. "Thank you, Lady Whiston, I should like that, but perhaps not just now." What an awkward way to meet, crashing to the floor and tripping him up like that . . . and with her disgraceful hair hanging around her like a deranged milkmaid's.

"Nonsense. No time like the present." Lady Whiston rose and called, "Woodbridge, my boy! Do come here."

"Lady Whiston, you don't have to—"

But it was too late. The young man had already turned back to them. He looked at Sophie intently, without smiling, and she was sure that her face must resemble her new dinner dress from Amélie's sari cloth.

"Falling over young ladies in my ballroom does not constitute an introduction," Lady Whiston said, only slightly archly. "You must let me remedy that. Lady Sophie, may I present the Earl of Woodbridge? Woodbridge, Lady Sophie Rosier."

Sophie took a deep breath and curtsied in response to Lord Woodbridge's bow. At least she could do *that* gracefully. "My father—I can't thank you enough for what you—that is, it was fortunate for him that you happened to be there. . . ." She gestured toward where Zeus had stood.

"For poor Palmerston, too!" Lady Whiston inserted. "Good heavens, if those two had been hurt by my Zeus, Napoléon would have been dancing a jig in Paris when he heard." She smiled at them both, then rejoined Lord Whiston and Papa.

The young man frowned at her retreating back and opened his mouth as if to reply. But then he seemed to think better of it and turned back to Sophie.

"I should probably confess . . . to be honest, I didn't just *happen* to be there." He hunched his shoulders slightly and suddenly looked very young. "I had, er . . . hoped someone would be kind enough to present me to you."

Yes, she definitely was blushing. What did one say to such a confession? "Oh—indeed? That is, I . . . we noticed you standing nearby."

He smiled and looked down at his feet for an embarrassed instant. "I hope I didn't stare you out of countenance. I couldn't help it, I'm afraid. You looked so—"

"Perry?" called a girl's voice, pleasant but imperious. "Good God, boy, what trouble have you gotten yourself into now?"

A young lady was pushing her way through the milling guests with cheerful unconcern for where her elbows landed. She was tall and dark-haired and beautiful in a distinguished, strong-featured way, like a sculpture of a medieval queen. Her deep blue dress was as elegant as Sophie's (but not more, Sophie was glad to note). She halted by them and glanced curiously at Sophie, then turned to Lord Woodbridge.

"Well?" she demanded, poking him with her fan. "By Jupiter, I can't let you out of my sight or else you're in it up to your neck, aren't you?"

Sophie couldn't help bristling. Who was this girl? Lady Whiston had mentioned that he had brothers, but not sisters— and even a sister wouldn't presume to scold so publicly. A sister wouldn't, but a *fiancée* might.

"I'm not in anything up to my neck, Parthenope," Lord Woodbridge said patiently, but a hint of annoyance edged his voice. "Instead of plowing in and jumping to conclusions, you might consider asking questions first for a change. It's astonishing what you can learn if you do."

Well, that didn't sound very loverlike, but one never knew. Some people quarreled by way of love talk, according to a few novels she had borrowed from Aunt Molly.

"I *did* ask questions, if you'll only think. You just haven't answered them yet." The girl turned to Sophie. "Really, he's impossible. Since he seems to have forgotten his manners, I suppose I must introduce myself—"

"I haven't forgotten my manners." Lord Woodbridge was definitely gritting his teeth now. "You just haven't let me get more than two words in—"

"Oh, abominable! I have so! You just said—let me see . . ." She began, very ostentatiously, to count on her fingers while muttering under her breath.

He ignored her. "Lady Sophie, though it pains me to do so, may I present to you my most vexatious and trying cousin, Lady Parthenope Hardcastle—though God knows she doesn't deserve the title of lady."

His cousin! An absurd feeling of relief flooded Sophie, followed by a tide of embarrassment. Why should she be so relieved that this girl was merely his cousin and nothing more? Of course, that didn't mean that they still might not . . . but somehow she didn't get the impression that they had the least amount of interest in each other in *that* way.

Lord Woodbridge was still speaking. "Parthenope, Lady Sophie Rosier, Lord Lansell's daughter. Behave yourself and be civil to her, or I swear on Grandfather's grave that I'll take a horsewhip to you."

Sophie waited for Lady Parthenope to explode at this shocking introduction, but she only laughed as she dropped a curtsy in response to Sophie's. "You'll have to catch me first. Don't listen to him, Lady Sophie. My manners are perfect, but his—" She broke into a tinkling laugh. "Do you recall that day two summers ago when you poured your tea down my back? Is that what you consider behaving oneself?"

"I was provoked, if you recall." Lord Woodbridge's voice remained calm, but his brows had drawn together threateningly.

"Ha, I like that! All I said was that if you were brave enough and really wanted to go to sea like your brothers, you'd surely have found a way—"

"Lady Sophie," Lord Woodbridge interrupted, "I trust the rest of your evening will be less alarming—though that is open to question in present company—and that I did not injure you in any way." He bowed to her, pointedly excluding his cousin, and stalked away.

"Oh ho! That still rankles, does it?" Lady Parthenope called. "Good night, Perry. I say, do call on my mother tomorrow if you have a moment. She said just today that she was sorry not to have seen you in town yet."

Sophie watched Lord Woodbridge's retreating back— he didn't turn to acknowledge his cousin's admonishment or even show that he'd heard it—and wanted to tread on Lady Parthenope's toes and hurry after him so she could hear what he had been going to say . . . well, insofar as she could hurry. Why had he hoped to meet her so much? Her first introduction of the season to a young man (and *such* a handsome one, too!), and it had to end almost before it had started. It was positively *maddening*.

"Heavens, he's gone all prickly," Lady Parthenope observed, staring after him. "Perhaps he's out of practice—we haven't seen each other to argue since Christmas. He's been in London,

Mama says, haunting Whitehall in hopes someone will employ him. He's mad to join the Foreign Office."

"Indeed?" Sophie couldn't keep a chill out of her voice, but Lady Parthenope didn't seem to notice.

"Oh, quite. Our families call us Oil and Water. We've always squabbled, partly because he's far too perfect and needs humbling, I think—of course, he thinks the same of me—and partly just for the fun of it. But he seemed different tonight . . . I don't know. Like there was something else on his mind and our war suddenly didn't matter anymore." She paused and peered at Sophie. "I say, your hair seems to have gotten rather tumbled. Let's go to Lady Whiston's room and I'll fix it for you. I love fiddling about with hair and I don't have any sisters, so I don't have anyone to practice on except Macky, and her hair is rather thin and gray and governessy. Which isn't surprising, I suppose, since she's my governess, but *still*, it's not like yours at all. Did you manage to find all your pins? No matter, we can always borrow some from Lady Whiston. Come on, I think it's this way."

Sophie blinked at this sudden change of topic. "You don't have to do that. I—"

"Yes I do. Besides, I don't know anyone here apart from Perry, and he's not talking to me, so it would be diverting to talk to you. This is my first time in London, you know. Papa and Mama haven't brought us till now, since I'm the eldest. Are you?"

"Am I the what?"

"The eldest in your family, of course. I suppose you must be, since I don't see any brothers or sisters here with you, though I suppose that could mean you're the youngest, too. Well, let's go. We can chat while I fix your hair." She linked her arm through Sophie's and took a step.

Sophie glanced over at Papa and Amélie, still the center of a small crowd, and Aunt Molly and the comte, still being glowered at by Aunt Isabel. No help could be expected from that quarter. Letting this dizzying young woman redo her hair seemed to be inescapable, so she let herself be pulled along.

After they had taken a few paces toward the ballroom's door, Lady Parthenope paused. "Are you all right? Did that great lummox Perry break your foot?"

"Oh, he wasn't a lummox! I—" Of course. How could she forget her limp? She opened her mouth to speak, then closed it again. This girl had just arrived in London and seemed determined to be friendly. Would she continue to be so once she'd heard gossip about hunchbacked, half-witted Sophie Rosier, even if it obviously wasn't true? Would a crippled Sophie be just as unacceptable? Quite possibly. Some people had foolish prejudices and believed that a bodily infirmity must reflect a spiritual or mental flaw as well. But there couldn't be anything wrong with an *injured* Sophie.

"Why, yes—I may have hurt something—it was such a hurly-burly." She took another step and pretended to wince. "Oww—I jumped up to try to warn my father and tripped on my hem, and then Lord Woodbridge fell over me—"

"Just what I said! A lummox!" Lady Parthenope looked amused but shook her head. "Wait till I see him next. I'll give him a good—"

"No! That is . . . please don't scold him." The last thing she wanted was for him to think that Parthenope's scolding came from *her*. "I assure you, it was all my fault. If he hadn't been there, my father might have been injured, or—or worse."

"Well, I suppose." Lady Parthenope sighed. "I do love having an excuse to cut the boy into thin strips, though."

"You need an excuse?" Sophie said, then bit her tongue.

But the girl only grinned. "No, not really. And I take dreadful advantage of being a girl, because he's got a chivalric streak as wide as the Channel and doesn't think he ought to abuse me the way I abuse him, even though he loves to. Which is a pity, because he can out-insult me quite handily when he puts his mind to it—or when I drive him to it, as you just saw. Wasn't he *good*? I wanted to pat him on the head and say 'bravo!' but it would have rather destroyed the moment. . . . Heavens, I shouldn't keep you standing here when you've got a hurt foot. Here, let's get you back to your seat. Your hair can wait, though I would *so* have liked to fix it for you—"

Still chattering about hair, Lady Parthenope helped her back to her seat, then boldly stepped up to Papa and Amélie. Lord Palmerston and Lady West had left, and the crowd around them had by now mostly dispersed. A pair of footmen had gathered up the pieces of Zeus, and the musicians were again playing, but Amélie still looked pale as she leaned on Papa's arm, sipping a glass of wine.

"Lady Lansell—Lord Lansell." Lady Parthenope curtsied. "I must apologize for my cousin. Your daughter seems to have been injured by his clums—"

Amélie blushed hotly and shook her head in protest. "Mademoiselle, you are mistaken. I am not Lady Lansell—"

"Aren't you?" Lady Parthenope looked interested.

"Sophie's injured?" Papa turned quickly to find her.

"Oh, not badly injured, I don't think," Lady Parthenope assured him. "He tripped over her, you see, and seems to have stepped on her foot. He isn't usually that clumsy, but I suppose the circumstances were extenuating. Anyway, I think it might be a good idea if you took her home and did something for it. Her foot, that is. A cold poultice, probably. My Macky always—she's my governess, you know, Miss MacTavish—anyway, Macky always puts an angelica root and oatmeal poultice on bruises—"

"Angelica root and *oatmeal*?" Aunt Molly had materialized behind Papa. "I've never heard it used for that before."

"It's a Scotch remedy. They use oatmeal for everything, I think. Oh, you must be Lady Lansell, then—"

"Goodness, no!" Aunt Molly shook off the suggestion impatiently. "Tell me, does she grind the angelica or does she just bruise it?"

Lady Parthenope stamped her foot in annoyance. "I don't know, and I don't care! Won't someone find Sophie's mama so that she can take poor Sophie home so her foot doesn't swell like a grape and keep her from dancing the rest of the season?"

Everyone stared at her except Amélie, who was looking at Sophie with raised eyebrows. Sophie returned her inquiring look with a pleading one. Amélie gave her a tiny nod. "*Vraiment*, mademoiselle, you are entirely right," she said crisply. "*Pauvre* Sophie, you must take my arm—or should I call for help? No? Very well. Monsieur le Marquis, won't you ask that the carriage be brought?"

"Under the circumstances, I think that is an excellent idea." Papa turned to find a footman.

Lady Parthenope looked relieved. "Thank you. I'll call tomorrow, then, to see how you do, Lady Sophie. Good night."

"Um, that would be lovely. Good night," Sophie said, clinging to Amélie's arm as Lady Parthenope swept away.

"Must we go so soon?" Aunt Molly asked plaintively, looking back at the comte, who hovered on the edge of the conversation.

"I too shall call tomorrow, if I may," he assured her, bowing with his hand over his heart. Aunt Molly dimpled.

"Sophie?" Amélie asked quietly as they moved slowly down the stairs. "What is all this? Are you truly hurt?"

"Yes—no—I don't know! I didn't know what else to say to her. She seemed to gallop over everything, and it was easier just to let her think what she wanted and . . ."

And her first ball had turned into an utter disaster, hadn't it? Sophie stared down at her hand clutching the banister. First her hair, then that Sir William being so unpleasant to Amélie, then overhearing that horrid man and Zeus nearly killing Papa and the mysterious magic she'd felt and the beautiful Lord Woodbridge being scared off by Lady Parthenope and . . . and *everything*. Her hand blurred through a film of tears.

"*Chut!* I am not scolding, *petite*." Amélie squeezed her arm as they gained the lotus-columned hall. Lady Whiston herself came fluttering toward them with their wraps and bid them good night. Amélie thanked her and took Sophie's arm once more. "This evening has been even more exciting than we expected, no?"

"Not exciting—horrible!" Sophie muttered.

"Are you all right, Lady Sophie?" someone asked.

Sophie looked up—and straight at Lord Woodbridge, who

was standing at the base of one of the columns. He was re-garding her steadily, brows slightly drawn.

"I—it has been a t-tiring evening, sir," she stuttered.

He bowed and stepped back, but Sophie was sure she could feel his eyes on her as they proceeded to the door being held open by a tall footman.

Lord Whiston accompanied them out to their carriage and handed her and Aunt Molly and Amélie into it. After Papa climbed in and gave the coachman the signal to start, Sophie looked out her window toward the house. She thought she saw a dark-haired figure in a blue coat standing with Lord Whiston under the torches by the door, watching their carriage clatter down Mount Street.

"Well," Amélie commented quietly, "perhaps not *entièrement* horrible."

"Indeed not," said Aunt Molly, sounding dreamy and far-away.

Chapter

4

Breakfast was barely over the following morning when the front door knocker rat-a-tatted loudly. A few moments later Aunt Isabel swept into the breakfast room, grim-faced above her enormous ermine muff. She fixed Papa with a steely look.

"Gilbert, we must talk," she announced, then turned to Aunt Molly. "And you too," she added. "*If* you feel that you can face us."

Aunt Molly blinked. "What did I do?"

"You have to ask?" Aunt Isabel demanded.

Amélie rose at once. "Good day, Lady Dow. You must talk, and me, I must write some letters, which I should have done many days ago." She glided calmly from the room, giving Sophie a meaningful glance.

Sophie rose too, ready to follow but wishing she could slide under the table instead and find out just what Aunt Isabel was so indignant about. It must have something to do with Aunt Molly's comte last night, but why had he so upset her? If Mama were alive, she would have stood up for Aunt Molly—she had always been protective of her, especially when Aunt Isabel was around. If only Sophie could . . . but first she had to know what Aunt Isabel's visit was about.

"I think the library would be more appropriate, if you do not mind, Isabel." Papa climbed reluctantly to his feet.

"Indeed," she snapped. "Come along, Molly."

Aunt Molly's vague blue eyes were troubled as she followed her sister, but her mouth had set itself in a line fully as stubborn as Aunt Isabel's own. Good for her. Now all Sophie had to do was wander upstairs as if she hadn't noticed the drama playing itself out in front of her, then set up a quick listening spell on the library—

Except that while Mama would approve of her wanting to help Aunt Molly, she would emphatically *not* approve of eavesdropping . . . and especially not of using magic to do so. And besides, by the time she'd concentrated hard enough to cast any spell, it would be time to dress for dinner. Which only left her one daunting option.

"Papa!" she called, as he was about to leave the room.

He paused. "Sophie?"

"Please—" She paused too, then said in a rush, "Please tell me what has upset Aunt Isabel so. Is it anything to do with Aunt Molly and the French comte we met last night?"

He frowned. "I am not sure that's anything a young girl needs to know about—"

"But I'm not a young girl anymore, Papa." She drew herself straighter and met his eyes. "If I am old enough to be out in society, then surely I'm old enough to know what is going on in my own family."

He looked at her then—really looked at her, she thought, as he hadn't for a long time—and let his hand drop from the door latch. "Yes . . . very well. But I shall have to give you the abbreviated version, or Isabel will be down here to drag me bodily up the stairs. When she was your age, your aunt Molly fell in love during her first season with a young Frenchman. He had escaped from the Terror, which had just gotten under way in France, and though he was heir to his family title and estate, there didn't seem to be any chance that he'd ever inherit any of it, since the aristocracy of France had been abolished. So your grandfather forbade them to meet, and . . ." He hesitated.

"Go on." Poor Aunt Molly!

Papa coughed. "Your grandfather arranged for the young Frenchman to be arrested and deported. It was not hard to do—there was concern that the Revolution might spread outside France, brought by secret agents, and in fact it was proven that the revolutionary government did try to encourage it here, to destabilize England and reduce any threat from us."

"So that's why she never married," Sophie said softly.

"Indeed. The, er, problem was that she very nearly succeeded in running away with him. There was rather a scandal that had to be smoothed over, and your Aunt Isabel is sure that it cost her an offer of marriage from a duke."

Ah. So *that* was what had Aunt Isabel so upset. Still . . . "But it's all so long ago!"

"True, but I do not think she ever forgave Molly, and it turned her bitter. Never bear a grudge, Sophie. It will eat up your soul. Furthermore, she now has your cousins to find wives for—preferably wealthy wives—and doesn't want old scandals revived. I expect she wants me to bundle Aunt Molly back to Lanselling and pretend we never met the comte last night."

"Gilbert!" Aunt Isabel's voice drifted down from the head of the stairs.

Papa grimaced. "That's it in a nutshell. I had better go before she has apoplexy."

"Wait, Papa—one more question. What will you say to them?"

He looked at her. "My sister—both my sisters—are adults. I can no more banish Molly than I could Isabel. She will have to live with that."

"Do you think Aunt Molly and her comte will—"

"I have no idea, Sophie. Time will—"

"*Gilbert!*"

Papa sighed. "We can finish this later, if you wish to discuss it further." He left, closing the door behind him.

Sophie sat back down and twiddled her cane thoughtfully. So this was the secret of Aunt Isabel's bad temper, especially toward her sister. Well, if the Comte de Carmouche-Ponthieux was going to be in London for any amount of time and was a bachelor, then she would do her best to see that he and Aunt Molly would have a chance to discover if they still cared for each other, Aunt Isabel or no Aunt Isabel.

She was still thinking about Aunt Molly and her comte that afternoon when the door knocker announced another caller.

Lady Whiston had already been there to see how they were, which was very good of her, and Lord Palmerston had left his card. Sophie hoped that this latest caller would be the comte, and looked up from her embroidery to make sure that Aunt Molly's cap wasn't askew or her gown streaked with dirt from her bad habit of dusting her hands on it after making the rounds of the greenhouse downstairs.

"Lord Woodbridge," Belton, their butler, announced at the door.

For a moment, Sophie thought, *Who?* Then realization swept over her as she caught a glimpse of a tall, dark-haired figure framed in the drawing room doorway. He wore a dark green coat this morning, with exquisitely cut pale buff-colored buckskin breeches and a simply but elegantly knotted neck cloth.

"I came to inquire after Madame Carswell and Lady Sophie and express my hope that they're quite over their shock of last evening," he said, advancing into the room and bowing to Amélie and Aunt Molly. But his eyes definitely kept flickering to her, Sophie realized with a little flutter.

"Woodbridge?" Aunt Molly echoed dubiously.

Amélie leaned over and murmured something in her ear. Aunt Molly's brow creased. "Did we? I don't recall—"

"—recall when I have been to a ball more *agréable*," Amélie said firmly, drowning out Aunt Molly. "I am quite recovered, but perhaps you should ask Sophie herself how she is." She looked pointedly at the empty chair next to where Sophie sat, which was slightly apart from the sofa she and Aunt Molly occupied.

Sophie watched him bow his thanks and turn toward her. After they arrived home last night she had lain awake for hours, reviewing every moment of the evening and thinking about what she *should* have done or said. There was some small consolation in the fact that she hadn't actually done any magic in public, but not much; the only thing that had kept her from it was falling over her own feet. She'd had to leave rescuing Papa and everyone to Lord Woodbridge. That might not have been so bad—according to those novels of Aunt Molly's, men seemed to like doing the rescuing while young ladies stood by in excesses of terror-stricken sensibility before melting into their saviors' strong yet gentle embraces. But any attempts at melting she might have made (even if she'd thought of it, which she hadn't) had been blown away by the breezy Lady Parthenope.

Lord Woodbridge gave her another short, polite bow before sweeping aside the tails of his coat and sitting down beside her. Was her hair tidy? Were the ruffles around the hem of her white muslin morning gown flipped up or lying smoothly? She stole a peek at him from the corners of her eyes and saw that he was regarding her gravely, brows slightly drawn again over those sea gray eyes. Oh dear, he must be the handsomest man in London this season. What did one say to such a paragon?

She glanced past him and saw that Amélie was looking at her, even while she nodded sympathetically at whatever Aunt Molly was saying. Then Amélie gave her a tiny, private smile, and lifted her chin ever so slightly. Sophie felt her own chin rise in response and, with it, her courage.

"It is most kind of you to call, Lord Woodbridge," she found herself saying with a smile. "Last night was quite an introduction to London society for me! I do find myself hoping other parties won't be quite so, ah, exciting. Or should I be sure to take care around the statuary in all my hostesses' ball-rooms?"

"I'm relieved to see you taking it in such good part, Lady Sophie," he replied. "I had feared that you would be more alarmed."

"You are very kind, but as you can see we are all . . . er . . ." Drat, she should not have kept looking at him; now she'd lost the lovely smooth thread of speech that had somehow begun to unwind itself from her tongue.

"You are putting a good face upon it for me, but I should have known, when you left early . . . that statue . . . and I blame myself for my inexcusable clumsiness."

Goodness, he was truly upset, wasn't he? "Was it clumsi-ness that saved my father and Lord Palmerston?" she asked.

He shrugged impatiently. "It was clumsiness that might have injured *you*. That is what I can't forget."

Another flutter in her midsection. Why did the thought of having hurt her, even accidentally, trouble him so? "But you didn't, sir."

"But I might have. How could I have been so careless? You, of all people. . . ."

"Please don't alarm yourself! You didn't at all hurt me. . . ." Then his words sank in—words that raised a sudden horrid sus-picion. "Me of all people? What do you mean?"

"Oh, er, nothing . . . nothing at all. Please forget I said it."

Her previous tongue-tiedness had vanished. "I am afraid my memory is quite unbiddable, sir. Pray say what you meant."

Oh yes, now he was definitely uncomfortable, suddenly absorbed in contemplation of the toes of his polished Hessian boots.

"I'd rather not," he muttered.

"Perhaps not, Lord Woodbridge, but you can scarcely stop now. Why is it that you felt it necessary to be so careful of a young lady who was a perfect stranger to you . . . or was she?"

He stared at his boots a moment longer, then sighed. "No, she wasn't."

Of course she wasn't. "Rumor travels faster in London than I thought," she muttered.

"Rumor? What rumor?" he asked innocently—too innocently. "My mother is—was—a good friend of your mother. I believe they were out together, though I expect my mother is a year or two older. She didn't come to London until she was nearly twenty, because—"

Sophie cleared her throat gently.

"Anyway, she was most shocked by you—by your mother's— by your family's . . ." He swallowed and looked even more uncomfortable. "She had to stay in Suffolk to nurse one of my brothers who is home from the war, but when she heard that Lady Lansell's daughter would be making her come-out, she asked me to look out for you and try to be especially ki—"

Sophie felt her face redden. "Try to be especially *kind* to the poor unfortunate child. Was that what she told you?"

"But that's not the only—I wasn't expecting you to be . . ."

So that was why this beautiful young man had been staring at her so intently last evening—except that he hadn't seen *her* at all. She remembered that he'd addressed her by name before Lady Whiston had introduced them. Of course he had, if he'd been on orders to "be kind" to the crippled daughter of his mother's old friend. Good God, she'd feared the Lady Lumleys of the world being gossipy and unpleasant to her and had

heard just what that gossip might entail, but it hadn't occurred to her that people feeling *sorry* for her could hurt just as badly.

Maybe even worse.

"To be so normal?" she finished for him. "Lord Woodbridge." A tremble in her voice only made her angrier. "Just because one of my legs is twisted and shorter than the other, it does not follow that I require your or your mother's or anyone else's condescension or pity . . . oh, I'm sorry. I meant to say your *kindness*."

It was his turn to flush. "She did mean it kindly, whether you believe it or not. And I was surp—that is, I was only concerned that I'd hurt you. You cannot be strong—"

"No? In fact, I am anything but fragile. If I had been, I would not have survived to be here, would I?"

He frowned. "I . . . I'd not thought of it that way. Still—"

Sophie resisted the urge to ball up her handkerchief and throw it at him, since sobbing into it just then would not have been acceptable behavior. Here she had been dreaming that perhaps he had, just perhaps, spoken to her last night and called today because he found her attractive . . . at least a *little*. But that hadn't been it at all.

Well, he wasn't the only one who could say hurtful things. Something Lady Parthenope had mentioned last night about him popped into her head. "Please, sir. You may save your kindness for someone else—though it might not be so easy to find someone to be kind to who also has a father with connections in Whitehall."

He stood up so quickly that his chair was nearly knocked backward. She caught it as he stalked to the window behind them and stared out into the street.

"That was unfair, Lady Sophie," he said, not turning.

"Was it? I am sorry. Cripples don't often get to go out in society and talk to other people, you see, so my conversation is perhaps not as polished as it might be." So there!

"You have no right to make assumptions about me." His speech was punctuated by another *rat-a-tat* from the front door.

Oh, lovely. More callers. Just what she wanted right now. "Nor do you about me, Lord Woodbridge."

"Sophie?" Amélie's voice drifted from the sofa, gentle as always but unmistakably inquiring. Sophie looked up and saw that she was looking at Lord Woodbridge with lifted eyebrows.

"We were just . . ." Sophie took a breath and hoped she wouldn't falter. "That is, we were discussing the Duchess of Kelling's's picnic tomorrow, and Lord Woodbridge was just looking at the sky to see if it might not be coming over rain."

"Oh, I shouldn't think so," Aunt Molly said comfortably. "My aspidistra would be drooping if it were, and it isn't. Rain always makes my aspidistra droop."

"Ahem." Belton coughed gently from the door. "Her Grace the Duchess of Revesby and Lady Parthenope Hardcastle."

He bowed the two women into the room—or tried to, but Lady Parthenope swept past him and up to Sophie. She wore an elegant short gray cloak lined with red satin and edged with fur, and a matching bonnet in red silk.

"How are you—no, pray don't stand up," she said breathlessly. "Did you try the oatmeal and angelica root on your poor ankle? Mama, here's Lady Sophie with the foot that my cousin quite stomped on—isn't she as pretty as I said she was? Oh, Perry! I say, I didn't see you there at first. How civil of you to call! London must be agreeing with you if you've learned to observe the niceties—"

She fell into abrupt silence as the duchess, who had been exchanging courtesies with Amélie and Aunt Molly, turned her head and ever so slightly raised one eyebrow before smiling and nodding at Sophie. Sophie scrambled to her feet to curtsy properly—one did not neglect to be polite to a duchess—and thought that Lady Parthenope's mother looked at her a little more keenly than the situation perhaps warranted.

But she was distracted by Lady Parthenope's coming round behind her and turning her chair slightly away from the others, then plonking herself down into the chair Lord Woodbridge had vacated. "Perry, you don't have to stand over there, you know. I promise I'll behave myself," she said, giving him a radiant smile. "Do bring up a chair and talk to us."

He bowed stiffly. "Thank you, but I think it is time I took my leave. Lady Sophie." He gave her the barest nod, then went to give the duchess a dutiful kiss.

"Huh." Lady Parthenope watched him make his farewells. "*That* was interesting. What's put him into such a temper? I barely had a chance to speak to him this time." She frowned and drummed her fingers on her knee, then turned to Sophie. "Anyway, now we can have a comfortable coze. How is your foot? I'm glad someone found you a cane to use till it's better." She nodded at Sophie's cane, hooked over the back of her chair.

Sophie folded her hands in her lap so that the other girl could not see that they shook. First that hideous encounter with Lord Woodbridge, and now this.

"Um . . . thank you, Lady Parthenope, but it's not going to get better," she said carefully.

While she'd tossed and turned last night, Lady Parthenope and the "injured" foot had been among the things she'd thought about, almost as much as wondering about Lord Woodbridge. She could not let the girl go on thinking her lameness was a transitory condition—the truth would out sooner or later. Probably sooner. It was time to confess her lie, but did it have to happen now, when she was still agitated from dealing with the abominable . . . the abominable *pity* of that man?

"I didn't really hurt it last night," she continued. "Well, it got a little wrenched, but nothing to speak of. I—um, I'm lame, you see. I have this cane because I need it, and was . . . I was too vain to bring it with me last night." If she was going to do this, she'd do it properly.

"Oh!" Lady Parthenope's cheeks grew pink.

"And I must beg your pardon for leading you to think otherwise," Sophie added conscientiously. "I have a frightful limp. I always will."

There. She'd said it. Now Lady Parthenope could gabble a few incoherent words of pity—more pity!—and think of an excuse to get her mother out of the house as rapidly as possible. And then Sophie could persuade Papa and Aunt Molly to take her back to Lanselling and never set foot in London again.

But that was not what happened. Instead, Lady Parthenope's eyes suddenly grew suspiciously bright.

"No—that is, I should be begging your pardon, Lady Sophie. I should not have been so . . . ." She paused as if struggling to find the right words. "I was far too bossy last night trying to drag you off to fix your hair without stopping to ask whether you even wanted my help."

"You were very kind to offer." Sophie lifted her chin. "But

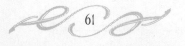

I should also confess that my hair didn't look that way because of my fall. That's how I wore it last night, to please my aunt. She did my hair the way she'd worn hers at *her* first party . . . except that was over twenty years ago. I know I looked ridiculous, but it was my choice to do so. Or maybe just my folly."

"No, it was all my folly! I had no idea that your mother—that she—wasn't there last night when I dragged you off to find her. Mama told me after, and I felt just—just horrid! Like I'd blundered all over everything, and made a mess of my first London party, and behaved just *dreadfully* to you." She blinked several times, then looked away.

Oh. Sophie felt her own eyes prickle with tears. "It doesn't bother you?" she asked abruptly.

"What doesn't bother me?" Lady Parthenope was digging in her reticule.

"The fact that I am crippled."

"Why should it?" She found a handkerchief—a ridiculous scrap of lace—and eyed it with misgiving before blowing her nose energetically into it. "Did my barging in and trying to take charge before I quite know all that I should and asking where your poor mother was bother you?"

Sophie hesitated. This was a delicate moment. She could be polite and effacing, or she could take a chance—

"Frightfully!" she said, making her face as disapproving as possible. "I declare, it was simply . . . *horripilatious.*"

Parthenope met her eyes, startled. Sophie struggled not to giggle at her expression, but her mouth *would* begin to quiver at the corners . . . and Parthenope burst into laughter. Sophie joined her and felt a large part of the worry and tension that she'd been cradling against her heart like an ugly, fretful baby melt away.

"Oh my goodness. I am so glad you said that," Parthenope declared, subsiding into giggles. "I positively *swore* any number of solemn oaths to myself that I would be all elegance and repose once I arrived in London, but being a languid miss just isn't possible for me, I think. And here you are, looking as cool and serene as I wanted to be, yet I find you're quite as naughty as I am, underneath. Now, tell me about your lameness," Parthenope commanded when they finally regained their breath.

To her surprise Sophie found herself telling her, much as she had Amélie. Parthenope listened without interrupting, to Sophie's further surprise, even when she added what had happened with Lady Lumley in the dressmaker's shop—leaving out the magic she'd done, of course.

"Your poor mama," Parthenope said, her voice gentler than Sophie had yet heard it. "And your little sister. . . . I can't imagine how dreadful it would be losing one of my brothers forever, even though I sometimes wish a few of them could be temporarily mislaid. And then that loathsome toad of a woman saying those things right to your face—it's a wonder you didn't box her ears or do something equally vengeful."

"Oh, er . . ." Sophie hoped she didn't look too guilty. "Don't think I wasn't tempted."

"I expect that I would have given in to temptation." Her eyes twinkled mischievously. "I know what we should do. We'll tell everyone that you injured yourself when attempting to save your father, and you can spend the rest of the season languishing on sofas being pale and interesting and ordering all the young men to bring you restorative glasses of champagne."

Sophie grimaced. Except for Lord Woodbridge, of course. Then again, if he were to bring her a glass of champagne, she'd probably throw it at him. "It's a lovely thought, but I don't think my aunts would approve."

Parthenope looked over at Aunt Molly. "Mm, perhaps not. What a shame. I expect you could have been quite the thing."

Sophie looked down at her hands in her lap. "Sometimes . . . sometimes I wish, if I had to be crippled, that it had happened when I was riding breakneck to hounds or something dashing and romantic like that. Then I suppose I could have tried your sofa and champagne idea. But having been ill is scarcely dashing. Besides, if I drink too much of anything, I won't be able to spend much time on the sofa, will I?"

Parthenope giggled. "Oh, I know. D'you know what my Macky told me? She said that I should eat and drink as little as possible when I'm out in the evenings, because I'm sure to muss something up about my dress if I have to use the convenience. I think you and I ought to make a pact—if we're at the same party, we'll neither of us go to the privy alone, just in case we get our petticoats in a twist. All I need to do is disgrace myself in public—I'll never hear the end of it from Perry."

"From—oh." She meant Lord Woodbridge, of course. Sophie hesitated, then said, choosing her words carefully, "I . . . um, I know he's your cousin, but . . . I must confess, I came very near just now to poking him in the eye."

"Really? Not Saint Peregrine! What did he do? I thought it rather interesting that he'd called—"

"He called so that he could tell me how sorry he was for me."

"What?" The smile on Parthenope's face vanished.

"It seems his mother knew my mother and told him to be kind to her old friend's crippled daughter. That's what he was trying to do last night at Lady Whiston's when you—er—"

"When I lumbered in on your conversation," Penelope finished for her. "Hmmph. He's usually a lot more diplomatic than that. I would have thought that he wouldn't say, 'I'm here to be kind to you'; he'd just . . . *do* it. There's a reason he wants to find a position in the diplomatic corps—he's *good* at being tactful and politic. So why be such a blunderbuss all of a sudden?"

"He claimed to be concerned that he'd hurt poor fragile me." Sophie shrugged. "I'm about as fragile as an old boot. Being crippled is not for the feeble—my leg may be too short and weak, but the rest of me has had to make up for it."

"I'd not thought of it that way, but you're right, aren't you?"

"Not everyone thinks so. My Aunt Isabel disapproves of my not behaving like a drooping blossom about to fall off its stem."

"What a dreadful way to want someone to behave." Parthenope looked thoughtful. "May I ask—can . . . that is, do you ride?"

Sophie hesitated, then told herself not to be touchy. Even many noncrippled ladies did not care for riding, after all. But on a horse's back was one place she didn't limp. "You should see my new riding habit. Aunt Isabel disapproves of it, too."

"I'll bet it's just splendid, then. Have you been riding in Hyde Park yet? It's quite the place to see and be seen. I say, let's ride there tomorrow. 'Tis a pity it's not last year, when the czar and the king of Prussia and half of the continent were here, but that doesn't mean London is quite empty. Do say you will!"

"Monsieur le Comte de Carmouche-Ponthieux," Belton intoned from the doorway.

"Oh, he came!" breathed Sophie. She hadn't even heard the door knocker, engrossed as she had been in talking with Parthenope.

"Goodness!" Parthenope murmured. "Who is that?"

The comte had entered and was bowing elegantly, though his eyes had gone straight to Aunt Molly. What a mercy Aunt Isabel wasn't here!

"It's a terribly romantic story," Sophie murmured back. "He's the Lost Love of my aunt's youth, come back from France after more than twenty years."

"Really?" Parthenope watched as the comte seated himself next to Aunt Molly on the sofa. "He's not already married and the proud papa of twelve back over there, is he?"

"Oh!" Why hadn't she thought of that possibility before? "I hope not! If he isn't, I am determined to see that they get the chance they didn't have twenty-whatever years ago."

"Playing matchmaker, are you?" Parthenope grinned. "That sounds like fun. May I join you?"

Sophie hesitated, then smiled back. "Please do!"

Chapter

5

At twenty-five minutes past four the next afternoon, Sophie and Parthenope on horseback, along with an elegant little barouche containing the Comte de Carmouche-Ponthieux, Aunt Molly, and Amélie, clopped through the gate at Piccadilly into Hyde Park and toward Rotten Row, the roadway that ran along the southern side of the park. It was before the magic hour of five, when the fashionable portion of London thronged the park to take the air, see, and be seen. But Sophie observed that there were already a number in carriages and on horseback as well as elegantly dressed strollers enjoying the pale afternoon sunshine shimmering down from a pearly sky.

Sophie had been delighted when the comte arrived at the house to take Aunt Molly and Amélie driving. Though it might have been preferable for him to take just Aunt Molly, she couldn't help liking him for including Amélie as well. This would do to begin with.

"It's perfect! We shall cut quite the figure together!" Parthenope had nearly shrieked when she saw Sophie's sapphire blue velvet riding habit. Hers was very similar, though in a reddish purple the color of a plum. Both were dashingly military, with frog fastenings and epaulettes and tall ostrich-plumed hats much like the shakos worn by soldiers. "Though I saw a lady two days ago with a habit rather like ours, but she'd gone and had gold braid put on it, so it looked like she'd pilfered it from an officer somewhere. *Too* much." She shuddered delicately.

"Lady Parthenope is a young woman of taste, I can see," observed the comte, with a twinkle in his eye. But Sophie had noticed that even when he smiled there was a sadness about his expression that made her feel sorry for him. Was it from being disappointed in his youth?

"Would you tell my Macky that? She hates half my new dresses and would much rather I was still in pinafores, I think." Parthenope looked disgusted.

"Try as I might, I simply cannot picture you in a pinafore," Sophie said to her.

"Oh, good. That makes me feel better."

"Unless it was quite grubby and had at least two fresh tears in it."

Parthenope laughed. "How did you know? Come on, let's canter."

Sophie glanced back at the carriage. Aunt Molly and Amélie sat side by side, facing the comte. It would have been better if Aunt could have sat next to the comte, but that would not have been proper. She and he were chatting happily, which was wonderful. Aunt Molly had always been a little vague, a little in her own world, but today she was obviously very present.

Sophie hoped that Amélie would not be bored and caught her eye. Amélie smiled and gave her a slight nod. Reassured, Sophie touched her horse on the flank with her crop and then cantered after Parthenope.

They had slowed after a few minutes—the increasing traffic made only short bursts of speed feasible—when Parthenope's face lit into a grin that was decidedly mischievous. "I say, could that be . . . ? Why, Cousin Peregrine! What a pleasant surprise!"

Peregrine! Sophie nearly groaned aloud as a rider a short distance ahead of them reined in his horse and turned. Why, of all people, did they have to meet Lord Woodbridge today?

Parthenope, however, had already trotted up to him, so there was no avoiding him. She made herself look at him and nod slightly—drat it, why did he have to be so good-looking in that dark blue coat, his hair tousled as he removed his hat? Cutting him dead would not be a polite thing to do in front of his cousin, much as she would like to.

"But . . . you're riding!" she heard him say as she drew in beside Parthenope. "I'd assumed—"

"That Lady Sophie could not ride, my lord?" she finished for him. "Lady Sophie can most certainly ride. She's ridden her entire life, and being lame hasn't altered that."

He flushed, and she saw his eyes turn toward Parthenope with an expression part pleading and part angry. Hmm. They hadn't arranged this meeting, had they? But why? Parthenope knew quite well what a bad impression her cousin had made. She glanced over at her new friend and saw that Parthenope looked exasperated as well as amused. Yes, very suspicious.

"Of course we're riding, dear Cousin Clunch," she said.

"How else could we show off our habits? Aren't we dashing? I think we cut quite a figure here this afternoon."

Lord Woodbridge seemed to have somewhat regained his composure. "You quite outshine anyone else here," he said, and Sophie realized that he was looking directly at her.

"Let's ride," she said, and encouraged her horse forward. No need for anyone to see the telltale warmth surely flushing her cheeks.

To her discomfort, he managed somehow to maneuver himself into riding between her and Parthenope. She sat stiff and tall in her sidesaddle and did not move her gaze from between her horse's ears.

"I think we should do this every day, don't you, Sophie?" Parthenope said. "It's hard being shut up inside so much, here in London. I say, Perry—who is that young man there? On the bench on the far side of that tree, reading—in the green coat. See him?"

Peregrine looked in the direction she'd indicated. "Who? Oh, that's Leland—James Leland, I mean. Very pleasant fellow, when he pulls his nose out of a book long enough to talk to you. He gets his share of ribbing for it at Boodle's, but never takes the least offense. From Hampshire, if I recall—old family. He'll come into a viscountcy eventually. Why do you ask?"

"Oh . . ." Parthenope paused to flick a fly off her horse's neck. "Just wondering. Anyway, Perry, it's lovely to see you here. Do you ride often?"

"As often as I can," he replied promptly.

"Perfect! You can be our escort, then—"

"Escort?" Sophie could hear the frown in his voice. "You

can't mean you're here alone without even a groom—? Parthenope, this is London, not—"

"Oh, pooh. Sophie's aunt and her friends are here too. We're not total madcaps," Parthenope said. "At least, I don't think we're madcaps, though it might be fun to—"

"Madcaps? Where? I adore madcaps. Bring 'em on!" a cheerful male voice called from behind them. "Oh, good day, Woodbridge. I thought it might be you selfishly claiming the attention of two such fair ladies."

Sophie suppressed an exclamation. She knew that voice, had heard it only a day or two ago, from behind a statue at the Whistons' ball, discussing her fortune and whether it would be worth making a try for it . . . and her.

"Underwood," Lord Woodbridge acknowledged shortly. He didn't seem particularly pleased.

The man pulled up next to her and swept his curly-brimmed beaver hat off his fair hair. He was handsome in a narrow-faced, foxlike way, and she guessed that he smiled a great deal—at least with his mouth. His green eyes, on the other hand, were cold and very alert as they swept over her.

"There. I've caught you, haven't I? Don't be greedy, now, old man. Won't you present me and let me take on some of the delightful burden of entertaining these charming young Amazons?" He leaned toward her till his knee nearly brushed her leg. She suppressed an urge to spook his horse and enchant it to toss its rider into the Serpentine, but that would not be kind to the poor animal. Besides, considering the state of her magic, she doubted she could do it. "I don't know that I've seen a handsomer turnout this spring, ma'am," he continued. "The Duke of

Wellington will be wanting you for aides-de-camp if he sees you, which means I shall have to buy myself a commission so as not to be completely shut out."

"I'll believe that when I see it," Lord Woodbridge said under his breath. No, definitely not glad to see him.

Parthenope made a tsking noise as she leaned forward to smile at the man. "How ungenerous of you, sir! Is it only our 'handsome turnout' that you are so struck by, or ourselves?"

"Why, yourselves, of course, but it would not be gracious to say so until I know whom I am addressing." The man raised an eyebrow at her, then leaned toward Sophie again. "Not that I don't know who you are at least, Lady S. How could I not remember such loveliness? But the niceties must be observed, mustn't they?"

Lord Woodbridge sounded reluctant as he spoke. "Parthenope, Lady Sophie, may I present Mr. Norris Underwood? Underwood, my cousin Lady Parthenope Hardcastle and Lady Sophie Rosier."

Mr. Underwood shot him an amused glance before somehow managing to bow while still seated in his saddle. "Enchanted and enraptured, mesdemoiselles," he declaimed, one hand on his heart. "Are you a Hardcastle of Revesby, Lady Parthenope? Woodbridge, I didn't know you possessed such illustrious connections."

"He doesn't like to admit we're related. Do you, Perry? Now, what have you heard about my family, Mr. Underwood? No one ever tells me the *good* stories, and I am persuaded you must know at least a few." She gave Underwood a coyly provocative look from under her lashes before spurring her horse

slightly ahead. He grinned and followed suit, which left Sophie riding beside Lord Woodbridge.

Well, she supposed it was better than riding with the horrid Mr. Underwood. And Lord Woodbridge certainly seemed to share her opinion of him. After a few minutes of silence, she asked him, "Will you tell me something, sir?"

"I—what is it?" he replied, sounding cautious.

"Is Mr. Underwood as big a scoundrel as I suspect he might be?"

He was startled into a laugh, which he tried to turn into a cough, then gave up. "Perhaps bigger. How could you tell?"

"Oh . . . the shocking manners do rather give him away. Is he a rake?"

He hesitated. "Worse. He's a fortune hunter of the first water."

Ah, that made sense. "Why is he so in need of a fortune?"

Lord Woodbridge chuckled mirthlessly. "I don't know how he's lasted this long without having to flee his creditors. He's heir to his uncle's baronetcy, but that's worth less than the ink it would take to write it out—Sir Cyrus is just as devoted a gamester."

"Oh—gambling." She wrinkled her nose. What a dull way to be profligate. "May I ask why, then, you are allowing your cousin to associate with such a known rascal?"

"Do you think I have much say over what Parthenope does?" he demanded. "Anyway, Parthenope is no headstrong fool. If Underwood should become bothersome, I expect she'll know how to put him in his place."

"I see." But some devil would not let her tongue be still. "Is that why you are riding with me? Because you did not think poor Lady Sophie would be capable of putting the bothersome Mr. Underwood in his place?"

He stared straight ahead. "You may think what you like. However, whether you choose to believe it or not, I am riding with you because I *want* to, and Underwood be damned. And whether you choose to believe it or not, I don't pity you."

"No?" She raised her eyebrows. This was starting to get interesting.

"No. In fact, I—"

"Oh, look!" Parthenope called over her shoulder. "There are your aunt and Madame Carswell and the comte, Sophie. Shall we ask them if we might perhaps ride a little longer?"

"Of course you wish to ride longer!" cried Underwood. "Why, we've barely had an instant here together. And you certainly cannot wish to deprive the gathered citizenry of the sight of your charming selves. I shall so enjoy the glowerings of envy cast upon me as I ride at your side."

Parthenope laughed. "You are quite absurd, sir. And I doubt anyone riding in Hyde Park right now would appreciate being called 'citizens.'"

Drat! She'd wanted to hear the rest of what Lord Woodbridge had been about to say. "Amélie or Aunt Molly might have had enough driving for one day," she said. "We should certainly ask."

Underwood twisted in his saddle to smile back at her. "I am sure your guardians can deny you nothing, dear Lady Sophie."

"I am sure you haven't any idea of that whatsoever, Mr. Underwood," she returned, barely smiling in return. Could the man be any more oily and insinuating, not to mention obvious?

No wonder he hadn't been able to persuade an heiress to marry him yet.

"Well, let us find out. Halloo there! Halloo-oo-oo!" Parthenope called, waving her crop at the carriage most conspicuously. The barouche began to edge to one side of the carriageway, heading toward them.

Lord Woodbridge sighed. "Parthenope, this is not a hunting field. Is it necessary to make such a noise?"

"That man had best look out. Completely oblivious," said Mr. Underwood disdainfully. "These fusty old fograms should keep to their firesides and out of Hyde Park if they can't be bothered to watch where they're going."

Sophie looked up. A lone horseman, gray-haired and sober-looking, rode hunched in his saddle as if absorbed in his own thoughts a mere few yards from the barouche. He didn't seem to notice that his course would rapidly lead him into collision with it.

"That's no old fogram, you idiot." Lord Woodbridge spurred his horse forward. "Hoy! Sir Walter!" he shouted, waving his hat.

Sophie urged her horse after him. There was something not quite right about the way this Sir Walter sat on his horse— something wrong, too, with the way his horse moved, as if it were completely unaware of its surroundings—

"Sir Walter!" Lord Woodbridge shouted again. But it was too late. The older man's horse shied violently, as if it had just then noticed the carriage nearly upon it, then half wheeled around and reared, squealing in anger and fear, tossing its rider to the ground with an audible thud. Somebody screamed, and someone else shouted. The comte's coachman cursed loudly as he tried to yank his horses' heads aside to keep them from trampling the stunned man, and wrestled them to a standstill.

Lord Woodbridge was there an instant later and slid from his horse. He shoved his reins at Sophie and dropped to his knees in the sandy path next to the man, who lay crumpled on his side. Woodbridge didn't try to move him, but loosened his cravat and felt for his wrist, calling his name.

"*Bon Dieu!* Poor man, is he breathing?" The carriage had wheeled around, and the comte was standing up in it, shading his eyes. "I did not even see . . . Samuel, what happened?"

"I'm sorry, sir—I didn't see him neither—*fust* he wasn't there and then he was, all suddenlike—" the coachman gabbled, setting the brake and jumping down to join the groom in soothing the horses, which stood in their harnesses, trembling and sweating.

"Do you know who it is? Is he—alive?" Aunt Molly said. Her voice quavered just a little. Amélie put a comforting arm about her shoulders.

"It's Sir Walter, all right—Sir Walter Benning." Lord Woodbridge bent over and listened near his mouth. "He's breathing. I think he's just been knocked unconscious, though he shouldn't be moved until we know if he's broken anything or not." He raised his voice and shouted, "Someone, get a surgeon!"

The comte had climbed down from the carriage and stood next to him, gazing down at Sir Walter, hat in hand. "*Parbleu,*" he said softly. "Why did he not see us?"

"Good God," Sophie breathed. She took off one of her gloves and held her bare hand outstretched before her as if feeling for raindrops . . . but it wasn't rain she was feeling tingling against her palm. Once again there was a residue of magic hanging in the air, like a whiff of cooking odors long after dinner had been served and cleared away, just as there had been in the Whistons' ballroom.

"Sophie?" Amélie had climbed down from the barouche and come to stand at her side. *"Ma chère*, what is it?"

Sophie gave herself a little shake. "N-nothing. I'm sorry to alarm you, Amélie." She let her hand drop. "Lord Woodbridge, what can we do to help?"

"Underwood could stop gaping at us and go find a surgeon, for one thing," he snapped, as Underwood and Parthenope reined in by them. Underwood grimaced, but obediently turned his horse and trotted through the gathering crowd toward Piccadilly.

"Brave lad. Don't dawdle!" Parthenope called after him. "Oh, good. Someone's gone and gotten the poor man's horse before it bolted to Kensington. I was about to go after it myself—"

"Here. Hold them for me." Sophie leaned over to hand her reins and Lord Woodbridge's to Parthenope. "Lord Woodbridge, oblige me by helping me down, please." She unhooked her right leg from the crook of the sidesaddle, kicked the stirrup from her left foot, gathered the trailing length of her skirt over her arm, and held out her hands to him.

"What?" He looked up at her.

Amélie knelt gracefully beside him. "Go help Sophie. I shall see if I may help the poor man here." She waved a tiny silver vinaigrette under Sir Walter's nose, murmuring, *"Allez, m'sieur. Tout va bien."*

"Oh, I wonder if there's any borage or lavender about? They're just the thing for a swoon, though it's a bit early for them to be in bloom." Aunt Molly too had climbed down to join the increasing crowd, though she still looked pale. The comte hurried to take her arm. "Pennyroyal too . . . d'ye think pennyroyal grows in Hyde Park?"

Lord Woodbridge hesitated, then rose and came to Sophie. Ignoring her hands, he caught her about her waist and swung her down from her horse.

"Thank you," she said, and limped over to where a tall boy stood holding Sir Walter's horse. The animal's sides were sweaty and heaving, as if it had just finished a race, and its eyes showed white around the edges.

"Had he run far?" she asked the youth.

"No, ma'am—just a few yards away, then stood twitching and trembling, like he'd been cornered by a lion. I don't think he's hurt, but . . ." The boy craned to look around her. "Is the old man dead?"

"Of course not. Don't worry. Ssh, my friend—nothing to fear." Sophie bent to give the horse's legs a cursory look, in case it had been lamed, then reached up to touch the horse's cheek with her ungloved hand. Yes, there it was, even stronger—the remains of a strangely misty, elusive, mirrorlike spell. Someone, somehow, had put an enchantment on this animal, and she wondered if Sir Walter, too, had fallen under it as well. An illusion spell, maybe, or a twisted sort of concealing spell: Both horse and rider had seemed unaware of anything around them, as if surrounded by a fog. But who could have placed such a spell, and why?

"Now, Sophie, what are you fussing about with that horse?" Aunt Molly called. "Leave him be, or he'll eat those feathers in your hat. I had a horse once that always ate feathers," she said to the comte. "The chickens went quite in terror of him . . . or was it a donkey? Not that went in terror of the horse, I mean—those were definitely the chickens, though I believe the turkey cock also took exception to him."

"Yes, Aunt Molly," Sophie said dutifully, and let her hands fall just as Sir Walter let out a groan.

"My head," he said fretfully, lifting a hand to it and struggling to rise. "Where . . . ?"

"What's this, good sir?" A man finished pushing his way through the crowd and came to crouch beside Sir Walter. "Easy, now. You've taken a bit of a fall. Let me have a look at you. Did your horse manage to find the only rabbit hole in Rotten Row to step in?" Norris Underwood had evidently returned with a surgeon.

Mr. Underwood himself followed a few seconds later. "I am quite unused," he announced, "to performing errands of mercy. They unsettle my digestion shockingly."

"A little fasting now and again never hurt anyone," Lord Woodbridge replied. "Be so good as to fetch a hackney, won't you? Sir Walter will need one."

"Oh, *non*, monsieur," the comte said. "He shall be taken home in my barouche with the surgeon, if he is agreeable. It is the least I can do for the poor man. I shall obtain a hackney for myself and Lady Mary and Madame Carswell."

"Ah, *c'est bon*," Amélie said, climbing to her feet. Lord Woodbridge hurried to help her. "And if you, monsieur"—she smiled prettily at Underwood—"would be so kind as to follow Monsieur le Comte's carriage and lead Sir Walter's horse home, we shall do *à merveille*." She hesitated, then turned her large blue eyes up to Lord Woodbridge and blinked. "Monsieur—if it

would not be too great a favor to ask—would you accompany Sophie and your cousin back to Monsieur le Marquis's house?"

Lord Woodbridge said promptly, "It would not be the least trouble, madam. Underwood?"

Mr. Underwood mumbled something under his breath about being outmaneuvered by a damned female Napoléon, but bowed his assent. Within a few minutes, Sir Walter and the surgeon had been established in the barouche and were steering a careful path toward the gate, followed by a glum-looking Underwood leading Sir Walter's horse. The comte offered an arm each to Aunt Molly and Amélie and prepared to stroll back to Piccadilly Gate. Just before she turned, Amélie caught Sophie's eye and winked.

"Well," said Parthenope, watching the departures as the crowd dispersed. "Poor old thing, I hope he won't suffer any lasting damage. Let's go. I feel an almost overwhelming need for a sustaining cup of tea and some even more sustaining gossip, and I shan't get either of them here."

Lord Woodbridge fell in beside Sophie again as they rode out of the park gates back into Piccadilly. "Was the horse all right?" he asked her.

"I beg your pardon?"

"The horse. Sir Walter's horse. You seemed concerned about it."

Drat, he'd noticed. "Oh, did I?" She tried to look confused. "That is . . . it's fine."

They clattered down the cobbles of South Audley Street to Lansell House. Lord Woodbridge gestured to a boy lounging on the steps of the house to take his horse, and dismounted to help Sophie and his cousin from their horses. As he lifted her down, Sophie said, "You seemed to know Sir Walter. Who exactly is he?"

He looked down at her in surprise. "Don't you know?"

"Should I?"

"I might have thought so. He works with your father in Whitehall in the War Office."

Chapter

6

Over the next few days, Sophie could not stop thinking about the incident with Sir Walter in the park. Two accidents . . . or were they? It looked suspiciously like someone was using magic to try to cause harm and make it look accidental, but who could be doing such a thing? Might there actually be a lady or gentleman in society who was also a witch or wizard with grudges to repay, or could it be a disgruntled servant or tradesman?

But that didn't make sense either. Why would anyone want to hurt men as harmless as Papa and Lord Palmerston or Sir Walter? All three seemed to be upright, honorable men, as far as she could discern . . . which admittedly wasn't far, as she had little access to society gossip. But she could vouch for Papa's character, anyway. . . . Oh, it made her head hurt, trying to puzzle it out. But ignoring it was not possible, either. If someone truly wanted to hurt Papa or any of the others, he or she might try again.

One other thing bothered her—the fact that all three were associated with the War Office. Was it merely a coincidence, or something else?

Lord Woodbridge hadn't seemed particularly concerned. After he'd told her yesterday as they were dismounting after their ride in the park, she'd taken a deep breath and said, "Lord Woodbridge, may I ask what might sound like an odd question?"

He smiled. "I am sure there will be nothing odd about it."

"I only hope you *will* laugh at me. Does it strike you as—well—odd that three members of the War Office have been in near-fatal accidents in a very short period of time?"

"Good heavens!" Parthenope slid from her saddle without assistance and handed her reins to the link boy who'd been lounging on the steps. "I hadn't thought about that!"

"What do you mean?" Lord Woodbridge asked.

Sophie gave him a quick glance. "My father and Lord Palmerston, then that poor Sir Walter, recently have all been in accidents that could have proven disastrous. They are also all ranking officials in the War Office—indeed, Lord Palmerston is Secretary at War. Do you think that is a coincidence?"

He smiled indulgently. "I do think it a coincidence, Lady Sophie. Sir Walter isn't even really a member anymore—he retired last autumn and is just back to help out in the present emergency."

She sighed. "I expect that you're right. It just seemed—"

"Odd," he'd finished for her, still smiling.

And odd she still thought it. Would he have dismissed the idea so quickly if he knew what she knew—about the surreptitious use of magic to cause the accidents? If only there were someone she could talk to about it! Mama would surely have been able to pinpoint the source of the spells at once, or at least have been better able to determine their intent. They could have worked together and made sure Papa stayed safe . . . but it was no use dwelling on that, or she'd make herself even more unhappy. If only there were someone—Amélie, perhaps. Or Parthenope.

It was novel to suddenly have a best friend, but Parthenope seemed determined that they would be bosom companions. Sophie could not help wondering why: It couldn't be her social position, because as a duke's daughter Parthenope held the higher rank, and her family was at least as wealthy as Sophie's. Perhaps it was their both being eldest daughters without sisters, or sharing a love of riding, or . . . or maybe it wasn't worth trying to understand why. Maybe it was just better to accept that Parthenope was her friend, and be grateful.

She wasn't the only member of the family with a new friend, though it didn't seem quite correct to call the Comte de Carmouche-Ponthieux a "new" friend. He called the day after the Sir Walter incident to report that the surgeon who had seen to him was sure that after a day or two of rest, he would be quite well again.

"Well, that is good news," Aunt Molly said. "Though I had thought about sending him a posset. Do you think I ought to, Augus—I mean, Comte?"

Sophie smiled to herself to hear her slip of the tongue, but Aunt Isabel, who was also there, scowled. Poor Aunt Molly would be in for a scolding after he left, if Sophie knew anything about it.

"I am sure he would receive it most gratefully, Lady Mary," he replied. "Your kindness . . . ah, but you have not changed."

Sophie was gratified to see Aunt Molly's usually pale cheeks grow pink. They suited her very well. "How long do you stay in London, Comte?" she asked.

He turned to her. "As long as my king needs me here, Lady Sophie. Until he is secure on his throne again."

"In that case, I hope he won't be for at least a little longer," Aunt Molly said, rather shyly.

Aunt Isabel made a disgusted sound, but the comte beamed at Aunt Molly. "I may not say that, of course, but my thoughts are my own, yes? In any event, when His Majesty King Louis is returned and all is at peace again in France, I will have leisure to do as I please—and spend time where I please," he added, looking meaningfully at Aunt Molly.

"Will His Majesty be returning to England?" Aunt Isabel deigned to ask.

The comte spread his fingers. "Who can say? It is hoped that the Allies will defeat the emperor quickly, and in that case, I expect not. At present he is safe in Ghent, so we watch and we wait."

Belton came to the door. "Lady Parthenope Hardcastle is waiting for you in her carriage, my lady," he said to Sophie. "Madame Carswell is ready as well."

Sophie rose. It was too bad Parthenope had arrived now— surely the comte would be leaving in a moment, and that would leave poor Aunt Molly subject to Aunt Isabel's tongue. She curtsied and limped down to the hall where Amélie waited.

"We've got to do something about Aunt Isabel," she said to her. "She's going to be horrid to poor Aunt Molly about the comte coming to call and taking her out in his carriage and everything."

Amélie pursed her lips. "What do you think can be done, *ma chère*?"

"I wish I knew!" She had thought about a few possibilities, namely making sure some minor accident happened to Aunt Isabel every time she came over—a spilled cup of tea on her skirt, a ripped hem, a broken shoe—so that she would have to leave almost as soon as she arrived. It might have been quite easy to manage—look how a tiny spell had routed the loathsome Lady Lumley in Mrs. James's shop . . . except that her magic could not be relied on.

But somehow she didn't want to do anything like that again. It might help chase Aunt Isabel away, but it was . . . well, it was a small-minded and petty way to do it. And even though Aunt Isabel was being small-minded and petty, it didn't mean that *she* had to be so. Wasn't she supposed to be an adult now? And Mama would most certainly have not approved of using their gift for such a purpose. She would have found another way.

"Well, there is one thing you might do," Amélie said slowly as they descended the stairs and crossed the pavement to the Revesby carriage, where Parthenope was bouncing on the seat in impatience. "But I do not think that you would care for it."

"What?" Sophie asked. "I'm willing to try anything. Don't you think it would be lovely if Aunt Molly and the comte—well, you do know that once, a long time ago . . ."

Amélie smiled. "So I have heard. You wish to play the matchmaker, then, and keep Tante Isabel from the lovers, yes? Then you must occupy her yourself."

"*What?*" Sophie paused halfway into the carriage.

Parthenope made an impatient noise. "What are you *doing*?"

"If you pay calls with her or ask her to go shopping with you, then she won't be able to pay as much attention to her sister, *non*?" Amélie said calmly.

Sophie plopped heavily onto the seat. "Yes, but . . ."

Amélie climbed in after her. "It was a suggestion, *petite*. You do not have to take it."

"What are you two talking about?" Parthenope squinted at her. "You don't look happy."

"Oh, nothing." Sophie sat back against the seat next to her friend. Drat it, Amélie was right—it would keep Aunt Isabel away from Aunt Molly. If she could bring herself to do it.

"Hmmph," Parthenope said, but did not question her further. "What are you shopping for? I need gloves."

"So do I." Sophie seized on the new topic eagerly. "I need gloves for my new evening dress to wear to the Hallidays' ball on Thursday. You'll be there, won't you?"

"Oh, yes. Perry's going to be there as well. He's coming to dine with us first." Parthenope paused, taking great care in arranging her pelisse over her knees. "I do hope you'll find him a little more agreeable that evening."

"That will be entirely up to him." Sophie regarded her friend more closely. "Why do you say so? You didn't say anything to him, did you? About me, I mean?"

"Of course not. But I know he's clever enough to realize

he's been an utter clunch . . . and I don't care to be known to have clunches in the family, so I trust he'll reform." She paused. "Do you dislike him that much?"

"N-no, not at all . . . that is, not at first." Sophie hesitated. Should she tell Parthenope her *first* impressions of Lord Woodbridge?

"Well, *that's* good," Parthenope said before Sophie could think of what else to say, but why did she sound relieved?

At their first stop Sophie found a shawl of silk gauze so delicate that it looked like woven moonlight, which Parthenope made her buy. At the glover's shop, Sophie returned the favor by convincing Parthenope to purchase two pairs of coquettish pink kid gloves to wear with her riding habit, and found the perfect gloves to match her new dress, adorned with a daintily embroidered edge of ivy leaves.

As they were examining the trays of gloves, Sophie watched Amélie sort through the selection of black gloves with an absent, melancholy expression in her eyes. "Amélie, when exactly did Mr. Carswell—when did you lose him?" she asked.

Amélie sighed. "It was only a few days after we left Madras. That was in the beginning of October, *ma chère.*"

Sophie did some quick counting. "More than seven months ago, then."

Amélie looked momentarily startled. "*Vraiment?*" She knit her brows for a moment, then nodded. "You are right. I did not think it had been so long," she said slowly. "The time has gone faster than I thought."

"So . . ." Sophie felt her way carefully, looking for the right words. "So I know you wear black ones now, but will you always?"

Amélie was silent, gazing down at the tray. "It is not something I can forget . . . ever," she finally said.

"I know that."

Amélie looked up swiftly then. "Of a certainty you do! I did not mean that I am the only one who knows what it is to mourn." She paused, and her expression softened. "When you lose someone that you love so much, you feel as if you will not ever again laugh or enjoy anything . . . and then when you do, you feel as if you must scold yourself for it. But I do not need to be telling you this, I am sure."

Sophie swallowed hard. "I thought it was just me," she said. "Sometimes I feel horrid for wanting to be here in London for the season, even though Mama is dead. She was supposed to be here too. We had it all planned, the fun we would have. . . . Then sometimes when I'm at a party or a concert, I wish I weren't, especially with this stupid, stupid leg, and I just want to go home and hide. And then I can't wait until the next one. It's as if I don't know what I want."

"You don't have to, Sophie," Amélie said kindly, and put her hand over Sophie's. "Some days you will want one thing, and some days another. That is just how things are when one is young, even when one does not have the burdens that you have, and for you, I am sure it is *encore plus difficile*. I promise, the day will come when—*voilà!*—you'll begin to understand what it is that you want."

"Did you?"

"Oh, yes. I did." For a moment her face had a faraway look; then she sighed and smiled. "And so for now, I will continue to wear my black gloves. But it will not be forever. And though your gloves are not black, at least to other people"—she squeezed

Sophie's hand—"someday, sooner or later, you will know that they aren't, and it will be acceptable to you that they aren't. You know that your *maman* would not want you unhappy."

"No, she wouldn't. But sometimes . . . sometimes I don't know how to be anything else."

"Do you like to cling to unhappiness just because it is what you know?" Amélie asked gently.

That felt almost like a little slap, but as much as she didn't like to admit it, Sophie knew it was a fair question. "Maybe," she said.

"It is a bit like your cane, I am thinking," Amélie said slowly, gesturing at Sophie's brown cane resting against the counter. "It is ugly, but it is all you have. Perhaps we must change that. Madame!" she called. "We are ready, *s'il vous plaît!*"

On their way home, Amélie requested that they stop at Mrs. James's shop so that she could pick up an order. But rather than sending the footman to get it for her, she herself went in. She emerged some time later, bearing a small parcel and a mysterious smile.

"What did you get?" Parthenope eyed the parcel with interest.

Amélie's smile deepened. "You will see!"

Chapter 7

Sophie did not repeat the mistake she'd made at her first party of the season; though she hated to, she brought her cane with her to Mrs. Halliday's ball. Nor did Aunt Molly's Bunty do her hair; Amélie sent her little maid, Nalini, as soon as she had done her mistress's hair. Nalini twisted Sophie's hair into a loose knot on the back of her head, leaving wisps of hair above her forehead and ears, then deftly curled them with a tiny curling iron and finished the whole with a fillet of pearls. Sophie smiled when the curls bounced against her cheek as she climbed the stairs to the Hallidays' ballroom on Amélie's arm.

"I hope there will be no falling statues tonight," she murmured. Should she try patrolling the ballroom, just in case—at least feel if there was magic in the air, even if she couldn't do anything about it?

Amélie smiled but shivered. "I hope so too, *ma chère*."

The Hallidays' ballroom was indeed free of statuary, featuring instead dozens of tall potted palms and trees spaced across the herringbone-patterned parquet floor to screen the musicians. Aunt Molly's eyes lit up when she saw the greenery, and she led them to seats by a large planter with odd, knobbed stems supporting long silvery leaves growing from it. "Bamboo!" she exclaimed. "I've always wanted to meet one!"

"My dear Amazon!" Norris Underwood, resplendent in an elaborately tied cravat and flower-embroidered stockings with his satin knee breeches, swooped down on them before Sophie had even sat. "How delightful to see you here this beautiful evening!" He made her an elegant bow, beamed at Amélie and Aunt Molly, then gave Papa a slightly more restrained greeting.

Papa caught her eye and ever so slightly raised an eyebrow at her. Drat! He couldn't possibly think she had any interest in this . . . this *rattle*, could he? "Mr. Underwood," she acknowledged as coolly as she could.

It didn't seem to daunt him. Indeed, he looked almost amused. "On second thought, perhaps I should say that the evening is a trifle chilly, but the weather is always changeable in April, isn't it? And where, may I ask, is your charming Amazonian comrade-in-arms? Is she not here?"

Sophie regarded him with slightly narrowed eyes. "I would assume she will be coming with her own family. And as you can see, we have just arrived, so I have not had time to see if Lady Parthenope is already here."

"But she *is* coming, is she not?"

"I am under the impression that she is, sir."

He laid one well-manicured hand over his heart. "Ah!

Then my evening will be complete. Pray tell her that I shall be devastated if she does not save me a dance. She promised me she would, when I spoke with her in Hatchard's this morning."

"Hatchard's Bookshop? I would not have guessed you were a reader, Mr. Underwood." Sophie kept her voice light and pleasant.

"You cut me to the quick! Do I appear such an empty-headed fellow to you? I adore Hatchard's; one may learn so much there—and not just from the books. Ah, I see Lord Wood-bridge looking this way. I shall leave you to his skillful pleas-antries. Those diplomatic hopefuls do love to practice their charming chitchat—especially on hard-hearted types." He gave her an impudent grin, bowed again, and sauntered away.

Sophie watched him go, wishing she could unravel his stockings with a dissolution spell. This interest of his in Parthe-nope was disturbing, if he really was the fortune hunter Lord Woodbridge said he was. Whether he was or not, she found his ingratiating-to-the-point-of-slimy manners tedious, and she couldn't imagine the straightforward Parthenope could like them, either.

But Lord Woodbridge was indeed approaching, with Par-thenope on his arm. She was talking to him—or perhaps at him—with great vehemence. Surprisingly, he seemed to be lis-tening without protest—nodding even. How odd, considering some of their past conversations she'd witnessed.

Papa looked much happier to see Lord Woodbridge than he had Mr. Underwood. "Good evening, Woodbridge," he said cordially. "I was talking to Lord Castlereagh about you just yesterday—"

"Well, that's the last we'll see of Perry for a while. Oh,

Sophie." Parthenope had detached herself from her cousin and stepped back a pace to survey her. "Yet another dress I'll have to figure out how to steal from you! Except green looks so much better on you than it does on me. And those gloves are perfect. If I didn't like you so well, I'd be perfectly seething with jealousy. You must come show it to Mama—I think I like your dressmaker better than hers."

Sophie sat down and smoothed the white satin skirt of her dress. The bodice, in moss green corded silk trimmed with lace and a frill of falling collar at the back, *was* flattering, she thought, but more important matters were at hand. "Never mind dressmakers now. You just missed Mr. Underwood. What a dreadful little toad-eater the man is! He asked me to tell you that his heart would be broken if you did not give him a dance tonight as you promised."

"Did he?" Parthenope looked unconcerned. "Well, I suppose I must, then. Goodness, what is your aunt doing to that plant?"

"Talking to it, I expect. Parthenope, do be careful with Mr. Underwood. He is not at all a respectable person."

"Isn't he? That makes him much more interesting. What has he done?"

"I'm more concerned about what he might do. Your cousin tells me he is a known fortune hunter."

"Then I shall be careful not to accept any proposals from him." Sophie's expression must have betrayed her, because Parthenope dropped her flippant tone and patted her hand. "Don't worry, Sophie," she murmured. "I have no interest in him, no matter how amusing he can be in conversation. Oh, look, here he comes. Good evening, Mr. Underwood. Was the book of sermons my Macky recommended to your taste?"

Mr. Underwood bowed. "Since that good lady is not here to be offended by my telling you, I must confess that it was not."

"And if she were here?" Sophie could not resist asking.

"Then I should say it was exactly the thing, of course." Mr. Underwood did not appear in the least fazed by her question. "Dear Lady Parthenope, if you will recall our conversation this morning, you promised me a dance. I see sets are forming for a country dance—might I claim it now?"

Sophie raised an eyebrow. "Goodness me, not waiting for a waltz? You are being circumspect this evening, Mr. Underwood."

"You underestimate me, Lady Sophie. I rarely overplay my hand. Lady Parthenope? Will your duenna here permit you to dance?"

Parthenope laughed. "You're a complete humbugger, Mr. Underwood, and though I should really make you ask my mother first, a country dance will do no harm. I say, Sophie, don't let Perry leave till I'm back—there's something I particularly wish to ask him."

Sophie watched them join the dancers, feeling discontented. She'd looked forward to a jolly evening with Parthenope, examining the dresses and coiffures of the passing ladies. What she'd forgotten was that Parthenope was not crippled as well. She could scarcely expect her to spend the entire evening at her side, not dancing with eligible young men . . . except that Norris Underwood was anything but eligible—

"Is my cousin not here?"

Startled, Sophie looked up at Lord Woodbridge. "N-no. She was asked to dance by Mr. Underwood."

"Oh." Lord Woodbridge frowned down at his feet for a moment. Unlike Mr. Underwood, he was dressed almost severely, in a dark blue coat and plain stockings with the knee breeches that were the expected evening wear for gentlemen, and yet Sophie was sure she knew which man eyes would follow if the two were to walk across the room together. At least, she knew whom *her* eyes would linger on. . . .

"It's not fair," she said, more loudly than she'd intended.

He looked up quizzically. "What is not fair? Did you wish to dance with Mr. Underwood?"

"Of course not!" Sophie nearly sputtered in indignation. "Do you take me for an utter peagoose?"

He laughed softly and sat down next to her. "Only at my peril."

Sophie regarded her fan in her lap. "Weren't you talking to my father?"

"Yes. But he's presently otherwise engaged. I hope I am not bothering you—please say if you'd rather be left in peace."

Sophie followed his gaze and saw that Papa was leading Amélie to the card room, to join those guests who were not dancing. Amélie, glancing back over her shoulder, caught Sophie's eye and nodded at her. In encouragement?

She picked up her fan and began to fan herself with it, more out of a need to do something than because she was hot. "Er, no, not—that is, Parthenope asked that you wait here for her, as she had something to ask of you."

"I see. One does not gainsay my cousin—not if one is wise."

"I thought you did so all the time—at least, that is what she told me."

"Our 'merry war' betwixt oil and water." He smiled again. "It lasted us for several years, but even the bitterest wars come to an end eventually."

"That's what we all thought about Napoléon," she said.

He laughed. "Very true."

Sophie was about to respond, but her attention was drawn by a pretty girl with cornsilk hair almost skipping toward them, like a graceful young muslin-clad deer.

"Lord Woodbridge!" she cried, halting in front of them and sketching a quick curtsy. "How lovely! Mama said you would be here, but I was sure you wouldn't come till later. Please, we need one more for our set, and the music's about to begin—won't you come dance with us?" She held out her hand to him. "We're simply *counting* on you."

"Good evening." Lord Woodbridge stood and bowed. "Lady Sophie, may I make Miss Susan Halliday known to you? Miss Susan, Lady Sophie Rosier."

"Oh!" Miss Susan blinked her large, rather watery blue eyes. "You're the one who's—that is, good evening, Lady Sophie." She turned back to Lord Woodbridge and caught at his hand. "Please, Woodbridge. Do say you will."

He inclined his head. "At any other time I should certainly be happy to oblige you—but I fear I cannot just now."

"Oh, er, of course." The girl looked at Sophie from under her lashes for a few seconds. "I understand, but . . . my dear Lady Sophie, do you like to play cards? You know, cards?" She pantomimed holding a hand of cards before her. "There's a very

cozy room just over here where lots of lovely people are playing—I'm sure they would be very happy if you would go and play with them. You can just watch if you don't know how to play the games. I'll take you there, shall I, so that Lord Woodbridge may dance for just a little while?"

Sophie stared at her. Was this girl truly addressing her as if she were feeble-minded? "I beg your pardon—"

"Shall I say it very slowly, as you do not seem to comprehend?" Lord Woodbridge said, an edge to his voice. "I . . . am . . . engaged . . . at . . . present . . . and . . . will . . . not . . . dance. There, now, wasn't that easier to understand? Would you like me to say it again?" He mimicked exactly the tone Miss Susan had used when speaking to Sophie about playing cards.

Miss Susan flushed, whether from anger or embarrassment it was impossible to tell. "I was just trying to be kind," she muttered, backing away a step.

"A lady would first have found out if such *kindness*, as you call it, was required."

This time her flush was definitely anger. "Why—of all the—"

"I do believe your dance has started, Miss Susan," Sophie said gently.

"Oh!" Miss Susan actually stamped her foot, then turned and hurried away, casting a venomous glance over her shoulder.

For a moment, neither of them spoke. Sophie wasn't sure what to feel: certainly angry and insulted at Susan Halliday's treating her like an imbecilic child. But what of Lord Woodbridge's behavior? What did it mean?

"You could have danced, if you wished. You didn't have to stay," she said, fidgeting with her fan.

"Yes, I did."

"Not . . . not really—"

"But Parthenope wishes to speak to me, if you will recall. You told me so yourself."

"Yes, but I'm sure—"

He cut her off in midsentence by leaning past her and addressing Aunt Molly. "Lady Mary, it's rather close in here, don't you think? We would be delighted to procure you some refreshment. Champagne? Ratafia? Lemonade?"

Aunt Molly looked up from the bamboo plant she was still examining, having progressed to the leaves. Sophie hoped she wouldn't climb up on her chair to get a better look at them. It was a pity the comte was not here this evening. "Eh? Oh, lemonade would do me just fine. I don't care much for nasty little bubbles."

"Certainly." He stood up and held his hand out to Sophie. "Will you accompany me?"

"What about waiting for Parthenope?"

"That set will last some time. I do not think we shall be missed if we go now."

Sophie accepted his arm and rose, glancing back at her cane as she did. Should she take it?

Something of her thought must have occurred to Lord Woodbridge. "I'm sorry—I thought a stroll—but if you—"

"I am quite capable of accompanying you to the supper room, sir."

He flushed. "Yes, you are. My apologies." He hesitated, then said, "Would the other arm be more useful to you?"

"Yes, thank you."

He moved around her so that she could lean on his left arm, supporting her right side, and they promenaded slowly around

the edge of the ballroom as Sophie tried to puzzle out Lord Woodbridge's behavior this evening. When he'd called at home, he'd been pitying; on their ride in the park, carefully agreeable. But tonight—

"I was about to tell Susan that I had already asked you for that dance," he said abruptly.

She stopped in surprise. "Why? It's obvious that I don't dance."

"But that doesn't mean I can't still want it . . . very much."

Sophie looked up at him. He was looking down at her with a hard, brooding expression in his eyes that made her feel odd, somehow, as if the bodice of her lovely new dress were suddenly a bit snug.

"I used to dance, once," she found herself saying as they resumed walking. "Before I was ill. We even had a dancing master come to us each year for a month in the summer to help us polish our steps. My brothers used to complain, but I never did."

"The way you carry yourself shows it. You miss it, don't you?"

His tone had been carefully neutral. She tried to match it. "I try not to think about it."

"Have . . ." He hesitated. "Have you tried?"

She laughed derisively. "Where? With whom? And how many of my fellow dancers will be willing to catch me when I stumble and fall? I thought at first I could manage a minuet if it were played slowly enough, but I doubt it, and I certainly cannot do anything as lively as a country dance. I'm sorry, Lord Woodbridge, but you shall have to put aside your wish to dance with me."

They had reached the supper room. Lord Woodbridge led her to a seat at a table and offered her a glass of champagne. She regarded it doubtfully, then took a small sip. Not too nasty, as Aunt Molly thought it, but the tickly sensation of the bubbles on her tongue was decidedly peculiar, like the feeling of magic hanging in the air after a spell had been done. She watched as he took a sip from his own glass and gazed fixedly at the linen-covered table, as if he were lost in thought. If only it were possible to reach over and lift up the top of his head, so she could see what those thoughts were.

"Would you be averse to a small wager, Lady Sophie?" he suddenly asked.

She looked down into the rising bubbles in her glass, then took another small sip. "A wager? But . . . I don't know. What are the stakes?"

"Stakes to be determined, but won't be claimed if disagreeable to the loser. The wager is this: that I will, within a year of this day, claim my dance with you."

She set her glass down on the table and looked at him levelly. "A few days ago you were astonished that I could ride a horse, an action which, I might remind you, is not at all affected by my lameness. And now today you say you will dance with me. It makes no sense."

It was his turn to look down at his glass, smiling faintly as he did. "Does it have to make sense?"

"With you? Yes," she said bluntly. "You have diplomatic ambitions. And Parthenope says that you are a fencer with words beyond compare, though I must say that I am not as impressed with your oratorical skills as she seems to be."

"Family prejudice," he murmured.

She made an impatient noise. "At the risk of being undiplomatic, Lord Woodbridge—what do you want with me?"

Again, a pause and that faint smile. "I want you . . . to—to give me a chance. We started out on the wrong foot—"

"The wrong foot," she repeated. "What an elegant way of putting it."

He looked up at her, smile gone. "Stop that. Not everything has to do with your condition, Lady Sophie."

That surprised her. She closed her mouth and looked at him thoughtfully. Good heavens, had she become so self-absorbed that a common turn of phrase would set her hackles up?

He took advantage of her silence to continue. "It was my fault. I . . . yes, I felt sorry for you, but it made me want to protect you. I guessed you'd be facing people like Susan Halliday and worse. It made me determined to—yes, be kind to you. Defend you, if you will."

She shifted impatiently in her chair. "I do not need that sort of kindness."

"I'm beginning to understand that. That is why I am asking if we can start again. Let us drop our—our preconceived notions of each other. Do you think it is possible for you to try that? Do you *want* to try?"

She looked down at her champagne again. Did she? It would be so much easier to say no, to clutch her anger to her and hate him and the rest of the world outside the safe little wall she'd made around herself, just as she'd said to Amélie, no matter how much she longed for it at the same time . . . which would only make her angrier and hate it more.

"I . . . don't know what to say," she finally said to her glass. "Please."

The word brushed her ear like a moth's wing. Its very delicacy made her flinch. "But I'm afraid," she whispered.

He was silent, and she was sure she could hear his quiet breathing despite the music and the chatter nearby. After a few breaths—were they his or hers?—she felt him take her glass from her and set it on the tiny table. Very carefully, he took her hand, barely holding her fingertips in the lightest of grasps, the way one might hold a silkworm's cocoon.

"I won't hurt you. I promise I won't," he said, then released her fingers. "Shall we take some lemonade back to your aunt?"

The set was just breaking up as they brought Aunt Molly her lemonade, gentlemen escorting their partners back to their chaperones or out to the supper room for refreshment. Parthenope, escorted by Mr. Underwood, beamed when she saw them. "Perry, I'm so glad you're still here! Won't you take me back to Mama for a moment so she knows where I am? We'll come right back, I promise, Sophie." She took Lord Woodbridge's arm before anyone could say anything and firmly led him off.

Sophie sat down, grateful for a moment to try to untangle her whirling thoughts. But to her irritation, Mr. Underwood, instead of taking himself elsewhere, seated himself beside her. "Thirsty work, dancing with your friend. I could use a glass of champagne."

"You are quite free to go and get one, sir," Sophie said pleasantly.

"Oh, I shall in a moment. Not polite to abandon you here."

"I assure you, I would survive."

Mr. Underwood ignored her. "Lady Parthenope's a lively chit, isn't she?" he said meditatively, after a moment.

"That's one way to describe her."

"Tell me about her family. Brothers or sisters?" he asked.

"Four brothers, no sisters. She's the eldest."

"Ah." There was a meditative look on his narrow face. "All younger brothers, then. None of them out yet? Away at school, I assume?"

"Of course." She frowned. "Why do you ask?"

"Oh, idle curiosity." Underwood shrugged. "Wasn't familiar with the family except by hearsay. So how is she taking?"

"She's the only daughter of the Duke of Revesby. How do you think good society regards her?"

"Oh, I'm sure the tabby cats at Almack's have decided she's quite acceptable." He still had that thoughtful look on his face. "What I meant was, what about her? Has she formed any attachments yet? Lost her heart to some gallant? Have any attentive swains making a nuisance of themselves underfoot?"

The suspicion that had slowly been sprouting in her mind as he spoke burst into flower. "Only one."

"Oh? Who is that?"

Sophie took a breath. "You. Keep away from my friend, Mr. Underwood."

Underwood laughed lightly. "Good God! I've stood up for one dance with her. Does that constitute a threat on her virtue in your book? Ask her if my demeanor was at all exceptionable—or ask any of the twenty other people in the set with us."

"I am very happy to hear that, sir. And I trust matters will stay that way."

He looked at her, one eyebrow raised. "I have the distinct

feeling that you do not like me, Lady Sophie. What have I ever done to deserve your aversion?"

What would he do if she told him what she had overheard him saying at the Whistons' ball? "Nothing, yet," she said. "But don't think I am not keeping an eye on you. Ah, there is Parthenope. Pray excuse us."

He did not protest this summary dismissal but bowed, one hand sardonically on his heart. "Cut to the quick, cruel lady," he murmured, and turned away.

The rest of the evening was uneventful, and might even have been enjoyable, had Sophie paid any attention to it. But she had too much to think about, between her conversations with Lord Woodbridge and Mr. Underwood. At least the latter had been straightforward; she had warned him off Parthenope. Whether or not he took her warning . . . well, that remained to be seen. She would be watching him, however, and if he tried to make one improper move, she'd . . . she'd do *something*.

Her conversation with Lord Woodbridge, on the other hand, had been anything but straightforward. She was still thinking about it as they clattered home through a fine misty rain and after she'd taken off her beautiful green dress and lace-trimmed petticoats and left them to air on a chair before being folded away in her wardrobe.

What should she think about him? Did she want to give him a second chance, as he'd asked?

Why did he want one, anyway?

She unpinned her hair—finally grown in as thick as it had been before she'd fallen ill—and let it tumble over her shoulders and down her back. She unknotted and loosened the laces of her corset and wiggled out of it, then went to stand in front of her mirror. Her hair shone in the candlelight, and she turned her head slowly to watch the play of light along it, then smoothed her chemise over her figure with her hands. Her breasts were full but not overlarge, her waist slender; Mrs. James had nodded approvingly as she measured her for her new dresses.

Then, taking a deep breath, she lifted her chemise and stared at her legs. They both began well enough at the top, long and shapely . . . or at least the left one was. Somewhere just above the knee, the right one started to seem off, some-how . . . and then, in the calf, it became awkwardly shaped, wasted, twisting inward to a splay-toed, flattened foot. What if Lord Woodbridge were standing behind her, looking over her shoulder into the mirror? What would he see—the lovely young body or the misshapen leg?

She turned abruptly away from the mirror.

Chapter

8

Late the following afternoon, Parthenope paid a call with her mother. She wore a large cloak rather than one of her more usual sleek pelisses and was walking with a rather peculiar hunched gait as Belton ushered them into the drawing room.

"Sophie! I've brought a surprise to show you," she announced, heading toward the corner of the room that had become their spot. "Are you ready?"

Ah, that would explain the cloak and the hunch. "I don't know. How surprising is it?" Sophie asked as she sat down.

"Silly. Do you think Mama would permit me to call with anything horrid?"

"No, probably not. Very well, what is it?"

Parthenope's eyes twinkled. "Close your eyes and put out your hand."

"Parthenope—"

"Just do it! I promise you'll like it."

Sophie closed her eyes and held up one hand, holding her breath. It was true that the duchess wouldn't let Parthenope do anything too outrageous, but still—

A slight weight settled on her hand, accompanied by a delicate, prickling grip on her forefinger. "Parthenope—"

"There! Open your eyes. Isn't she darling—or he—we're not quite sure which it is."

Sophie opened her eyes and found that she was holding a bright green bird with a long tail and a most attractive reddish purple head. "Good heavens!" she exclaimed.

The bird looked at her, cocking its head slightly, then reached up one clawed foot to scratch near its yellow beak. "Turnip!" it announced.

"Oh, you naughty little girl. Why can't you say anything other than that?" cooed Parthenope.

"*What* is *that*?" Aunt Isabel, who had arrived just in time to prevent Aunt Molly from driving out with the comte, gasped from the sofa.

"Don't worry. It's just Hester," Parthenope explained. "Isn't she the sweetest thing you've ever seen?"

"Parthenope insisted on bringing her new pet to show Sophie," the duchess said soothingly to Aunt Isabel. "Believe me, she's quite tame and won't make messes on the carpet—the bird, I mean."

"Thank you for clarifying," Sophie murmured. Parthenope put out her tongue at her.

Amélie's laugh rang out. "*C'est une perruche!*" She smiled at Parthenope. "I saw many of these in India. But I am afraid that this is a monsieur, not a mademoiselle. The females have a head that is gray-blue, not this color of a plum."

"Oh." Parthenope looked crestfallen, then brightened. "But *he* doesn't know that Hester is a girl's name, does it, my precious little angel?" She screwed her face into a coaxing grimace.

"Turnip!" Hester announced again.

"Is that all it can say?" Sophie brought the parakeet closer to examine its handsome plumage.

Parthenope looked nettled. "No, of course not!"

"It also says 'cabbage,'" her mother added helpfully.

"I suppose it could be worse," Aunt Isabel said, faintly.

Parthenope's eyes suddenly gleamed. "It could, couldn't it?"

"Don't get any clever ideas about new words to teach it, dear." The duchess turned back to the aunts and Amélie.

Sophie brought her attention back to Hester and found that he seemed to be examining her in turn, tilting his head thoughtfully from side to side—or at least he looked thoughtful. Did birds have thoughts? "Don't call me a turnip again," she warned him.

He didn't. Instead, he opened his mouth, bobbed his head as if in greeting, and said, "Good day, Mistress Witch."

Sophie nearly dropped him, but Parthenope guffawed. "Ha! I think I'd prefer being called a turnip! What a beastly name to call my friend, you bad-mannered thing."

Sophie held him out to Parthenope, her hand trembling. Had that been a coincidence, or had the bird actually meant what he said? And if so, how could he know? Birds were said to be particularly sensitive to magic, but she'd done so little of that lately that she wasn't even sure she could call herself a witch. "He's . . . um, charming. Where did you get him?"

Parthenope put the bird on her shoulder. Hester leaned over and began to nibble at her ear. "Wretched bird. You know that tickles. See? I told you he knows more than 'turnip.'"

"Turnip," Hester agreed, sidling down her arm onto her hand.

"Enough turnips," Parthenope said firmly. "And I don't know where he came from, at least, not officially. The butler found his cage on our steps this morning, with a tag addressed to me that said, 'To the fair Amazon, whose beauteous head oft wears feathers of a similar hue.' There was no signature."

Sophie wrinkled her nose. "I think I'd rather secret admirers left me flowers."

"Oh, you've no poetry in your soul!"

"And you do?"

Parthenope grinned. "No, not a particle. My guess is that it was Norris Underwood. Who else calls us Amazons? And my riding habit is the same color as Hester's head, don't you see?"

Sophie did see, and frowned. "And you're keeping it—er, him?"

"Why should I not? I like him."

"Whom? Hester or Mr. Underwood?"

"Well, really! Hester, of course, though Mr. Underwood can be an amusing companion."

Sophie glanced over at the adults and pitched her voice low. "You do remember what Mr. Underwood is, don't you?"

Parthenope rolled her eyes. "Do you take me for an utter flat? No, leave my ear alone, Hester! How many times do I have to tell you?"

"Then accepting his gifts hardly seems like the proper course—"

"But I don't know it's from him, do I?" Sophie's expression must have affected her, for she leaned forward and patted her arm. "Believe me, Sophie, I have Mr. Underwood quite in hand. Nothing bad, or even terribly *interesting*, will happen. I promise."

"Hmmph. Has your cousin made Hester's acquaintance yet?"

Parthenope looked annoyed. "Since Hester just arrived, no. And he doesn't need to, either."

"Meaning you don't want him to know about Mr. Underwood's gift."

"Turnip," Hester commented.

"My thought precisely," Parthenope declared. "So, shall we ride tomorrow afternoon?"

Sophie let her get away with changing the subject. "I don't know. Probably not."

"Why?"

Sophie looked at Aunt Isabel talking with great animation to the duchess. "Because I've decided the best way to let Aunt Molly have a chance to see her comte is to keep Aunt Isabel busy myself. I've asked her to take me out to make calls tomorrow, and I can't promise we'll be back in time to go riding."

"You," said Parthenope, shaking her head, "are a saint. Or maybe just addled. I'm not quite sure which."

"Well, it was all I could think of," Sophie answered irritably. "If you have any better ideas, do let me know them."

"Tur—" Hester began, but Parthenope stood up quickly and drew her cloak back over him.

"Quite enough of that, young man," she said. "Or my friend may wring your little purple neck."

Aunt Isabel was in a rare good mood when she picked up Sophie the next afternoon for their first round of calls—in such a good mood, in fact, that she didn't even ask what Aunt Molly was doing. Which was just as well, as at that moment Aunt Molly was happily on her way to Richmond with the comte for the afternoon. The look of utter satisfaction on her face below her modish new parasol as they'd clattered down the street had been of some consolation to Sophie.

"I am very glad you're taking a proper interest in society," Aunt Isabel said as they in turn drove down the street. "It is just what one does in our position, and I think it particularly important for you, my dear, to show the world that you really are quite an ordinary young lady, despite your affliction."

Why, thank you for that charming compliment, Aunt, she thought a little sourly. But to some degree, Sophie had to admit that Aunt Isabel was right. If it were more widely seen that she was prettily behaved, could speak intelligently on a range of topics, and did not drool or twitch, perhaps the gossip and stories that she was feeble-minded or simple would die out.

Aunt Isabel was surveying her through her quizzing glass. "Your dress is . . . acceptable," she said after a moment. "Did you choose it?"

Sophie knew that 'acceptable' was Aunt Isabelish code for admiring something excessively but not wanting to admit it and kept her face straight as she replied, "Thank you, Aunt. Amélie did, with a word or two from Mrs. James."

"Hmmph."

"You look very nice too, Aunt," she said, after a moment's reflection. Aunt Isabel usually did dress very well and would in fact be a handsome woman, if only there weren't that perpetual frown between her brows and downturn to the corners of her mouth.

To Sophie's relief, their first stops were just to leave cards and not go in. But after that, Aunt Isabel decreed that they must go into Lady West's house. Perhaps it wouldn't be too bad; at least Sophie had already made her acquaintance at the Whistons' ball.

There were already two carriages in front of the house. Aunt Isabel peered at the crests on their doors. "Lady Whitbury and the Countess of Parrington," she said. "They came out more or less when I did. The countess has a son. . . ." She looked at Sophie speculatively, then shook her head.

Lady West seemed pleased enough to see them. "London air would appear to agree with you," she said to Sophie with a smile after she made introductions and waved her to a seat on a sofa with two older ladies—the Ladies Whitbury and Parrington whom Aunt Isabel had mentioned, though Sophie hadn't quite caught which was which. They gave her a thorough examination—one (Sophie thought it might be Lady Parrington) peered through an enormous quizzing glass—then proceeded to ignore her and resumed conversing in low voices.

Sophie began to count inside her head. Calls were supposed to last fifteen to twenty-five minutes, unless one was visiting a particular friend. She supposed she ought to try to make conversation with her sofa mates, but neither seemed inclined to acknowledge her continued presence, much less talk.

And so it went for five more visits, with slight variations. All of the houses at which they called belonged to people Sophie knew at least slightly, so she began to conclude that Aunt Isabel was actually trying to be kind in an unobtrusive way. This was unexpected and somehow disconcerting. When had Aunt Isabel ever been either kind or unobtrusive?

While the hostesses they called on were always pleasant, the same couldn't be said for fellow callers. Some, like Lady Whitbury and Lady Parrington, ignored her. Others stared; still others avoided meeting her eye while trying to surreptitiously examine her shape. For her supposed hunch, she assumed. She agreed several times that the weather had been pleasant this spring, that the entertainments of the season had so far been most amusing, if not as glittering as last year when the czar and the king of Prussia had been in town, and that it was a shame the Duke of Wellington had to be so taken up with that monster Napoléon that he would not be showing his face in London till God knew when.

On the way home, Aunt Isabel actually looked at her with approval. "Your manners were very good, my dear . . . perhaps a little quiet, but one does not like to see a girl in your position being too lively or, heaven forbid, *hoydenish*."

"Heaven forbid," Sophie murmured.

"What was that?"

"I was just agreeing with you, Aunt." She leaned her head back against the cushion. How could spending the day sitting in either a carriage or in various drawing rooms be so exhausting?

"I think it would be advisable for us to make another round of calls the day after tomorrow," Aunt Isabel announced as they drew up to Papa's house.

"Oh—um . . ." But Sophie thought about Aunt Molly and said, "Yes, thank you." As soon as the footman had opened the door, she was through it, anxious to leave before Aunt Isabel took it into her head to accompany her.

Belton met her at the door. "Is my aunt in yet?" she asked him.

He cleared his throat. "No, Lady Sophie. But Madame Carswell requests that you come up to her room when you are able to."

"Thank you, I will." Aunt Molly must have been having a good time with her comte, if she hadn't returned home yet. Sophie mounted the stairs and thought about stopping in her room to take off her hat and pelisse, but as she passed Amélie's room, the door opened to reveal Nalini, Amélie's maid, in a soft violet sari. "You come, Lady!" she said, a wide smile on her small face.

"Ah, Sophie! How were your calls with Tante Isabel?" Amélie stood by her bed, smiling also. A large, brightly patterned cashmere shawl was spread over the white counterpane next to her.

"Er, tolerable," Sophie answered, eyeing it. "Amélie—"

"So? Nalini and I, we have been busy. Tell me, *petite*, what dress do you think you shall wear tomorrow for the opera?"

Sophie blinked. "I don't know. The pink one, perhaps, with the little lace cape and the deep flounce on the bottom. Why?"

"Ah!" Amélie smiled and turned to the bed, bent over, and peered under the shawl. "*Voici!*" she exclaimed, pulling something long and thin out from beneath it, and holding it out to Sophie.

It was a walking stick, thinner than her heavy brown cane, but still sturdy enough to lean on. Entirely wrapped in woven ribbons of alternating pink and white that would exactly match her pink opera dress, and finished with a starched lace bow, it looked like it belonged to an elegant shepherdess from a Meissen porcelain figurine. Sophie stared at it, speechless.

"I think you shall not be ashamed to carry this!" Amélie said. "Will it not look well with your dress?"

"Oh, Amélie!" Sophie took it from her. It was exactly the right length, and the smaller crook fit her hand better than her old cane. "It's perfect!"

Amélie's smile lit up her face. "And these?" she asked, flipping the shawl aside.

Sophie gasped as she came to stand next to Amélie. A dozen—no, more!—canes lay on the bed in a rainbow of colors, all made to match several of her new dresses. Some were cased in a sheath of plain fabric cut tight or gathered into ruches. Others were wrapped in ribbon like the pink one for her opera dress and finished with jaunty bows. A few were lacquered a deep, shiny black and decorated with hints of gold, blue, and red, rather like the Egyptian columns at the Whistons' house or the Chinese decorations she'd seen in pictures of the Prince Regent's home in Brighton. One very grand one was of gilded bamboo set with tiny seed pearls.

"It was time to make a virtue out of necessity, I thought," Amélie explained, head to one side. "If you must carry a cane, why not make it a thing of beauty? *Parbleu*, perhaps you will set a fashion!"

Sophie thought of Susan Halliday sporting a cane at her mother's next party and laughed. "I don't quite see that."

"No, perhaps not. But you will set a fashion for yourself, and others will respect that and admire you for it. They will wait to see what kind of cane the Lady Sophie will be carrying at every ball and *soirée*, just the way they wait to see what fashion Monsieur Brummell will introduce next." Amélie's smile twinkled at her. "And Nalini and I, we had *tellement de plaisir* making them! Did we not, Nalini?"

The maid stepped forward and bowed slightly, hands together before her. *"C'est vrai, madame. C'était un plaisir de les faire pour Lady Sophie,"* she said in her piping voice.

Sophie looked again at the bright array on the bed, then threw her arms around Amélie. "I never thought . . . I hated my old cane, but I didn't think there was anything to be done but try not to use it," she whispered.

"But the cane is your friend. It helps you walk straight and upright, which is good for your posture and keeps you from tiring too quickly . . . not to mention that it keeps you safe." Amélie hugged her back. "So—you will promise me that you will use these, yes? And when you get new dresses, we will make new ones to go with them. And speaking of new dresses . . ." She paused and gave Sophie an impish smile. "Mrs. James delivered the carriage dress that had not been quite ready. Which is a thing very good, I am sure, as you will be needing it."

"Did she? Oh, good." Sophie had bent to admire the canes again, but Amélie's last sentence finally penetrated. She straightened and looked at Amélie. "Why shall I be needing it?"

"A certain young lord stopped by this afternoon to ask if he might take you driving. As it happened that you were out, he left his card and asked if he might call again soon with the same intention." She produced a small rectangle and handed it to Sophie.

Sophie swallowed and looked down at it. *The Earl of Woodbridge*. "Oh, Amélie, should I go?"

"Why should you not?"

"Because . . . because I'm afraid!"

Amélie raised both eyebrows. "Why? He is not . . . not *une canaille* like that Monsieur Underwood, is he?"

Sophie laughed uncertainly. "Of course not, but . . ."

"But?" Amélie looked at her, head tilted to one side.

Sophie looked away to avoid her bright, curious gaze. What was she afraid of? Lord Woodbridge had asked, very graciously, if they might not try again to be friends. A ride in Hyde Park was an excellent way to start—it offered plenty of material for polite conversation, and being so obviously in public precluded the possibility of a quarrel or unpleasant scene.

No, it wasn't driving in the park with him that she feared. What she feared was the note in his voice when he'd said "please" to her that night at the Hallidays' ball . . . and the feelings it had raised in her.

"I'm afraid I'll begin to like him too much," she said to her shoes.

"And what would be the wrong in that?"

"Because . . ." Because she could not be sure that he didn't still feel sorry for her, at some level, and it would be too humiliating to fall in love with someone who felt sorry for her. But she could not say that out loud.

"Sophie." Amélie tilted her chin up to look at her face. Her eyes were kind as she said, "Do not—how does the expression go?—do not go borrowing trouble. You do not have to think about liking him too much, or even at all. Go, and have a pleasant ride. That is all you must do for now. *D'accord?*"

"Brilliant!" Parthenope almost shrieked when Sophie met her in the passage behind the balcony boxes at the King's Theatre in Haymarket the following evening. "Where did you get it?"

Sophie twirled her pink and white cane, eyeing it with satisfaction. "Isn't it perfect? Amélie made it for me—in fact, she made one for practically every dress I own."

"I wish I'd thought of it. We shall have to promenade about the foyer so people can admire it." Parthenope reached for it and examined it closely. "Well, that settles it. If I were you, I'd make your papa marry her immediately. She'd be a perfect stepmama for you, I think."

Sophie smiled but shook her head. "I don't know that Papa will marry again. He's barely taken notice of anything—or anyone—because he's been so busy with the war—"

"Oh, pish. Goodness, Sophie, it would be perfect! He's a widower, and she's the widow of his childhood friend. It would be terribly romantic, don't you think? Most important, she's fond of you. You don't want him to go and marry someone who might not like you, do you? Only think how dreadful *that* would be! No, you'll all deal monstrous well together, so you'd best get busy and make it happen. Surely you can get him to propose to her before the season's over—"

"Hush! They're right behind me!" Sophie scolded, but couldn't help laughing. She glanced back, but only Aunt Molly was there, chattering to the comte; far behind them, Papa and Amélie were talking to a man she didn't know. She pulled Parthenope farther down the passage. "You wretch!" she whispered. "What if they'd heard!"

"So what if they did?" Parthenope looked utterly unconcerned. "Your father was too far away, and your aunt likes Mrs. Carswell too, doesn't she?"

"I suppose so, but that's not important!"

"Isn't it?" But Parthenope's attention had been drawn by a box, the fourth over from Papa's. She stepped inside in and squealed. "Goodness, look at this!"

Sophie followed her through the opening left by the looped-aside curtain. Instead of the usual complement of chairs, the little room held only a broad, purple-velvet-covered divan heaped with cushions at one end, along with a tall gilt candelabrum. "So?" she asked.

"Don't you see? It's scandalous!" But Parthenope sounded anything but scandalized. "I'm sure some rake is planning a seduction in here. How shocking!"

"Planning a seduction *here*? Don't you think there are perhaps slightly . . . er . . . more suitable places for a seduction than a box at the opera?"

"Not if you want to make sure the entire fashionable world knows about your latest conquest. I wonder whose box it is?" She craned her neck to look back down the passage at approaching operagoers. "Maybe it's Lord Byron's—can't you see him owning an opera box with a purple divan in it? Very Turkish!"

Sophie snorted. "Or maybe it belongs to an invalid who loves music. Aren't you getting a little carried away?"

"An invalid wouldn't come to the opera and lie on a purple velvet sofa. It's not at all—*invalidish* enough."

Sophie struggled to maintain a straight face. "That's true.

A serviceable brown canvas would be much more appropriate for an invalid," she agreed.

"Stop quizzing me. I'm sure that I'm right." Parthenope peered across the theater to the boxes on the opposite side. "Oh, famous! I shall be able to see here quite clearly from our box."

"Shall you? What a happy thought," Norris Underwood's voice said pleasantly behind them. "Does that mean I may count upon your undivided attention for the evening?"

Sophie turned. He stood with one hand on the arched door frame, an inscrutable expression on his face that shifted smoothly into a smile as Parthenope turned too and held out her hand to him.

"A delight to see you here. So do the fair Amazons pay tribute to Apollo of the lyre as well as to his sister Diana the huntress?" he asked, raising Parthenope's hand to his lips. His pale green eyes never left her face.

"Well, we can't always be on horseback, can we?" Parthenope winked at Sophie and asked, "This couldn't be *your* box, could it, Mr. Underwood?"

"I have the pleasure of its use for the evening, thanks to the kind offices of a friend who is unable to attend tonight," he returned.

"Unusual furnishings your friend has provided," Sophie couldn't help saying.

He turned to her and bowed. "Good evening, Lady Sophie. Yes, they are unusual, but most comfortable, I am assured. I believe I saw your father in the passage a moment ago, looking for you. Will you permit me to escort you both to your respective families?"

Sophie took his arm, feeling relieved. For a moment, she had feared he was trying to get rid of her so that he could have Parthenope alone, but if he was offering to accompany them both to their boxes . . . She gave herself a mental shake. After all, what possible mischief could Mr. Underwood get up to at the theater, apart from his usual flirtatious banter with Parthenope?

"I'll come see you at the interval," Parthenope called over her shoulder as they left her at Papa's box. "I think Peregrine's coming in at some point this evening—I'll fetch him along if he does." Norris Underwood murmured something to her, and she laughed as they swept away.

Papa looked up at her from his seat beside Amélie with one eyebrow raised as she slipped around the curtain.

"I'm sorry—Parthenope," she mouthed, and took her seat at the end of the group of chairs, next to the comte. Papa nodded and turned his attention to the stage, where the curtain had been drawn back and revealed the interior of a Roman palazzo and a plump, elegantly dressed woman clutching a letter to her heart and appearing to sob. There was a scattering of applause and loud comments from the pit.

As the soprano launched into a passionate aria pledging awful revenge for the capture and banishment of her betrothed by her own father, Sophie scanned the boxes opposite theirs. Where was Parthenope's, and was she safely back in it? She lifted the tiny set of mother-of-pearl opera glasses Papa had bought for her and squinted through them at the other side of the theater, looking for Parthenope's gold gown and cap adorned with a rakish plume curling around her dark hair. Finally Sophie spotted her, peering through her own set of opera glasses.

She swiftly dropped them and waved. Sophie waved back. Well, at least Mr. Underwood had kept his word. She could relax for now and enjoy the opera.

But Parthenope's comments about Amélie and Papa, seeming so flippant at the time, kept coming back to her. Was it so far-fetched an idea, Papa proposing to Amélie? She wasn't sure she was ready to consider the idea of anyone taking Mama's place, but it was true that there couldn't be anyone she'd like better to do so. Papa had grown so . . . so *absorbed* in his work that it felt as if he sometimes forgot how to be himself rather than the devoted servant of the state.

Parthenope was waving at her again. Sophie could see the feather in her cap nodding violently. She raised her glasses again and saw her friend moving her hands about as if trying to pantomime a message . . . at least until the duchess caught one of them in midair and pressed it firmly back into her lap, murmuring something into her daughter's ear. Sophie grinned—evidently Parthenope had something interesting to relate to her at the interval—and turned her attention to the stage once more as the soprano fainted elegantly into the tenor's arms. A murmur of sympathy rose from the audience until someone in the pit below shouted, "Loosen her stays, then! That'll bring her round!" Sophie giggled and turned to look at Parthenope. She'd clapped the back of one hand to her brow and was shaking her head.

"Poor girl," Aunt Molly whispered as the curtain came down. "Why doesn't he fetch her some spirits of hartshorn? He doesn't look very *steady*, if you ask me. And that poor girl is going to be sorry if she doesn't do something about her father. What proof has he got? It's not fair to keep her away from Don Umberto like that. I shall complain to the manager."

The comte smiled. "You are *sentimentale, mon amie*."

"Well, it's just like us, isn't—"

"It's just a story, Molly," Papa interrupted her. "Oh, Patten. Glad you found us. La Bertinotti is certainly in voice tonight, isn't she?"

Sophie turned. A young man had pushed aside the curtain enclosing their box. He bowed, then stepped inside to shake Papa's hand, and she recognized him as the stranger who had been speaking to Papa and Amélie before the opera. "As I was saying before, she ought to be. She gets paid enough to be so," he said coolly.

Papa chuckled. "I still think you should be working for the treasury and not for me. Sophie, I don't believe you had the pleasure of meeting Mr. Patten earlier."

Sophie nodded politely but she did not care for Mr. Patten's cravat, which was too fussily tied for her taste, or his eyes, which were too close-set and which were lingering on her.

"Are you enjoying the opera, Lady Sophie?" he asked. "Your father says it is your first visit. Most young ladies of sensibility seem to find it very appealing."

"I don't know what is more entertaining—what is happening on the stage or off it," she answered politely, choosing to ignore his reference to "young ladies of sensibility." Did she look like someone who would swoon at an opera?

"We are fortunate to be hearing Signora Bertinotti tonight. Many prefer Catalani, but her acting skills leave much to be desired, in my book. She always smiles, even when singing tragedies." Mr. Patten moved closer, leaning casually against the box's ornate railing.

"I think you are right, Sophie. The audience is as *amusant* as the singers," Amélie put in. She raised one eyebrow slightly, then cast her eyes heavenward. Sophie stifled a laugh and looked away.

Mr. Patten went on as if she hadn't spoken. "Mr. Braham is always a pleasure to hear, though he sounds a trifle off tonight—perhaps the weather disagrees with him. We shall see how Don Umberto does—"

A sharp cracking noise cut off his speech. Sophie looked up and saw his horrified face and upflung arms as he started to tumble backward. The carved wooden front of their box had splintered.

Chapter
9

Sophie gasped and grabbed for Mr. Patten's flailing arm. Her gloved hand slid down his smoothly sleeved arm but gained purchase on his hand, and his fingers closed round hers in a desperate grip. She leaned backward, but in her half-seated position could not get the leverage needed to pull him back, even if she'd had strength enough.

"*Mon Dieu!*" she dimly heard someone exclaim. Then the comte was there, yanking Mr. Patten back into the box, and the three of them stood, panting, while Papa and Amélie and Aunt Molly stared at them.

Aunt Molly spoke first. "What happened? Why are you all standing like that?"

"Monsieur, are you injured?" The comte had gone very pale.

Mr. Patten opened and closed his mouth a few times, like a beached fish. Sophie felt a pang of sympathy for him in the midst of her own shock. "I . . . I am quite unharmed. Thank you, sir . . . I . . ." He turned and looked behind him, and for a moment looked as though he would fall all over again. "I . . . excuse me!" He clapped a hand over his mouth and plunged out of the box into the passage.

"What *happened*?" Aunt Molly asked again, plaintively.

"The—the railing appears to have been of poor manufacture," the comte said, breathing hard. "Lady Sophie, you just saved that young man from a nasty accident."

"Not at all. You were the one who pulled him back." Sophie nearly collapsed into her chair. Her heart felt as if it were about to pound its way out of her chest.

"If you had not caught him first, I should not have been able to." The comte bowed, then he too sat down abruptly.

"Auguste! Are you all right? Would you like my vinaigrette?" Aunt Molly started digging in her reticule.

"Sophie?" Amélie put a hand on her shoulder and bent over her.

"I . . . I'm fine. Just a little shaken." She pressed Amélie's hand and winced. Her right hand—the one Mr. Patten had grasped—felt bruised and sore. She peeled her glove off and tentatively flexed it.

Papa was examining the front of their box. "You caught him before it broke quite through— fortunately for the people sitting below us, too. But it will definitely require replacement."

"Perhaps the wood is rotted," Amélie said, watching him.

"Or beetles—they can eat right through a chair in a twinkling. I *know*," Aunt Molly said ominously, handing the comte her open vinaigrette. He grimaced and shook his head.

"I see evidence of neither," Papa said, sounding grim. "I shall certainly have to speak to Mr. Waters about having this repaired." He rose and turned to the comte. "I must thank you, sir."

The comte waved him away. "It is your daughter you should thank, my lord."

Papa looked at her, and his face softened. "Are you all right, Sophie? Do you want to go home?"

"I'm fine, Papa." She tried to smile, but her mouth felt trembly.

"That's my girl. But I think I had better go check on Patten." He touched her shoulder briefly, then twitched the curtain aside and left.

"Sophie, I insist." Aunt Molly handed her the vinaigrette. "If it wasn't beetles, then what could have made it happen?"

Which was a very good question. Sophie leaned forward and reached out to touch the splintered wood. A cold tingle pricked at the bare fingers of her right hand. A familiar cold tingle—

"Oh!" she exclaimed, and sat back in her chair.

"What is it, *petite*?" Amélie turned to her quickly.

"Um . . . it's Aunt's vinaigrette . . . it's rather, um . . . pungent!" Sophie sniffed and blinked her eyes as if they watered, and snapped the vinaigrette shut.

"Of course it is, dear. That's the point." Aunt Molly beamed at her. "It's got wild onion and stinking cabbage powder in it. Feel better? You might want to sit quietly for a minute until the stinking cabbage wears off."

"Yes, I think I shall." Sophie handed it back to her and sat down, closing her eyes and resting her head against the wall as if overcome.

Magic again! That icy prickle still vibrating through the wood had been unmistakable. Someone had intentionally made it break, probably with a dissolution spell, though her touch had been too brief to tell. But how—and when? All of them had touched the railing at some point this evening. Why, she herself had leaned on it briefly as she sat down. The thought made her shiver, as did another, close on its heels: Mr. Patten also worked in the War Office.

"Lady Sophie," the comte said softly. Sophie opened her eyes and looked up to see him bending solicitously over her. "Shall I try to find for you a drink of water—or something a little stronger if it can be found?"

"It was just . . . so sudden," she said. Which sounded almost foolishly inadequate, but he nodded.

"*C'est vrai.*" He looked at the broken railing and frowned. "It was ill done," he said, more to himself than aloud.

"I beg your pardon?" Sophie asked, but at that moment Papa pushed aside the curtain to the box.

"The footman could not find Waters—I'm sure he's backstage just now—so I'm afraid we shall have to wait to speak to him till later. I did find poor Patten and put him in a hackney. He looked completely done up." He looked at Sophie. "He's Sir John Patten's grandson—there's a good property in Shropshire. I believe he was rather taken with you, Sophie—asked me to tender his apologies for his abrupt departure."

Sophie grimaced, but only said, "That was kind of him, Papa."

He raised an eyebrow. "Are you sure you wouldn't like to go home?"

"N-no. Really, I'm quite well. And I should like to see more of the opera." She paused, then added, "Even *if* Mr. Braham is a trifle off tonight."

Papa chuckled. "Point taken—*both* points, in fact. And there is the curtain, so you shall have your wish." He resumed his seat next to Amélie and murmured something to her that Sophie couldn't hear.

Sophie sat back in her seat and slowly wiggled her glove onto her hand as Signora Bertinotti resumed being agitated at stage left. She would have liked to run her hands over the splintered section of railing again and try to feel the magic that had been used, to find some hint—anything!—of who had done it and why. Sometimes the emotion of the person performing the magic would make its way into the magic and could be sensed by others. It might be informative to know if these had been the acts of an angry or vengeful person. But it would be too difficult to explain away what she was doing . . . and besides, she wasn't sure she wanted to get that close to the broken place. Heavens, what would Parthenope think when she came at the interval—

Except that the interval had already happened. And Parthenope hadn't come.

Sophie found her opera glasses—undamaged after tumbling from her lap onto the floor when she'd risen to save Mr. Patten, thank goodness—and scanned the boxes opposite them. Yes, there was the Revesbys' box. . . .

There was no sign of the gold hat and its outsized feather.

Sophie lowered her glasses and frowned. So Parthenope wasn't in the box with her parents and the guests she'd seen there before. What was so odd about that? Perhaps she had needed to go to the necessary or had stopped to talk to an acquaintance on her way to visit and been detained.

But it just didn't seem like Parthenope not to have at least poked her head in to say hello—at least, not after all the purposeful gesturing and waving she'd done during the last act. She'd definitely looked as though she had something to say. Perhaps she'd seen something amusing taking place on Mr. Underwood's purple velvet sofa.

She stood up abruptly and bent to whisper in Amélie's ear. "I should like to go use the necessary. I'll be back directly."

"Of course—we did not have a chance for that after . . ." She gestured at the broken railing. "Do you wish me to come with you?"

"No. That is," Sophie amended conscientiously, "not unless you wish to."

Amélie patted her hand. "I am not in need. Go, then, *ma chère*."

Sophie nodded, and taking her cane, slipped into the passage. Once there, she paused, leaning against the wall. The thought of Mr. Underwood and his sofa suddenly seemed as worrisome as magically splintering railings. What if Parthenope had been waylaid by him on her way to visit Sophie? Highly doubtful, yes . . . but she could not get the thought of it out of her brain. If only she had a mirror in her reticule—then she could ask it to show her Parthenope. But she didn't. And what made her think she could do a scrying spell anyway? The only thing for it was to go to Mr. Underwood's box and see if Parthenope was there. If she wasn't, she could apologize for intruding. Quite simple, really . . . except that the last thing she wanted to do was visit that box.

But the memory of the purple velvet sofa and the way Mr. Underwood had looked at Parthenope as they stood there earlier propelled her away from the wall and down the passage. Mercifully, there were no lingerers in the passage—evidently those of a more social bent had already ensconced themselves in their friends' boxes for visits. Sophie walked as quietly as she could, not letting her cane tap on the parquet floor, until she arrived at the fourth box down from Papa's. The curtain was indeed drawn over the entrance. Sophie drew close, listening, but Signora Bertinotti and Mr. Braham were engaged in a passionate duet onstage, which obscured every other sound in the theater. Taking a deep breath, she parted the curtain and peeked inside . . . and found herself almost nose-to-nose with a wild-eyed Parthenope.

"Sophie!" she gasped. "Thank God! Help me!"

Sophie goggled at her and realized that her friend was hanging bodily over someone's shoulder. Parthenope squirmed furiously and beat at her captor's back and posterior with both fists, exclaiming, "Put me down!" in an outraged whisper.

Two things occurred to Sophie. The first was to say "I told you so!" in an insufferably smug tone.

But that wouldn't help Parthenope, which was the second and far more important thing. If she didn't do something quickly, the entire theater would soon notice that there was something much more interesting going on in this box than onstage.

"*Figere!*" she commanded, dropping her cane and pointing at Parthenope's assailant.

To her surprise, it worked. Instantly the figure froze in place, ceasing its attempts to restrain Parthenope . . . and so did Parthenope's attempts to free herself. The spell had worked too well, and frozen them both.

Sophie edged her way to the front of the box and twitched the curtains closed, then peered out the crack left between them. To her relief, she didn't see any opera glasses turned in their direction.

"I'm tempted to leave you there and fetch your mother to see you in this position, Parthenope Hardcastle," she said severely, turning to look into the face of Parthenope's captor. As she expected, Norris Underwood glared back at her, equal parts of fear, anger, and disbelief showing in his eyes. Thank heavens the spell immobilized his mouth as well, or she was sure she would be the recipient of some extremely strong language just now.

She hobbled around to face Parthenope and retrieved her cane, then looked at her thoughtfully. Parthenope also stared, her mouth as immobilized as Mr. Underwood's, but her eyes were eloquent.

"I know, I know," Sophie said to her. "Give me a moment. I have to think about this. Magic can be tricky sometimes." Or in her case, all the time. Attempting a releasing spell while Parthenope and he still touched would be risky: assuming it even worked, there was no telling what he might do once they were released.

Parthenope's eyes widened, and an idea came to Sophie.

"Yes, I said magic," she said, walking around them to face Mr. Underwood. "Were you attempting to publicly compromise my friend so she would have to marry you, Mr. Underwood?" she asked him. "That was rather crass, don't you think? You must be quite desperate to have attempted such a thing. Lord Woodbridge said you were ridiculously in debt, and I believe it. Only a desperate man would have thought up such a scheme."

He glared at her.

"A duke's daughter! Think of the scandal! It might have worked, but there was no way for you to know that her best friend was a witch, now, was there?" she continued in a soothing voice. "Though I expect you may have called me that name or worse, in your mind." She paced around until she faced Parthenope. "Get ready," she mouthed, pantomiming setting something free, then circled back to where Mr. Underwood could see her.

"Now, listen to me well, you," she said, leaning toward him in as menacing a fashion as she could manage. "I stopped you just now, and I can stop you again. In a moment, I'm going to release you. You will set my friend down—gently, mind you— and then you will leave this box without saying a word, to us or to anyone. After that, you will have twelve hours to get yourself out of London, and you will stay out of London for . . . for a year and a day, or my magic will hunt you down and freeze you once more, and the next time, I might not be around to free you. Do you understand?" She pushed her face against his until they were nearly touching—she could smell fear coming off him in acrid waves.

"I'll take that as a yes," she said, pulling back, and then made herself smile at him almost tenderly. "You do believe me, don't you? And if you ever—*ever*—try to tell anyone of what has happened tonight, your throat will close on your own breath." She paused and said, "You know I can do it, don't you?"

His eyes bulged.

Now came the hard part. She moved to the side where neither could see her—she was not sure she could do anything with Mr. Underwood's angry eyes or Parthenope's pleading ones on her—and raised her hands. *Mama, help me,* she said in her mind, and pointed at them. "*Liberamini,*" she whispered.

Nothing happened.

Panic, dry and cold like a winter gale, surged up her throat. "*Libera—*" she began, more loudly.

Without warning, Mr. Underwood crumpled to the floor as if his bones had suddenly dissolved. Parthenope collapsed on top of him, and for a moment Sophie wondered if she had done something hideous to the two of them. Then Parthenope jumped up awkwardly, backing away from Mr. Underwood as if he had smallpox.

"You villain!" she cried, patting her chest. "You broke my busk! If it tears my corset, you will *pay*—do you hear me?"

Mr. Underwood was trying to lift himself to his feet, but had only made it to hands and knees. "You . . . you *bitch*!" he spat, staring up at Sophie.

She ignored him. "Are you all right?" she said to Parthenope, touching her arm.

"No!" Parthenope squeaked. "This was my favorite busk! It was carved ivory with my initials—" She stopped and looked down at Mr. Underwood. "What did you just say?"

He had managed to regain his feet and stood swaying slightly and glaring at Sophie. "You cursed little whore!"

"Nobody speaks to my friend that way, Mr. Underwood, and I suggest you stop or I shall make you," Parthenope said to him as she put up her fists and set her feet. "I am told I have a quite punishing left jab for a female."

"Parthenope! You can't mean you know how to box!" Sophie wasn't sure whether to be scandalized or amused.

"Of course I do." Parthenope continued to watch him with narrowed eyes.

Mr. Underwood's left eye was twitching oddly. "You crippled bitch! Think you can best me, you miserable—"

Parthenope sighed, shifted her stance slightly, and punched him.

He tottered back a pace, swearing again and feeling his nose. A shocking spatter of blood crimsoned his snowy neck cloth.

"Dear me, I'm so sorry," Parthenope said pleasantly. "Did I say it was my left jab that was so noteworthy? I meant to say my right, of course. So silly of me." She took a step toward him, smiling widely. "May I suggest you close your potato-trap and leave this box now, Mr. Underwood, before I see what I can accomplish with my left? Your hat is on the floor there—I seem to recall having kicked it during our earlier discussions."

Mr. Underwood looked as though he would have liked to say something to her too, but Sophie stepped forward.

"Twelve hours," she said, raising her hand and pointing at him.

He scowled, made a grab for his hat, and almost lunged for the curtain enclosing the box.

"Safe journey!" Parthenope called as he flung the curtain aside and dashed into the passage.

Sophie let out her breath in a whoosh and tottered over to the purple velvet sofa. "I do wish you hadn't made me do that," she said, collapsing onto it.

Parthenope sat down next to her. "You can do magic!" she said. "You can truly do magic!"

"No," Sophie said, slightly crossly. "I'm just so terrifying that Mr. Underwood was paralyzed with fear."

Parthenope snorted. "You're not going to fob me off with that, you. Sophie, you're a witch!"

"And you've yet to explain to me how you got yourself into this situation. How could you, Parthenope? You were the one who said this box looked as though it was the setting for a seduction. Why did you let him drag you in here?"

"Because he said *you* were in here," Parthenope snapped.

"What?"

"I was on my way to your box just at the end of the interval—I'd been waiting for Perry to come, but he didn't arrive—and Mr. Underwood suddenly stepped out as I passed. He said you were inside and that there was something wrong—that you'd fainted or fallen or something. So of course I rushed right in, and then he grabbed me. How could he *lie* to me about such a thing? I was nearly speechless with worry!" She sniffed.

Sophie wanted to laugh, but was so touched by Parthenope's concern that she didn't. "I suppose I have to forgive you, then."

"You certainly do. Now come on, Sophie Rosier—it's your turn. Tell all."

Sophie shifted uncomfortably, then stood up and went to the box's entrance. "Can't it wait? I'm going to be missed if I don't get back to Papa's box soon, and I'll bet you will be too."

Parthenope scowled at her but stood up. "Fine. But you'd

better be ready tomorrow to talk." She threw back the curtain and stepped through, then gasped, "Why, Perry!"

Sophie, though not sure how she did it, managed to melt away to one side of the entrance and slip behind the curtain as Parthenope stepped through it. Of all people, why Lord Woodbridge *now*?

"Parthenope!" she heard him say. "What in blazes have you been doing? I was just nearly knocked down by Norris Underwood with blood running down his face, looking like the hounds of hell were after him and muttering something about not letting her get him."

"Oh." Parthenope let out a tinkling little laugh. "Why, that was me, of course."

"You—"

"I drew his claret quite properly! Remember how I made you teach me to throw a punch two years ago after you started taking boxing lessons with Gentleman Jackson?"

"Are you saying that *you* bloodied Underwood's nose?" Lord Woodbridge said incredulously.

"Of course I did. He was behaving very badly, so we—" she broke off, then continued, "Umm . . . so I . . . well, I couldn't very well let him get away with it, could I? I'm so glad I didn't forget how to set my feet and put my weight into it, like you showed me."

"Parthenope, why did you have to punch Underwood in the face like that?" There was a pause, and then she heard, "Good God, Parthenope—there's a sofa in there. You don't mean that you—"

Sophie held her breath, willing him not to enter the box.

"Don't worry about that," Parthenope said hastily. "Where

were you? I thought you said you'd be round to see us before the first interval—"

"Would to God I had been. Then maybe you wouldn't have gotten into Underwood's clutches. What possessed you to enter this box with him? Do you want the entire world to think you're letting him—"

"Of course not, silly! Why do you think I punched him?" Parthenope's voice had begun to take on a decidedly sulky tone. "Aren't you impressed that I bloodied him? I thought I handled him rather well."

"Handled him well? The only way to handle a hellhound like him is to leave him strictly alone. But no, not you. You've been so busy trying to stage-manage my addresses to Lady Sophie that you haven't paid a whit of notice to your own—"

Sophie stiffened. Had she heard him correctly?

"Not so loud!" Parthenope cautioned him. "Do you want the entire theater to hear us?"

"I don't care if they do. It's no more than you deserve!"

"But I've *only* been trying to help—goodness, you'd made enough of a mull of wooing Sophie on your own. And you didn't want Mr. Underwood trying to woo her, did you?"

"Good God, no!"

"I didn't think so." Sophie could almost see her nodding smugly. "That's why I had to draw his fire myself. Now, pay attention. Don't you think Sophie is the loveliest, most charming girl in London?"

Sophie closed her eyes and leaned against the wall.

"That has nothing to do with—"

"*Do* you?" Parthenope demanded.

"You know I do. What—"

She went on as if she hadn't heard him. "And didn't you fall head over heels in love with her the moment you saw her, so much so that you could hardly speak to her when you met? That's what you told me!"

"Yes, I did, but—"

"And don't you want to fix your interest with her before someone else besides Mr. Underwood realizes what an enchanting creature she is and crowds you out? Hmm?"

"Stop poking me! God knows I do—but not if you're going to get yourself caught by a villain like Underwood in the meanwhile. I can attend to fixing my interest with her without your help, thank you."

"Well, I would suggest that you bestir yourself, young Peregrine," Parthenope said, sounding ludicrously grandmotherly. "Sophie is coming to spend the morning with me tomorrow—" She cleared her throat and repeated, "At least, I believe we have determined that she is *definitely* coming to spend the morning with me tomorrow as *soon* as she is possibly able, but you should certainly come riding in the park with us later in the day if the weather is fine."

"No."

"Why not?"

"Because I intend to take her driving myself tomorrow afternoon, and a chaperone is not needed, thank you. And now you must promise me something."

"Oh, *all* right." Parthenope sounded grudging again, but Sophie could hear the edge of glee beneath her words. "What is it?"

"That you undertake to promise that you will not receive Underwood anymore. No calls, no dancing, no riding with him, no more than the merest civilities if you should meet. Nothing more."

Parthenope sighed. "Oh, Perry, you're such a—"

"Promise me."

"Very well. I solemnly promise that I shall have nothing more to do with Mr. Underwood. You drive a hard bargain, dear coz." Sophie wondered how he couldn't hear the laughter in her voice. "Now I think it's probably time we went back to Mama's box. She has guests, and it helps if I take over poking Papa if he begins to snore too loudly, so she can concentrate on playing hostess."

"Can't you go without me? I was intending to visit the Lansells' box before I was so unexpectedly detained."

"Were you? Good boy. Now, don't forget what I told you last time. If you should see her, don't be afraid to let her catch a hint that given a chance, you'd like to drag her into the nearest alcove and kiss her senseless."

"Parthenope!"

"Well, wouldn't you?"

"That is nothing I want to discuss with a chuffy-faced chit like you," he said repressively. "Besides, what would you know of such things?"

"Nothing. I'm utterly heartless and impervious to male blandishments and gallantry. Hadn't you noticed?"

"I'd noticed the utterly heartless part."

"Pooh. Well, if you don't see Sophie, I shall tell her you were looking for her when I see her tomorrow. In the morning, *bright and early*."

Chapter 10

Sophie spent another nearly sleepless night, her mind bouncing from one to another of the evening's events, trying to sort through them. Foremost among those were revealing her magic to Parthenope (and Mr. Underwood!) and over-hearing (if that was the word—she was quite sure Parthenope had intended her to hear every bit of it) the conversation between Parthenope and Lord Woodbridge.

What should she do when she arrived at Parthenope's "bright and early," as her friend had so loudly and distinctly directed? Throttle her or embrace her?

When she'd heard Parthenope say Lord Woodbridge's name last night, she wasn't sure she'd ever missed having full use of her magic so much: a translocation spell would have been very useful. She'd already had quite enough drama for the evening, thank you very much, between Mr. Patten's near accident and evidence that magic had played a part in it and then vanquishing Mr. Underwood . . . and Lord Woodbridge had definitely seemed ready to enact a dramatic scene with his cousin.

To hear that her best friend had been directing Lord Woodbridge's wooing had left Sophie torn between laughter and indignation. But then to hear him matter-of-factly agreeing that he thought her the prettiest girl in London, that he'd loved her on first sight, and that he needed to secure her affections before someone else did . . . well, was it to be wondered that her eyes would not close?

Amélie looked at her sharply when she came into the breakfast room that morning. "Did you not sleep well, *petite*?"

"Hmm? Oh, I . . . no, I slept perfectly well, thank you." Sophie helped herself to a cup of chocolate.

"Is that all you're having? I hope you're not coming down with green-sickness," Aunt Molly said, leaning forward and peering into her face. "Perhaps I had better mix you up a spring tonic. I wonder if I can find some centaury flowers at the apothecary? The *Domestic Encyclopedia* says that worsted stockings should be worn by those suffering from green-sickness, rather than cotton or silk. What sort are you wearing?"

"Thank you, Aunt, but I don't think I'm ill." Sophie helped herself from the platters of eggs and fried mushrooms and beef on the table, and rapidly began eating. "But I shall go up and change my stockings directly I'm finished, if you wish."

Aunt Molly beamed. "You're a good girl, Sophronia."

As it happened, however, her cotton stockings were never changed, for only moments after Sophie had finished eating, Belton came to the door of the breakfast room. "Lady Parthenope Hardcastle presents her compliments, my lady, and says she is here to convey you back to her house for the day," he said, looking as amused as he ever permitted himself to.

"My goodness!" Sophie rose from the table and hurried into the hall. Parthenope stood there in her gray and red short cloak, whistling and tapping her foot.

"I'll give you ten minutes," she said cheerfully, by way of greeting. "After that Belton has promised me he'll drag you downstairs and lift you bodily into my carriage."

"He did no such thing," Sophie said, a little crossly. "Might I be permitted to clean my teeth and comb my hair?"

"He did too. Very well, you may do the teeth, but your hair looks fine to me. Oh, stop looking so disapproving and tell me that you're not dying to talk."

Sophie relented. "All right, I am. Won't you go sit with Aunt Molly and Amélie while I get ready?"

Once they were ensconced in the Revesbys' carriage, Parthenope sighed. "Thank heavens you didn't take any longer. Your aunt thinks I am coming down with something called green-sickness and says you are as well. She asked me what kind of stockings I wore and threatened to dose me with some hideous-sounding tonic. Lord, if I'd known you were contagious, I would have just sent the carriage for you and waited at home."

"Green-sickness isn't contagious. It's just some old wives' tale way of saying we both look haggard." Sophie paused. "I'm not surprised—I don't believe I slept very much. What happened last night after you left the box with Lord Woodbridge? You left earlier than we did."

"Absolutely nothing happened. Mama took pity on my father and we left, and that was that. It was dreadfully anti-climactic."

"Did you really want more excitement last night?"

"N-no, I suppose not." Parthenope eyed her. "You did hear all of my conversation with Perry last night, didn't you? I thought you were behind the curtain, but I didn't see you. Did you do some sp . . . um . . . do something and sneak away?"

Sophie knew she was thinking of the groom perched up on the seat behind them, staring straight ahead as was proper but surely able to hear their every word. She gripped her reticule more tightly. "I was there."

For the rest of the short drive to Curzon Street, they were silent. Sophie felt a tension in the silence and hoped it was due to the fact that they weren't alone, rather than that Parthenope had begun to realize just how Sophie's magic set her apart.

Once they arrived at Revesby House, Parthenope led her up to her bedchamber, handsomely done in shades of rose and pink. "I gave Andrews the morning off," she announced, closing and locking her door behind her. "We'll have a bit of luncheon at two, but until then we won't be disturbed."

"Another tot of gin, Mab!" said a cheerful voice.

"Oh, you good boy!" Parthenope exclaimed, crossing the room. "You said it quite plainly that time."

Hester the parakeet sat placidly on a perch by a window, preening his feathers. Sophie regarded him warily as she put off her pelisse and removed her hat. "Is he going to start going on about turnips again?"

"I hope not. I've taught him a few much more interesting things to say. Don't tell Mama, though." Parthenope took a walnut meat out of a bowl on the sill and gave it to him. "There you go, my precious."

"Doesn't he, er, remind you of Mr. Underwood?"

"As a matter of fact, he does. The poor man did turn a rather peculiar shade of purple after I popped him in the nose last evening." She turned back to Sophie and took a breath. "I thought about what you did half the night—I didn't think I'd dreamed it."

Sophie hesitated, then said, slowly, "Before we talk about this anymore, you have to swear to me that you will tell no one else. No one! If anyone should find out—"

"Good God, of course I would never tell anyone!" Parthenope pulled a pair of chairs closer to the window and dropped unceremoniously into one, the violence of her motion lending emphasis to her words. "Why do you think I sent Andrews away and locked us in here? Your magic saved me from a dreadful scrape last night—the very least I can do is to keep your secret for you!"

"Yes, but . . ." Sophie stopped. Parthenope obviously understood the necessity for secrecy. She also understood, far more deeply than Sophie herself seemed to, what was due to a friend.

"Then yes, I'm a witch," she said, exhaling. "Or at least, I sort of am. Was. My mother—"

"*Was?*" Parthenope interjected. "That certainly looked like magic to me, last night!"

"Yes, I know. But I was lucky it worked. Ever since I was ill, my magic has been as crippled as my leg. It's better than it was. For a year, I couldn't do anything. But I can't rely on it— I'd just tried to immobilize Mr. Underwood last night, not both of you—"

"Wait!" Parthenope held up her hands. "I think you had better go back to the beginning, or else I might burst into flame."

Sophie smiled and told her about Mama and her lessons,

about little Harry, about her illness. Parthenope's eyes grew wider and wider as she spoke, until she got to the day that Papa had come to her and told her in a broken whisper that her mother was dead.

"I'm so sorry," she said softly when Sophie ran out of words. "Losing them was doubly bad, wasn't it? They weren't just family—they were the only ones like you." She frowned, opened her mouth, closed it, then appeared to make up her mind. "I beg your pardon if this is a rude question, but . . . well, if your mother had this power, then why couldn't she stop your illness, or keep your leg from becoming lame? Why couldn't she help your sister?"

Sophie sighed. "Don't you think she tried? But it doesn't work that way. There are limits. I could very probably heal a broken bone if I tried—I know I can heal a cut or take away a wart . . . or at least I *could*, once. But that's because I know what a cut or a wart or a broken bone is. What is sickness? How can we stop it if we don't know what it comes from? I remember her trying to bring down my fever, and afterward trying to help keep my leg from twisting and shrinking. I don't know if what she did helped or not. Maybe I would be even worse if she hadn't. But I've thought about it for a long time, and I always come back to this: Why else would she have fallen into despair and illness herself, if she could stop it?"

Parthenope nodded slowly. "That makes sense, in a way, but it still seems quite godlike to me . . . or goddesslike, I suppose. And then losing it . . . why do you think that happened?"

"I don't know! I don't know if it's because it too was somehow harmed by my illness, or something else, because sometimes it does work, like last night—"

"Thank heavens for that! When you did whatever you did last night, and we couldn't move . . ." She shook her head. "I had tried to get a chance to hit that scoundrel, but he grabbed me so suddenly that I could not—"

"Yes, and I can hardly believe that you know how to box!" Sophie said. It was a relief to change the subject for a few minutes, though she was sure they would come back to her magic. "I was sure you were hoaxing when you put up your fists like that!"

"I would never hoax about such a thing! I thought it only fair to warn him. Perry taught me, of course—or I made him teach me when I found out he was taking lessons. I *knew* it would be useful someday," she added, sounding smug.

"Speaking of whom . . ." Now that Lord Woodbridge had been mentioned, it was Parthenope's turn to do some explaining.

"Who? Perry?" Her eyes twinkled. "Why, what about him?"

"Parthenope!"

She laughed and held up her hands in surrender. "Don't bite my head off! Wasn't it just perfect, last night? I'm astonished that I didn't laugh and ruin it all. You heard him, didn't you? Well?"

Now that they'd finally begun to speak of it, Sophie didn't know what to say. "Well . . ."

"Don't you dare go all missish on me! I knew from that first day we called on you and he was there that he was smitten. He's quite gone about you, you know. I must admit I'm finding it monstrously amusing, the way it's made him so cowhanded. And I don't think I'm wrong in thinking that you're not indifferent yourself, am I?"

Was she? She thought of the way he had looked at her at

the Hallidays' when he asked if they could start again and the tingle it had sent down her back and into her middle. "I don't know. Don't you remember what he said to me, that first day when you called? I don't want anyone offering for me because he feels like he needs to protect me or because he feels sorry for me."

"Of course you don't," Parthenope replied promptly. "That would be abominable, not to mention shockingly tedious. But think—when he said he loved you as soon as he saw you, he didn't know who you were. That wasn't until after, and he said it gave him such a turn because he couldn't see anything to feel sorry for you about—"

"Until we tripped over each other and he understood what it was. Oh, God, Parthenope, I don't know! He's . . . yes, when we were presented I was . . . not indifferent—"

Parthenope snorted. "I should think not. He's excessively handsome, in case you hadn't noticed."

"Yes, and so why would he settle for a cripple?"

Parthenope stood up and took a few paces, then turned and stared down at her, hands on hips. "Sophie Rosier, that is the stupidest thing I've ever heard you say. He's in love with you. With you. I think he would be if you had three crippled legs. Why can't you accept that?"

"I don't know." Sophie shrank down in her seat and stared at the toes of her slippers miserably. "But it must matter, at some point. It always does. That's just the way the world is. Didn't you hear the rumors about me, at the start of the season? Half of society had decided that if I was lame, then I must be half-witted as well, or hunchbacked, or possessed of a squint. My aunt Isabel told me I should be lucky to find an impoverished younger son or a half-pay officer to offer for me and that it was fortunate my dowry would be so large. Do you wonder that I'm suspicious, then, if the best-looking man in London suddenly seems to be taking an interest in me? I know it's not for my dowry—he'll be a marquis someday and doesn't need my money . . . so what can it be, except a mild attraction inflamed by sympathy? You yourself were the one who said he's got a chivalric streak as wide as the Channel."

Parthenope sat down again, her face softer. "Might I give your aunt a taste of my boxing skills, next time I see her? Is that what you think is going on here?"

"Isn't it?" Sophie felt in the sleeve of her dress for the handkerchief she'd tucked there.

"No, it isn't," Parthenope said, very firmly. "But I'm not sure how to convince you of that. Perry's *dying* to go to your father and ask his permission to pay his addresses to you, but he won't until he thinks there's a chance you'll say yes or at least not refuse him outright. What would you do if he came to you tomorrow, asking for your hand? What would you say to him?"

A flutter of excitement burned in Sophie's throat at the thought, cooled by a wisp of doubt. He was handsome and very eligible, fashionable without being a fop or dissipated, serious and clever without being schoolmasterish. He and Papa already got along . . . why, he was even attentive to Aunt Molly. And yet, would that niggling little doubt that he regarded her as a strong, whole person in her own right ever go away? "I—I don't know."

"Well, that and the fact that you good as confessed you hardly slept last night tells me his cause isn't completely lost. I should tell you, by the way, that I am quite determined to have you for a cousin." One corner of her mouth quirked humorously. "If you're still concerned about him feeling the need to protect you, we could always tell him about what you did to Mr. Underwood last night. That would—"

"Don't you *dare* tell him!"

Parthenope made a face. "You know I won't! But what if you do marry him? Will you tell him then?"

"I—I don't know. Considering that I can barely do a spot-lifting spell—"

"Ooh, what's that? Will you show me!"

Sophie couldn't help smiling. Parthenope sounded like a child begging for a treat. "Do you have something with a stain on it? A dress or a—"

"Do I?" Parthenope leapt up and went to her bed, burrowing under the counterpane and lifting her mattress with a grunt. "Here. I sneaked some strawberries up to Hester yesterday and got an enormous red smear on the skirt of this muslin because *somebody* was not being a very dainty eater, was he?" She laid a white bundle on Sophie's lap and gave Hester's tail a small tug.

"Piddle," he commented.

"Don't you dare, or it's back in your cage with you. Well? I was going to try to clean it myself so Andrews wouldn't sigh patiently at me—she's terrifying when she sighs patiently." Parthenope perched on the edge of her chair, looking expectant. "What are you going to do?"

Sophie took out her handkerchief and shook out the dress. A couple of large red spots, along with some smears, marred its whiteness. "What am I going to *try* to do, you mean? Move the stain from your dress to my handkerchief."

"Move it? Why not just . . . you know—make it go away?" Parthenope waved her hand vaguely.

"Because it's a lot simpler to move it from one place to another than to make it cease to exist. Trust me." She took a deep breath and rubbed her finger across the red stains, closing her eyes as she did. "*Migrā*," she murmured.

"Oh!" Parthenope whistled softly. "I can see that magic could be very useful."

Sophie opened her eyes. The stain was gone . . . she'd done it!

But wasn't it pathetic that she should be so excited by such a trifling spell?

"By the pricking of my thumbs!" Hester said, fluttering down from his perch onto Sophie's knee and scratching gently with his talons at the place where the stain had been.

"You don't have thumbs, feather face." Parthenope reached down and forced her hand under him so that he had to hop onto it, then set him back on his perch. "Get back up there and behave yourself. So where's the stain?"

"Here, for now." Sophie held up her forefinger. The pad of it was bright red. "And now, here." She brushed her finger across her handkerchief. It remained unstained. She rubbed it again, a little harder. "Oh, the devil!"

"Umm . . ." Parthenope looked sympathetic.

"This is what it's been like!" Sophie balled up her hanky and threw it to the floor. "I never know whether even the smallest bit of magic will work or not. It's infuriating! I limp when I walk, and I limp when I do magic. I'm useless."

"No." Parthenope took her dress and held it up. "My dress is clean. And Norris Underwood is probably halfway to Scotland or somewhere by now because of your magic. Stop being so hard on yourself."

"You don't understand." Sophie pulled herself to her feet and went to stand by the window.

"Maybe I don't. Or maybe I see my friend chastising herself for no very good reason and want her to stop."

"Parthenope, listen. If I can't get my magic to work, someone might die."

Parthenope snorted. "Now you're just being dramatic—"

"Am I? Do you remember the statue falling at the Whistons' ball, when we met?"

"Of course—"

"And Sir Walter's horse throwing him in Hyde Park?"

"Yes, but what—"

"What do they have to do with my magic? Those weren't accidents. Someone used magic to make those things happen. And last night, they tried again." She explained about the railing in their box at the opera and Mr. Patten.

Parthenope listened intently and exclaimed softly when Sophie was through. "So that's part of what rattled you so badly that night at the Whistons' ball . . . and in the park, too! I remember how you went to Sir Walter's horse."

"I think he'd been spooked with an illusion. So that's why I need my magic. If someone's trying to hurt my father—and the others . . ."

Parthenope patted her chair. "Get back over here and talk to me. I don't doubt that you felt magic had been used, somehow, but why should someone be trying to hurt them?"

Sophie sat down. "I don't know, except that all of them just happen to be members of the War Office."

"What? All of them?" Parthenope looked at her very intently. "You're saying that someone is using magic to attempt to hurt members of the War Office, but trying to make it all look accidental?"

Said that way, Sophie wasn't sure if it sounded even more sinister, or too far-fetched for words. "Well . . . yes."

"But why? Unless . . ." Parthenope's eyes widened. "Unless it's the French!"

"We've been at war with the French for years. Don't you think they would have already used their magic to help themselves, if they had it?"

"Oh, stop being so logical. It's much more interesting if we think it's them!"

Sophie stared at her incredulously. "Is that what you think this is? Something 'interesting' for us to think about? My father was nearly killed by whoever is doing this, and so were three other men, and there isn't anyone but us who knows what's really going on." She reached up and rubbed her forehead. "I don't know. Maybe I'm wrong. Maybe it's just coincidence—"

"It can't be—what about the magic you felt? And I'm not being frivolous. Who else hates the War Department as much as the French?"

"The Russians and the Austrians, because we're the only ones who never knuckled under to Napoléon? No, don't take that seriously—but maybe there's some other reason someone hates Papa and these men, and the War Office part is accidental. Maybe it's someone who wanted to work for them and was turned away or lost his position."

"I suppose that's possible, though I'm not convinced. Hmmph." Parthenope looked thoughtful. "There's no way to tell where the magic might have come from? Like being able to figure out the direction from which a gun was fired?"

"It doesn't work that way."

"Drat." Parthenope drummed her fingers on her knee, brows knit. "Sophie—you haven't done any kind of magic yourself those times, have you?"

"No—I told you, I can barely do any magic these days. Why?"

"Maybe that's for the best," Parthenope said slowly. "The last thing you want to do is draw the attention of the person who is doing this onto yourself. I don't know how many people out there can actually do magic, but it can't be that many. And if whoever it is knows you can, I'm willing to wager that War Office members won't be the only ones in danger."

Sophie wasn't sure she could face driving with Lord Woodbridge that afternoon, but Parthenope threatened all manner of dire consequences if she did not. Which was how she found herself beside him at five, trotting smoothly down South Audley Street.

Lord Woodbridge drove his curricle and pair with a quiet precision that she found pleasing. It was very unlike the showiness of some young men she'd observed who tried to demonstrate their skill by flicking flies off the backs of their horses with their whips or taking corners far too quickly whilst talking far too much.

In fact, he was being rather quiet, which suited her well

enough while they still drove on the street. But once they entered the park, surely they would have to talk. After overhearing him last night, what could she possibly say? Perhaps, *So tell me, Lord Woodbridge—do you truly think I'm the loveliest girl in London?* Or, maybe, *Do you truly intend to ask me to marry you?*

Very well, she knew she was being silly. After all, he had no idea she'd heard him say those things and more. All she had to do was pretend she had no idea.

Ha.

"Your cane is very handsome," he observed. "Is it new?"

Sophie looked down and realized she was gripping the handle rather tightly. She forced her hands to relax and held it up: It was one of the black-lacquered ones enlivened with Egyptian decorations picked out in red, gold, and blue. "Yes. Isn't it wonderful? Amélie made it for me."

"Amélie—?"

"Oh, I'm sorry. Madame Carswell, I mean. Our guest."

"Ah, yes." He drove in silence for a moment. "She's French, isn't she?"

Sophie frowned. "Well, I suppose she is, if only by birth. Her family was French, but she has lived much of her life in India and married a dear friend of my father's out there. She still has family in France and in Belgium whom she'd hoped to have a chance to visit, though now with the war back on . . . perhaps she might still be able to visit Brussels, though."

"But for now she is staying with you."

"Yes, and I'm so glad she is. She's been such a—a friend to me."

"Does it . . . has it been awkward at all—her nationality, that is, and your father's position in the War Office—"

"Only when we're forced to deal with bigoted bullies," she interrupted. "Amélie was married to Papa's friend for over twenty years. She is an Englishwoman now, despite her French accent."

"Of course. I would never suggest otherwise," he said quickly.

"Thank you." Sophie fell silent. She'd been perhaps a little too vehement in Amélie's defense, but his questions had made her uncomfortable. Why wouldn't everyone just accept Amélie as who she was—a lovely, warm, perceptive person?

To her relief, he broke her silence. "Oh, there's Lady Cowper, in the barouche over there. Have you been introduced?"

"Not yet." Sophie regarded the approaching carriage. "We go to Almack's next week—I presume she'll be there, as one of the Lady Patronesses. Oh, isn't that Lord Palmerston with her?"

"They're, er, very good friends," he said, turning slightly pink.

"Oh." Oh! Sophie realized what he must mean and felt herself blush as well.

Lord Woodbridge cleared his throat. "Odd he's out driving, after the news from his office."

Sophie sat up straighter. "From the War Office? What news?"

He didn't speak for a moment, but drove in silence wearing a slight frown. "I'm sorry. That was clumsy of me," he finally said. "I forgot that you were there—"

"Please—what happened?"

He sighed. "Sir Walter Benning—you remember, from the park—"

"Yes, of course! Go on!"

"I'm afraid he"—he looked at her from the corners of his eyes, as if to gauge what she might do—"he died this morning."

"Oh." Sophie swallowed. He covered her right hand with his left for just a moment, a quick reassuring pressure. Sophie remembered the strawberry stains on her fingers and was grateful for her gloves.

"What happened?" she asked, after a moment. Good God, please let it not be another accident.

"He was stricken at his home this morning—his valet was helping him on with his boots, and he just collapsed. They said he'd not been quite right since his fall, so perhaps it isn't such a surprise—is there something wrong?"

Sophie realized that she was gripping her cane again. She made her hands relax. "Do—do you remember once when I asked you if it didn't seem odd that three War Office ministers had been in near-fatal accidents recently?"

"Did you?" He thought a moment. "Yes, I remember. Coming back from our ride in the park that day, after Sir Walter's accident."

"What would you say if I told you that there had been another incident . . . and now poor Sir Walter on top of that?"

He continued to look straight ahead, but she could sense his interest. "What was the other incident?"

"A colleague of my father's came to visit our box at the opera last night. As he leaned against the railing, it broke beneath his weight—and no, he is not in the least a large man. He didn't actually fall—we were able to grab him in time and pull him back. But it was a near thing."

"What a fright for you. And for him too, I suppose, but I can't see how a railing breaking at the King's Theatre could be anything but an accident—an unfortunate one, but still an acc—"

"It wasn't an accident," she said, trying to keep her voice steady. "None of them were. They were quite deliberately caused."

"How can you know that?" He sounded politely incredulous.

"Could you—just for the sake of discussion—accept that they were?"

He looked at her, frowning, for a few seconds, then nodded. "Very well, for the sake of discussion. In which case, who do you think is responsible for these . . . intentional accidents?"

"That's what I want to know. Who could bear such a grudge against the War Office that he would try to murder its members—and why?"

"The logical answer would have to be the French, of course," he answered promptly, just as Parthenope had.

"Yes, but—" But she certainly couldn't repeat the conversation she'd had with Parthenope about the French using magic. "Besides the French, is there anyone else who might wish to hurt the War Office?"

"Well, there are the Americans, though we're theoretically at peace now. Then there are Turks and the Barbary States, who are in a constant state of semi-war with our navy in the Mediterranean. That's it for any possible active belligerents, for now. And then there are the Allies."

"*The Allies?*"

"Quite. Just because we joined with them to defeat

Bonaparte doesn't mean that we like or trust each other. The Russian czar is insanely jealous of our navy and resents our holdings in India—I've a feeling he thinks Asia should be his exclusive playground. The Prussians also envy our commercial wealth—their treasury is, for all intents and purposes, empty. And the Austrians dislike us on principle, if only because they are a Catholic nation and we are a Protestant one."

"Oh!" She sat back against the seat. "So it *could* be anyone, really."

They drove in silence for a moment. Then Lord Woodbridge took a deep breath. "Lady Sophie, if you know of some threat to the government—though I can't imagine what or how—shouldn't you speak to your father about it? Tell him what you know?"

She had been afraid he would say that. "What if I tell him and he doesn't believe me? What then?"

"*I'll* believe you."

"You can't know that—"

"Very well. I'll trust that you believe it, and do what I can to help."

He spoke with such surety, such confidence, that it was very tempting to tell him about all of it—the magic . . . and her. But she couldn't, not yet.

Soon, perhaps?

Chapter

11

Sophie knew that Almack's Assembly Rooms were regarded as the social heart of fashionable London. It was the most exclusive venue in town, ruled by seven despotic society women who didn't hesitate to deny admission to anyone they disapproved of, no matter how wealthy or wellborn. To be approved by them for a voucher to purchase tickets to the Wednesday evening subscription balls meant that one *mattered*. She knew all this—Aunt Isabel had drilled it into her—but now that she was here, she knew something else as well.

It was numbingly *dull*.

For one thing, conversation was careful and decorous. No one wanted to give offense to the Lady Patronesses and be denied a voucher in future, after all. For another, the narrow-eyed, unsmiling mamas and aunts ranged around the room in knots, gossiping about whose daughter might catch which eligible bachelor, were positively hair-raising. How had such an uncomfortable and uninteresting place become so important?

Aunt Isabel, on the other hand, was in her element. She glided majestically through the crowd on Papa's arm, Sophie and Amélie following in her wake. While they'd waited on the pavement outside the house for Amélie to come down, Aunt Molly had suddenly claimed a sick headache, though she whispered to Sophie before they left that she had a great deal to do in the conservatory, putting down her sovereign anti-aphid mixture. Sophie wondered if the sick headache was a sham and the comte was coming to help her with the foul-smelling mixture of coffee grounds and cayenne pepper in olive oil. Then again, maybe not. It would hardly be a romantic occasion with that ghastly concoction around.

"Ah," Aunt Isabel said. "There's Lady Jersey. Come along, Sophie. You must be presented."

"Yes, Aunt," Sophie murmured. Where was Parthenope? She'd hoped to find her first and lay claim to a secluded corner to escape this very thing, but evidently luck was not going to be with her tonight.

"Do not just bare your teeth, *petite*. *Smile*," Amélie admonished her softly as they approached "Queen" Sarah, Countess of Jersey, the all-but-anointed sovereign of Almack's.

To her surprise, Lady Jersey was not in the least queen-like. She greeted Aunt Isabel with a certain amused glint in her eye, it was true, but received the rest of their courtesies with polite warmth. She was much younger than Sophie had expected and quite handsome.

"I like your cane," Lady Jersey said forthrightly, nodding

at the white and gold one she carried today. "I understand you've got them to match every outfit?"

"Thanks to Madame Carswell, I do." Sophie smiled at Amélie.

"How clever! I'm sure you'll not mind if I say this, Madame Carswell, but leave it to a Frenchwoman to come up with such an idea. Of course it's a shame that you have to use them at all, Lady Sophie, but I do declare, it's the perfect way to make the best of the situation. Such a pity you didn't live fifty years ago! Canes were quite the favored accessory then, though for myself I expect the ladies carried them as weapons—the young men in those days were shockingly *louche*, if you know what I mean—quite dreadfully so! Not at all like dear Lord Woodbridge here—how do you do? And Lady Parnethope, too!"

Sophie turned as Parthenope and Lord Woodbridge joined them. "ParNEthope?" she mouthed.

"Don't you dare laugh, you," Parthenope muttered out of the corner of her mouth as she curtsied to Lady Jersey.

Fortunately that lady's attention had been momentarily attracted by the musicians in the balcony. "Oh, they're getting ready to play. A set must be forming. It's such a shame you can't dance, Lady Sophie, or I should certainly recommend Lord Woodbridge here as a partner. Have you been introduced?"

"We have, thank you," Sophie replied demurely, looking at him. There was a faint sparkle of fun in his eyes as he bowed to her.

For a moment, Lady Jersey got a calculating look in her eyes. "Then in that case, Woodbridge, I'll leave you to entertain Lady Sophie during this set. Dear Lord Lansell, might you care to escort Lady Dow and Madame Carswell to the card room? Now, I promised Maria I'd find a partner for her cousin. Come along, Lady Parnethope. I should like you to make a certain young man's acquaintance." Looking pleased that she'd arranged them all, she took Parthenope's arm and neatly detached her from their group.

"Parnethope. I shall have to remember that," Sophie said, watching them go. Parthenope cast an agonized look back at them over her shoulder.

Amélie chuckled. *"Méchante enfant!* She will be very cross if you do." She took Papa's arm. "I think Sophie and Lord Wood-bridge will entertain each other quite *agréablement*. Shall we?"

"But—" Aunt Isabel looked indecisive as to whether she felt she ought to permit Sophie to remain talking unchaper-oned with a young man, but Papa neatly captured her arm and led her firmly away.

Sophie glanced up and met Lord Woodbridge's eyes. He was looking down at her with an expression that made her feel as if it had suddenly grown warm in the room. She looked quickly away and pretended to be scanning the dancers in the center of the room with great interest. "Oh, there's Parthenope, dancing with—with—oh, dear." She bit her lip, trying not to laugh.

A grim-faced Parthenope was dancing with a young man—a very plump and spotty young man, perhaps at his very first adult social event—who barely reached her shoulder.

Lord Woodbridge flashed his cousin a brilliant smile and bowed. She ignored him. "Vanquished by Silence Jersey," he said lightly.

"Silence?"

"It's what everyone calls her, because she's anything but. She takes it all in good part, though. Some people say she's all sound and no substance, but I rather think there's a great deal going on behind the chatter."

If there was, she hadn't used it as far as poor Parthenope was concerned. "I wonder if we'll ever get her to Almack's again this season. Poor thing, she looks unhappy."

"Nonsense. It was about time someone managed her for a change, since she's so fond of managing everyone else."

Sophie felt herself flush slightly, remembering the conversation she'd heard between him and Parthenope. She looked around the room, hoping to think of something else to talk about, and her eyes fell upon a handsome but vaguely rumpled-looking young man standing alone, watching the dance. "Oh, look! It's him," she exclaimed.

"Who?"

"Over there—the young man standing on the other side of the room, by that pillar."

"Where . . . oh, do you mean James Leland?"

"Yes! You're acquainted with him, I believe you said?"

"We're members of a few clubs together."

Sophie gave him a measuring look as an idea came to her. "How would you like to try your hand at a little managing of your cousin?"

"With James Leland?" He thought about it for a moment. "You think that she has an interest in him?"

"Don't you remember that she asked about him when we were riding together in Hyde Park?"

"Did she?"

"Yes."

He grinned. "It would give me great pleasure to manage Parthenope a little, but are you sure? I can't see that asking about someone in the park means very much. Don't you think she would have already done something about meeting him, if she were as interested as all that?"

"Of course not," she replied promptly. "That wouldn't do at all. Not in the least romantic."

"Romantic? *Her?*" He snorted. "I've met Cockney coal merchants who are more romantic than my cousin."

"On the contrary. I would say she's extremely romantic," she said.

He raised one eyebrow, but didn't disagree. "Very well. What do you suggest?"

"Let's go over and engage Mr. Leland in conversation, and make sure Parthenope sees us. When the dance is over, she'll make her partner bring her to us, and then we shall undertake to make Mr. Leland dance with her. It shouldn't be too hard, I hope."

"Have you been taking managing lessons from her?" he asked, offering her his arm.

To Sophie's delight, it worked just as she'd planned. Lord Woodbridge introduced her to Mr. Leland, whom she liked immediately for his gentle manners and kind eyes. She did her best to chat vivaciously with him, keeping an eye on Parthenope, and discovered that they were, in fact, distant cousins on her mother's side.

Parthenope indeed saw them. As soon as the dance was over, she practically dragged her partner over to them, then neatly dismissed him . . . and stood silent and, Sophie was pleased to note, faintly pink-cheeked.

"Parthenope, only fancy! I have found a new cousin! May I make Mr. Leland known to you?" she said.

"A cousin—how . . . how interesting," Parthenope murmured, curtsying. The pink in her cheeks surged into rose.

"Parthenope, you look a little overheated. Perhaps a glass of lemonade is in order," Lord Woodbridge suggested. There was a note in his voice that could only be described as teasing.

Mr. Leland brightened. "I should be happy to escort you to the supper room," he said, holding his arm out to her. "I'm sure we can find you something refreshing there."

Parthenope gulped—actually *gulped*—and took his arm. "That would be most . . . most . . . I thank you, sir." She paused only long enough to send Sophie a darkling look over her shoulder and mutter, "We'll discuss this tomorrow morning, you. Expect me at half past ten."

Sophie watched them go, managing to keep her face sober until they were at least ten paces away. Lord Woodbridge bent and murmured, "You terrify me, Lady Sophie. I don't think Parthenope herself could have handled that better."

"You are too kind," she replied, matching his tone. "I must say that I begin to see why she enjoys it so much."

"That's even more terrifying."

"Oh, pooh," she said, imitating Parthenope's characteristic expression. He laughed, and she joined him. There was a warm, intimate feeling in the shared laughter that she rather liked.

"There you are!" Lady Jersey materialized in front of them. "Your aunt was wondering where you were, Lady Sophie. I told her I should find you for her."

Thank you *so* much, Aunt. "I'm very sorry you were put to such trouble, Lady Jersey."

"Nonsense. I'm the one who said that Woodbridge should entertain you for the nonce." She looked at them keenly and asked, "Or should I have pretended not to have been able to find you a little longer?"

Sophie felt herself blush. Lord Woodbridge held his arm out to her. "I'll take you right to her, Lady Sophie. Excuse us, madam." He bowed to Lady Jersey slightly and led Sophie away.

"But we don't know where my aunt is," Sophie said, pausing to turn back.

He gently urged her on, weaving through the milling crowd. "I know we don't. Why do you think I hurried away from Silence so quickly? We shall be obliged to wander about for at least another quarter hour, looking for her."

Sophie laughed, but underneath it, she felt a little jump of happiness. Things were changing between them, weren't they? Maybe she was getting over her distrust of him after all. "In that case, I am quite sure she can't be in the card room," she said.

"Probably not. I should not be surprised if—"

Sophie stopped walking. Had she just heard someone nearby say "Lord Lansell"?

"Lady Sophie?" Lord Woodbridge looked concerned.

"I thought I heard . . ." She looked quickly around. It had sounded like a woman's voice. Eavesdropping was, of course, an unpardonable breach of manners, but if someone was talking about Papa, she needed to hear what was being said, just in case. She released Lord Woodbridge's arm and took an awkward couple of steps backward, straining to sort through the competing conversations around them.

"—she acting as hostess for him since Frances Lansell died? That seems odd," a female voice, not the first she'd heard, said.

"What is it?" Lord Woodbridge followed after her, reaching for her elbow. "Are you well? Can I—"

"No, I—please. . . ." Without thinking, she grasped his arm with a quelling gesture.

"Why should she?" said the first voice. "She has her own household, after all. No, Molly is doing the honors, from what I hear. You do remember the dreadful business over her, don't you, and what happened with Isabel?"

They weren't talking about Papa, then. But oh, why did someone have to bring up gossip about Aunt Molly's past now, just when it seemed like she might attain the happy outcome she'd missed as a young woman? She glanced warily around, but there were at least five nearby pairs of chatting ladies. It could be any of them.

"Hmm . . . was that when—no, that was someone else. . . ." said the second voice, which obviously didn't remember but would be quite happy to be reminded.

"Molly Rosier was the younger sister," said the first voice patiently. "She ruined it all for Isabel, of course, when she tried to run off with a Frenchman during the Revolution. They tried to hush it up, of course—old Lord Lansell was such the stickler and would never have let her marry him."

"So how did that ruin anything for Lady Isabel?"

"My dear!" The first voice tittered. "Don't you know who was paying court to her at the very same time?"

"Who?"

"Why, the Duke of Mowbray! He'd just come into the title

the year before and was very full of himself—not that *that* has changed! He'd been quite attentive to Isabel all season, and according to my brother, betting was even in the betting book at Brooks's that he'd propose by June. But once the business with Molly came to light, he dropped her like a stone. Couldn't allow any breath of scandal to touch his sacred name, you know."

"My goodness! That must have been a shock for her," the second voice said, not unsympathetically.

"Oh, I'm sure it was. She disappeared from view for the rest of the season, supposedly because of a sprained ankle, and by autumn was engaged to Dow. Do you know"—the voice dropped slightly, so that Sophie had to strain to catch its next words—"some said she actually cared for Mowbray and was nursing a broken heart, not an ankle. She was certainly out of looks when I happened to see her once that summer, so it just might be true—she had been quite pretty. Fancy falling in love with that windbag! But I suppose he was good-looking enough back in those days—"

"Lady Sophie." Someone touched her arm, and she jumped. Lord Woodbridge still stood there, looking at her quizzically. "Is there anything wrong?"

What could she say? "Pardon me, there was a conversation I had to eavesdrop on"? Certainly not . . . perhaps pretending nothing had happened would be best.

"Er, not at all," she said, taking his proffered arm. She thought she heard the second voice say something, but Lord Woodbridge was already leading her away, and anyway, what more was there for her to hear?

Good heavens! Had Aunt Isabel been in love with the

suitor who'd abandoned her? She'd assumed Aunt Isabel's disappointment at not becoming a duchess had been what soured her disposition and turned her into the unpleasant person she was today. But if she'd actually been in love with the duke, and he'd treated her so coldly, dropping her at the least sign of scandal in her family rather than standing by her—well, it might go some way toward explaining her bitterness toward poor Aunt Molly—and toward the world.

"They were talking about your aunt," Lord Woodbridge said abruptly.

Sophie was startled. But he had been right there next to her—of course he would have heard. "I think, yes, they were."

"Mowbray . . . his wife left him years ago, you know. They say she's living in an Italian convent—not even with a lover. Your aunt may have had a lucky escape."

Had she? Had turning into a bitter, discontented woman really been a lucky escape for Aunt Isabel? If she hadn't fallen in love with the wrong person and then lost him, might her life have been different? Or was she doomed to be unhappy, just because that was who she was?

I won't be like her, she thought fiercely. I won't let anything turn me into an Aunt Isabel. Not losing Mama and Harry. Not even being crippled. Or falling in love with someone who might not love me as much as he thinks he does.

She spent most of the remainder of the evening watching the dancing, sitting with Amélie and Parthenope's mother and Lord Woodbridge while Parthenope danced—twice with Mr. Leland, Sophie was happy to notice. Sophie could not help wondering if the duchess remained with them so that Lord Woodbridge, as her nephew, could sit with them without setting the gossips astir—at least not *too* astir. Sophie said as much to Amélie as they waited for their carriage when Aunt Isabel could finally be dragged away.

"I would not be surprised," Amélie agreed. "I too am grateful for her presence. It was very kind of her to sit with me."

"Kind of her to sit with you? Why?"

Amélie hesitated. "It is nothing, *petite*."

"Amélie, please tell me."

She took a moment to fuss with her pelisse before answering. "I am being a—a—what do you call it—a vaporish miss, I am sure. But some people here, they are not comfortable with a person whom they think is French." She shrugged.

"Was someone rude to you?" Sophie asked, aghast.

"Not exactly rude . . . ah, I have upset you, *ma chère*. There is no need—"

"That's why you stopped playing cards when I came in, isn't it? Someone was rude to you there."

Amélie sighed and nodded.

And the duchess must have seen, and by being openly friendly to Amélie was making it clear that she did not hold any silly views about being pleasant to a Frenchwoman. Just as Parthenope had had no qualms about befriending Sophie. The apple hadn't fallen far from the tree, had it?

Sophie brooded about the matter on the carriage ride home and was still thinking about it as the footman opened the door for them and bowed them into the front hall. Perhaps she should talk to Papa about it . . . and maybe about her other concerns as well—

"You're back early." Aunt Molly appeared at the top of the stairs, squinting down at them in the light of the candelabrum left burning in the hall for their arrival. Even from here, Sophie could smell coffee. Evidently the aphid destruction program had occurred on schedule.

"It's nearly one, Molly. Not all that early," Papa said, pulling off his gloves. "You didn't have to wait up for us. How is your head?"

"Oh . . . er, much better, thank you. And I didn't wait up. Auguste happened to call and stayed to help me with my plants, and we've just finished. I was about to ring for tea. Auguste!" she called over her shoulder.

Sophie concealed a grin. So the comte *had* come to keep her company over her plants! Wouldn't it set tongues wagging if Aunt Molly were to catch a husband this season . . . especially the husband she'd first wanted twenty years ago?

The comte appeared a moment later behind her, smiling a little sheepishly down at them. "Your pardon, Monsieur le Marquis. I did not intend to stay so late, but—"

"But we got all the plants taken care of, and you'll never guess what we found! I must show you—in the conservatory—and then we can have a nice cup of tea together and you can tell me all about your evening," Aunt Molly said, all on one breath, and started down the stairs.

"Marie, wait—" the comte said, starting after her.

"I'll be right back, Auguste," she called over her shoulder. "I simply can't wait to show—you'll *never* guess, Sophie—oh!"

That gentle "oh!" was the only warning that something was amiss. In the next instant Aunt Molly pitched forward, arms thrown before her to break her fall. A ghastly cracking sound, not very loud but horribly clear, was followed by Aunt Molly crying out sharply.

"Molly!" Papa gasped, and the comte cried, "No!" But it was too late. She tumbled limply down the rest of the staircase, coming to rest in a pitiful huddle on the marble-tiled floor.

Chapter 12

Papa said afterward that he wasn't sure how they would have managed without Amélie, and Sophie heartily agreed. It was Amélie who got to Aunt Molly first and gently suggested that the footman fetch a surgeon and that Papa summon Belton and the other servants. It was she who reassured the shaking comte and asked for his carriage to be brought, promising to send word first thing in the morning as to Aunt Molly's condition, and she who comforted Aunt Molly's maid, Bunty, who burst into loud hysterics when she saw Aunt Molly's still, white face and motionless form.

"She's dead!" Bunty wailed. "An' the pineapple in the conservatory was just about ready—she was so happy, and now she'll never—"

"She's not dead," Amélie said calmly. "*Voyez?* She is breathing—no, do not touch her until the surgeon comes—but if you could bring a blanket to cover her and some smelling salts. . . ."

The surgeon arrived quickly, thank heavens, and ascertained that Aunt Molly had escaped with a broken arm and a lot of bumps and bruises.

"Go to bed," Amélie told Sophie as they watched the footmen and Papa carry a faintly moaning Aunt Molly upstairs on a hastily improvised stretcher, followed by the surgeon and a still-sniffling Bunty.

"But you're doing everything. Isn't there some way I can help?" Sophie protested.

"You can help by being rested in the morning. Your *tante* will need someone to sit with her, and Bunty and I will need you to do that so we can rest." Amélie gave her a little hug. "I must hear what the surgeon says we should do to take care of her. Go. Your work will begin tomorrow."

Sophie reluctantly did as she asked, following the little procession up to the third floor and watching as it disappeared into Aunt Molly's room. What a dreadful end to the day! Had she caught her heel on a carpet rod or missed her footing in the dim light? The poor comte had looked positively devastated as he rushed down to her. . . . Oh, dear, she hoped this wouldn't put a crimp in their romance, which had seemed to be coming along *so* well.

The next morning Sophie slipped into Aunt Molly's room after knocking discreetly and hearing Amélie's quiet *"entrez!"* She was shocked to see that Amélie still wore her black crepe evening dress and slippers.

"Haven't you rested at all?" she demanded in a whisper.

Amélie shook her head. "I am going now, *petite*. I made Mademoiselle Bunty go to her bed just now, though she did not wish it. I promised her that you would call her immediately if Lady Molly needed her, but I also made her drink a cup of tea with a drop or two of the laudanum the surgeon left. She too needs her rest. If you feel you need help, I will be sending Nalini to sit out in the hall. She can get me."

"How is she?" Sophie moved closer to Aunt Molly's bed. The curtains were drawn over the window, but a fire in the grate and a shielded candle gave enough light to show that she lay straight and still under the blankets, like an effigy on a tomb, and totally unlike her usual cheerful if muddled self.

"The surgeon set her arm and left us laudanum to give her for the pain and an *onguent* of arnica to put on her bruises. She just had some and will probably sleep most of the morning. If she seems uncomfortable, you might bathe her forehead, but if she grows hot as if falling into a fever, you should call me *immediatement*," Amélie said, and yawned.

"Now it's my turn to tell you to go to bed," Sophie said. "Go on. I'll be all right."

"I know you will." Amélie squeezed her hand, took one more look at the still form under the blankets, and left, closing the door gently behind her.

Sophie sat down in the chair next to the bed and studied Aunt Molly. Her cropped hair stood up every which way, and she was very pale, but someone had managed to get her out of her dress and corset and into a soft flannel nightdress. At least she would be comfortable, the poor old dear. Had Amélie had

a moment to send a note to the comte? Perhaps she ought to remind her before she retired—

Aunt Molly stirred slightly and sighed. Sophie bent over her to feel her forehead, and she opened her eyes, blinking as if they weren't working quite right.

"Who is that? Oh, Sophie." She twisted her mouth into a grimace that Sophie supposed was meant to be a smile.

"Hello, Aunt. How are you? May I get you anything?"

"Thirsty," she whispered.

Sophie poured half a glass of water from the pitcher on her bedside table and managed to lift her head slightly without disturbing her arm so that she could drink. Aunt Molly took a few sips, then turned her head away. "Where's Bunty?" she asked, trying to peer past Sophie.

"Sleeping. She was with you all night, and now I'm sitting with you while she rests."

"Was she?" Her brow creased, as if she were trying to remember something. "I—fell."

"Yes, you did. Last night, on the staircase."

"Last . . . night? It's morning now?"

"It's a little after ten, yes."

"The stairs . . . ," Aunt Molly said, frowning again. "I remember. They . . . they pushed me off. Down. I . . . it was . . . very *rude* of them." Her voice squeaked and broke.

Sophie looked at her anxiously. She wasn't getting agitated, was she? Surely that would be bad for her arm, splinted and bandaged though it was. Best to humor her. "I'm sure they didn't mean it, Aunt," she said, patting her good hand.

Aunt Molly shook her head fretfully. "Oh, they did . . . I felt them. They wanted me to fall. They'd been . . . told." She closed her eyes.

A cold prickle started somewhere between Sophie's shoulder blades and crept down her back. "Aunt Molly, what do you mean 'they'd been told'?" she asked, leaning forward. But Aunt Molly's eyes remained closed, and her chest had begun to rise and fall rhythmically with her breath. The laudanum Amélie had given her had done its work.

Sophie sat back in her chair and watched her sleep, then got up and hobbled to the window to flick the curtains open a crack. The morning was a fine one, but she didn't see the washed-blue sky above the budding trees in the square below.

The stairs had made her fall. Someone had told them to.

Very well. Aunt Molly might be muddled from the laudanum and have dreamed or imagined that the stairs had intentionally thrown her. Or she might be saying precisely what had happened, that someone had told the stairs to make her fall. Which was entirely possible . . . with magic.

But that would mean someone had managed to sneak in somehow last evening while they were at Almack's and Aunt Molly was happily ensconced with her comte in the conservatory. How he or she had managed it with Aunt or the servants liable to wander through the front hall at any time, it was difficult to say.

Or could it have been one of the servants themselves? Someone with a grudge against Aunt Molly? That seemed difficult to believe . . . unless the magical trap had been laid for someone else. Someone like . . . Sophie gripped the fabric of the curtains very tightly. Someone like Papa.

One thing was certain: She had to go examine those stairs, and soon. There might still be some residue of magic left on them, something that might give her a hint of who might have done such a thing. Or why.

Opportunity to do so arrived sooner than she'd hoped. About a half hour later, Nalini, Amélie's maid, tiptoed in. "I sit with mademoiselle *la tante*," she whispered. "Ladee Sophie go—her friend is here."

"My friend?" Sophie blinked at her, then remembered. Parthenope had said she would visit this morning, hadn't she? "Thank you, Nalini. Aunt should stay asleep, but if she wakes, please call me—let your mistress rest."

Nalini pressed her hands together and bowed, and Sophie grabbed her cane and hurried out.

Parthenope was still in the front hall, unbuttoning her pelisse. One of the footmen stood next to her, holding an arm stiffly in front of him. Hester perched on his outstretched hand, looking about him with interest.

"There you are!" Parthenope called up the stairs to her. "Stay there. I'll be right up." She finished unfastening her pelisse and looked expectantly at the footman, waiting for him to help her off with it. He looked from Hester to Parthenope, and a look of desperation crossed his face.

"Oh, for heaven's sake." Parthenope wiggled out of her pelisse, took Hester from the now red-faced footman, and then handed him the garment.

Sophie waited until he disappeared into the cloakroom with it. "No, wait," she said as Parthenope reached for the banister. "Don't come up till I tell you."

"What? Are you going to send me away just because I

brought this miscreant?" Parthenope set Hester on her shoulder. "I promise he won't engage in any behavior unbecoming a gentleman. Well, he probably won't. I hope."

"It's not that." Sophie tried to remember which stair Aunt Molly had fallen from. About a third of the way down? Maybe a little less? She went down a few steps, then clinging to the banister, sat down on the tread and slid herself over to the center of the stairs.

"What are you doing?" Parthenope demanded. "And I was worried about *Hester* behaving strangely."

"Aunt Molly fell on the stairs last night," Sophie said tersely, running her hands over the carpet.

"My goodness, did she? I'm so sorry. Is she injured?"

"Broken arm." No, nothing on this step. She slid down to the next one and repeated her search.

"And you're . . . looking for a trip wire?" Parthenope asked, head to one side.

"After a fashion." Sophie moved down to the next step.

"Really?"

"Yes—ah!" There it was, very faint, just a prickle under her fingertips.

"You found it?" Parthenope's voice rose with excitement. "Where? May I come up?" She set a foot on the bottom stair.

"Yes, but don't touch anything, for heaven's sake." Sophie ran her hand over the spot again. It was hard to find the edges of the remains of the spell, hard to read the intent inside it.

Parthenope sat two steps below. "I don't see a wire," she said, peering at the carpet under Sophie's hand. "And anyway, who would want to do something so awful to poor Aunt Molly? She wouldn't hurt a fly, unless it was eating one of her plants."

"It's not an actual wire that tripped her. I think it was magic . . . and that it was meant for someone else."

"Ohh." Parthenope's eyes widened, and she leaned forward. "Like for your papa, perhaps? Where is it? What does it feel like?"

Hester uttered a small, annoyed chirp and fluttered from her shoulder down to the step. He took a hop toward Sophie, then stopped. "By the pricking of my thumbs," he said, scratching at the rug.

"None of that, sir," Parthenope admonished and reached for him, but Sophie stopped her.

"Wait a moment," she said. "He's said that before."

"He's said a lot of things before, the little wretch, many of which I heartily regret teaching him."

"No—he said that when I did the spell to take the stain out of your dress."

"Did he?" Parthenope was staring at the step as if she could discountenance the spell into showing itself. "I know it's from *Macbeth* since Macky made me read that one because it's about Scotland, and because there are a lot of deaths and people getting chopped into pieces with swords and stabbed and so on. She says I have a bloodthirsty streak."

"Have you?"

"Of course I do," Parthenope replied promptly. "Hadn't you noticed?"

"Hmm." Sophie put her hand out for Hester to hop onto her finger. "I wonder . . ." She trailed into silence.

"What?"

"I don't know. It's just a guess, but 'by the pricking of my thumbs' is something one of the witches in *Macbeth* says."

"So you're saying that he's read *Macbeth* too? My clever boy!"

Sophie made a face at her. "I'm saying that I wonder if he isn't sensitive to magic. Birds often are, for some reason. Someone must have taught it to him. I wonder where Norris Underwood got him?"

"I'm not about to write the cad and find out," Parthenope said firmly.

"You don't have to, silly. But if Hester *is* sensitive to magic, he might he useful."

Parthenope brightened. "That's true. I've been wanting to do something a little different. Wearing Hester on my shoulder to balls and parties will let us keep an eye out for any more magic as well as set me apart—"

"And your mother will have you sent to Bedlam if you do. Besides, Hester's purple and green will clash with some of your dresses." She handed him back to Parthenope, who looked crestfallen.

"I hadn't thought of that. Still, I expect having Hester about to sniff out magic will prove handy someday—"

The metallic clunk of the door knocker interrupted her. The footman who'd taken Parthenope's pelisse came scurrying from the cloakroom to open it.

"I am here to inquire after Lady Mary's health," said a familiar voice from the stoop outside. "And to bring her a small trifle that I hope might cheer her."

The comte! Had anyone sent him word about Aunt Molly? Sophie sat up. "Peter, please let the comte come in." The poor man must be frantic if he'd gone to the trouble of calling himself.

The footman opened the door all the way, and the comte stepped in, bearing a large bouquet of hothouse lilies.

"Good morning, monsieur," Sophie called down to him. So what if she and Parthenope looked odd, perched on the stairs as they were? "It is very kind of you to call about Aunt Molly."

He glanced up, and his brown eyes, which Sophie had often thought resembled a sad spaniel's, narrowed angrily. "What are you doing?"

Parthenope rose and set Hester on her shoulder. "Why, looking to see which carpet rod is loose," she said. "It would be terrible if someone else were to trip, don't you think?"

The anger seemed to leave him as quickly as it appeared. "If only she had not," he replied softly, taking out his handkerchief and wiping his brow. His eyes were once more sad and slightly drooping at the corners. "To see you there—it reminded me again of that horrible moment . . . please, how is your aunt?"

Sophie thought about trying to rise and decided against it. "Her arm is broken, and she's rather buffeted and bruised. She's asleep just now, but she'll be so pleased to hear you called." If only she could sneak him up to see her, but that would hardly be proper. Anyway, poor Aunt was so pale and fragile-looking that it would just make him worry more.

He shook his head and looked even sadder. "You will give her these?" He held out the flowers to the footman. "Please . . . tell her—tell her I am very sorry that she was injured. And that I shall call again in a day or two to see how she is." He turned back to the door.

"Of course I will." Poor man. Sophie almost wished she could hug him. "Good-bye, Comte."

He turned and looked back up at her, and a fleeting

expression she could not quite decipher crossed his face, then was gone. *"Au revoir*, Lady Sophie."

That evening Sophie took a deep breath before knocking on the door to Papa's study. This was not going to be easy.

After the comte had left that morning, she and Parthenope had retreated to her room to talk about Sophie's discovery of the spell on the stairs.

"What if whoever did it decides to come back and try again?" Parthenope asked. "Once he hears it was Aunt Molly and not your papa who fell, he might."

Sophie shivered but shook her head. "How could he get into the house without anyone noticing?"

"He already did, didn't he—no reason why he couldn't again. He's a *spy*. They're supposed to be good at that sort of thing," Parthenope said patiently, as if she were explaining something to a very young child. "Sophie, I think it's time you talked to your father about this. After all, it's not just he who's in danger— it's Lord Palmerston and heaven knows who else. What if someone tries to assassinate the Prince Regent? Or the king?"

It was that last argument that persuaded Sophie to discuss their suspicions with Papa. The only problem was that, try as she might, she still hadn't figured out how to tell him about their concerns without revealing the magical aspects of the situation. Mama had said that magic was a secret that had to be kept, even from one's closest and dearest; she had never told Papa what she was, nor had she told him about Sophie or little Harry. If even Mama hadn't been able to tell him, Sophie knew that she couldn't. She took another breath, and knocked.

"Ah, Sophie," Papa said when she opened the door. He was sitting at his desk, looking through a stack of invitations. The curtains were drawn, and the lamplight on the gilt titles of the books in the bookcases and on the old mahogany furniture gave the room a cozy feel—perfect for confidences, she hoped.

"I'm glad you're here," Papa continued. "With your aunt laid up for the next few weeks, we have to decide who can chaperone you. Isabel, of course, and perhaps Madame Carswell would be willing, though—"

"I'm sure she would, Papa," Sophie interrupted.

He regarded her for a few seconds with one eyebrow slightly raised, then nodded at the chair before his desk. "You have something you want to talk about that's more important than parties, I gather."

"I'm sorry I interrupted you, but yes, I do have something I want to discuss with you."

He smiled and nodded. "Go on."

Sophie hesitated. She'd rehearsed this in her head over and over, but now that it was time to actually do it, all her prepared words fled. "It's just that . . . well, we've been thinking, and we thought you ought to know—"

"We?" he interrupted.

"Parthenope and I. Anyway, we . . . well . . . we wondered if you hadn't thought it odd that so many of your friends in the War Office had had accidents recently."

"Runs of bad fortune generally *are* odd, mercifully. What—"

"But what if it wasn't just bad luck? What if it was intentional?"

His smile slipped, just a little. Good; that meant she had his attention. "Are you saying that the accidents and near accidents weren't accidents? That someone somehow engineered them?"

Sophie drew a breath. "Yes."

"Who? And how? A falling statue in a ballroom, a spooked horse, and a rotted wood balustrade—I'm afraid I can't see how any human agency could have effected those. Or why."

If only she could tell him! For now it would probably be prudent to sidestep the how and focus on the why and who. "The why is obvious. We're back at war again, and the stakes are higher than ever. I'm sure the emperor would grasp at anything that would give him an advantage—and wouldn't disabling the War Office of one of his chief enemies among the Allies give him an enormous advantage?" She ignored the growing incredulity in his eyes and pressed on. "Whoever has tried has already succeeded with poor Sir Walter. . . . What if he keeps on trying? What if Lord Palmerston or . . . or *you*—"

"Sophie." Papa leaned across his desk and held out his hand. She put hers in it and he squeezed gently. "Sophie, I think maybe you're a little overwrought."

"But Parthenope—"

"Must be a highly imaginative young lady in her own right. No, Sophie, there are no plots or spies or Bonapartist agents lurking in the shrubbery, trying to decimate the War Office. And even if someone were, which is *very* unlikely, it's not a matter for a girl to concern herself with."

Sophie regarded him miserably. "But—"

"No buts." He patted her hand again and rose. "No one has attempted or will attempt to murder me or Palmerston or anyone."

"But I *know* it's true that someone's been trying to hurt you!" she persisted.

His brows drew down, but his voice remained gentle. "How, Sophie? What makes you so sure?"

What indeed? What if she told him about the spell she'd sensed at the site of every "accident" . . . and most recently on the stairs, right here in his own house? He would accuse her of concocting fairy tales, or worse. "I just am," she muttered.

"And I know it's true that you have had a difficult few weeks dealing with being in London and are perhaps in need of some rest." He looked down at her consideringly. "Perhaps we ought to find you some other young ladies to befriend besides Lady Parthenope. I do not think she has been a good influence on you."

"Papa! She's my best friend!"

He shook his head. "A 'best friend' is not a desirable commodity. One should hold all of one's friends in equal esteem, if they are worthy to be called friend. I suppose that without your mother's guidance, you—well, never mind that for now." He felt for his watch in a gesture she knew well, opened it, and sighed. "Late again. They'll be wondering what's happened to me at White's. Off with you, Sophie."

There was no gainsaying that tone of voice. Sophie rose obediently and left, leaning a little more heavily on her cane than she usually did just because she felt so . . . so deflated. That would be it, then. She and Parthenope could expect no assistance from Papa—or even expect to be listened to, by him or anyone else. They were on their own.

Sophie did not go to any social events for the next three days. Amélie felt that she should stay with Aunt Molly in the evenings so that Bunty could rest before sitting up all night with her mistress, which meant that Amélie could not go anywhere with Sophie. And while Sophie felt more in charity with Aunt Isabel since overhearing those two cats at Almack's discuss her disappointments, it did not mean that she wanted to have to spend long swaths of evening sitting with her at a ball, watching others dance.

On the surgeon's advice, Aunt Molly remained mostly asleep for two of those days while the worst of her bruises and discomfort slowly subsided. Bunty single-mindedly concocted comfrey poultices for her arm and glowered at anyone who came near, including the surgeon, though she was less hostile to Sophie. On the third day, when Aunt Molly was more awake, Sophie managed to steal a few moments alone with her to ask her again what she'd felt before she'd fallen, but this time, she had no memory of it at all. Frustrated, Sophie left her to Bunty and a fresh poultice and went to ignore her embroidery in the drawing room. Only when Belton announced Parthenope did she brighten.

"This is getting ridiculous!" Parthenope announced, pausing dramatically on the threshold before entering. "Do you know how *bored* I was at Lady Mansfield's rout last night, not to mention the Killingsleys' ball the night before? My dear Lady Sophie, pray tell me why did your aunt choose to injure herself at the height of the season?"

Sophie laughed. Parthenope's presence seemed to fill the room with much-needed fresh air. "One must rely on one's inner resources at such times, of course. Hasn't Miss MacTavish told you that?"

"Several times, but it's my firm opinion that inner resources are on the whole vastly overrated. Especially mine."

Parthenope dropped her reticule on the sofa and presented Sophie with a tight little bouquet of violets that she'd been hiding behind her back. "For your aunt. Aren't they perfect? I've never seen such large ones as they have down here. The violets up by Revesby Castle always seem terrified, as if they suspect it might snow on them if they dare grow very large."

"She'll love them." Sophie set them on the table. But Parthenope wasn't finished.

"I've also got a very interesting article for her in the *Lady's Magazine* about the rhododendrons of Asia Minor and the Black Sea, and one about the *Orchidaceae* of North America, whatever those are, and the agricultural report in the most recent number of Ackermann's *Repository*. What is barley, anyway? Do you eat it, like wheat?"

"No. I think you stuff it down the throats of people who behave nonsensically."

"Pooh." She dropped the magazines next to the violets. "I'd thought about bringing Hester to distract her too, but I'm afraid he's in disgrace."

"What did he do?"

Parthenope grinned. "I brought him to Lady Mansfield's last night, and while I was playing whist, he went for a little jaunt onto the old Countess of Exton's shoulder, took a look at her cards, proclaimed, 'Fancy that! Five kings!' then made a mess on her new French silk shawl. I guess I'm in disgrace too, for bringing him, but not as much as the countess."

"Did she really have five kings in her hand?"

"She certainly did."

Sophie laughed, but her laugh faded into a sigh. Parthenope frowned at her. "What? Don't worry—they'll forgive me eventually, but I shouldn't probably expect her grandson to be asking me to dance anytime soon. Not that I'm devastated or anything."

"It's not that. Come sit, and I'll tell you." She told Parthenope about her talk with Papa.

"Ah," Parthenope said when she'd finished. "Well, I suppose I can't much blame him—it does sound rather far-fetched. And if you'd told him about the magic, it would have been even worse."

"I know. And now I don't know what to do next. If no one will listen to us—"

"Ahem." Parthenope was regarding the toes of her slippers. After a pause, she looked up. "I had an interesting conversation myself last night."

Sophie waited and, when Parthenope didn't continue, prodded her friend with the tip of her cane (today the green-painted one wrapped with lace, so that the color showed through the pattern). "And?"

Parthenope eyed her. "You won't be angry with me?"

"How can I be, if you don't tell me?"

"That's hardly inducement to talk. Very well, I told Peregrine about our suspicions. I was worried after your aunt's accident, and I had to do something. Not that it helped."

Oh. That wasn't so bad. "Did he say it was outrageous fudge?"

"No. That's what worries me. I was sure he would, because I . . . er, have been known to be economical with the truth with him in the past, but he said that you had spoken to him about something similar. I pretended not to know that. Anyway, he didn't tell me not to be a codfish. He only looked very serious and thoughtful. Goodness, if *Perry* thinks there might be something to worry about . . . Sophie, you have to talk to him again. He might actually believe you."

Sophie sat back. Of course she had to, but life would be so much easier if she didn't. She and Peregrine—er, Lord Woodbridge—had reached a—a place of balance. They had finally begun to trust each other after their spectacularly bad start, and she was afraid to do anything to jeopardize that delicate equilibrium lest their trust be destroyed a second time. But if he would actually *listen* to her. . . . "The last time we spoke about it, he suggested I speak to my father."

"And you did, and it didn't help. You can tell him that when you talk to him." Parthenope looked at her, all traces of laughter gone from her face. "Which I hope you'll do soon. In the meanwhile, please be careful. I don't want to have to bring you violets and articles about the progress of this year's barley crop because *you've* gotten caught in a magical trap."

Chapter 13

Sophie's chance to talk to Peregrine came a few days later, when Aunt Molly was deemed well enough that Bunty no longer had to sit up with her at night and Amélie could go out in the evening again. Indeed, Aunt Molly was feeling sufficiently improved to talk of getting out of bed in a day or two to check on her conservatory and see if the aphid mixture had done its job. Bunty sniffed dubiously at these signs of returning vigor, but Sophie was delighted. Perhaps in another day or two, she'd be ready for callers. Wouldn't the poor comte be happy to see his Marie?

So she and Amélie and Papa were free to attend Viscountess Montashton's musicale that night. Parthenope would be there, and she'd assured Sophie that Peregrine would be too, although as they were ushered into Lady Montashton's reception rooms, crowded with rows of small gilt chairs rapidly filling with guests, Sophie still wasn't entirely sure how she would broach the topic of the attempted murders with him. Trying to discuss anything of such a sensitive nature in a crowd like this would be almost impossible. But she had to try.

She was pleased to see the comte, who came to bow over her hand and ask after Aunt Molly. His smile when she told him that Aunt would probably be well enough for visitors soon lit his whole face. Less pleasing was the attention—or lack of it—which she saw being paid to Amélie. Two ladies (though they hardly seemed to deserve the name) quite pointedly cut her while gushing over Papa, and others were distinctly chilly, greeting Sophie and Papa in a friendly fashion, then barely acknowledging Amélie.

"This is outrageous!" she murmured as they seated themselves. "What have you ever done to anyone, besides be incredibly kind?"

Amélie lifted her shoulders. "I exist, *ma chère*. We have discussed this before—why do you still let it trouble you?"

"Because it's horrible and unfair!"

"They think they are being *patriotique*, Sophie. It does not trouble me. Please, do not permit it to trouble you." She patted Sophie's hand. "See, there is Parthenope. It looks as though she is trying to gain your attention."

Sophie scanned the crowd and spotted Parthenope waving at her enthusiastically from partway across the room while the duchess tried to catch her sleeve. Sophie nodded to them, and the duchess looked relieved as she captured Parthenope's arm and brought it down. Parthenope grimaced, then began to jerk her head to one side in a most pointed manner. Sophie smiled, wondering if the duchess would try to grab her head, and looked where Parthenope had indicated. And saw Peregrine Woodbridge sitting alone, his eyes fixed on her.

The music was probably very good, as Lady Montashton was known to be something of a connoisseur, but Sophie heard very little of it; every time she allowed her gaze to wander over to where Peregrine sat, she saw that he still watched her. As soon as the applause had died away and the quartet had laid down their instruments, she saw him rise and begin to make his way toward her. There was a seriousness and purpose in his stride that made her heart beat a little more quickly.

He greeted them all, then asked Papa, "May I claim the pleasure of your daughter's company in the supper room?"

"If Sophie wishes it, then by all means." Papa smiled indulgently and turned away with Amélie on his arm.

"Lady Sophie?"

He was regarding her steadily. She made him a small curtsy and replied, "Thank you, sir."

He held out his arm. "I was very sorry to hear about your aunt's accident. I assume that your being here means she's improving?"

Oh, good. This sort of polite social exchange she could handle . . . but why was he still looking at her so intently? She could almost *feel* the weight of his regard. "We hope she might begin to come downstairs soon. She was rather battered by the fall and is just feeling better."

"I'm glad to hear that." He was silent for a moment as they followed Papa and Amélie and the rest of the crowd toward the dining room, then said, simply, "I've missed you. It's been fiendishly dull and flat without you. I thought about calling, but I didn't want to disturb your household, so . . . so I've been waiting for you to return. I think it's been the longest week of my life."

Sophie dropped her eyes and wished she could hide behind her fan, but using her cane got in the way. What reply was one supposed to make to such a statement? And how was she supposed to discuss possible assassins with him when he said things like that?

"I—I am flattered, Lord Woodbridge," she said carefully. "In fact, I am especially glad to see you, as there's something that I would like to dis—"

"Sophie." His voice dropped, and he glanced around them as if to make sure they were not overheard as he drew her arm a little closer. "Not being able to see you this week made up my mind. . . . I know it's not the usual thing, but I . . . I thought this way was the best. I would like to speak to your father about paying my formal addresses to you."

Sophie would have liked to stop and try to make sense of what her ears were telling her, but the press of guests behind them was too great. He had said . . . he was more or less asking her to— But he was still speaking.

"I am asking you first if . . . if you would not mind if I did. Under the circumstances, I would not wish to speak to him if you find the idea repugnant. That would just distress the both of us. So . . . would it be all right with you if I do?"

Would she be able to take another step without collapsing from sheer shock . . . and from sheer happiness? More important, could she give him a coherent answer without dying of embarrassment? Preferably one that was gracious and polished and elegantly phrased. . . .

"Yes, please," she murmured, and felt her face burst into flame.

She knew in a distant sort of way that they had made it into the supper room, and knew too that Peregrine left her at a table with Amélie while he and Papa went to fetch ices and *marrons glacés* and tiny cakes. Gradually her breath came back to her along with the ability to think . . . and an enormous happiness. He *did* love her. Of course, now it would be impossible to discuss her concerns about Papa's safety: Her inability to think about anything but the enormous shiny bubble of joy inside her had seen to that. But they could talk tomorrow. Surely he would be willing to go driving or riding with her in the park—

"Something has happened," Amélie observed quietly.

Startled, Sophie met her eyes. "What?"

But Amélie only smiled and adjusted her gray gauze shawl more snugly about her shoulders. "I should not have spoken. It is too soon, I am thinking. Ah, Monsieur le Comte." She nodded graciously as he strolled up to their table. "I am happy to say that your friend is looking forward to receiving callers again in a day or so."

"So I have heard from Lady Sophie." He bowed. "It is news that makes me very happy, you may be sure, and I will plan on calling the day after next, if you think it will not be too soon." For a moment he looked pensive, then brightened. "Ah, but might I be of service to you ladies? I shall be happy to procure some champagne." He turned and spoke to a footman, who nodded and disappeared.

Papa and Peregrine reappeared then with several little

plates of delicacies and convinced the comte to join them. Peregrine sat down next to Sophie; she was deliciously aware of his proximity, of how he was able to gracefully arrange his long limbs on Lady Montashton's silly little chairs, even of his breathing. She stole a glance at him from the corner of her eyes and saw that he watched her too. Was he thinking thoughts similar to hers? Someday—the thought gave her shivers— someday she would ask him.

The footman appeared with a tray of glasses. Sophie idly watched him set them down in front of Amélie and her and Papa and—there was something wrong with Papa's glass.

Sophie leaned forward, gazing at it, ignoring the sprightly conversation being conducted around her. The glass looked just the same as the others, but it wasn't: a feeling of wrongness, of badness, radiated from it like stink from a pile of manure. What could it—

And then Papa picked it up and began to raise it to his lips.

"Papa!" she shrieked, scrambling half to her feet, and pointed at the glass. It broke in his hand, the bowl cracking away from the stem and falling into halves, as if cleaved by a sword.

For a second there was stunned silence at the table and at the tables around them. Then everyone seemed to move and speak at once.

"*Mon Dieu*—Gilbert!" Amélie cried, jumping up and grasping Papa's sleeve.

"My dear marquis," the comte exclaimed. "Are you injured?"

"What—Sophie, what happened?" Peregrine turned to her, helping her back down into her seat.

Sophie thought fast. "Papa—your glass—I saw it crack!" she said loudly, then pretended to collapse in her seat.

"Thank God that you did," Amélie said fervently, trying to hand her dainty, black-edged handkerchief to Papa. He took it from her, glanced at it wryly, and used it to blot some of the champagne from his hand. Sophie winced as she looked at the liquid that bespattered the table, and wondered what would happen if, say, a mouse were to happen along and drink some of it. . . .

Except that she didn't have to wonder. Papa's champagne had been poisoned. That's what the sense of badness she'd felt meant.

They left for home early, of course, as Papa was drenched in champagne. Sophie sped matters along by coming down with a convenient headache. She didn't want Papa wearing those clothes any longer than he had to.

The ride home was a quiet one. Sophie sat with eyes closed and head back because of her supposed headache; she thought she felt Amélie watching her, but she was too preoccupied with trying to figure out how this latest attempt on Papa's life—for it had to have been one—had happened. Magic had not been used—at least, she didn't think it had. It looked as though it had been a straightforward attempt to poison him. But who had managed to get the poison in the right glass? If only there were some way for her to go back and question Lady Montashton's footmen . . . but there wasn't. To the rest of the world, this had been a simple incident of a breaking glass, and that had been her doing. No one else knew what she did . . . except the person who had arranged it. If she hadn't sensed the wrongness about it . . .

Which was another matter, less worrisome but just as mysterious: Was her magic coming back at last? She had sensed the poison and destroyed the glass so quickly and easily—the spell had just rushed out of her, almost without conscious thought or intention, *almost as her magic had before her illness*. It made her want to bounce in her seat with excitement; as soon as she got home and was safely alone in her room, she would have to see what else she could do.

And then there was Peregrine . . . good heavens, her head was practically awhirl with it all. Would he come as soon as tomorrow to speak to Papa?

But on their arrival home, Amélie took her arm. "I know you have *un mal de tête*, Sophie. But I should like to speak with you for just a small moment before you retire, *s'il vous plaît*."

Sophie's heart sank, but she said, "Yes, of course." On the way up the stairs, she again felt Amélie's eyes on her, as she had in the carriage on the way home.

Once in Sophie's room, though, Amélie seemed nervous and distracted, refusing a chair but setting her candle down and choosing to stand, fidgeting slightly—so not her usual calm, smiling self that Sophie asked, as she tossed her shawl on her bed and sat down at her dressing table, "Is there something wrong, Amélie?"

"Wrong? No . . . at least, I do not think, not yet. . . ." She pressed her lips together, as if to keep herself from saying more, then sighed. "*Ma chère* Sophie, may I ask you to make me a promise?"

Whatever she'd been expecting Amélie to say, it wasn't this. "Er . . . what promise is that?"

She came to Sophie's bench and knelt beside it, taking her hand. "That you will use at all times the canes Nalini and I have made for you. It is *very* important."

Sophie blinked and looked at the cane she had carried tonight. It was one Aunt Isabel had given her a week or two ago, inspired perhaps by a desire not to be outdone by a mere houseguest, and was of wood and ivory inlay. "Of course I shall, if you wish, but may I ask why it is so important?"

Amélie hesitated. "It is . . . I am not sure that I am able to explain, *petite*. Will you just take my word for it that it is?"

It seemed an odd thing to ask, and yet Amélie had been so kind, so understanding, that it seemed churlish to demand an explanation. "If you wish it, then I will, Amélie."

Amélie looked relieved and gave her hand a squeeze. "Thank you, Sophie. You set my mind at rest." She stood up, then to Sophie's surprise, bent and kissed her forehead. "Now, *petite*, to bed. It has been an evening *très occupé*, I am thinking." She took up her candle and left the room.

Sophie sat for a moment after she left, thinking. That had been very strange—why should it be so important to Amélie that she use only her canes? She rose and went to the large brass umbrella stand she'd appropriated from the hall to store them in, and pulled one out at random—a delightful confection of woven pale blue and rose pink ribbon and tassels—then took it back with her and sat down to examine it more closely.

It looked perfectly ordinary. Poking the ribbon aside, she could see plain brown wood underneath it, and it had been perfectly serviceable when she had used it last. She examined it carefully, standing to lean all her weight on it, and sighting along it to make sure it was straight. It was. At last she laid it across her lap and closed her eyes as she ran her fingertips along its length . . . and there it was. A faint something—not quite a tingle, but something smoother, like brushing the surface of running water.

She sat staring at it for several minutes after that. Was that magic she felt? If so, it was unlike any other magic she'd felt before—and so subtle that she wasn't even entirely sure it was there.

She set it aside abruptly and began to unpin her hair. But despite all the events of the evening—or more likely because of them—it was a long time before she could sleep.

Two days later, Sophie sent Parthenope an urgent note, summoning her to come over that afternoon if at all possible. Parthenope did not disappoint her. They were all in the drawing room when she arrived: Aunt Molly lay on the sofa, directing Sophie and Bunty as they crocheted soft woolen yarn into plant ties.

Parthenope crossed the room and knelt beside Aunt Molly, taking her good hand. "Out of bed so soon? You are a marvel, ma'am."

Aunt Molly bridled. "Oh, no, not really. But I do have a very strong constitution, if I do say so myself. I think it comes of living in the country. Very salubrious air at my house, you know, and the flues draw wonderfully. I declare, if only my arm weren't broken, I'd order my carriage this very minute and go back to Lilac Cottage, so I could recuperate in peace and quiet!"

"Flues. . . ." Parthenope tapped her chin in thought. "That reminds me. I can't be *positive*, but I *did* think I smelled something not quite right coming from the direction of your conservatory when the footman let me in. Are the flues drawing well down there?"

Aunt Molly's eyes widened. "Did you hear that, Bunty? I thought they were, but perhaps we had better go and see. My dwarf oranges are just fruiting!" She cast aside the rug tucked over her legs and gestured to Bunty, who scurried over and helped her to her feet, then supported her from the room.

Sophie regarded Parthenope. "You're utterly shameless, you know."

"If you're going to make a cake, you've got to break some flour, or something like that." Parthenope fixed her with an exasperated look as she took off her bonnet. "Now, what's so vital that we discuss it today? I hope you don't ever decide to take up espionage on a regular basis, you hulver-headed peagoose."

"Why?"

"'An afternoon of needlework,' sent in your aunt's name? Sophie, she's got a broken arm. Just what will she be doing? Hemming petticoats with her toes? It's a good thing Mama has a sense of humor and knew it was just an excuse for us to chat."

Oh, drat. That had been careless, hadn't it? "Well, never mind that now. Something very important's happened."

"I'd guessed." Parthenope pulled a chair close to her and looked expectant. "It had better be good, though, if you want me to give over teasing you."

"I don't know that I'd call it good. Papa received an invitation from the Prince Regent yesterday. He's holding a special reception at Carlton House for government members who are closely involved in the war effort."

"Really." One of Parthenope's eyebrows rose.

"Yes. Papa and Lord Palmerston and all of them—"

Both eyebrows were up now. "All together at the Prince Regent's house."

"It's the perfect opportunity for our assassin to do a great deal of harm."

"Isn't it, though?" Parthenope had lost her skeptical air and now looked excited. "You're going, of course? All we have to do is figure out how to get me in. Perhaps I could disguise myself. . . . Hmm, can't pass myself off as Amélie, too tall for that. Do you think I could pretend to be Aunt Molly if I put my arm in a sling and stooped a bit and . . . er, cut my hair and gained a couple of stone in the next week or so?"

Sophie laughed. "Don't be silly. I'm sure I can persuade Papa to bring you as one of our party."

"Yes, I suppose so. But it would have been much more fun to come in disguise." She brightened. "Do you think I could bring Hester? He'd be very useful if we're there to guard against magical attacks."

"Parthenope, you *cannot* go to the Prince Regent's party with a parakeet on your shoulder. Countess Lieven and Princess Esterhazy will be there, and you'd never get into Almack's again if they saw Hester."

Parthenope wrinkled her nose. "Why do you always have to be so practical?"

"One of us has to. That reminds me—I wish you'd brought Hester with you today."

"I thought about it, but wasn't sure Aunt Molly would

approve. Why? Are you that fond of the wretched little thatch-gallows?"

Sophie smiled. "What did he do to deserve being called that?"

"Took four or five bites out of a new chip bonnet I'd left on my bed. I came *this* close to wringing his little purple neck." She held up her thumb and forefinger a hair's breadth apart. "Want a new pet? I'm sure he'd do splendidly at keeping you entertained."

"No, thank you. I shouldn't like to deprive you of your bosom companion. But I would like him to have a look at this." She held up the cane she'd examined the night Amélie visited her room.

Parthenope looked at it curiously. "Is it new?"

"No, just one Amélie and her maid Nalini made."

"It's splendid, but why do you want to have Hester look at it? Do you think there's magic in it?"

"I don't know," Sophie said slowly. "That's why I'd like Hester's opinion. There's something odd about it—about all of the ones they made me—a very faint feeling that might be magic, but if it is, it's like nothing I've ever seen before. It could be I'm imagining things—"

"Who's imagining things?" Aunt Molly came in, followed by Bunty, who was holding her hands behind her back. "Certainly not you, my dear," she said to Parthenope. "My gracious, I'm so glad you've such a sensitive nose!"

Parthenope looked stunned. "The flues? There *was* something wrong with them?"

"No, not at all, though I can perfectly understand the confusion. No, the coal wagon had just made a delivery, which is probably what you smelled. But I did find that Bunty had neglected to open the ventilation window this morning, and it would have gotten far too warm in there and blasted my oranges. So I thought, well, if anyone deserved a reward, it was you. Close your eyes and hold out your hands!" She motioned for Bunty to sidle over to them, still keeping her hands behind her back.

"Er . . ." For once, Parthenope seemed bereft of words.

"I insist!" Aunt Molly was beaming.

"Is one of the orchids in bloom?" Sophie asked, trying not to laugh.

"Even better! Come along, child," Aunt Molly urged.

Parthenope said something under her breath that Sophie didn't quite catch, closed her eyes, and held out her hands. Bunty turned slightly, so that Sophie couldn't see what it was she was putting into Parthenope's hands. Then Parthenope exclaimed, "What the deuce!" and Bunty stepped aside.

Parthenope was still seated, her face a study in consternation and her hands cradling a large, perfectly formed pineapple.

"There!" Aunt Molly said, beaming. "Isn't it beautiful?"

"It's *dripping* on my dress!" Parthenope's voice came out somewhere between a squeak and a moan.

"That's hardly surprising. Bunty just cut it from its stalk. Don't worry, it will wash out of that muslin without a bit of bother. Unless . . ." Aunt Molly suddenly looked uncertain. "Don't you *like* pineapple?"

Parthenope took a deep breath. Sophie could almost see her light upon and reject half a dozen sarcastic answers to the question. "I adore pineapple," she finally said. "Would it be possible to have someone put it in a basket for me to take home?"

As soon as Aunt Molly and Bunty had left the room again with the offending fruit, Parthenope collapsed back in her chair with a gusty sigh. "If it hadn't been your aunt, I don't think I could have done that."

"I was lost in admiration of your self-control."

"Fiddlesticks. You came within inches of laughing like a hyena, and you know it." She gazed down at the sticky juice dribbles on her lap. "I wish your magic were working reliably. Then at least you could have wiped that grin off your face and got rid of these for me, Madame Witch."

Sophie gave her a haughty look and brushed her fingers across one of the dribbles. It vanished.

"Sophie!" Parthenope looked almost as thunderstruck as she had when Bunty gave her the pineapple. "You—you did it just like that!"

"Yes, I know," Sophie replied, trying to sound bored. She pulled out her handkerchief and transferred the stain to it.

"But—last time you had to try like anything. Is your magic working again?"

It was becoming too hard to restrain her glee. "I think it is. Ever since the other night when I broke Papa's glass with the poison in it, I've been able to do more and more. Look!"

She tossed her handkerchief into the air and whispered a word. It vanished.

Parthenope blinked at the space where it had been. "What did you do with it?"

"Look beneath you," Sophie said, smugly.

Parthenope twitched aside, then lifted the hem of her gown. "I don't see it."

"Stand up."

Parthenope did, and looked behind her at the seat of her chair. A handkerchief marked with Sophie's initials was there. She picked it up and touched the fresh pineapple juice stain on it, then regarded her with narrowed eyes. "Hmm."

"What?"

"I find it very interesting that your magic reappeared when it did."

"In time to save my father?"

"I think saving your father was coincidental. So has Perry called recently?"

Sophie felt her face grow warm. "What does that have to do with my magic?"

"Everything, possibly." Parthenope leaned forward. "He spoke to you that night, didn't he? He asked you if you would not mind if he spoke to your father about paying his formal addresses to you, yes?"

"Parthenope, that's—"

"Humor me. I'm trying to make a point."

Sophie relented. "Well, yes."

"Aha! And what did you tell him? Never mind—you're blushing like a beet." Parthenope grinned. "I knew we should be cousins someday! Anyway, don't you find it interesting that your magic should suddenly come back the very night my cousin as good as proposes to you?"

"What do you mean?"

"I mean that, just maybe, part of your problem with your magic is dependent on how you feel. When Perry spoke to you, were you happy or not?"

"Do you want the rest of this pineapple off your dress or not?"

Parthenope laughed. "Very well! I concede. But I still think I'm right. Here." She held the skirt of her dress stretched out so that Sophie could remove the sticky pineapple sap more easily. "She doesn't have a whole pinery in there, does she? I won't have to go through this again?"

"No, just a few plants. But it could have been worse, you know," Sophie said, not meeting her eyes.

Parthenope snorted. "How?"

"I believe she's trying to raise trout in the goldfish pool down there."

Chapter 14

To Sophie's relief, Papa agreed that Parthenope could attend the Prince Regent's reception as a member of their party. She and Sophie spent the next ten days huddled together at one or the other of their houses, planning what they would wear (Parthenope) and what they should actually do that evening at Carlton House (Sophie). Would they be free to roam about keeping an eye on the assembled guests, or would they be forced to sit demurely in one spot with Aunt Molly?

"We simply have to stay together all evening. That way we won't need a chaperone and can wander about," Parthenope declared.

"What if James Leland is there?" Sophie asked.

"Pooh," Parthenope said severely, though a slight blush crept up her cheeks. "Anyway, this isn't a social event for us. We'll be *working.*"

"Then why are you having such a hard time deciding

whether to wear the fawn-colored dress or the blue one and whether to wear flowers in your hair or ostrich plumes?"

Parthenope ignored her.

She did, however, bring Hester to examine Sophie's canes. Sophie found herself holding her breath as she laid one across her knees and Parthenope gently brought the parakeet down and encouraged him to hop onto it. But instead of his usual Shakespearean pricking thumbs announcement, Hester whistled softly. "Like," he murmured, bending to pluck at one of the tassels decorating the cane, and he could not be convinced to hop off again until offered a sugar lump.

"You're not being helpful, bird," Parthenope said to him. "So what conclusion are we to draw from that?"

"I don't know." Sophie watched Hester tug at the tassel again and set it swinging, his purple head cocked to one side. He hadn't seemed alarmed in any way by the cane, which she had to assume was a good sign, but then again, it could just have been that he thought it was a lovely new toy. "I suppose I could have imagined it. Why should Amélie give me enchanted canes, anyway?"

"Well, if she did, could it be because it's a good enchantment? Why else would she be so insistent about your using them all the time?" Parthenope fixed her with a stern look. "Sophie, do you truly think she's a witch?"

Sophie bit her lip. "N-no. I don't. We're together almost constantly every day, and I've never gotten the least hint that she might have any magic. I don't suppose that's proof positive, but . . . no, I don't think she is."

"Then stop worrying," Parthenope commanded. "We've got our Carlton House campaign to plan."

Their endless discussions of just how they were supposed to guard an assembly of two or so hundred people from a person or persons unknown took Sophie's mind off the fact that Peregrine's calls had suddenly become far less numerous in the last week. Nor was she the only one who'd noticed a change.

"Milor' Woodbridge does not seem to be himself, I am thinking," Amélie commented one afternoon after he'd paid them a brief call. To Sophie's surprise, he had been nearly rude to Amélie, giving her the shortest of bows and addressing all his conversation exclusively to Sophie.

"N-no," she said, slowly. "I also thought he seemed a little . . . off."

"You have not had a disagreement, have you? He does not call as often of late." Amélie's voice was light, but Sophie felt her eyes examining her curiously.

"No," she said, trying to sound assured. "He did say that he'd been to wait upon Lord Castlereagh several times over the last week or so, though he didn't say why. Perhaps he is finally to get the position in the Foreign Office that he has always wanted."

"Ah, that may be it," Amélie agreed. "I hope that he will have good news soon—in many parts of his life." She smiled gently at Sophie, who couldn't help coloring slightly. At the few calls Peregrine *had* made recently, he mostly sat staring at her with a distant, faintly worried expression on his face that she couldn't decipher. Had something happened to change his feelings? Had he decided not to speak to Papa after all?

Perhaps she should ask Parthenope to find out . . . but as dear as she was and as staunch a friend, could she be trusted to handle such a mission with any degree of subtlety at all?

Finesse was not Parthenope's strong suit, at least where her cousin was concerned. No, Sophie would have to wait and see, but the tension of this added to worrying about the Prince Regent's reception was nearly unbearable.

Sophie had driven past Carlton House, the Prince Regent's enormous London residence in Pall Mall, St. James, dozens of times since arriving in London and thought it looked like a cross between a Greek temple and Versailles. But its outside, grand as it was, had scarcely prepared her for the splendor of its inside.

"It's . . . um . . ." Parthenope whispered to her, wide-eyed, as they were ushered in the main door by one of the prince's equerries, clad for tonight in a hussar's uniform of scarlet and gold with green facings.

Sophie sympathized with her uncharacteristic speech-lessness. The anteroom they had just entered was striking in bright blue and dazzling with multitudes of candles. The light reflected off the rich burnished gold of the elaborate moldings and picked out the gold fleurs-de-lis of the carpet.

"If you think this is impressive, wait until you've seen the rest," Papa murmured to them. "The crimson drawing room makes this look like a monastery, and the conservatory is beyond description."

"It is . . . a little goes a long way, I am thinking," Amélie replied quietly.

"Nonsense," said Aunt Isabel, who had announced that she would be accompanying them as soon as she'd heard of the invitation. "I think it's charming."

"I should like to see this conservatory," Aunt Molly said wistfully, and a little too loudly, from Papa's other side. Her turban, adorned with a spray of gilded wheat ears, bobbed gently as she nodded.

The equerry bowed. "The prince will no doubt be delighted to have it shown to you, madam, but for now, will you be pleased to follow me to the gardens? There are temporary rooms set up there for some of the celebrations His Royal Highness is holding this summer."

Parthenope's eyebrows rose. "Temporary rooms? Aren't there enough permanent ones in this ridicu—"

Sophie took her arm and gave it a warning squeeze. They had agreed (reluctantly, on Parthenope's part) that tonight they were going to try to be as unobtrusive as possible, which meant dressing simply, comporting themselves quietly, and otherwise pretending to be meek, well-behaved nobodies. Parthenope gulped and nodded.

"As this evening's reception is not large, not all the rooms have been lit," the equerry explained as he conducted them through a covered walkway hung with green cloth and decorated with illuminated scenes painted on fine silk. "Just the main ballroom, the Corinthian temple, and a few of the supper tents."

Parthenope rolled her eyes at Sophie. "Is that all? I declare, I'm feeling quite—oh!"

Her whispered comments dissolved in a gasp as they entered what appeared to be a gigantic tent at least a hundred feet across, a tent lit with a dozen glittering chandeliers and scores of mirrors to reflect their light. Gold cords and tassels decorated the muslin-hung walls, and even the ceiling was draped with cloth.

"It's *trompe l'oeil*," the equerry explained, following their eyes upward. "Just painted to look like cloth. Terribly clever, really. The whole building is actually brick. The Prince wanted it to feel very light and airy, and I think he succeeded. May I ask you to join the queue so that His Royal Highness may say his welcomes?" He indicated a line of guests snaking toward a raised dais on which several glittering, uniform-clad figures stood, bowed, and hurried back down the passage, presumably to escort more new arrivals.

Parthenope linked her arm in Sophie's. "This is going to be harder than I thought. How can we be in six places at once? I wish I'd brought Hester after all."

"Hush. We'll do our best," Sophie whispered back, hoping she sounded more confident and bracing than she felt. "We shall just have to move around a lot, like guards on patrol."

"Well, I wish we had more help. Can't we tell Amélie and recruit her into guard duty?"

"What help will that be? She's not a witch, so she won't be able to sense any magical attacks, and there will be plenty of the Prince Regent's servants about to protect everyone from nonmagical threats. Anyway, it's really only the royals and a handful of War Office people we have to keep our eyes on. I think we can manage that."

"But what if the Prince Regent decides he wants a bite to eat and goes to a supper tent and Lord Palmerston wants to have a look at the Corinthian Temple and your papa wants a chat with someone else in the ballroom? Hester could have perched on a chandelier and at least watched this room for us," Parthenope said pensively.

"Yes, and more than likely made a mess on Princess Mary or

something equally dreadful." Sophie sighed. "But you're right. Just now, I wouldn't much care if he messed on her dress and tried to nest in the Prince Regent's wig, if he were here to help."

Parthenope patted her arm. "You're worried, aren't you?"

"Yes . . . and I don't know if it's for a good reason, or if I'm being vaporish."

They made it to the head of the receiving line in not too much time, to Sophie's relief. The Prince Regent greeted Papa in a most gracious manner.

"Ah, Lansell," he said jovially, taking hold of his shoulder while he shook his hand. "This war—will it ever end?"

"We're working on it, sir. May I present my family?"

The prince turned slightly and smiled at them as he bowed. "A pleasure! Will you all go to Brussels, then?"

"Brussels?" Parthenope murmured to Sophie as they sunk into curtsies. "Why didn't you tell me you were going to Brussels?"

"This is the first I've heard of it," Sophie murmured back. Was Papa being sent to Brussels to help supervise the War Office's activities there? It was rumored that the Duke of Wellington himself was due to arrive in Brussels momentarily from Vienna, ready to take command of the British and Dutch forces gathering northeast of France in case Napoléon should choose to reopen his war with the Allies there. Would Papa want them all to come? But what about the season? She couldn't miss anything now that she had Parthenope to do it all with. And what about Peregrine?

Papa glanced at her. "We haven't discussed it yet, sir. It's only just been decided."

"From what I hear, I understand they're having an even livelier season there than ours in London. I'd go myself, if I could get away from the pressures of state here. You shall have to enjoy it for me." The prince smiled at her, and Sophie knew he saw her cane and didn't care that she was crippled. Suddenly she could see why, despite his ludicrous wig and enormous corseted belly, he'd once been considered the handsomest and most charming prince in Europe.

"Well, that went very well," Aunt Isabel said after they'd left the prince and moved to the side. "Did you see how he looked at me? I declare, it made me feel all aflutter."

"I did see that! They do say he definitely has a *tendre* for older women, though, so I'm not at all surprised," Aunt Molly agreed wisely. Amélie took her arm and hastily led her several yards away to look at a potted azalea.

Deprived of blasting Aunt Molly into pieces, Aunt Isabel turned on Papa. "And why did you not tell us about going to Brussels, sir?"

Papa sighed. "I just learned about it myself, Isabel, if that makes you feel any better."

"But when do you leave? One does not just up and make a journey like that on a moment's notice—"

Parthenope tugged Sophie's arm, so that they turned slightly away from Aunt Isabel's tirade. "Let's leave them to it. No one will dare hurt your father when your Aunt Isabel is there. Shall we stand guard on the prince or go looking for miscreants and assassins?"

"I trust His Royal Highness had the wit not to invite any of those tonight," someone said behind them, "but one never knows."

"Perry!" Parthenope dropped Sophie's arm and whirled. "What are you doing here?"

Sophie turned too, her heart feeling as though it had fluttered up into her throat, but curtsied smoothly enough as he bowed. Peregrine wore a black coat and plain linen and white stockings with his knee breeches, like the Regent's friend Beau Brummel. The splendid dark simplicity of his clothes set off his cool gray eyes even more noticeably.

"That's not a very gracious greeting." Peregrine's mouth quirked humorously, but Sophie noticed that the smile never reached the rest of his face. "I'll overlook it for now, though, as I have quite an excellent reason for being here. Probably better than you have, coz."

"Pooh," said Parthenope. "I'm here as a guest of Lord Lansell."

"And I'm here as a new secretary to Lord Palmerston."

Sophie was unable to repress a gasp. "In—in the War Office?"

"That would be where Lord Palmerston works," he agreed.

Parthenope grabbed his arm. "But—but you can't! I thought you wanted to be in the Foreign Office?"

Sophie wished she could grab his arm as well, to have something to hold on to. First Brussels, and now this—what other bombshell of news would drop on them tonight?

"I would have preferred the Foreign Office, but can hope to transfer there in the future, once we've got Napoléon at bay again." He hesitated, and looked at Sophie. "Your father—"

"Sophie, tell him—you can't work there, Perry!" Parthenope looked as though she was close to tears.

"Stay here and watch my father. Don't let him drink anything, if you can." Sophie patted her shoulder and turned to

Peregrine. "Will you walk with me? I think that perhaps we ought to talk."

He bowed and took her arm. "The garden?"

There would be less opportunity to be overheard there. Sophie nodded and let him lead her through the crowd toward one of the open doors.

Could this be what had kept him so busy the last week, and so distracted? Quite probably, but why choose to enter the War Office when his heart was in diplomacy, not battle? Yes, he could surely transfer when the war was over . . . *if* it ended.

He was silent as he led her as quickly as she could manage from the ballroom and into the cool, dark blue dusk of Carlton House's back garden. Torches set in high wrought-iron sconces lit the scattered supper tents and refreshment rooms, and from another small templelike structure on the far side of the ball room, the sounds of an orchestra playing marches could be heard. Here and there party guests—mostly couples—flitted about in the torchlight arm in arm, or stood together in the shadows in close conversation. The tents, the music, the torches, the equerries and servants in their hussar uniforms, all lent the gardens a romantically military air that Sophie knew was false; a real camp of soldiers preparing for battle would be anything but romantic. But she couldn't help feeling a tension in the air—was it only hers?

Peregrine paused. "Over there. We can use one of the supper tents."

He led her toward a tent in the far corner of the garden. It was unlit, but a nearby torch threw enough light into it to show rose-colored draperies and a display of regimental colors on the walls. Haphazardly stacked chairs and tables piled with candelabra and folded linens, in readiness for the prince's next grand party, occupied much of the space. Peregrine seized a candle from one of the candelabra and lit it at the nearby torch, then came back, set it in the candelabrum, and to her astonishment, took her in his arms.

"Sophie," he murmured, and kissed her hair.

Sophie tried to make herself think of frozen ponds and drifting snowflakes, but everything below her ears seemed to be thinking of warmth and melting instead. It would be wonderful to bury her face against his shoulder and just drink in the feeling of having him so close to her, but this would not do. There were too many questions to be answered.

"Peregrine, what—"

He drew back slightly and laid a finger gently on her lips. "I've spoken to your father—did he tell you? He seemed happy to give me his consent to speak to you."

A half hour ago, she would have let her head drop back onto his shoulder and enjoyed the moment. But this was now. She turned her head to evade his hand and said, "The War Office—why? Why did you go there?"

He looked surprised. "Is that what you want to talk about? I went there in order to find out who's trying to kill your father and the others, of course."

His voice was so matter-of-fact that it took her a moment to comprehend his words. "Then you do believe Parthenope and me?"

He hesitated. "I didn't at first. But the more I thought about it, the more it troubled me. Parthenope and I may have a history of—of disagreement, but I know she's no fool. And neither are you."

"And what if *you* get hurt or killed?" Sophie demanded.

His arms tightened around her. "I promise I won't. But it's better than you or Parthenope coming to any harm."

"No, it isn't. Besides, why should we? We don't work there."

"Which is why *I* need to be there. It's rather difficult for you to investigate it from the outside, don't you think?"

"Yes, but you don't know—" Sophie stopped.

He frowned. "What? Is there something else? Has something else happened?"

Sophie thought furiously. She couldn't tell him about the poison in Papa's champagne, could she? No one knew about that except her and Parthenope and the person who'd put it there. And she couldn't tell him about the magic. . . .

Or could she? He'd finally come to believe that there was some kind of plot—but would he believe that magic was behind the actual attempts, camouflaged to look accidental?

"No," she said slowly. "But I don't like the idea of you putting yourself into danger."

He smiled and touched her cheek gently. "And I repeat— what kind of man would let a pair of defenseless females face danger, if he could prevent it?"

A little stab of annoyance made her speak sharply. "I'm not as weak and defenseless as I might look, as I believe we've already discussed in the past."

"Of course you're not defenseless," he said quickly. He hesitated, then said, "And besides, I have a feeling I already know who is responsible. My joining the War Office may aid in drawing our villain out, but I'll need your help especially to catch her."

Her? "You think it's someone I know?"

He nodded and looked past Sophie at the jumble of furniture. "Maybe we should sit—I'm afraid this might not be easy for you—"

Sophie shrugged impatiently, but let him lead her to a chair. "We're talking about my father's life, for heaven's sake! Who do you think it is?"

He stood before her, hands clasped behind his back, and looked down at his feet as if he wasn't looking forward to telling her. "Your houseguest, Madame Carswell."

For a moment, Sophie wasn't sure she'd heard him correctly. "Mada—Amélie? You think it's Amélie?"

"Sophie, think about it. Who has been there at all of the attempts?"

Why hadn't she foreseen this possibility? Because it seemed so utterly ridiculous? "Yes, Amélie has been there at all of them . . . and so have I. So why don't you think I'm responsible, then?"

"Because you are not French, and she is," he explained patiently. "We're at war with the emperor of France. I know I spouted some nonsense about the Allies and the Americans, but truly, nobody else has a reason to want to remove important members of our War Office except someone sympathetic to Bonaparte's cause. Except that I think it's far more than that she sympathizes with him. I think she's an agent sent to do just this."

"But she's not French anymore. She's been British ever since she married Papa's friend—"

"Do we know that? All we have is her word that she's John Carswell's widow—"

"My father, who was Mr. Carswell's friend, seems to think she is as well," Sophie replied frostily.

He shrugged. "Very well. But before that, she was French. Her father was in India as an official of the French government. Why shouldn't she be loyal to her home country?"

Good God, he had an answer for everything—a wrong answer, she was sure, but— "And what if she is still fond of her home country? Wouldn't you be?"

"Yes," he replied. "Which is why I suspect her." He knelt by her chair and took her hand. "I know it's hard for you to believe—"

"You're quite right, I can't believe it. She has been wonderful to me—to us. Even Aunt Isabel likes her—"

Peregrine was shaking his head. "Of course you all like her. How could she remain in your house without making herself as agreeable as possible? Do you think all spies walk about rubbing their hands together and acting like a villain in a farce? There's no reason she can't be trying to kill your father and be kind to you at the same time—"

"She hasn't just been *kind*, as you call it," Sophie said angrily. "Do you have any notion of what Amélie has done for me? She's helped me understand that I don't have to be ashamed that I'm a cripple. That being lame doesn't make me stupid or ugly or half-witted. That I can wear pretty dresses and go to parties and be just like any other girl. That while I'm limited in a few things, I can be just as good as anyone in others, or better. That isn't being kind to me—it's making me see I don't need to agree with how other people might see me, or accept their 'kindness'—or their 'protection.'"

"Of course you are. That's obvious to everyone—"

"No, it isn't. Was it obvious to Susan Halliday and all the others like her who've been rude or condescending or just looked straight through me because I make them uncomfortable with my limp and my cane? Was it obvious to *you*?"

He had the grace to look shamefaced. "They're wrong to behave so."

Sophie swallowed back a sarcastic retort. "If it weren't for Amélie, I would still be hiding behind the potted palms at every party I go to. She is not trying to kill me or anyone else. You have to take my word for it—we must keep looking for who really is responsible."

This was madness, but how could she say, "I know it's not Amélie, because whoever's doing it is using magic, and I would know if she were a witch"?

"It's not Amélie," she said more calmly, measuring her words to lend them weight. "I *know* it isn't."

He sighed and took her hand again. "How do you know that?"

"Because . . . because I do."

He was silent for a minute. "Because you don't want to believe it?" he finally said.

"No!" she cried, snatching her hand away. "Do you think I'm such a—such a gull that I'd convince myself of something just because I don't want to believe the truth? Don't you think I've had enough experience in my life facing difficult truths? I've lived in the same house with her for many weeks now. I *know* it isn't Amélie."

"Then I will believe you, if you tell me your proof."

Her annoyance withered. "I—I can't. If I could, I would. Can't you just believe me?"

"Can't you just trust me?"

"Of course I trust you!" She held her hand back out to him.

He didn't take it. "Just not enough to tell me how you know it's not Madame Carswell."

Peregrine's words fell on her ears like a glove thrown down in challenge. "No—I don't know! Oh, you don't understand!"

"No, I don't." He climbed to his feet and stood over her, close enough that she could see the agitated rise and fall of his chest. But when she looked up to meet his eyes, she couldn't read the expression in their cool grayness. "Sophie, I have to do what I think is right. And quarreling with you isn't helping. When you feel you can tell me how it is you are so sure that Madame Carswell is innocent of trying to murder your father, I will be happy to listen to you."

"I—"

"But I have to say that it doesn't make me feel exactly comfortable to know that the young woman I—I had every intention of making my wife can't trust me with her secrets."

She stared at him, trying to think of something—anything!—to say. But it suddenly felt as if her thoughts were squeezing through a tiny hole in her mind, one word at a time, so that she couldn't string them together. Peregrine seemed to blur and waver as he stood before her, and with painful slowness she realized that her eyes were full of tears.

Because he was right. She should be able to tell him why she thought Amélie was innocent, but she didn't trust him enough to tell him about her magic. Not yet. She still hadn't gotten over how he'd hurt her at the start of their acquaintance, and now she still wasn't sure she knew him well enough to trust that he wouldn't regard her as unnatural or evil . . . or if her magic failed, as freakish or insane. And if she couldn't tell him about it, could she, in all conscience, let him continue to court her?

"Sophie?"

His voice sounded as if it were coming from miles away, which she supposed, in a way, it was. "I'm sorry," she whispered, and sniffed . . . but no. She wasn't going to sit here and cry at him. At least she could be dignified about the matter.

She set her cane and stood up, ignoring the hand he held out to her. "You're right, Lord Woodbridge. I can't stop you from suspecting that Madame Carswell is some kind of Bonapartist assassin. And I can't tell you why it's quite impossible that she is, because what you said is true. I can't trust you with my—my secrets." She paused to steady her voice and looked down at her hands clutching the crook of her cane, because she didn't dare look at him. "Perhaps it would be best if . . . if we agreed that under the circumstances—"

His voice broke across hers, and each word sounded chipped from January ice. "So you're willing to stand by and wait until another War Office member—your own father, perhaps—is killed? Or will it take two or three of them dying to bring you to your senses and stop you from clutching your secrets like a—like a cane? And in the meanwhile, will you enjoy seeing England's ability to make war on the emperor compromised?"

"Why, you can't—" she gasped, feeling as if all the air had been sucked from her lungs.

In the candlelight she could see the lines of his face shift as his jaw clenched, relaxed, clenched again. "I can, and I will, because I have evidently made a grievous error in judgment.

Forgive me, madam, for taking up your time." He bowed, a short, cold salute, then turned on his heel and stalked from the tent.

"Peregrine," she said, but her throat had turned hot and scratchy, so it came out in a low croak. He wouldn't hear her . . . and anyway, did she want him to? She'd made her choice. She was even certain it had been the correct one. So why did it feel as if her heart had been yanked from her chest and cut into thousands of tiny, bleeding slivers?

She leaned heavily on her cane for support. If only she could make the clock run backward . . . but what good would that do? They would still reach this point of impasse.

She had hurt him terribly, she knew. Perhaps it would have been kinder to stab him with a knife than say to him what she had. But she was hurt too. Had it been necessary for him to say those horrible things about her wanting to kill Papa?

Suddenly that tent was the last place she wanted to be. She blew out the candle and stumbled out into the dark, but not to find Peregrine. All she wanted now was to find Papa and claim a headache, and ask if she could go home. Parthenope would surely—

Oh God, Parthenope. How was she going to tell her that she and Peregrine would not—Parthenope had spent the last two months doing her best to bring them together . . . and now this. Parthenope would forgive her—eventually. But just now she could not face her, as much as she loved her.

At the perimeter of the brightly lit supper tents, she paused, wishing the flickering torches wouldn't make her eyes water so. At least, that's what she preferred to believe . . . not that tears were running down her face for any other possible

227

reason. She was dabbing at them with the corner of her shawl because it was too hard to juggle cane and fan while fishing a handkerchief out of her reticule when something—a movement off to her left, caught her attention. A man stood there, his back to Sophie, a few feet behind one of the tents, which seemed jammed full of guests, to judge from the noise and the laughter issuing from it. As she watched, he raised his hand and seemed to say something.

"Monsieur?" Sophie called. "Monsieur le Comte?" She took a few tentative steps toward him. Who had he been talking to?

The Comte de Carmouche-Ponthieux started and whirled around. "Lady Sophie!" He wore an odd expression that she could not quite decipher in the torchlight.

"I didn't know you would be here tonight, sir," she said. "My aunt will be so pleased to see you."

"Marie is here?" he asked. "I did not think—" He leaned toward her and frowned. "But you are not well, mademoiselle. Will you take my arm? May I help you?" He gave her his arm, then without comment handed her a large, snowy handkerchief.

Sophie took it with a murmured thank-you. He waited while she used it, then said, "You have gotten lost, perhaps, in this very large garden? May I escort you to your family?"

"Thank you, that would be . . . no, wait. Could you find Aunt Molly for me? I have a—a dreadful headache, actually, and I should like to go home, if she wouldn't mind—"

He inclined his head. "At once. I shall call my own carriage, and drive you both back to your house on my way home. I too am finding the evening somewhat . . . disappointing." He smiled and shrugged. "You will be all right to wait here? Can I not take you into the tent to sit down?"

"No, I'll be fine here—really I shall." The last thing she wanted was to see someone . . . like Parthenope. Or Parthenope's cousin.

The comte was back more swiftly than she'd thought possible with Aunt Molly in tow.

"Poor child," Aunt Molly said, peering at her in her near-sighted way. "You look quite dreadful. I think it's the decorations, myself. They're making me bilious. You were very right to fetch me, Auguste." She dimpled at him. "Though I am cross with you for not telling me you'd be here, beastly thing."

They bundled Sophie into the comte's carriage—Aunt Molly enjoining the coachman to avoid all bumping and jarring on the cobbled streets—and set out for South Audley Street. All the ride home, Sophie gazed out at the shadows in the unlit side streets and alleys and longed to bury herself in a quiet dark place like them, where memory and thought could no longer find her to rip at her.

Chapter 15

Sophie awoke slowly, savoring the faint lavender scent and comfort of the featherbed and soft linen sheets surrounding her. And the quiet too—no shouting innkeepers or coaches clattering on cobbles had broken her rest this morning. This was by far the nicest inn they'd stayed at since leaving London—

No, wait. She opened her eyes and remembered: This was no inn but the house Papa had rented, just off the rue Ducale near the Parc in Brussels, where they'd arrived late last night. The room was bright with dainty white-painted furniture and blue bed hangings and curtains, and the blue-and-white-tiled fireplace framed a cheerful fire to take off the chill of early morning—goodness, she'd slept right through the maid tiptoeing in to rebuild it, hadn't she? The only discordant note in the room came from Parthenope, still sound asleep next to her and snoring gustily.

Sophie watched her for a minute, smiling, then sighed. If

only she could fall back into sleep as well, where memory couldn't follow her, but it was too late. At least today, though, she would have the flurry and excitement of settling into Brussels to take her mind off her misery.

It had been nearly two weeks since the Prince Regent's party, two weeks since she'd seen the icy anger in Pere—in Lord Woodbridge's eyes, right before he walked out of her life forever. Sometimes the memory of that night jabbed her like a knife; other times, it smothered her in a heavy blanket of wretchedness. Only getting ready to depart for Brussels had taken her mind off it. Papa had actually tried to convince her to stay in London with Aunt Isabel so that she wouldn't miss the rest of the season, but missing the rest of the season was precisely what she wanted to do. She couldn't face the thought of running into *him* at some ball or party, and watching him cut her or, worse, bow to her with polite indifference.

She'd been surprised that the duchess had permitted Parthenope to come with them to Brussels, especially without her old governess, Miss MacTavish, and on such short notice. But Sophie knew Parthenope could be extremely persuasive, and since Brussels was almost as full of London's best society this spring as London itself and both Aunt Molly and Amélie were there to chaperone them, there was little reason for the duchess to say no. Besides, Parthenope confessed on the boat over to Ostend, she'd told her mother she'd be going whether she got permission or not.

As if she'd heard her thoughts, Parthenope gave a particularly loud snore, followed by a start and a faint mumble of protest. She opened her eyes and squinted at Sophie. "What'd you do? You woke me up."

"I did not. You woke yourself. If I were possessed of any conscience at all, I'd write James Leland immediately and inform him that you snore."

"Pooh." Parthenope yawned and rubbed her eyes, then dropped her hands and looked at Sophie with a small frown. "*Do* I snore?"

"Abominably. But then again, he might too, so you'll drown each other out."

To her eternal credit, Parthenope hadn't said a word of reproach when she told her about what had happened between her and Peregr—dash it, Lord Woodbridge. In fact, all her rancor seemed reserved for her cousin: She expostulated at length on his pigheadedness and foolishness at not having consulted her. Sophie knew Parthenope hadn't given up hope that there would be a reconciliation between them—but she couldn't think about anything like that right now. The wound was still too fresh, not to mention compounded by her anxiety about him working at the War Office.

Parthenope snorted and sat up, plumping her pillows and leaning back against them. "Twaddle. So what are we doing today?"

"I suppose that's up to Papa, but I should think we'd be able to at least go for a walk in the Parc or something like that. I assume he'll be calling on the Duke of Wellington and the ambassador and other people today."

"The duke. . . ." Parthenope got a dreamy expression in her eyes.

"The duke is quite married, if you'll recall," Sophie said, poking her. "And what about Mr. Leland?"

"I don't want to marry the duke, silly. I just want to see

him. He's a hero, remember?" Parthenope sat up and flung aside the bedclothes. "Anyway, I have a list of people Mama wants me to call on, so I suppose we could see about getting some of them out of the way. The sooner we call on them, the sooner they'll start inviting us to parties, right?" She paused and looked back at Sophie. "How are you today?" she asked, more gently.

Sophie shrugged. "I was wondering, in the carriage yesterday on the way here . . . do you think we can finally stop worrying about Papa? Do you think he's safe now that we're out of London?"

"I suppose we'll find out," Parthenope said lightly. "If something bad happens here, then—" Sophie's face must have changed, because she leaned over and pushed at Sophie's shoulder. "And you can get that expression off your face. I'm not implying that Amélie had anything to do with any of it, the way my bacon-brained cousin seems to think she did. All I'm saying is that we ought to watch out for him a little longer. If nothing happens, we can assume whoever was responsible is still in London." She sighed. "I confess, I don't like to think about Perry there if that's the case, bacon-brain though he is."

Neither did Sophie, but she couldn't admit it just yet. Not even to Parthenope.

⁓

By the time they'd dressed and found their way down to the small breakfast room, the rest of the family had gathered there. Papa already had his nose buried in a newspaper.

"*Bonjour, mes chères!*" Amélie called gaily from behind a pair of silver pots. "Did you sleep well? Come, sit! Would you care for coffee or chocolate?"

Amélie had been delighted to accompany them to Brussels, where she had a cousin she had not seen since her childhood. Sophie knew she'd also guessed that something had happened between her and Lord Woodbridge. Though Amélie had not mentioned his name, she'd been particularly gentle and sweet.

"I should have the chocolate if I were you," Aunt Molly said from her seat on Papa's other side. "And besides, it's better for you. Young girls should never drink coffee."

"Good morning. Coffee for me, please," Parthenope said as if she hadn't heard Aunt Molly. Sophie looked at her and guessed that she hadn't; she was ignoring the chair the footman had drawn out for her and was making a beeline for the birdcage in the window. "Hester, *ma choucroute!*" she murmured, scrunching her face and making kissing sounds. "How is *maman's* darling? Did you sleep well too?"

The footman made a small choking sound that he tried unsuccessfully to turn into a cough, and Amélie laughed. "I think you are meaning *chouchoute*, which means 'pet,'" she said kindly. "*Choucroute* means 'pickled cabbage.'"

"Does it? Oh, dear." Parthenope opened Hester's cage and held out her hand. He hopped readily onto her finger, and she set him on her shoulder, where he started tugging at her ear. "Ow! All right, you little beast! You shall have some breakfast in just a moment. Pickled cabbage, you say? I rather like that. It fits his temperament. Come along, *ma choucroute*."

Though Papa had been perfectly willing for Parthenope to accompany them, Sophie didn't think he'd expected Hester as well. But Parthenope had already established his cage in their barouche the morning they left, and their poor butler Belton had looked mutinous when Papa attempted to hand the bird into his care.

"This room stays warm all the night, so I thought he should be comfortable in here," Amélie said. "He looks as though travel agrees with him."

Papa snorted slightly from behind his newspaper. Parthenope pretended not to hear him and said brightly, "Oh, yes, I believe it does. He's learned several *very* interesting French words recently, thanks to the boot boy in the inn at Ostend."

Amélie's eyes twinkled. "Ah, I am sure that he has. May I pour coffee for you too, Sophie?"

"Sophie, child, I must insist you have the chocolate. You must keep up your strength," Aunt Molly interjected.

"Yes, aunt," Sophie agreed meekly. "Chocolate, if you please, Amélie." It had been quietly decided that Amélie would be taking over the role of mistress of the house while they were here in Brussels, as neither Aunt Molly's French nor her strength, what with her arm still in a sling, were up to the task. It was pleasant to see Amélie presiding over the coffee pot, just as Mama once had—

"It would appear that half of English society truly is in Brussels right now, from what I read here," Papa commented, lowering his paper.

Amélie nodded. "Madame Mabuse—she is the housekeeper—says that you were fortunate indeed to get this house. There's not another available in Brussels. The city has been overwhelmed not only with its own tourists but with many who fled Paris after the emperor's return."

Parthenope came to the table and sat down. "Cowards,"

she said, busily stirring cream into her cup. "I suppose they're all composing stories to tell when they get home about what brave, clever fellows they were to evade old Boney. Utter rubbish." She took a large gulp of her coffee, burned her tongue, and said a word that possibly even Hester didn't know. Yet.

Amélie smiled. "Your confidence is refreshing. Madame Mabuse says that many in Brussels are quite sure that the emperor is poised to fall upon Brussels at once and lament that there are so few troops to protect them."

"They assume we keep soldiers laid away tidily in bandboxes until needed, too," Papa said drily. "But I expect in a few weeks' time they'll be complaining that the town is overrun with them."

"No they won't—they'll be too busy flirting with them," Parthenope whispered to Sophie.

"I can see that might be so. However"—Amélie hesitated—"I must say something, and I hope you will not misunderstand. You should know that many Bruxellois would welcome the emperor's return. Of course the British here feel differently, but it . . . it is perhaps best to avoid discussion of the matter if you are not sure of the sentiments of your company."

Parthenope's eyebrows shot up, but Papa nodded easily. "I'm not surprised. Your point is well made, madame."

"Why would they prefer to have Napoléon back?" Sophie asked.

"Because here in Brussels, the people feel more French than they do Dutch. If Napoléon again wins, they can be part of France. If he does not, they must be part of the new Netherlands under the Dutch king William," Papa explained, dropping the newspaper on the table and pulling out his watch. "And speaking of Napoléon winning, I think I ought to call upon His Excellency the Duke this morning—"

"Oh, look here," Parthenope said, picking up the newspaper. "It says there's a British literary club in the city. That sounds interesting—I expect all the newspapers from London will be there—"

Papa made an odd coughing sound. Glancing up at him, Sophie saw he was trying to conceal a laugh. "I can't say if the newspapers are all there," he said, "but I hear that a great many *notes* are exchanged among the members."

Amélie laughed. Aunt Molly looked confused. "Why are they exchanging notes? Is no one allowed to talk while reading the newspapers?"

Parthenope grinned. "It's a gaming hall, isn't it? Oh, famous! I've always wanted to see one. May we go?"

"Certainly not." Papa rose. "I'm taking the carriage, but can send it back for you if you wish. This afternoon we ought to all call on the Duke of Richmond and a few others. Does that suit you?"

"We're going to walk in the Parc, aren't we, Sophie?" Parthenope announced.

"A park! Well, I shall like to see how the Belgians do with their plantings," Aunt Molly said placidly, and poured herself another cup of chocolate.

The Parc turned out to be more on the scale of a London square than like Hyde or Green Parks ("It's not so much a Parc as a Parc-lette," Parthenope declared), but what it lacked in size it certainly made up for in beauty and charm.

Aunt Molly was in transports as they strolled about, her bonnet-enclosed head whipping from side to side as she exclaimed at the fine trees and lush shrubberies. Walking slowly arm in arm behind her and Amélie, Parthenope and Sophie exchanged glances when she made them stop and admire a rhododendron with large, glossy leaves and fat buds.

Parthenope leaned toward Sophie as they walked on ahead of Aunt Molly and Amélie. "Too bad the comte isn't here. I think she's a little less . . . *botanical* when he's around."

"He told me before we left that he might try to arrange a visit, but that he's very busy with his work. Maybe he'll be able to combine a trip here with a visit to King Louis—he's just in Ghent." Sophie hoped so. Someone needed to have a happily-ever-after, and it didn't appear that she herself would be that someone.

They left cards on Lady Capel, who was a friend of Parthenope's mother, and a few other important British ladies who lived by the Parc. "Mama said most of them are here because it's far cheaper to live here than England," Parthenope commented. "The Capels are related to half of the aristocracy back at home, but she said they don't have two farthings to rub together. Even the Richmonds are here in order to save money, and he's a *duke*, for heaven's sake. They still manage to entertain a great deal, though. The Duchess of Richmond is always having parties, they say, at the Duke of Wellington's request."

"The duke didn't bring his wife?"

"No. One hears tales that they're not in the best of—oh, drat!"

A small, muddy dog had come galloping down the path toward them, followed by a small and equally muddy boy, whooping loudly. The dog hurtled straight into Parthenope, staggered, shook itself, and gave her an annoyed look before resuming its flight. The boy never even paused.

Sophie looked down at Parthenope's white skirt, now considerably less white. "It's a good thing we were done paying calls," she commented.

But Parthenope shrugged. "Can't you just—you know"— she glanced back over her shoulder to make sure Amélie and Aunt Molly weren't in earshot—"magic it away? Where's my hanky?" She started to root around in her reticule.

Sophie didn't answer.

Parthenope made a small triumphant exclamation and flourished a lace-edged white square. "Here we a—"

"I can't."

"What?"

Sophie stared straight ahead as she walked. "I can't. It's gone."

"Gone? Your magic's gone? Good Lord!" Parthenope's voice rose to a squeak. She cast another guilty glance back at Aunt Molly and Amélie and asked more quietly, "You mean, totally gone? Since when?"

"Since before we left London." For a day or two, Sophie had been too preoccupied and too busy packing and getting ready to leave to take much notice of her magic. But when she'd tried to put a locking spell on her trunks, nothing had happened, and nothing happened when she tried a concealing spell or a fire-starting spell or, the most basic of all, a summoning spell.

"Oh, Sophie . . . that's . . . you're sure?"

"I'm sure." Sophie didn't have the heart to talk about the

dozens of times since then that she'd tried to do something as simple as lift a dropped snippet of ribbon with magic. All that she'd been able to do was cause it to twitch a couple of times . . . and even then, she wasn't entirely sure that a stray current of air hadn't been responsible.

Parthenope was silent for a moment as they continued down the gravel path. Sophie hoped they'd go back to the house soon; the gravel was difficult to walk on, and she was tired after paying calls on foot. She stole a look at her friend and saw that Parthenope was frowning, as if deep in thought.

"Why didn't you tell me?" she finally asked.

"What was there to tell?" Sophie sighed. "So my magic is gone again. Maybe this is the way it will be from now on: It will come and go. I don't know, and there's nothing I can do about it anyway."

"I'm not so sure about that," Parthenope said thoughtfully.

"What do you mean?"

"Well, think about it, Sophie—oh, good God almighty!" Parthenope halted abruptly. "Do you see who that is?" She nodded toward a trio approaching them on the path coming from the pavilion at the Parc's center.

Sophie looked. A gentleman accompanied by two ladies strolled slowly down the path toward them, one wearing a large and rather overtrimmed bonnet. As they drew closer, Sophie saw it was the younger of the two, a pretty girl of probably her age, so fair as to seem almost transparent. Her older companion was more soberly but just as richly dressed, handsome but with such dark hair that Sophie doubted they were blood relations. "Who? I don't know the ladies—" Then the gentleman laughed, throwing his head back as if overcome with mirth, and Sophie got a clear look at his face.

It was Norris Underwood.

For a moment Sophie clutched Parthenope's arm just as hard as Parthenope had hers, and the pleasant midday sun felt less warm on her shoulders. The last time they'd seen him had been at the theater in Haymarket, his nose bloodied and his eyes wild as he'd stumbled from the box with the purple couch. He'd certainly kept his promise to leave London, but why, oh why, had he fled to Brussels, of all places?

Because, said a calm voice in her mind. *Parthenope just said it. Brussels is where all the English nobility in financial difficulties come.*

"What should we do?" she whispered to Parthenope. Should they cut him—pretend not to know him—or acknowledge the acquaintance? Oh, if only her magic worked, she could do a spell to make them look like someone else, or to keep him from noticing them.

Parthenope's eyes had taken on a devilishly mischievous glint that made Sophie nervous. "Why, wish him good day, of course! One should always greet a fellow countryman when in a foreign place, don't you think?"

"Not if he's a scoundrel of the first water!"

"Pooh. Anyway, the best way not to call attention to anything we know about him is to be polite. We're bound to see him about—I'll bet all the British in Brussels know each other—and if we go about cutting him dead, people will notice. Now, hush—I think he's seen us."

Sophie looked up and saw that Mr. Underwood was looking directly at her. He was still smiling after his laughter, but

his complexion had paled, and his eyes gone wide and wary. She tried to school her own face into polite indifference, but wasn't convinced of her success.

"Why, what a surprise!" Parthenope said loudly. "Isn't that Mr. Underwood, Sophie? But how charming to see you in Brussels, sir!"

As Parthenope spoke, Amélie and Aunt Molly joined them, looking inquiringly. Mr. Underwood's pallor was suddenly replaced with a flush, but he released his companions' arms and stepped forward. His bow was more correct than it had been in London, less affected and sweeping. Could it be he'd learned something since their last meeting?

"Lady Parthenope—and, uh, Lady Sophie—what a pleasant surprise indeed!" he said. "Have you been in Brussels long?"

"Just arrived yesterday," Parthenope said. "We were just—"

"Were you in Paris?" exclaimed his younger companion, stepping forward eagerly. "My stars, how frightening! Did you see Bonaparte? We were supposed to go there in a few weeks, but not now. Not now!" She placed one lilac-gloved hand on her breast, which heaved in agitation. "I fear for our safety even here. No one on the continent shall be able to find a moment's peace while that monster is at liberty!"

"Kitty," murmured the older woman reprovingly.

Mr. Underwood seemed suddenly to recall their presence. "Miss Barker, you know that you and your aunt are safe whilst I am here," he said, turning slightly to smile at her. "I will have horses ready to bear you to Antwerp at a moment's notice, if the need should arise."

"Mr. Underwood is nothing if not resourceful," Parthenope agreed.

He shot her a look, but she was smiling blandly at Miss Barker. That seemed to remind him of his duty. "Lady Parthenope, Lady Sophie, may I present Mrs. Barker and her niece Miss Barker? Mrs. Barker, Miss Barker, Lady Parthenope Hardcastle and Lady Sophie Rosier."

Miss Barker's eyes widened as she made her curtsy, and stayed wide as Aunt Molly and Amélie were introduced as well. "My stars! You have a prodigious lot of important acquaintances, Mr. Underwood! But then you're going to be a baronet yourself someday, aren't you?"

"Kitty," Mrs. Barker said again, a little more sharply.

The girl flushed. "I'm sorry. It's just that we've met so many people of consequence since we came to Brussels—so many more than we knew at home in Russell Square. Haven't we, Aunt?"

Mr. Underwood smiled down at her. "You are a person of consequence to all who know you, Miss Barker."

She blushed prettily, peeping up at him through her lashes with guileless coquetry, and Sophie immediately understood. The Russell Square address, the handsome if slightly over-fussy clothes, the artless manner—Mr. Underwood had found himself a new heiress, probably one with a fortune sprung from trade . . . one whom he might entangle more easily than, say, a duke's daughter like Parthenope.

At first Sophie was amused. Mr. Underwood wanted money, and Miss Barker (or her family) wanted a social step up, which they would get if she became Lady Underwood someday. But another look at the girl's open, trusting countenance fizzled her amusement. A wave of protectiveness washed over her, and she heard herself say, "Miss Barker, I don't know how consequential we are, but we should be delighted to call on you, if your aunt will permit it."

Mr. Underwood's eyes widened again, then narrowed, but Miss Barker clasped her hands ecstatically. "Oh, would you? I am sure Aunt Barker will be honored"—she paused, took a breath, then continued, more restrainedly—"that is, most pleased to welcome you. Won't you, Aunt?"

Sophie felt Mrs. Barker's regard and met her eyes. They were cool and appraising, and she guessed that while the niece was an unworldly innocent, the aunt was not.

"Of course we would be honored if Lady Sophie called," Mrs. Barker said. "We have taken rooms at the Hôtel d'Angleterre in the rue de la Madeleine. You are welcome at any time."

"Well, this is very jolly," Mr. Underwood said, "but we mustn't keep you from the calls you have to pay now by planning future ones." He held out his arms to the Barkers with such a commanding air that they took them without demur. "Good day," he said, nodding at them all, and firmly propelled his companions down the path.

"Good day!" Miss Barker called back at them from over her shoulder. "I shall look forward to seeing you very soon!"

"Well!" Parthenope said to Sophie in an undertone when they had resumed walking. "What was that all about? Call upon that infant?"

"Oh, like you're such an aged old beldame. Don't you see? She's Norris Underwood's new quarry!"

"I'm decades older than she is, in experience, anyway." Parthenope tried to look world-weary and dissolute, and failed miserably. "Yes, I'd come to the conclusion that she's his new object of pursuit too. So?"

"He'd make her miserable! She thinks he's Sir Galahad and Beau Brummell rolled into one, and when she finally realizes he isn't, it'll be too late."

"Twaddle. She'll be so happy being addressed as 'your ladyship' that she won't even notice. You don't have to solve the entire world's problems, Sophie. Besides, I'll venture a guess her aunt knows just what he is."

"But—"

"We'll call on the chit, but I'm not doing any rescuing. I've got enough other problems to sort out."

"Like what?"

For some reason, Parthenope blushed. "Never you mind what. All right, go ahead and save Miss Barker if you want to. Just don't expect me to help."

Chapter

16

The problem soon became not *if* they would keep Sophie's promise to call on the Barkers, but *when*. The calls they made that afternoon on the Richmonds and the Capels were soon reciprocated and redoubled, and invitations began to pour in. Both the Richmonds and Capels were large families with several sons and daughters close in age to Sophie and Parthenope, so the girls found themselves included in riding parties, picnics, impromptu concerts, and more, all liberally attended by young officers, among them the Hereditary Prince of Orange, heir to the new throne of the Netherlands. Brussels society suffered from that most delightful of problems: more gentlemen than ladies.

One of those gentlemen, Lord March, the Richmonds' eldest son, raised Parthenope's ire by making clear that he found Sophie's company very pleasant. As he had been seriously wounded in the Peninsula while serving as one of the Duke of

Wellington's aides, he often sat out the dancing at parties and soon sought Sophie's company whenever sets began forming.

"You're going to get talked about, you know," Parthenope said to Sophie severely one night after they returned from a small party at the Richmonds' house in the rue de la Blanchisserie.

"Me? Whyever should anyone talk about me?" Sophie sat down at their dressing table in her wrapper to unpin and comb out her hair. Before she could start, Parthenope took the hairbrush from her.

"That March stripling. He spends far too much time with you. I'm sure everyone is starting to notice." Parthenope set to brushing Sophie's hair vigorously. Sophie gritted her teeth and held on to the edges of the stool.

"He's not a stripling, and if everyone in Brussels weren't so dance-mad, he wouldn't spend so much time sitting them out with me. And anyway, he spends no more time sitting with me than Lord Hay does dancing with you," she countered. "It's quite shocking, and I'm sure everyone is starting to notice."

"Lord Hay is a great hobbledehoy, as well as an old friend of my brothers'. We practically grew up together. And don't try to distract me, you, because it isn't working. You have to tell March to behave himself."

"He does behave himself. He's perfectly pleasant and tells very entertaining stories about all the high jinks he and his friends got up to in Spain with Wellington. Besides"—she twisted on the seat to look up at Parthenope—"why shouldn't I be allowed to enjoy his company? It isn't as if I'm engaged to be married, am I?"

"But—" Parthenope frowned and closed her mouth, then

hesitated before replying, "Well, no, but I still don't like it. It doesn't feel right."

Sophie felt a lump rise in her throat. "Parthenope, I'm sorry that Pereg—that your cousin and I didn't suit after all. I know you'd hoped . . . but I can't wear the willow for him forever. I wish him happy." At least happy in his work. She wasn't quite sure she was generous enough to wish him happy with, say, a beautiful, amiable, wealthy young lady of impeccable family or anything like that. "But I have to wish myself happy too, now. If Lord March is kind enough to find my company pleasant since neither of us dance, is there any harm done?"

"There might be," Parthenope muttered darkly, resuming her brushing, and wouldn't respond to any of Sophie's entreaties to explain what she could possibly mean.

Parthenope was fortunately in a better mood the following morning when Sophie proposed that they finally pay their promised call on the Barkers. "It will quite likely put Norris Underwood's nose out of joint if we do," Parthenope said brightly as they set out in the carriage for the Hôtel d'Angleterre.

Sophie considered this. "Is that necessarily a good idea?"

"Why not?"

"Because he's afraid of us. We know things about him that could discredit him with the Barkers, but he knows things that could discredit us—well, me."

Parthenope shrugged. "We're at a stalemate, then. And I don't think we need worry about him. He's a coward at heart, really, and cowards don't like to attack first."

"Cornered animals are the most dangerous, they say."

"Then we need to be careful not to make him feel cornered. Stop worrying, Sophie, and help me think of some polite things to say to these Barker people. You do appreciate the sacrifice I'm making by coming with you, don't you?"

"Is it my imagination, or have you become even more absurd lately?"

"If it makes you smile more often, then I'll be as absurd as I possibly can. Good heavens, we're here. Brussels *is* small, isn't it?"

The Hôtel d'Angleterre was one of the more elegant hotels in the city and, just now, very full. As they crossed the crowded front salon and climbed the stairs to the Barkers' rooms, following an officious maid, Sophie leaned close to Parthenope. "Behave yourself, if you please," she said in a low voice.

"What if I don't?"

"If you don't, I'll tell James Leland that you think he dances like a plow ox," Sophie told her.

Parthenope gasped. "You wouldn't!"

Sophie was saved from having to answer by someone's throwing the door open while the maid was still knocking. The someone was Kitty Barker, who beamed at them.

"Lady Sophie! And Lady Parthenope, too! Why, what a pleasant surprise! Do come in—thank yo—er, mare-see, Jeannette. That will be all." She nodded to the maid, bustled Sophie and Parthenope inside, and shut the door, calling, "Aunt, do come—we have callers! You know," she said to Sophie in a confiding tone as she ushered them across the comfortable-looking parlor, "it really isn't a surprise. I was looking out the window and saw you drive up to the hotel and was so hopeful you were coming to call on us! Aunt will be along directly—I sent her to change her cap because she will wear one of her old ones sometimes, instead of the new lace ones we just bought. The lace here in Brussels is just heavenly, don't you think? I should like to have a whole gown made of it, but Aunt says it isn't appropriate for someone my age to wear all lace. I declare, I don't know who makes up these silly rules about how old one must be to do things, do you?"

Sophie stole a quick glance at Parthenope, who was looking bemused. *Please don't say anything cutting*, she thought hard as Parthenope drew breath and opened her mouth.

"I do know, as a matter of fact," Parthenope said. "It's a trio of elderly Scottish spinsters who've never left Aberdeen in their lives, but saved up enough to have bought the license from the Crown decades ago to decide who may wear what, and no one's ever figured out how to get it away from them."

Miss Barker stared at her blankly for a moment, then burst into peals of laughter. "Oh, my stars, Lady Parthenope, you're such a quizzer! For a moment, I thought you were— Wait till I tell Aunt! Aunt, where *are* you? I can't imagine why she's taking so long. . . . Won't you please come and sit down?"

"Aberdeen?" Sophie whispered to Parthenope as Miss Barker hurried to the sofas by the fireplace to plump up the cushions, then to rap smartly on a door at the far side of the room, still calling her aunt.

"I don't know. It's what popped into my head." Parthenope looked a little wild-eyed. "Good God, I can almost feel sorry for Norris Underwood. Does he have any idea what he's letting himself in for?"

"Probably not. Then again, he tried for you."

Parthenope wrinkled her nose and stuck her tongue out at

Sophie, then quickly composed her face as Miss Barker came dancing back. "Lady Sophie, won't you sit here? May I fetch you another cushion, or a footstool? No? Lady Parthenope, you must sit here by me and tell me more about these ladies of Aberdeen."

Sophie was about to nervously suggest that she herself sit by Miss Barker when Mrs. Barker emerged from her room, followed by a maid carrying a daintily arranged tea tray. She directed the maid to set it down on the table between the sofas, then murmured her greetings and seated herself next to Sophie.

"Oh, Aunt, thank you!" Miss Barker said, clapping her hands. "I should never have remembered to order refreshments on my own. Shall I pour? Lady Parthenope, will you take a dish of tea?"

Under cover of tea pouring and questions of did they prefer Chinese or Indian, Sophie had a chance to examine her hostesses more closely. Kitty Barker was aptly named, for she indeed resembled a kitten, with the same small features and wide-eyed interest in a world she was sure must love her. Right now she was chattering to Parthenope, leaving few enough gaps requiring response in the conversation that Sophie felt it was safe to turn her attention to Kitty's aunt, who was dabbing the excess tea from her saucer where Kitty had mispoured.

"Have you been traveling on the continent long?" she opened tentatively.

"No, Brussels is our first stop. Friends assured us we should wait till spring was advanced before we thought about traveling any farther, if we didn't wish to jar our carriage to pieces on the roads. I thought it might be wise to stop here and let my niece get a little more accustomed to going out in society." She spoke matter-of-factly, but when she met Sophie's eyes on her last sentence, there was a distinct twinkle in them.

"Her manners are charming," Sophie assured her. "Too many girls are so tongue-tied on first coming out because it is all so new and confusing. I know I was."

"A thread or two restraining her tongue might not come amiss, but then, she has always been as you see her. Her mother died young, and she was indulged by my late husband's brother until his death last year, right after my Ned went."

Ah, so she'd been right—Mrs. Barker was Kitty's aunt by marriage. "How sad for both of you. But at least you have each other, and Miss Barker certainly seems fond of you."

"Fond enough, as I am of her. But it's a husband she's wanting, if you'll pardon my plain speaking. Which is why we're here."

"Are you looking for a foreign husband for her?" Sophie asked, startled.

"Goodness, no!" Mrs. Barker chuckled. "Especially as Kitty's French—what little there is of it—was learned from a schoolmistress who spoke it with a Yorkshire accent. No, I thought that she might acquire a little polish if we went abroad, and I myself have always had a hankering to see something of the world, which I couldn't do till Bonaparte had his teeth drawn. Of course, he seems to have grown them back, so I expect our junketing about will come to an early end and we'll have to go back to London."

She paused and looked at Sophie consideringly, as if deciding whether to say more. Sophie tried to look earnest and discreet, which seemed to work, for Mrs. Barker continued, in a lower voice, "I daresay you know exactly what we are and where we come from, Lady Sophie. We're what you nobility like to call cits. I'm all right with that. I'm proud of the way my Ned and his brother worked to build the business and become successful, and now half of London uses Barker Brothers paper and ledger books. I only wish they could have lived longer to enjoy their money. But it means Kitty will find herself mixing in a different world from what she's used to, because these days nobs are discovering that cits' gold is just as shiny as anyone else's. So, here we are, trying to polish Kitty up so she's as shiny as the guineas in her marriage portion."

"Yes, I—I can understand that." Sophie couldn't help feeling a little taken aback at this rush of confidences. But she liked Mrs. Barker's concern for her niece's happiness. "Is—does Kitty—has she accepted that she might be sought out because she's an heiress?"

Mrs. Barker looked troubled. "She might have done. But I don't like to bring it up in quite such a bald way and take all the moonlight and roses out of looking for a husband. There'll be time enough for that if the situation arises."

She was far kinder than Aunt Isabel had been. Sophie took a breath, choosing her words carefully. "So if someone were to pay her marked attention, she might not understand if—if his interest was inspired purely by her or by . . . ?"

"Her money?" Mrs. Barker looked at her sharply. "She might, or she might not. It's something I am keeping my eyes open on, though."

They both fell silent and sipped their tea. Across from them, Kitty Barker continued to talk at Parthenope, who was maintaining her countenance admirably.

"I trust you won't mind Kitty calling on you in turn," Mrs.

Barker said, watching them also. "There'll be no stopping her now. She seems to have taken quite a violent liking to Lady Parthenope. Not all the ladies in Brussels have been so kind to her."

"We shall happily receive her—and you, ma'am."

Mrs. Barker smiled at her.

They stayed a cordial half hour, and Kitty promised to return the call as soon as possible, for she quite longed to make the acquaintance of Lady Parthenope's dear, sweet little bird, Hester.

"You know that Hester's going to say one of the words you've taught him when she calls and give her a fit of the vapors," Sophie said as their carriage took them back around the Parc.

"No, he won't. He's very well trained. Anyway, I have decided."

"Decided what?"

Parthenope looked pleased with herself. "That once you and Mrs. Barker have made sure that Mr. Underwood doesn't get his claws into Kitty Barker, I shall introduce her to one of the Duke of Richmond's sons. They're all young sprigs of nobility in desperate need of rich brides, and she's a rich bride in search of a noble husband. She would suit them admirably."

Sophie kept her face straight. "What, all of them?"

"No, Miss Goose-cap, just one, thank you. She'd make a properly adoring little wife."

"Except that the duchess wouldn't hear of one of her sons marrying a cit's daughter, no matter how much money she has. And besides, Mrs. Barker and I haven't planned anything about Mr. Underwood. His name was never even mentioned between us."

"It didn't have to be. Besides, I overheard a good part of your talk. Kitty's conversation doesn't require much attention, so long as you smile and nod frequently. Or reassure her that Napoléon is not going to march into town the day after tomorrow, which she seems to think likely."

"She's not the only one. Papa says rumors like that have been flying everywhere the last few days." Sophie couldn't help shivering slightly.

But Parthenope only laughed. "She needs a good dose of Wellington, then. Once we get her into society, she'll get that well enough."

Parthenope was as good as her word. Within a few days of her mentioning to two of the elder Richmond daughters, Jane and Georgiana Lennox, that Kitty Barker was an heiress, Sophie was pleased to see her firmly in the center of a group of admiring young men when they arrived at a rout at the Richmonds' house.

"What about the duchess and her horror of cits?" she asked Parthenope.

"Who knows? Maybe practicality won over snobbery." Parthenope bent to shake out her skirts, crumpled in the carriage ride over. "How is she doing?"

Sophie studied the group. "Well, I think. She's wearing a very pretty gown and is listening to something John Lennox is saying and gazing at him as if he's the Delphic oracle."

"And no Norris Underwood in sight. Famous. If she keeps that up, she'll have one of those boys wrapped around her finger in no time."

Should she hug Parthenope, or shake her? "I thought you weren't going to do any rescuing of Kitty Barker, you soft-hearted fraud, you."

Parthenope sniffed. "I'm not. I'm giving her the means to rescue herself, of course. Oh, look who is over there!" She grabbed Sophie's arm. "It's the duke!"

"Of course it's the duke. I don't think he's missed a party yet." The Duke of Wellington indeed seemed to be at every party, dinner, or ball that they attended, along with his "family" of well-born young aides-de-camp.

"Pooh. It's good for morale for him to be seen everywhere, so silly people will stop panicking," Parthenope said loftily. "But he does look to be in fine form tonight."

"He's always in fine form," Papa commented from behind them, a little sardonically. "He's the one all Europe's trusting to stop Napoléon, and he's well aware of the fact." He coughed slightly. "I also know he's reputed to be extremely, ah, gallant with the ladies."

"Yes, isn't he?" Parthenope stared after him, starry-eyed.

"You just haven't gotten over his winking at you at Lady Charlotte's dinner the other night." Sophie tsked in mock disapproval. "I think I ought to write to James Leland and tell him his future wife has been flirting with the Duke of Wellington."

Parthenope was spared answering just then because Kitty Barker had caught sight of them and came hurrying over to greet them. "Lady Parthenope! Lady Sophie!" she cried happily. "I'm so pleased to see you! Lady Jane Lennox invited me—such a dear girl, isn't she? And Lady Georgiana, too—oh, all of them, though I do find her grace, their mama, rather terrifying! I'm so glad the duke is here and will keep us safe from that horrid Bonaparte, because I should be so sad to have to leave Brussels just now when I am finding so many agreeable new friends!"

"Of course you shouldn't leave Brussels now, just when it's getting exciting," agreed Sophie. Hmm. Did she dare probe a little about whether Kitty was seeing much of Norris Underwood lately? How could she question her without being too obviously inquisitive? It was delicate—

"So have you seen much of Mr. Underwood lately?" Parthenope asked.

"Oh, yes," Kitty said, unconcerned. "He called just yesterday morning to ask Aunt and me to the theater tonight, but I was already engaged here, of course, and then he wanted to take me for a carriage ride tomorrow, but Aunt had already arranged for a fitting at a new mantua maker that Lady Sarah recommended, since we shan't be going to Paris anytime soon, more's the pity! I was very sorry to have to tell him I was busy, as he seemed a little put out, but then he sent the loveliest flowers this morning, so I hope he isn't too vexed with me, because he's been so kind and attentive. . . . Oh, dear Jane is waving at me. We must talk more later." She scurried back to her group.

"There's your answer," Parthenope muttered to Sophie as they went to make their curtsies to the duchess. "She'll have forgotten him inside of a week."

"I'm not so sure. Look over there." Sophie gestured to a side door with a tilt of her head.

Parthenope followed her gesture and swore under her breath. "I thought he was going to the theater?"

Norris Underwood stood in the doorway, adjusting the set of his sleeves. Evidently he'd refused to cede the field to the Lennox brothers and had decided to crash the party.

"He looks rumpled. Did he climb the wall holding his coat in his teeth?" Parthenope asked, not without admiration. The Richmonds' home had once belonged to a carriage maker and was actually several buildings grouped within a walled yard.

"He must have." Sophie continued to watch him. He finished his sleeves and felt his cravat to assure that it had not sustained damage, then scanned the room. She saw his faint smile when he spotted Kitty, followed by a drawing down of his brows when he saw her entourage. A look of something that might have been desperation crossed his face. Taking Parthenope's arm, Sophie turned away.

Sophie was awake early the following morning and left to go down to breakfast while Parthenope was still putting up her hair with the nervous help of the housemaid. She was still troubled by the thought of Norris Underwood. Cornered dogs tended to bite, and when he found out—as he surely would from the artless Kitty—that she and Parthenope had been the ones to introduce her to the Richmonds, then there was no telling what he might do for revenge.

What, tell the world that you're a witch? Why should they believe him? Especially since it seems you aren't one anymore. You're useless, so he can't hurt you that way.

But what if he did something to hurt Parthenope? That was more worrisome . . . and without her magic, what if Sophie couldn't help save her friend again? She halted in front of the door to the breakfast room and glared at its white-painted panels, leaning on her cane. *Open*, she told it. *Aperī!*

It didn't move. She slapped it open with an angry swipe of her hand.

"Sophie!" Papa exclaimed.

He and Amélie were sitting together at the table in a pool of early morning sunshine, drinking coffee, and with them was the Comte de Carmouche-Ponthieux.

"Monsieur!" Sophie exclaimed involuntarily.

He looked tired and unshaven as he rose to bow, and she wondered if he'd just arrived in town. She came forward to take his hand. "How lovely to see you, sir! You were able to come, then."

He shook her hand and smiled at her. "You see me as I left London. I did not dare linger after receiving permission from my superiors, lest they change their minds. I came to leave my card, and Madame Carswell saw me and graciously invited me to breakfast before I go to my hotel."

"I hope you'll be able to find a room," Papa put in. "Brussels is bursting at the seams."

"Ah, but I have friends here. I am sure I shall." He smiled again.

"Good morning, *petite*. Since your *tante* is not yet here, may I pour you some coffee?" Amélie asked with a smile.

"I won't tell," Papa said, winking at her.

Oh, poor Aunt Molly! Should she go up and get her? It was just so *sweet* that the comte had come here directly on arriving in town. But Aunt Molly might get flustered. It might actually be better to surprise her.

"Yes, thank you," Sophie said, and sat down. Amélie handed

her a filled cup and pushed the cream pitcher toward her as Papa asked the comte about the political talk in London. Sophie thought about asking if he'd seen Peregrine and how he seemed, then remembered that she wasn't supposed to care about him any more than any other acquaintance in London. She took a sip of coffee instead and almost enjoyed the pain as it scorched her tongue.

Parthenope breezed in a moment later and dropped a letter in the tray on the sideboard so that Madame Mabuse, the housekeeper, could post it later. She'd been doing an awful lot of letter writing lately. Sophie had teasingly asked if she was writing to James Leland, but Parthenope had only sniffed and looked superior.

"Oh, goodness!" she said, catching sight of the comte. "Well, Aunt Molly will be happy now, won't she?"

The comte laughed. "Ah, I hope so."

The footman came in just then with the butter and jam, and Hester squawked indignantly when he passed his perch without stopping. Parthenope went to the bird and lifted him onto her shoulder. "Someone's been slipping you treats, hasn't he?" she crooned. "Naughty man. I'm the only one allowed to dispense treats around here."

Papa cleared his throat. "Perhaps not," he said.

Parthenope raised her eyebrows. "Would you like to feed Hester treats too, sir?"

Papa actually smiled. Usually conversation about Hester had the opposite effect on him. "No, thank you. The treat I'd been thinking about is more for you girls. We have accepted so many invitations that I think it time we considered giving our own entertainment."

"Oh!" Parthenope clapped her hands, and Hester squawked again. "Yes, please! I think it's a splendid idea! A ball? Might we manage a small one here? It would just do perfectly. There are definitely people we need to invite."

Papa looked slightly taken aback. "Er . . . well, I'd thought—"

"Oh, Sophie and Amélie and I will take care of the whole thing, won't we?"

Amélie smiled. "If Monsieur le Marquis says so—"

"He will," Parthenope declared. "Won't he?"

Chapter
17

"*We must* get the musicians who played at the Grevilles' dance, don't you think, Amélie? And the refreshments— can Cook deal adequately with that, do you think, or will she need help brought in? I am sure Madame Mabuse will do a fine job overseeing getting the ballroom ready, but perhaps another man to help polish and wax the floor would be helpful," Parthenope said later that day, frowning down at her scrawled list and tapping her pencil. "And footmen—I'm sure we'll need a few extra footmen."

She had been as good as her word, and declared a planning and strategy meeting for the afternoon with all the concentration of a general planning a military campaign.

"Madame Mabuse has an alarming number of nephews, who I am sure can be brought in to help," Amélie said. "I am not sure about Cook, though. It is something that must be ascertained."

"Maybe Madame Mabuse has an equal number of nieces who can help in the kitchen." Parthenope scribbled something on her paper.

Amélie's eyes twinkled. "I should be surprised not at all if that is so."

"Now, about the wines—is there a merchant here that we trust? I suppose we ought to draw up a guest list before deciding how much we must order. . . ."

Sophie half wondered if they shouldn't have asked Aunt Molly to take part in their planning. But she was out driving with the comte and would probably be gone all afternoon. The expression that had spread across her face that morning when she finally came down for breakfast and caught sight of him had been one of utter happiness; Sophie couldn't help wondering if, had they been alone, Aunt Molly wouldn't have thrown her arms (well, arm—one remained in a sling) about his neck and kissed him. Instead she'd contented herself with a heartfelt "Auguste!"

It was beginning to look more and more likely that they'd return from Brussels with Aunt Molly betrothed or even married. Surely the comte would not have come here to Brussels unless he truly loved her. Maybe someday, twenty years from now, she and Peregrine might—

"—invitations, Sophie," Parthenope said.

"What?" Sophie blinked at her.

Parthenope poked her in the arm with her pencil. "Sophie, if we're to get anything accomplished, you'll have to stop woolgathering and pay attention. I said we ought to draw up a list of people who will be sent an invitation. Apart from the obvious, like Sir Charles Stuart and the Richmonds and Capels and so on, whom do you think?"

"Oh. Er . . ." Inspiration struck her. "Why, the Duke of Wellington and his staff officers, of course. What party would be complete without them?"

"The duke . . ." Parthenope's eyes went dreamy. "Of course. He'll have to dance with us if he comes, since we're hostesses— well, sort of, anyway. I'll be able to tell my daughters about it someday. I suppose we ought to invite Kitty Barker and her aunt," she said, then smiled evilly. "And maybe Norris Under- wood, too, to make a point? Do you think he'd come?"

"I'm not sure we want him," Sophie replied, with a small shiver.

"Nonsense," Parthenope said briskly. "I'm sure he'll liven things up, and an extra man is always a good thing to have at a ball. Now, who else ought to come, Amélie?"

Amélie suddenly seemed very interested in the toes of her slippers. "I know someone I should like to invite," she said slowly. "But he is not in Brussels just now."

Parthenope opened her mouth, then closed it and began to nod. "Definitely. I'll put him on the list and write directly," she said.

"Who?" Sophie asked.

"Never you mind. Go back to daydreaming." Parthenope scribbled something on her paper and smiled at it in satisfaction.

The next few weeks flew past, preparations for the ball and the continued round of parties and balls that they attended speeding the time. Parthenope was cast into transports when the duke "accepted with pleasure" their invitation, along with a great many of his staff officers. He even offered to send over a few stout soldiers if they could use some extra hands.

Acceptances came in a steady stream. Sophie rather hoped that Norris Underwood would decline, but he did not; the Richmonds would be there in force, as would the Capel sisters and Lady Caroline, who was just a few months away from bringing yet another little Capel into the world and would probably refrain from dancing and restrict herself to cards.

Kitty Barker came in person to accept, bringing her aunt with her and turning it into a call. While Amélie and Aunt Molly entertained Aunt Barker, Kitty pounced on Sophie and Parthenope.

"Are you excited? I declare, I know I am. I've not yet been to a ball in Brussels, though dear Lady Jane promises she'll make sure I am invited to her mama's next one. Will you have the waltz? I know it's still not entirely the thing back at home, though Lady Jane assures me that *everyone* here does it, and without the least breath of—well, not scandal, but—oh, you know what I mean!" she said to them. Sophie resolved to watch closely next time to try to detect when Kitty managed to breathe in the midst of one of her speeches.

"Yes, we'll waltz," Parthenope said. "The Duke of Wellington and his staff officers will all be here, and they're supposed to be the best waltzers anywhere."

"Oh! Well, if the duke waltzes, then it must be all right. I must be sure to let Aunt know—she still doesn't quite approve of the waltz, but if the duke does . . ." Kitty trailed off, hesitated, then said, "I wonder . . . if I might ask . . ."

"Yes?" Sophie prompted when she fell silent again.

"Well, it's just that . . ." She took a deep breath and said, "It's my dress. Aunt made me choose it and says it's in the pink of fashion and exactly right for a girl my age, but . . . but when someone says a dress is just right for someone your age, don't you get suspicious?"

Parthenope's lips quirked, but she kept her countenance. "What sort of dress did you want?"

"It's just . . . I had thought . . . well, I read a description of a dress that Lady Caroline Lamb wore to a ball once, and I've always wanted one just like it. It sounded so dashing."

"Lady Caroline," Parthenope pronounced, "is not perhaps a good person on whom to model one's fashions."

"Or any other behavior, for that matter," Sophie added. "She's rather *fast*. Half of London doesn't like to receive her."

"Oh, no!" Kitty's face reddened. "No wonder Lady Sarah Lennox looked at me oddly and Lady Jane tittered and spoke of something else when I asked if they knew her and said how much I should like to make her acquaintance."

Before they left, Mrs. Barker beckoned to Sophie to sit beside her. "I need to thank you," she said quietly. "The, ah, situation we discussed not so long ago has improved greatly of late."

"Yes, I thought it might," Sophie agreed. "But that was Parthenope's doing more than mine."

"Was it? Then you must thank her for me, if you think it fitting. The problem person has not gone away—that would be too easy! But he has sufficient competition now that Kitty's head is no longer in a way to be turned."

"To be honest, it isn't that Lord John or any of the others aren't just as interested in Kitty's fortune," Sophie said. "But they are far better behaved and respected in society, and wouldn't make her unhappy the way I suspect Norris Underwood might."

"Yes." Mrs. Barker sighed. "She's young enough to fancy herself in love with any handsome young man who pays her marked attention. An older, wiser woman might be able to manage him quite well, but not Kitty." She stared pensively down at her gloved hands for a moment, then said briskly, "Well, we mustn't keep you longer."

And then there was the question of what to wear, as giving a ball of course required a new toilette. Sophie chose a dress in her favorite green, a soft and springlike shade, overlaid with a gauze overdress trimmed at the bottom with rows of lace flounces; Parthenope's dress was identical, but of a pinkish shade almost the color of a peach. Amélie bought them fans of Brussels lace and took them to a shoemaker who dyed his own leather to make them slippers to match their dresses. Sophie could not help feeling wistful, as he carefully measured her feet and murmured the numbers to his apprentice, and again when the slippers arrived a week later, wrapped in tissue paper and trimmed with a tiny frill of lace. Her dancing slippers would never dance, but at least they would look elegant with her dress.

Dancing slippers weren't the only thing that made her feel wistful. Though she tried daily, her magic seemed all but dead; only occasional glimmers of it showed when she practiced simple spells. It was almost as bad as the months after she'd first recovered from her illness, when the same thing had happened. Would it gradually return, the way it had then?

At least she hadn't needed it: No threats to Papa had occurred over the weeks they'd been in Brussels. Parthenope agreed that it must mean that whoever had been trying to kill him and the others was still in London, which was a comfort as far as Papa was concerned, but not as far as others were. Parthenope once mentioned that she'd gotten a letter from Peregrine and offered to read it aloud, but Sophie refused. Why pick at the wound? But at least she knew that he was safe so far, and also that no other accidents had occurred to other members of the War Office. It was as if the assassin had vanished . . . or was biding his time. The last thought made her shiver.

At least Aunt Molly was happy. She was always humming as she took her daily stroll in the Parc to visit the rhododendrons, and she took more pains with her hair, so that she looked less like a hedgehog. The comte came daily to take her driving or bring her flowers or just to call for a few moments in the morning, if he was on his way to report to King Louis in Ghent.

On one of those mornings, Sophie found him in the drawing room staring out the window into the street, waiting for Aunt Molly to come down before they went for a drive out the Allée Verte toward Laeken. He turned and smiled at her as she hesitated in the doorway. "Ah, mademoiselle! Your aunt, she must make herself beautiful before we go out driving, where the wind will disarrange her once again."

"Is she making you late? Would you like me to have her called?" Sophie started toward the bellpull.

"No, no, not at all! I simply like to tease her about it and started a little too soon." He looked at her speculatively. "I am under the impression that she has not often been teased over the years."

"No," Sophie agreed. "Papa does not know how, and my Aunt Isabel . . ." She shrugged; it would not be polite to say anything bad about Aunt Isabel, and knowing now what she did about her past, she could only feel sorry for her.

"Poor little Marie," he said softly, looking down at his hat gripped hard in his hands. He made a visible effort to uncurl them from around the brim. "She was such a—such a merry girl, once. I cannot help feeling responsible for how she has . . . changed."

Sophie hesitated. It would be fascinating to hear the story of their romance from him. All she knew of it was what Papa had told her. Would it be prying into private matters that didn't concern her? On the other hand, she was dying to know more. . . . "Please—what was she like, when she was young?"

The comte leaned against the edge of the window embrasure and smiled, a faraway look in his eyes. "She was just what I said—merry. I had just come to London from France, where one was afraid to breathe, even—much less smile. We had very little, my younger brother and I, though we had left a handsome house in the Faubourg Saint-Germain and estates in Auvergne. My father stayed behind, at our country estate, where he hoped that he would be safe among our people."

"Was he?"

"No."

"I am sorry."

The comte waved a hand. "I am not the only one who lost family. At least my father died knowing that his sons lived safe in England. And I met your aunt." He smiled. "You wished to know what she was like? I will tell you how I first saw her. I was at a reception at the Duchess of Allston's house—the duke

was a friend of my father's, and they were very kind to Ambroise and me when we first came. The reception was out of doors, in their garden, which made me both pleased and displeased—I had not gotten over my nervousness after leaving Paris and felt safer out of doors, but the daylight showed more plainly how shabby my clothes had grown. So I kept to the further edges of the garden even though I longed to be among the other partygoers, who all seemed so happy and carefree. And as I walked, I nearly tripped over your aunt."

Sophie couldn't help smiling. "What was she doing?"

"She was crouched in the path, drawing a flower in a tiny sketchbook that she had with her. She scolded me for standing in her light, and when I apologized, she looked up at me and laughed. But not at me. It was a happy laugh, and she said, "Listen to me. I sound like Isabel practicing to be a duchess. You could stand there, you know," and pointed to a spot just a little to the right. "Then you could hold my parasol for me."

Sophie laughed. It had always been hard to imagine a young Aunt Molly; the picture the comte was painting of her was unexpected, but not entirely so. "So did you hold it for her?"

"I did." He smiled, but his eyes seemed to see some other place. "You must understand, I had come from Paris, where the etiquette at court and among the nobility was still stifling, even though it had relaxed since my father's youth. But there I was in England, with your aunt, who was obviously a lady of importance, or she would not be at the duchess's party. Back at home, Frenchmen were killing other Frenchmen for being of a different social class . . . and here your aunt was on her knees, sketching a flower that had taken her fancy and asking me to hold her parasol. Can you wonder that I was bemused?"

"And then?"

"And then?" he repeated. "And then we walked around the garden together for hours. I was in love with her by the time your grandfather's carriage came for her and your family. I walked home to my lodgings above an apothecary's shop across the river and did not stop thinking of her. She—her soul was filled with sunshine. I had seen so much darkness, and now all I wanted was light."

"Oh." Sophie couldn't help sighing. It was terribly romantic, but it was also plain to see that he had suffered, poor man. It was no wonder that his eyes always held that sad expression. "I am sorry that—that . . ."

"That a penniless refugee did not become your uncle?" he finished for her, with a lopsided smile. "I am too, Lady Sophie. It took me a very long time to recover from losing my *petite* Marie—a long time to be able to see it from your grandfather's viewpoint. What kind of life could I have offered her, not knowing if my father was dead or alive, or if our lands and property had been seized and destroyed? What good was it being a vicomte, heir to an old and proud name, when all that gave it meaning was gone?"

"What kind of life did she end up having?" Sophie asked.

He looked down at his hat again. "I try not to ask myself that question. It is why it took me so long to forgive your family, even after the Directoire restored my name and some of my estates."

She wanted to ask him, "And now what?" but that was not

a question a young girl could ask her elders. She certainly knew what she hoped would happen. Would the sadness be finally banished from the comte's eyes if it did?

The day of the ball dawned clear and sunny. At breakfast Madame Mabuse came in to inform them that the weather would hold fair, according to her prophetic right knee, which never failed to warn her when rain was coming.

"How useful," Aunt Molly commented when she left. "I should rather like one of those so I knew when the garden needed watering. But I can't help wondering what her left knee has to say."

"Perhaps it warns when rain isn't coming," Parthenope suggested.

Aunt Molly nodded. "Yes, you're probably right, dear."

They were not permitted to linger at table discussing Madame Mabuse's oracular rheumatism, for that good lady wanted them out of the breakfast room so that her nieces would have a place to set out the freshly washed wineglasses they'd borrowed from Sir Charles at the British embassy.

The entire household had been bustling about since sunup; Sophie and Parthenope shooed Amélie away to oversee the other hundred tasks that needed doing, set Aunt Molly to arranging the buckets of ferns and early lilies delivered by the flower seller's boy, and helped iron napkins and tablecloths. Even the comte helped; after going up to the ballroom to admire Aunt Molly's arrangements, he took her out for a long ride. At Parthenope's request, they went in search of a dozen new packs of cards for the card players—which kept Molly from pruning the rented potted ferns and palms into "more natural" shapes.

At about four o'clock, Parthenope suddenly remembered an errand she'd forgotten and went running out of the house without her shawl to do it. Sophie called her back to give it to her, then slowly climbed the stairs. A nap would be nice, as tonight would be busy, but first she would just go up to have one more look at the ballroom and make sure Madame Mabuse's nephews had watered the flowers as directed. So she continued past the second-floor landing to the third . . . and stopped in the open doorway to the ballroom.

Amélie was there, but not checking flowers or that new candles had been set in readiness in the chandeliers. Instead she was kneeling on the floor, running her hands over it. Next to her was her maid, Nalini, frowning. She said something in Hindustani, and Amélie nodded.

"*Est-il ici?*" Amélie said in French, waving her hands in the air as if delineating something over the floor.

"Is something wrong?" Sophie asked, walking into the room.

Both Amélie and Nalini jumped. Amélie scrambled to her feet and hurried to Sophie. "Eh, *petite*, you startled us! No, nothing is wrong—that is, not much. Nalini thought the floor might be in that place—what is it the word?—rough and splandered—no, splintered."

"Oh dear. Did one of the Mabuse nephews nap on duty?" Sophie stepped over to where they'd been standing, but Nalini got there first. "It is just a very, very little," she said in her lilting voice, but planting her feet firmly. "I tell those boys, they come up and fix smooth."

"I—I'm sure they will." Sophie said, slightly taken aback. Why didn't Nalini want her to see the spot?

She took a half step forward, and felt it: a whiff, a hint of . . . of *something*. She glanced down at the floor below Nalini's sandaled feet. It was as bare and smooth as that in the rest of the room.

"Was there something you needed, Sophie?" Amélie asked.

"Um . . ." Sophie dragged her attention away from the floor and back to Amélie. "No, not really. I just wanted to check the flowers and make sure they were watered before I went to have a rest. Parthenope just went out, but said she would be back shortly."

Amélie nodded, as if unsurprised by Parthenope's vagaries. "A little sleep would be a good thing for you. You have worked hard today, and I am grateful. A daughter could not have done more." She slipped her arm around Sophie and gave her a little hug. "You are ready for tonight? Is there anything I may do for you?" Amélie gently steered her through the door and toward the stairs. "I shall send Nalini in to help, if you think you may need her."

"No, I think we shall deal famously." Sophie realized, too late, that she had been neatly maneuvered away from the ballroom and down the stairs. What didn't Amélie want her to see? What had they been looking at on the floor? What was it she had felt?

"Ah, *très bien!* Well, here is your room. Go and have that little *sieste* now, so that you will be fresh for tonight." She paused. "I shall do the same—for I think that tonight I will dance."

"You will?" Sophie forgot for a minute about whatever

Amélie had been up to in the ballroom. "Oh, Amélie, that's wonderful! That is . . . if you're ready to put off mourning now."

"I will never put off mourning inside, Sophie—I know you understand that. But I think that maybe I can begin to on the outside." She smiled and touched Sophie's cheek in a part pat, part caress, and opened her door.

"Thank you, Amélie." Sophie stepped into her room, shutting the door behind her, then leaned against it. She would wait ten minutes before going back upstairs to the ballroom. The little scene she'd witnessed bothered her: Both Amélie and Nalini had obviously been concerned about something. And she had felt something—something not quite right. If either of them was there when she went back up, she could say that she hadn't actually checked the flowers and had returned to do so.

Ten minutes had never seemed so long. Just before Sophie opened the door to slip into the passage, her patience was rewarded by the sound of Amélie and Nalini conversing quietly as they passed, followed by the *snick!* of a latching door. She counted to twenty and left her room, moving as quickly and quietly as she could.

In the empty ballroom she stopped first to check the flowers in their vases on the sills of the tall windows just in case, then turned to survey the polished floor, trying to estimate where Nalini had been standing. When she thought she'd found the approximate location, she awkwardly lowered herself to a kneeling position and ran her hands over the wood, just as Amélie had, and—

There! Under her outstretched palms, faint but definitely present, was the unmistakable tingle of magic against her skin. She began gingerly to explore it, looking for its borders and pattern. It wasn't like any spell she'd ever made with Mama; not necessarily more complex or powerful . . . just *odd*. There was a feeling of space inside it, a cold sort of openness, but that was all she could read of it.

Sophie sat back on her knees and stared at it. What was it doing in the middle of a ballroom floor, and who had put it there? An image of Amélie as she had appeared just a short time before, hands outstretched over it, filled her mind's eye—

But that was impossible. She had known Amélie for months, lived in the same house with her—and never had she gotten the least inkling that Amélie might be a witch. But . . . but . . . her eyes widened. That did not mean Nalini . . . might *she* possess magical abilities? That might perhaps account for the strangeness of the magic she felt—if it were Indian, based on a different set of teachings. . . .

Except that it had been Amélie running her hands over the floor, not Nalini.

Could she have been wrong and just not noticed that Amélie was a witch? That could not be ruled out, especially if she had learned, as Sophie herself had, to be extremely cautious and circumspect about using magic. Her experience in London during the season had certainly taught Sophie that caution was the—

"Oh my God." She breathed the words aloud. London, during the season. Magic.

Far below she heard the bang of the front door. Parthenope must be back from her errand. She scrambled to her feet, leaning heavily on her cane, and another memory struck her in the face: the canes that Amélie had made for her. She and Hester had both noticed something about them, a flavor of magic.

She resisted the impulse to fling the cane from her and made her way as quickly as she could out of the ballroom and down the stairs.

Parthenope was just emerging from their room as Sophie reached the bottom of the stairs. "*There* you are," she said, pausing in the doorway with one hand on her hip. "I distinctly recall telling you before I left to go have a nap."

"Never mind that. We have to talk." Sophie unceremoniously pushed her through the door, locked it behind them, then pulled Parthenope to the far end of the room, as far from the door as she could manage.

"Good heavens, what's happened?" Parthenope said, amused. "Let me guess—you've just discovered that all those strapping nephews of Madame Mabuse are actually her bas—"

"Will you be quiet?" Sophie said, so sharply that Parthenope looked at her face and fell into obedient silence. Glancing nervously back at the door, Sophie told her about Amélie and the ballroom floor. Parthenope listened with a puzzled frown creasing her brow.

"So you think Amélie—or Nalini—might be a witch. Apart from it being a coincidence that you and she are both witches, I don't understand why you're so upset."

Sophie restrained an urge to shake her. "Don't be a dunce! Remember London? All of Papa's colleagues from the War Office nearly being killed—and Papa too—with magic? Who is going to be among the guests tonight—someone rather intimately connected with the war?"

Parthenope whistled. "The Duke of Wellington! Good God, you don't think—"

"I don't know. But I'm afraid."

Parthenope continued to frown, staring at the floor and tapping her foot. "You're sure you felt something magical up there?" she asked.

"Yes! Why do you think I'm so overset?"

"Well, why don't we take Hester up there and let him have a look? Here, better yet, I'll carry him up and you lie down. You look absolutely done in." She pushed Sophie toward the bed and went to Hester's perch, where the parakeet was hunkered down with his head tucked under his wing. "Come on, lad. We've got some work to do," she crooned, pressing her finger against his feet. He raised his head and regarded her with an almost palpable air of displeasure, but stepped onto her hand and let her carry him out of the room.

Sophie sat down on the edge of the bed, and then stood up again in agitation as another thought struck her. Peregrine . . . he thought that Amélie was responsible for the accidents to Papa and the others, and she had dismissed his accusation as being groundless because Amélie could not do magic. But what if she'd been wrong? What if Amélie was a witch and had been trying to kill Papa and the others, as Peregrine had guessed?

Then she'd lost him for no very good reason, and might have put Papa back in danger again—not to mention England and all of the Allies, if something were to happen at the party tonight to the Duke of Wellington and his officers. On the ballroom floor, where tonight Amélie would be dancing. . . .

Amélie—Sophie could not imagine her ever hurting anyone, much less trying to kill someone. But that was what spies were supposed to do—blend in, be the last people one would suspect of wrongdoing. If Amélie were a witch, of course she would be at great pains to conceal it. And as Peregrine had said—oh, God, *Peregrine*. . . .

Parthenope was back in a very few minutes. "I walked around the room with him till we found the spot. Yes, he definitely thinks there's something there—did the pricking thumb speech and everything," she announced, stroking Hester's feathers. "And whatever it was, he didn't like it. Said it was cold, or something like that. Poor baby, you're shivering. Come sit in the sun, little man." She moved his perch closer to the sunshine by the window and set him on it, then turned to look at Sophie. "Oh," she said, and sat down next to her on the edge of the bed, then handed her a handkerchief.

"I'm sorry," Sophie said a few minutes later, still sniffing. "I just realized exactly what I've done."

"What?"

"Per—your cousin. He was right all along, and I refused to believe him. My only consolation is that at least he's safe back in London. I'd been worrying about him, even though I knew it was foolish of me."

"Twaddle," Parthenope said firmly. "It wasn't foolish of you. And to be honest, whatever is in the ballroom, I don't believe it's Amélie's doing."

"If it isn't her, it's Nalini, which comes down to the same thing. But I don't think it's her. She wasn't at any of the accidents, and Amélie was. And Hester's right. It's what I felt too—like there was some large, cold space hidden in the spell." Sophie shivered. "It was—I wish I could describe it. So what should we do?"

"I don't know. If only your magic were working, so that you could make it go away," Parthenope said, sounding hopeful.

Sophie shook her head. "I wish I could. But even if I did, I couldn't get a clear look at what the magic does. If I can't see its purpose, I can't change it or nullify it."

Parthenope blew out her breath in a sigh. "Then we can't do anything, can we?"

"But—"

"But we don't know what the magic is, or who did it. It could have been Nalini, you know, and you just came in too late to see her do it. For all we know, it might be something protective, not harmful. Unless we know Amélie is responsible for it and that its intent is malicious, we shouldn't say anything to her. It's a case of—oh, how does it go? *Cum . . . cum hoc ergo propter hoc.* It's Latin, and it means thinking that just because two things happen near each other, one caused the other—but that's not true." She slipped an arm around Sophie's waist. "And I'll say it again—I don't think it was Amélie. Peregrine's wrong."

"How can you be sure?"

"Because . . . because I *am*." She jumped up from the bed. "Why don't we just plan to keep a close eye on things? I'll set Hester's perch up there for the evening. He loves parties, and if there really is magic being done, he'll sense it. Now, I've got something important to discuss too." She crossed to the wardrobe.

"As important as a possible threat to the Duke of Wellington?"

Parthenope pursed her lips, but said firmly, "Yes. Here, try these on. I want to make sure they fit properly." She pulled a paper-wrapped parcel from under her shawl, which she'd tossed carelessly on a chair, and brought it to Sophie.

"What is it?" Sophie untied the string securing it and unfolded the paper. "My—my shoes for tonight. Why shouldn't they fit?"

"Dunce," Parthenope said, a little crossly. "Look at them again."

Sophie looked, and realized that the sole of one of the slippers was now much thicker than the other. Her breath caught in her throat.

"It was Amélie's idea," Parthenope said, a little hesitantly. "She and the shoemaker between them thought it up. I just did the trotting back and forth to the shop. The shoemaker had to estimate how thick to make it so that it matched your good leg, of course, but he was pretty confident he got it close to right. He said to come back so he can measure you properly and maybe alter your other shoes the same way if you're happy with these." Parthenope touched the shoe. "It's cork, by the way, covered with leather, so that it won't be very heavy for you. I don't know that you'll be able to do completely without your cane, at least at first, but maybe with time, you won't need it at all and will only limp a little bit. Come on, put them on. I'm dying to see if they work."

Sophie's eyes weren't working right; the shoes in their paper nestled on her lap had gone blurry as Parthenope's words echoed in her head: *Maybe with time, you will only limp a little bit.*

"Sophie?" Parthenope stooped to peer into her face.

"Parthenope!" Sophie wailed, threw her arms around her friend's neck, and burst into tears again. For a minute they hugged each other, and Parthenope sniffed furiously several times before pulling away.

281

"We must stop this, or we'll have red eyes for tonight," she scolded.

"I don't care." Sophie touched the shoe with the built-up sole. Why had no one thought of this before? Not her aunts, not Papa . . . not even herself.

Parthenope whisked them off her lap and knelt in front of her. "Very well. If you won't try them on, I'll try 'em for you." She pulled off Sophie's slippers and gently fit the new green ones to her feet. "He added ribbons to lace them around your ankles so that you wouldn't step out of them," she said, crossing the ribbons and tying them neatly. "Just like regular dancing slippers."

Dancing slippers. Sophie felt a little dizzy at the thought. "Do you think I'll ever be able t—"

"Let's make sure you can walk before you think about anything else." Parthenope rose and held her hand out to Sophie, who took it and stood up. "How is it?"

"I . . . don't know." Sophie felt as if her center of balance had shifted violently to the left; accustomed to trying to pull herself straight, having her shoe do it for her made her feel distinctly odd. "I think it will take some practice."

Parthenope looked anxious. "Do they hurt? Is it—"

"No, it's not that at all! But it's like learning to stand and walk again." She held on to Parthenope's arm and took tentative steps around the room. "I think I'd maybe better use my cane tonight, but even so . . . oh, don't scold, but I think I need to cry again."

"Pooh." Parthenope led her back to the bed, then handed her a handkerchief. "You may cry for precisely two minutes, but that is all."

Sophie laughed through her tears. "Horrid thing. How can I ever thank you?"

"And Amélie—I told you it was her doing. Do you see why I don't think she's our assassin? Why should she care so much about trying to help you if she's trying to kill your father? Now, are you going to have a rest, or do I need to club you over the head with your cane and make you take one?"

Sophie smiled, reached down to unlace and remove her slippers, and obediently lay down on her side of the bed. But even after Parthenope had done the same and was gently snoring, she could not rest; the same unanswerable round of thoughts whirled and tangled in her head.

She knew what she had seen that afternoon: Amélie kneeling on the floor, Amélie distracting her to get her out of the room, the strange magic she'd found there . . . and also the shoes that would help her walk more normally and keep her from standing out like a freak at a village fair. Could the woman who'd done that for her as well as so many other kindnesses be a murderess? Parthenope was right: It didn't seem to make sense.

But what if it was Amélie? Not only would that mean Papa might be in danger once more, as well as the Duke of Wellington, but . . . but it would mean she had been wrong and sent Peregrine away because of it, and she wasn't sure which made her feel closer to despair.

Chapter 18

Four hours later, a still-unhappy Sophie stood with Papa and Amélie and Aunt Molly at the head of the stairs by the ballroom to greet their guests. Not even the knowledge that she was looking her best could counteract the uneasiness that had taken hold of her since that afternoon's discovery.

Of course, Amélie had complimented Sophie on her appearance and asked her anxiously if she liked the new built-up slippers when she came down to dinner. Half of Sophie had wanted to throw herself into Amélie's arms to thank her, and half wanted to demand an explanation for what she had been doing in the ballroom. Neither happened, of course. Instead she'd mumbled her thanks, and felt even more miserable at the expression of concern tinged with hurt that Amélie tried to hide.

She shifted uncomfortably, which did not escape Parthenope's notice. "Are your shoes pinching?" she asked, craning her neck to see who was ascending the stairs.

"They're perfectly comfortable. It's the rest of me that isn't." Sophie surreptitiously tried to stretch without being obvious. As she'd guessed, the new shoes were making her carry herself differently. Her body was so used to the slightly twisted posture caused by her shorter leg that it would take time to accustom itself to straightness again.

Of course, trying to twist herself so that she could see into the ballroom from their place by the stairs wasn't helping matters either. Parthenope had brought Hester's perch up and set it near the magicked spot so that he could give the alarm if anything strange happened on it, but she needed to keep a watch out in case he did.

Parthenope peered down the stairs. "I say, there are the Barkers . . . and, oh, lud, Norris Underwood is with them. How did he manage that? I would have thought he might have fallen by the wayside what with the Richmonds about, but evidently not."

"You're the one who wanted to invite him," Sophie murmured. "He doesn't give up easily, as you might recall."

While he and Mrs. Barker exchanged pleasantries with Amélie, Kitty Barker made a beeline for Sophie and Parthenope. "It's so perfect!" she chirped. "I declare, I think this house must be the perfect size for a ball—just enough people to make a little crush, but not too bad . . . and your dresses are just perfectly—"

"Perfect." Norris Underwood finished for her as he came up. He bared his teeth in something passing for a smile as he nodded to Sophie and Parthenope and continued, "I was not aware you were such great friends."

"Of *course* we're great friends," Kitty said. "Why, it was

Lady Sophie and Lady Parthenope who introduced me to all the lovely people I know now, like Lady Jane and Lady Georgiana and their brothers. . . . Oh, let me tell you quickly, before she comes—Aunt didn't say no when I told her that Lord John had asked if I would give him a waltz tonight! I don't know that I can do it very well, but he promised he would hold me very tightly and not let me fall if I got dizzy. Wasn't that perfectly kind of him?"

Parthenope did not trouble to conceal her grin. "Most gallant," she agreed. "And I am sure your aunt will let you waltz—in fact, I shall speak to her myself about it. It's much better to learn at a private party, I expect she'll agree."

Mr. Underwood shot her a venomous look, then turned back to Kitty. "In that case, then I must claim one too."

"Yes, if you like," Kitty agreed carelessly. "Oh, look! There's Jane and Georgy! I must just go see which dress Jane chose—she wasn't sure if it would be the lilac or the blue. Excuse me. . . ." She fluttered away from them.

"So," Mr. Underwood said, staring after her, "I suspected as much, but now I know whom to thank for setting the foxes on the chicken." There was a peculiarly unpleasant note in his voice.

"Really, you're becoming quite ridiculous. If we'd thought you'd held her in the least bit of esteem, we would have been happy to stand by," Parthenope said, sounding bored.

"There are plenty of other cits' daughters with comfortable fortunes. Go find yourself one who knows exactly what kind of a husband she'd be getting, not one who might fancy herself in love," Sophie added.

"How do you know she wasn't in love?" he demanded, drawing himself up.

Parthenope snorted, but Sophie shook her head. "If she loved you, she'd never have fallen to the foxes, as you put it. She'd be here with you right now, looking forward to her first waltz. I am glad she escaped with her heart intact."

"Indeed," he sneered. "I was not aware you knew anything about hearts, Lady Sophie."

Next to her Parthenope moved sharply, and Sophie knew she was a bare second from slapping him across the face. She reached out to take Parthenope's arm—Norris Underwood was not worth the days of gossip smacking him would lead to—and said, not looking at him, "My heart has nothing to do with this. I merely think Kitty deserves to keep hers."

"Or is yours just made of wood? Isn't that what you witches—"

"Good evening," someone said quietly. Mrs. Barker had appeared at his elbow. She nodded to Sophie and Parthenope. "You are both very handsome tonight, as Kitty said you would be. Has she already been to make her duties to you?"

"Yes, ma'am." Sophie inclined her head toward the ball-room doors. "She vanished with Jane and Georgiana Lennox in that direction. I expect you'll find her safe with them."

"I'm sure I will find her quite safe." Mrs. Barker's voice remained blandly polite, but Sophie understood her double meaning clearly. "Mr. Underwood, won't you give me your arm so that I may see for myself?"

He had no choice but to do so, and pointedly did not look at Sophie and Parthenope as Mrs. Barker gave them a last smile and turned to the ballroom.

The comte arrived then, and Sophie was glad to turn from

the unpleasantness of Norris Underwood to the pleasure of greeting him. Aunt Molly would not let him go into the ballroom, but looked mutinous as she peered down the stairs. "Don't you think everyone's arrived by now? Do I really have to stand here any longer?"

"Yes," Parthenope whispered to Sophie. "Otherwise she'll start pacing back and forth in front of the potted ferns muttering to herself and making the musicians nervous. She's afraid someone will jostle them once the dancing starts—the ferns, that is, not the musicians."

Sophie smiled, as Parthenope seemed to expect it, but a loud laugh drifting up from the front door caught her attention. Only one person in Brussels possessed such a distinctive guffaw. She had a moment to wonder if it had anything to do with his equally distinctive nose . . . and then the Duke of Wellington was on the top stair, elegant in evening clothes and smiling jovially, trailed by several of his dashing young aides-de-camp in their bright uniforms.

"Lady Mary! Madame Carswell!" He bowed over their hands with practiced grace. Though not particularly tall, he had a presence that made him seem larger. "Delighted to be here! You will set a high bar for entertainments in Brussels tonight, I expect! Good evening, Lansell." He shook Papa's hand. "You know Lieutenant-Colonel Gordon and Captain Hill and Lieutenant Cathcart, don't you? Ah." His eyes lit on Sophie and he moved toward her. "Lady Sophie, I hear from George Lennox that you're tying his brother March around your finger. A smile from you is bringing him down, when years on the Peninsula couldn't. Maybe I need you and your friend the Hardcastle girl on my staff, eh?"

Next to her Parthenope made a small sound. Sophie hoped she wouldn't swoon. "I'm sure we would set you all to rights very quickly, sir, given half a chance," she replied demurely.

He laughed. "So you would! I'd better let my boys know the danger they're in. Ah, there you are, Lady Parthenope. What do you say? Report to me at headquarters tomorrow at eight sharp, so we may give you your orders." Chuckling, he wandered into the ballroom, and Sophie watched the inevitable wave of movement toward him that always occurred as soon as he entered a crowded room.

Parthenope grabbed Sophie's arm. "Did you hear that? We should show up in our riding habits tomorrow morning and tell him we're reporting for duty. Maybe he'll invite us for breakfast."

"I don't know about you, but I intend to sleep until noon if we get through this evening without incident," Sophie muttered back. And suddenly wished she could go find a quiet place to hide from the cheerful bustle and just be alone. But a quiet space would have to wait. "I think I ought to go watch the duke in the ballroom, don't you?" she said to Parthenope.

"One of us should," Parthenope agreed. "You go. And sit down for a few minutes. You're no good to us if you exhaust yourself before the ball has barely started. If anyone asks, I'll tell 'em you needed to use the necessary."

"You'll do no such thing, or I'll send Hester out here to make a mess on your shoulder."

"Of course I won't, goose-cap." Parthenope looked at her with concern. "Are you sure your shoes aren't hurting you?"

"They're fine. I'm just—"

"Worried," Parthenope finished for her. "Don't be. It will

be all right. Go watch Hester and the duke and make sure they both behave."

All seemed as it ought to in the ballroom—two of the musicians playing softly, little groups of guests (and the one large group centered on the Duke of Wellington) chatting amicably. Sophie edged her way around the room to where Hester sat on his perch. "Seen anything, Hester?" she murmured to him.

He looked at her with his head cocked to one side, then turned to scratch and smooth the feathers on top of his wing.

"I'll take that as a no, shall I?"

"Good evening, Your Grace," he said, swiveling back to scan the room. "How are you this evening, Your Grace?"

"The duke's over there, silly bird. I'm Soph—oh, all right. Watch him, then." She sat down in a chair next to him with a sigh of relief. Maybe she shouldn't have worn her new slippers tonight, but they went so well with her dress, and Parthenope had been so excited about giving them to her, not to mention Amélie—

No. She would not think about Amélie right now, so she scanned the room instead . . . and saw Lord March approaching her chair, smiling.

"I believe the dancing will be starting shortly, so I thought I'd find my favorite nondancing partner to open the ball with," he said lightly, sitting down beside her.

"Turnip," Hester said.

"Hester," Sophie said warningly. Dratted bird! "Don't mind him," she said to Lord March. "He might have said something much worse."

"Has Lady Parthenope tried to train him out of saying them?" March examined Hester with interest.

"Heavens, no! She taught him most of them."

He laughed. Though it had been more than a year since he'd come back from serving with Wellington in Spain, he still seemed tanned from the Iberian sun, and his teeth flashed white in his handsome brown face. "Lady Parthenope is quite a character. My sisters are not sure whether to adore her or be terrified of her."

"They're wise women."

"But you seemed to have tamed the lion—or lioness, as it were."

"No, I don't think so. It's just that the lioness took a violent liking to me."

"I don't blame her." His blue eyes were warm as he looked at her. "I have too."

Sophie smiled and looked down at her lap. The Richmonds were all charming—they must have inherited their charm from their ancestor King Charles II, who had been almost too charming, it was said. But Lord March had the Richmond charm in extra measure. All his sisters doted on him, which wasn't surprising. But his brothers did as well, which was less common, and Wellington was said to love him like a son. He would eventually become Duke of Richmond on his father's death, and though the family was not wealthy, they held several estates in England and Ireland. He was, by most counts, a splendid catch, and she liked him very much.

But that was all. She couldn't see him as anything but a friend—perhaps a dear one—but not anything more. She wasn't sure that she'd ever be able to look at any young man with anything but a sisterly eye . . . except for one. And he was lost to her.

"Ah, there they go. Your aunt's injury seems much better since your arrival," March said.

Sophie looked up. The sets to open the dancing were forming. On the other side of the room, Papa had taken the Duchess of Richmond, as the female guest of highest rank, as his partner to lead his set. Directly in front of where Sophie sat, Amélie had done the same with the Duke of Wellington. Just behind them were Aunt Molly and the comte.

"Oh dear, Aunt has left off her sling. I hope she won't strain her arm," she said.

"I'm sure her partner will take care that she isn't hurt," March said soothingly. "And I'm here with my nondancing partner," he added with a grin. "Where's your friend the lioness? Isn't she dancing?"

The musicians had finished tuning, and the lead violinist looked inquiringly at Papa. He nodded, and they played the opening measures of the dance.

"I don't know." Sophie scanned the edges of the room. That was odd—where had Parthenope got herself off to? They had agreed that she'd dance the first dance, for appearance's sake, then join Sophie in guard duty. "Perhaps I should go find her."

March rose at once and offered her his arm. "Please allow me—I should like to try my hand at lion hunting. Or lioness hunting, rather."

The opening measure ended, and the dancers began to move, bowing and curtsying, then beginning the figures. Sophie tried to ignore them as she let Lord March help her up—it was still difficult to judge how to move with these new slippers. This was the moment of a ball that always hurt the most—the first dance of the evening, when everyone was fresh and eager and smiling, able to do what she longed to do again, but never would.

But before she and March had taken a few steps, the line of dancers nearest to them had suddenly faltered, and the dancers at the head of the line stopped entirely.

"Why—where did the duke go?" someone—Aunt Molly, it sounded like—said in bewilderment.

A shock of fear froze Sophie in place for a few seconds. Even though she and Parthenope had been afraid something would occur, the reality of its actually happening was overwhelming.

"What is it?" Lord March asked, looking down at her.

"I don't know." Her voice sounded almost ridiculously calm in her own ears. She let go of his arm and turned back.

The entire line of dancers had now stopped, looking befuddled. "The duke—he just vanished!" someone else was saying loudly above the murmurs of confusion.

"The duke!" The name moved down the line like an ominous breeze. Now the other set of dancers had paused and looked toward the first set in confusion.

Sophie pushed her way through the milling crowd. At its center was a small clearing. Amélie stood there alone, looking stunned.

"Nonsense," a man said, from farther back. "People don't just disappear."

"But he did!" a woman cried in response. "I saw him—and then he wasn't there!"

A few people were looking about them, as if the duke had suddenly taken it into his head to play a game of hide-and-seek.

Everyone had stopped dancing now, and the musicians had ceased playing and had risen in their seats to peer over the ferns to see what the matter was. One or two ladies here and there started to cry.

"See here—you were dancing with him. What happened?" A man stepped out of the crowd and pointed at Amélie.

She opened her mouth, closed it, then finally said, "I do not know," in a very small voice.

"He just—wasn't there all of a sudden." Aunt Molly stepped forward, her vague blue eyes wide. "We were right behind them, weren't we, Auguste?"

The comte was just as pale and shocked looking as she. "It is so." He snapped his fingers. "Like that—and he was gone. Madame, surely you must have seen," he said to Amélie.

Sophie turned away. She didn't need to hear anything more, and she didn't want to see Amélie's face. What had she done to the duke? And why had she chosen to do something so public and obvious as to make him disappear in front of an entire roomful of guests?

What should she do? Should she confront Amélie right now, in front of everyone? What would Amélie do if she accused her of sorcery against the Duke of Wellington—and would anyone believe her?

"Sophie!" A hand caught her arm. "There you are! I've been looking all over for you!"

Parthenope! Sophie turned. "What do you mean? I've been look—"

Parthenope looked flustered and excited, but it was the person standing just behind her who stopped Sophie's words, and her breath. Peregrine Woodbridge stood there, looking at her steadily. "Please excuse me—I didn't intend to crash your party tonight," he said.

Breathe, Sophie, a cool voice in her mind reminded her gently. Why had he come here—and dressed in buckskin trousers and dusty boots and traveling coat, as if he'd just arrived in town? She gulped and wished she could sit down, but there was no time for that now. "N-not at all, Lord Woodbridge. Will you please excuse us? I have to talk to Parthenope now—"

But Parthenope was already pulling her, none too gently, to the edge of the crowd. "Sophie, you've got to hear. Perry's just ridden straight from Ghent, and he's got something to tell you."

Sophie shook her head. "It will have to wait. It happened—the duke is gone! Amélie's done it, right in front of everyone!"

Parthenope and Peregrine exchanged looks. "Tell her," Parthenope commanded.

Peregrine swallowed. "Lady Sophie, please excuse my appearing like this. I'm not quite sure how to start—"

Parthenope groaned. "Oh, never mind all that now. Sophie, you were wrong—or rather, you were right!"

Sophie was starting to become annoyed. "I have no idea what you're talking about. Parthenope, we have to *do* something—"

Peregrine spoke, forestalling his cousin. "She means that you were right about Madame Carswell not being responsible for trying to kill your father and the others."

Sophie shook her head impatiently. "No—Amélie already did something to the duke—"

"Sophie, please listen to me," Peregrine interrupted. "You know I started working at the War Office after we—after you left for Brussels. Lord Palmerston assigned me to keeping his correspondence with King Louis's Minister of War—"

"Oh, for heaven's sake, skip all that!" Parthenope demanded. "Sophie, Peregrine has found something out about the Comte de Carmouche-Ponthieux."

Sophie blinked. "What does he have to do with any of this?"

"It turns out that he's not working for the king after all," Peregrine said. "In fact, no one at the king's court has ever heard of him, including the king himself. All his credentials to Lord Palmerston are forgeries. I went to Ghent myself to make absolutely sure and came straight here."

Sophie felt as if she were trying to think through treacle. What did this matter now, when the duke was gone? "I don't understand—who could he be working for, then?"

"Whom do you *think* he might be working for?" Parthenope looked exasperated. "You were right that the assassin isn't Amélie. It's the comte! We wondered who might have been responsible for trying to kill the War Office people . . . well, wasn't he also there at every attempt—in the park and at the opera and all? It all fits together! He already knew who your family was—what would have been more natural than for him to 'discover' the lost love of his youth in London while posing as an envoy for the king? It gave him the perfect opportunity to be in the center of things, with access to your father and all the—"

Sophie closed her eyes. "Parthenope, aren't you forgetting one vital piece of information?"

"What you saw this afternoon isn't proof that it's Amélie!"

"Isn't it?"

"What information?" Peregrine asked.

Parthenope looked at Sophie for a few measuring seconds, then turned to Peregrine. "The fact that whoever tried to kill Sophie's papa and the others was using magic to do so."

"Parthenope!" Sophie grabbed her arm. Oh, how could she have said that?

"He has to know, because we need to do something *now*," Parthenope said firmly. "Sophie is a—"

Sophie dug her nails into Parthenope's arm. Parthenope winced. "I mean, she can sense when magic is being done."

"Magic," Peregrine said carefully.

"Yes, magic." Parthenope shook off Sophie's hand. "Sophie sensed it at all the other attempts in London and thinks she saw Amélie putting an enchantment here in the ballroom."

"The murder attempts—they were accomplished by magic," he repeated.

Parthenope patted his arm. "You're really taking this very well, you know. I'm impressed."

Sophie agreed that he seemed to be accepting this with remarkable composure, but there wasn't time to think about him now. "I didn't just think I saw Amélie," she said angrily. "What about Hester? He felt it too—you're the one who—"

Parthenope's face lit up. "Hester! Of course!" She hurried away from them.

"Parthenope, what are you doing?" Sophie called after her. Parthenope ignored her.

Peregrine cleared his throat gently. "Sophie, I'm sorry. This is . . . this is not how I would have chosen to come and apologize to you."

Sophie felt faint again under his pleading gaze. "You don't

have to apologize to me. It was—I was the one who was wrong. Amélie—I didn't want her to be a spy for Napoléon."

"But I don't think she is."

"And I don't think it could be the comte. That would mean—" She looked away, blinking back tears. That would mean that he'd deliberately insinuated himself into their family . . . and back into poor, innocent Aunt Molly's heart.

She felt him touch her arm. "Sophie, can you—is magic real, then? Can you really sense it?"

It was as if his question had opened a yawning chasm before her. How should she answer him? Should she tell him what she was—or what she once had been? What would he do if she did?

Well, she would find out, before he apologized to her . . . or before she let her feelings for him out of their tight little prison. She took a deep breath. "Yes, but it's more than just—"

"Here we are!" Parthenope pushed her way between them, one hand raised, on which perched a grumpy-looking Hester. "Come on, Sophie." She took Sophie's hand and pulled her along.

"What are you doing?"

"If he can find spells, then maybe he can find the person who made the spell," Parthenope said. "Will you believe *him*?"

"A spell?" she heard a woman say behind her. "Did that girl just say it was a spell? Witchcraft? Someone's done a spell on the duke?"

"Now you've done it," Sophie muttered to Parthenope.

"Twaddle," Parthenope said, still pushing through the crowd, but her usually pink cheeks were pale.

"A witch?" someone else called. "She's a witch! It must be that woman—the one who was dancing with him."

"Foul sorcery!" an older woman cried, and fainted.

"Nonsense!" someone said loudly. Sophie looked up.

Papa strode into the middle of the circle just as they reached its edge. He walked up to Amélie and took her hand. "Are you listening to yourselves?" he asked contemptuously. "Muttering about witchcraft and spells? Are we living in 1815 or 1615?"

"Papa," Sophie whispered to herself. Should she shout to him to run? That he was putting himself in the direst of danger?

"Well?" he said again.

No one answered him, though there was muttering. He ignored it. "I say again, it's utter nonsense. Madame Carswell is not a witch and has not harmed the duke in the least."

"Then where is he?" a tall woman called.

"I don't know. Moreover, neither does Madame Carswell. Do you, madame?"

She shook her head. *"Monsieur le Duc . . . c'est incroyable . . .* I do not know—I did nothing. He was here, and then—" She turned and buried her face in his shoulder.

Papa looked around at the crowd. "You heard her. She has done nothing ill tonight. The duke's officers and I will—"

"She's a Frenchwoman!" she heard someone shout. "Why should we believe she's done nothing to our duke?"

"A Frenchwoman! What does anyone know about her?"

"A widow from India, someone said."

"A convenient story . . ."

"You don't think she's—"

Sophie and Parthenope had reached the edge of the crowd.

Just beyond Papa and Amélie, Sophie could see Aunt Molly clinging to the comte. He had put a comforting arm around her shoulders.

"All right, little man." Parthenope brought Hester close to her face and spoke in an unnaturally high voice. "Someone here did the big cold spell you showed me today. Will Mama's little love show me who made it, pretty please?"

"Oh lord, Parthenope, he won't—"

Parthenope glared at her over Hester's head. "You're not helping. That's my good little boy. Go show Mama now?"

Hester twisted around and scratched at his back with his beak, then looked, unblinking, at Parthenope.

"Go, Hester!" Parthenope threw her hand up in the air.

Hester flapped in place for a minute, and Sophie was sure he'd settle back down on Parthenope's shoulder and call her a turnip. But then he began to circle the crowd, his purple head and green wings bright under the chandeliers. He glanced down at Sophie; she could see his dark, sparkling eye examining her. Then he circled again, seeming to search the crowd.

"Oh, what a darling little bird! Such pretty plumage!" a lady in a feathered turban cried loudly. Heads turned from Amélie and Papa.

"Don't you even think about it," Parthenope growled under her breath. "Come on, Hester!"

Hester did one more circuit of the room to the accompaniment of more exclamations of surprise. Then his wings slowed, and he arced down . . . down . . . and came to rest on the comte's shoulder.

"By the pricking of my thumbs!" Hester proclaimed.

Chapter 19

"*Hester!*" Parthenope cried. "You *good* little boy!"

"Silly bird!" Aunt Molly scolded, twisting out from under the comte's arm to look at him. "What are you doing here? Now, don't go doing to my Auguste what you did to poor old Lady Exton. You quite ruined her shawl, you know."

Sophie stared at the comte as he turned his head slowly to look at the bird on his shoulder. It *was* him. Thoughts and memories of the last months began to rearrange themselves into a new pattern. How could she not have even suspected him, even after what Peregrine had just told them?

Because she hadn't wanted to.

Before she could think anything more, the comte said something, very quietly. Hester stiffened and tumbled from his shoulder.

"Hester!" Parthenope launched herself across the floor and

scooped him up, holding him against her breast. "If you've hurt him, you—you—"

"*Sorcier*," Sophie finished for her, stepping into the circle as well.

The comte looked at her, and a slight smile touched the corners of his mouth—but not, she noticed, his eyes . . . his eyes that she had always thought so sad and sincere. "Ah, Lady Sophie. I think I am not wrong in saying that it takes one to know one."

Sophie lifted her chin. It wouldn't do any good to deny it, and it would do even less good for him to know that just now, her magic was all but nonexistent. Let him think there was at least someone present who could possibly oppose him. "What if I am?" she said haughtily.

"I suspected as much," he said, nodding. "When I saw you on the stairs after Marie's fall, I wondered. And when the glass broke in your father's hand at Lady Montashton's—"

"It was poisoned," Sophie said. "I could tell."

"Sophie, what is going on here?" Papa asked. "What poison? What are you talking about?"

The comte glanced at him and made a small gesture, and Papa clutched at his throat, eyes wide. Sophie stepped forward, but the comte shook his head. "I am not hurting him—merely keeping him from disturbing our conversation." He glanced around the crowd staring at him fearfully, inching away. "I shall be happy to do the same to anyone else."

"Let them leave," Sophie said. "No one else here matters."

"On the contrary." The comte bowed ironically, one hand on his breast. "I am pleased to give them a little sample of what I can do. It will make it easier for them to be docile when His

Imperial Majesty returns to Brussels in the not-very-distant future."

Sophie felt Peregrine come up behind her, shaking with repressed emotion. She put a warning hand behind her and felt him take it and squeeze it gently, then release it. His touch somehow made her feel braver. "So you admit that you work for the emperor," she said.

"But of course. I am a little surprised that no one suspected me until now. You are very credulous, you English."

"And the duke?"

The comte smiled. "The duke is quite unharmed. He is just elsewhere. His presence here in Brussels was thought . . . *unnecessary* by my emperor. That is why I was sent here, you will understand—to remove him, by whatever means came to hand." He nodded to Amélie. "It was nothing personal, madame. You were simply a convenience."

She stared at him in horror.

"And I suppose my aunt was a convenience as well," Sophie said.

The comte shrugged, but a slight flush told Sophie that she'd scored a hit. "You are correct . . . but maybe a little more than a convenience. More—let me see—more a chance for retribution. It was a—an added bonus to the task."

"Retribution against an innocent woman who loved you?"

"Against her family who kept us apart, who thought I was not good enough for her. She herself was no longer important, except as my tool."

Aunt Molly was staring up at him. "Auguste," she said, and there was little of her usual vagueness left in her eyes.

"I am sorry, Marie," he said. "It has been pleasant, seeing

you again. Perhaps once, all those years ago . . . if your family had not been so proud, things might have been different."

"I had thought they would be different now," she said, her voice cracking. "You made me think that we would finally be—that you loved me."

He shook his head. "Of course I had to make you think that. I had a job to do. But it was nothing more. My wife is a patriotic woman, but she would not be pleased if I were to turn bigamist, even for the emperor's cause."

"Your wife. . . ." Aunt Molly's face seemed to change somehow, as if the bones beneath it were disintegrating.

"My wife," he agreed. "Did you really think I had stayed single all these years, after what your father did to me? It was a pleasure to come back and try to take my revenge on your family, all in the name of working for my emperor."

Amélie, who had still been staring at him, straightened her shoulders, gave him a defiant look, and put her arms around Aunt Molly, drawing her away and turning her back on him. It was a magnificent gesture, and Sophie would have cheered if her anger hadn't almost choked her. How could he have been so cruel? Being a spy was one thing, but to deceive poor innocent Aunt Molly—

"And now what?" she asked, when she thought she had mastered her voice.

"Stalemate," the comte replied calmly—almost too calmly. It told Sophie that he felt in complete control of the situation, even with her there. "Now you know what I am, but only I know where milord the duke is."

"I've been trying to figure out how you did it," Sophie said. It seemed wise to keep him talking, to buy time—or in hopes that he would let some secret about the duke's whereabouts slip. "I know there was a spell on the floor here. I found it this afternoon—"

"Ha! Do you not remember that I called this morning, to take your aunt driving?" He looked smug. "It was only the work of a few minutes to set up the spell, while she went to put on her hat."

Parthenope made a strangled sound. The comte smiled at her. "Yes, you invited me to see the flowers and let me come up alone. It was very kind of you to give me the opportunity on a silver platter, as it were." Then his attention shifted back to Sophie. "So you found it, did you? That is very interesting. I had thought I had hidden it well enough. You are a very clever young witch, mademoiselle. I have perhaps underestimated you. It was a mistake on my part."

Behind her, Sophie felt Peregrine move slightly and tried to ignore him. "It was keyed to work only on the duke, wasn't it? That way, all he had to do was walk over it, and you would not have to do anything else. You could pretend to be as shocked as any of us and shift the blame to Amélie."

He nodded slowly, looking at her. "You are mostly right. I set it that way, in case I could not manage the job in person. But that does not mean that I cannot use it in other ways, if need be." He smiled and raised his hand, crooking his finger at her. "Like—*this.*"

Sophie landed hard on her hands and knees on a cold stone floor, feeling shaky and weak. She stayed there for a moment, trying to catch her breath; she felt winded, the way she had the first time she'd fallen from her horse as a small child. It was a horrid feeling.

How could she have let the comte catch her off guard like that? She must have been standing right in front of his trap for the duke, but she had been so intent on him that she hadn't paid attention . . . and he had yanked her through it before she could even react. She should have known that he would not stop at anything—look at how he deceived poor Aunt Molly.

When she was mostly sure that she wouldn't faint or throw up, she struggled awkwardly to her feet, wishing she had her cane, and looked around her. She was in an enormous rectangular room made of gray stone, its ceiling lost above her in shadows. Doorways pierced the walls at irregular intervals, leading into what looked like passageways, though the dim, grayish light that permeated the space made it difficult to see very far. It was cold, and a strong breeze blew from somewhere, ruffling her hair. There was no sign of the duke.

"Sir!" she shouted. "Are you here?"

Her voice echoed against the stone and was shredded by the wind. Had he fallen as he passed through the portal and hit his head? He might now be wandering in a daze down one of the passages. "Duke!" she shouted again. "Can you hear me? Duke! Please come back!"

No sound but the wind. She turned her head slightly so that it didn't blow so loudly in her ears and cupped her hand to her mouth to shout again. It sounded weak and thin, though she put all that she had into it. Why couldn't she be like Madame Catalani or the other opera singers she'd heard, who could fill any room, no matter the size, with her voice? "Duke!"

Nothing. The solitude of this echoing room seemed to mock her. "Duke?" she screeched, and hated the desperation edging her voice. "Here! In here!"

"*Hoy!*"

Had she heard that, or was the cruel wind playing tricks on her ears? "Duke!"

And then she didn't have to shout again, because he came striding, almost running, from one of the doorways.

"Good God!" he exclaimed, checking at the sight of her. "Lady Sophie! What are you doing here? How—"

She held her hand out to him. It trembled with relief—at least she had found him. Being alone in this strange, cold room had begun to unnerve her.

He came forward and took it. "What devilment is this?" he said. "Where are we?"

"I don't know, sir. It's not anywhere that I know." She hesitated, then added, "I'm not even sure that it exists on a map."

He looked at her down the length of his distinctively hooked nose. "It's some kind of witchery, isn't it? I've always thought it a hum, but I see that I was wrong. Who's responsible for it?"

"The Comte de Carmouche-Ponthieux. It seems that he's working for Emperor Napoléon. He tried to kill Lord Palmerston and my father and others in London, and then came here to get rid of you."

The duke whistled. "Working for Bonaparte! So the emperor's found himself a wizard to do his dirty work, has he?" He frowned. "You should not have come after me. It was a foolish thing to—"

"I didn't." Sophie wished she hadn't had to say that. It

would have been much less humiliating if she'd actually been trying to rescue him. "I'd hoped to find some other way to get you out, but he caught me instead when I wasn't watching. I didn't have a chance to block his spell."

He raised an eyebrow. "Then you're a—"

"Yes."

"Here, you're shivering," he said after a minute and started to take off his coat.

"I'm not cold," she said stiffly. She'd failed him; a kindly gesture on his part somehow made her feel worse.

He looked at her for a moment, then shrugged. "Let's get out of this wind. If we stand in one of those doorways, we can escape some of it and still keep an eye on this room, since it seems to be the way into this cursed place."

Sophie followed him, feeling numb—and not just from cold, though her bare neck and arms above her long gloves felt as if they'd been turned to marble. What would they do? She did not think they would find a way out if they followed any of the doorways . . . and as he said, this room must be the entrance point to this horrible place.

What would happen? Had the comte just abandoned them here, eventually to die a slow death? What was happening back in the ballroom in Brussels? Would anyone try to apprehend the comte, or were they all too frightened? Surely he would try to escape . . . and some of the guests—the duke's aides, surely— would try to stop him, hoping they could force him to release the duke . . . and her.

But could she count on that? All he had to do was refuse to say or do anything; they would never hurt him, as he was the only one who could bring the duke back. And in the meanwhile,

Napoléon would find it much easier to march on Brussels and secure his northeast border again—all his borders, really. With the duke gone, the heart would be wrenched from the Allied armies. No other general in Europe commanded such faith and respect.

The comte had declared they were at a stalemate, but that wasn't true. He had won. The only way to keep Napoléon from running roughshod over Europe again was for her to figure out how to get the duke out of here. And how could she, when she had no idea where "here" was . . . and not enough magic to lift a pin?

The duke led them a few feet inside a passage, then took off his coat and put it over her shoulders. This time she didn't protest; being proud wouldn't help matters. He held out his hand and gestured to the floor. "I think it time we talked about what we can do, Lady Sophie," he said. "Tell me more about this comte and the rest of it."

Sophie sat, her back against the cold stone wall, and huddled into the duke's coat. Talking was the last thing she felt like doing right now, but there was no gainsaying the Duke of Wellington. So she told him about meeting the comte at Lady Whiston's ball and the falling statue, and about all the other times he'd tried to kill Papa and the others . . . and about her illness and her mother and her magic. He nodded, asking an occasional question, but she could not tell what he thought, as his heavy-lidded eyes gave away very little.

"Your magic—it's come and gone, has it? Why do you think that is?" he asked when she ran out of words.

"I don't know. If I had any idea, I would have done something about it," she said wearily.

He climbed to his feet and paced a little ways up and down the passage. Watching him, Sophie realized that the gray light that suffused the space did not diminish farther down its length, but was uniform everywhere, with no visible source. Then they couldn't be anywhere real, but had to be in a magical place of some kind. The realization was not reassuring.

"I don't think you ever lost your magic," the duke said suddenly, stopping before her.

"No?" she said, trying to remain polite. "I'm afraid I don't see why you'd think that. Believe me, I've tried."

He crouched next to her. "You say it's something that runs in families—that your mother had it too, yes?"

"Yes," she said, listlessly.

"Just as fair hair may run in a family. Someone can dye it, but it will still be fair."

"I'm afraid I don't see the analogy, sir."

He blew out his breath in an impatient sound. "You're an intelligent girl, Lady Sophie. Use your wits. Dye may cover fair hair, but it's still fair. And your grief after your illness and losing your mother may have covered your will to do your magic, but it must still be there as well."

She shook her head. "Don't you think it more likely that since illness damaged my leg, it might have damaged my magic as well?"

"You don't know that it did."

"I don't know that it didn't, either," she snapped.

He ignored her, and after a moment rose and resumed his pacing, perhaps to help keep himself warm. Sophie drew her knees to her chest and wrapped her arms around them, hiding her face against them.

"Lady Sophie, how do you think I became what I am?" he asked, stopping beside her after a few moments.

She raised her face and looked up at him. "I don't understand, sir. You are what you are."

"That's exactly right—and so are you. But I could have been someone else, once." A shadow seemed to cross his face. "When I was your age, no one would have thought I'd turn out to be much of anything at all."

She stared up at him. "But—"

"Do you know what I did for most of my seventeenth year? Lay about playing with my dog and practicing the violin. I didn't do much more than that for the next few years, either. Not until I was in my twenties did I begin to make anything of myself. Do you know why?"

"N-no."

"Because I decided it was time to."

"So you think that it's my fault that I can't use my magic because I'm too busy feeling sorry for myself. No, sir. I don't think it works that way."

"Why shouldn't it? I had abilities, but until I determined to use them, they did nothing."

"But I've tried," she nearly shouted at him, trying to clamber to her feet. He held out his hand, but she ignored it, pulling herself up and balancing against the wall. "Don't you think I've tried?"

"I just saw you stand by yourself because you wanted to, despite your lameness," he replied coolly.

"Because Parthenope gave me shoes to make my legs the same length."

"What does that signify? You still did it."

311

Sophie turned away. Thinking about Parthenope giving her the shoes was making her want to cry. Would she ever see Parthenope again . . . or Peregrine? He'd come back ready to admit that he'd been wrong about Amélie. Had he also come back hoping that she still had some feeling for him? "She thinks as you do," she muttered.

"What, the Hardcastle girl? I knew she was a clever chit. What does she say?"

"She says—" Sophie swallowed the lump in her throat. "She thinks that I—because I was able to do magic again after—after Lord Woodbridge asked me if he could speak to my father about . . . about—"

"Woodbridge—Lord Rendlesham's son, is he?" The duke raised an eyebrow. "What do you think?"

"I don't know!"

He looked at her steadily. "Lady Sophie, I think you *do* know. But it's easier to blame what's wrong with you on everything around you, rather than on yourself—"

"Oh, so becoming lame was my fault, was it?"

"Of course not, you little fool. I am not surprised that your magic left you for a while after your illness and loss. But I think it might have become a habit to think of yourself as someone who's suffered and lost."

"So how am I supposed to think of myself, if you please?"

"As who you are—and who you want to be. If I had waited for someone to tell me to be Duke of Wellington, I'd still be on that couch scraping my cursed violin. You're the only one who can make you what you ought to be."

Sophie turned away and stared into the bleak stone room, the retort she'd been about to launch at him withering away unspoken. She'd hated Aunt Isabel treating her like damaged goods, unlikely to find a husband . . . hated the people like Lady Lumley, who'd seen only her lameness, not her. But could she have been accepting their view of her after all, without thinking? Had she let them define her as broken, and believed them?

"I—I don't know what to do," she whispered.

"Good God, Lady Sophie, do you think I do?" he asked. "Now, if you will excuse me, you may be content to stay in this godforsaken place and feel sorry for yourself, but I have a city to protect."

Turning in time to see him stalk from the passage and back into the large, echoing room, she stood transfixed. How dare he say such a dreadful thing? What did he possibly think she could do?

Try? asked a small voice in her mind.

The duke was crawling on hands and knees back and forth across the width of the room, staring intently at the stone floor, when she finally made herself follow after him. She watched him for a few moments and scraped up enough courage to ask, "What are you doing?"

"Looking for where we came in. I think it was here somewhere—at least, on this side of the room. If you say there was an entrance—or exit—back in the ballroom in Brussels, then I expect there has to be one here."

Sophie didn't tell him that magic didn't necessarily work that way. "How will you find it?" she asked instead.

He didn't bother looking up. "I don't know, but I know

that I have to at least try. I'm not about to roll over and play dead for Napoléon, by God."

A lump formed in her throat. She ignored it and walked over to him. "Will you help me down?" she asked shyly.

He glanced up at her, nodded, and held out his hand. She used it to lower herself to kneel next to him and looked around the room, trying to picture precisely where she'd landed after the comte pushed her magically through the portal. A little to the left, maybe? She paused to pull off her long evening gloves so that nothing interfered with her ability to feel any possible whisper of magic, then began to imitate the duke's crawl, running her hands over the roughly dressed stone of the floor. She tried not to think about what she would do if she found the portal, but that led to wondering what would happen if she didn't find it, which was infinitely worse.

In fact, she nearly didn't find it. It was much more subtle than the spell in the ballroom, not so much a portal as a memory of one, like a physical doorway that had been bricked and plastered over but was still visible. She didn't say anything to the duke, but found when she looked up that he was sitting back on his knees, watching her.

"You've got it," he said. It wasn't a question.

"I . . . *think* so," she replied cautiously, brushing the flats of her palms in a widening circle around it. "There's not much of it, but . . . I'm fairly certain there's something here."

He came over to crouch next to her. "Yes, this looks like about the right part of the room. What are you going to do?"

Sophie stared down at the place. Nothing about it looked different from the floor all around it. Had she imagined what she felt? Even if she hadn't, what could she do with it?

"I'm not sure," she finally said.

"You're not sure," he repeated slowly. "Very well. Do you intend to find out? Caution is no bad thing in a commander. But it can't keep him—or her—from taking action, Lady Sophie."

Sophie looked up at him. This wasn't the duke who loved to go to parties and laugh too loudly at jokes and flirt with pretty women that she'd come to know in Brussels. It was the iron-backed general who'd harried Napoléon's army out of Spain and Portugal and chased his marshals all the way into France, and wouldn't brook hesitation from anyone. Including a frightened, uncertain young witch.

Because she was a witch. She would not be here if she weren't. The comte had feared her enough to imprison her here, hadn't he? Then maybe it was time for her to justify his fear. The duke, for all his bravery and skill on a battlefield, was powerless here, and he knew it. But he also knew that she wasn't.

"Yes, sir," she said, and took a deep breath, trying to push the doubt, if not out of her mind, at least to its margins. *Just examine it*, she told herself. *See if there's anything to learn about it. You don't have to do anything immediately.*

She spread her hands again and moved them slowly over the floor. Yes, there was the place where they'd come through: She could still feel their passages, the duke's and her own, like the wake of wind left behind a swift rider. If only she could follow that wake back along its path! She pushed against hers, exploring its course backward, probing further—

And then suddenly it wasn't there anymore. Light and warmth and sound seemed to explode around her. She squinted, trying to understand . . . and realized that she was kneeling in the middle of the ballroom in their house in Brussels.

Chapter

20

The room was in an uproar. Sophie realized that she was toward the back of the large crowd that had originally formed around Amélie, but the open space that had been at its center had disappeared, and everyone had pressed forward into one seething, chattering mass.

"Sophie!"

All at once Parthenope was there, eyes enormous. Before Sophie could say anything, she'd pulled her to her feet and thrown her arms around her, hugging her fiercely. "You came back!" she squealed directly in Sophie's ear.

For a moment, Sophie gave herself over to a huge wave of relief. She'd done it! Somehow she'd managed to follow the trail of the spell back here.

Fast on the heels of that thought came another one. "Where's the comte?" she asked, pushing Parthenope away slightly and looking anxiously around.

"Ha!" Parthenope's eyes lit up with triumph and mischief. "Being carried downstairs with his hands tied up in someone's sash and a napkin stuffed in his mouth, thanks to your aunt Molly!"

"Sophie!" Papa seized her from Parthenope's grasp and enveloped her in a tight embrace. "Dearest child—what happened? You—you vanished!"

Sophie gulped. Relief at having escaped was giving way to the realization that she still had a great deal to face here . . . not to mention the duke to rescue.

"Sophie! My word, you gave me a turn, popping off like that!" Now Aunt Molly was there, followed closely by Amélie, who looked enormously relieved. Sophie wished she could spare a moment to apologize to Amélie, but it would have to wait.

Aunt Molly was still talking. "You figured out how to escape Auguste's witchery, then! I must say, I think it was extremely rude of him to try to enchant my own niece, but there, he wasn't a very *good* man, was he?" Her blue eyes suddenly clouded. Amélie put an arm about her shoulders.

"Well, you certainly gave him what for!" Parthenope said to her bracingly. "I don't think he was expecting—"

"Please, will someone tell me what happened to the comte?" Sophie interrupted.

"Well, after you disappeared, everyone stood there looking terrified and then started backing away," Aunt Molly said. "He was ever so proud of himself—I could tell by the way he stood there—"

"He wasn't going to stand there for long. In fact, he was definitely about to bolt," Parthenope inserted. "He bowed and said, 'And now, if you will excuse me—' but never got a chance to finish because your aunt stopped him with an enormous vase of lilies—"

"I walloped him over the head with it, pet!" Aunt Molly said, beaming at Sophie. "He never even saw me behind him, and he went down like a—like a—"

"It was just before you got back," Parthenope told her. "Once he fell, no one lost any time in getting him tied up. I think they're taking him to the duke's headquarters—"

"They've already got him more securely tied and into a carriage," an unfamiliar voice said.

Sophie looked up at a man in uniform—one of the duke's aides, who'd come to stand behind Aunt Molly. Captain Hill, maybe? But it was the man who stood next to him who captured her attention.

"You're safe," Peregrine Woodbridge said, his eyes shining. "Oh, God, Sophie—when you disappeared like that—"

"I came back" was all she could say, as a queer fluttering sensation seemed to have seized her throat. It seemed to be enough, though.

"Yes, but the duke didn't," Parthenope said sharply. "What *happened*, Sophie? Did you see him? Do you know where he is?"

"Well, of course she must have," Aunt Molly said. "I do believe she's wearing his coat."

"Please, ma'am," the captain said urgently. "The duke—is he all right?"

Sophie looked down in surprise and saw that she was indeed still enveloped in the duke's coat. Why hadn't she given it back to him before she tried to find the way back? The poor man must be freezing in that horrible place. "He's in perfect health," she said to Captain Hill. "Only . . . only I don't know where."

"But surely—" Parthenope began. Amélie and Peregrine shushed her.

"What I mean is, I know we were both in the same place. I just don't know where it actually is. I didn't expect to be able to find my way out of it—it was almost an accident that I got out," Sophie said.

"I do not think it an accident." Amélie spoke for the first time.

Sophie turned to her in surprise. What did she mean? Unless— "Amélie, I saw you this afternoon. Did you know the trap was here? Had *you* found it?"

"I had not," Amélie said. "But my Nalini did. She insisted I come to look at it, but I could not feel it. Me, I have no magic."

"But she does," Sophie said.

Amélie nodded. "Yes—how did you know? Your canes— she put a protective spell on them. Did you feel it? But we had no idea that *you, ma petite—*"

"May I ask why you don't think Sophie's escape was an accident?" Papa asked.

Amélie shrugged. "As I said, I do not know magic. But I do know Sophie." She smiled warmly. "Sophie brought herself out of Monsieur le Comte's *sorcellerie* because she is strong and will not let such a thing stop her. And I do not doubt that she can do the same for his grace the duke."

"Can you?" Captain Hill demanded. Another of the duke's

aides—Lieutenant-Colonel Gordon, she thought—had joined them and was staring at her hopefully, along with a growing number of guests. She could hear sibilant whispers of "Lady Sophie! She's back!"

"You found him once," Captain Hill continued. "Can't you go back and bring him with you this time?"

Sophie wished they would all stop looking at her so hard. Because despite what Amélie seemed to think, she wasn't strong or brave or any of those things. "I don't know. The spell that transported him was created especially for him. He himself set it off, so to speak. I just went there because the comte pushed me into it—" A sudden thought stopped her. The prison had been designed specifically for the duke, but the comte had been able to put her there with a conscious effort. Had his being knocked out allowed her to escape it?

But if so, what bearing did that have on rescuing the duke?

"Well, isn't the spell likely still in place?" Parthenope asked. "Can't you use it to go back to him?"

"Yes, it's probably there," Sophie agreed. "But the duke's the one who makes it work. It's like having the correct key for a lock."

"Oh," Parthenope said, glumly. "Too bad he doesn't have a twin brother handy. We could use him to open the door."

"That wouldn't work. It has to be him," Sophie said slowly. An edge of an idea had raised itself in her mind . . . if she could muster enough magic to do it. "But . . . maybe something be-longing to him—that might be enough to give me a fingerhold to pry it open—"

"Like his coat?" Aunt Molly said brightly.

Parthenope laughed aloud. "We should be quite lost without you tonight, ma'am! Sophie, do you think you can do it?"

Sophie thought of the duke's stern face. "I have to," she said.

"Sophie, I won't allow you to go back to—to wherever it is," Papa said angrily. Peregrine nodded agreement.

"But the duke—" Captain Hill began, just as angrily.

"I have to, Papa," she said again. "No one else can do it."

"But what if you can't come back?" he said, and she was surprised to see tears in his eyes.

Parthenope clutched at Sophie's arm. "Do you have to go all the way through again? Can't you just sort of open the door so that he can come in, rather than you going out?"

"I'm not sure it works that way. I'd never seen anything like this before tonight." She glanced at her father. Well, he'd have to know sometime, now. "My mother used to make windows so we could see other places, but never doors that we could go through."

Papa looked at her, opened his mouth, and closed it. Poor Papa; she would have a lot of explaining to do to him once this was over. If it ever would be over.

"Well, that's simple," Parthenope said. "Don't go all the way through. Can't you just poke your head in and call him to come out while you hold it open?"

Sophie started to protest again that she wasn't sure it would work, but changed her mind at the stubborn expression on Papa's face and the equally determined one on Captain Hill's. She looked at Parthenope and understood that she was thinking the same thing: Trying to open this doorway might or might not work—she might or might not be able to find the magic to do it . . . but there was nothing else she could do except try.

"I'll do it," she said softly.

Parthenope nodded. "You did it once. You'll do it again. Would it help if we held on to you, to make sure you don't go all the way through?" She turned to Peregrine. "Will you help? After all those boxing lessons with Gentleman Jackson, you're surely quite strong."

Sophie waited for him to protest like Papa had; wasn't she the young woman he'd thought he needed to protect? But he met her eyes and straightened his shoulders. "What do you want me to do?"

"Take my hand. I'll need one to find the spell with." She wasn't convinced that this would work—would it even be possible to be in two different places at the same time?—but it might. She held her left hand out to him and he took it, then grasped her wrist with his other hand so that he held on to her with both.

"Sophie—" Papa began.

"I'm sorry, Papa," Sophie said, because trying to argue him out of protesting would take too much time. "I think it would be helpful if everyone could move back a little," she said. "I need to find the exact edges of the spell again."

Captain Hill and Lieutenant-Colonel Gordon set about moving people back with alacrity. Papa looked mutinous, but to Sophie's surprise let the captain usher him aside. The crowd around them had grown, and whispered conversations filled the ballroom like wind rustling the leaves of a forest. *What's she doing? Where's the duke? Why didn't she bring—? Fancy that crippled little thing—* She wished they would stop; the buzz of half-heard words made it hard for her to concentrate as she felt the air around her with her free hand, pulling Peregrine with her—

There it was. When she'd found the comte's spell that afternoon, there had just been a line of magic on the floor. Now she found that it had unfolded and hung suspended above the line on the floor. She ran her fingers over it, trying to find the boundaries, and eventually described a large, wide oval. Evidently the comte had wanted to make sure that it was big enough to catch the duke if the dance lines did not form precisely where expected.

"It's here," she said to Peregrine, and stood a moment longer, ostensibly still defining its edges but actually trying to steel herself to begin trying to open it. What if she failed, here with a roomful of people—not to mention Papa, Amélie, Peregrine, and several of the duke's aides—watching her? It would be difficult enough to deal with society whispering that she was a witch . . . but to have it whispered that she was an incompetent one, or worse, that she had lied about her power?

And this wasn't just anyone she had to rescue. It was the Duke of Wellington, whom all of Europe was counting on to save them from Napoléon. She thought about the way he'd looked at her so sternly just a short while ago. Well, if he was going to save Europe, she was going to have to save him. She slid her hand into the sleeve of the duke's coat so that it, and not her fingertips, would be first to touch the edge of the spell.

As soon as she touched the spell again with her cloth-covered hand, she felt it stir, as if it were a curtain moved by a breeze. She grasped at that image and held it in her mind; all she had to do was draw aside the curtain and the door would be opened. Slowly, her eyes half closed, she pushed her hand to the side, and the air seemed to waver before her as a cold breeze struck her face.

"Good God," Peregrine whispered behind her, squeezing her wrist, but she didn't have time to acknowledge him. A stronger blast of cold wind washed over her, and there it was: the gray stone room with its shadowy doorways, bathed in that cold gray light and, huddled on the floor in front of her, head bowed on his knees—

"Duke," she called. Would he be able to hear her? If only he'd look up—surely he would be able to see that the door had been opened . . . ?

"The duke!" Dimly she heard her cry taken up by others in the room, but she couldn't attend to it now . . . only trust that Captain Hill could keep the crowd under control so they didn't surge into her.

"Duke!" she shouted, more loudly. But the figure on the floor never lifted his dark head. He was probably wondering what had happened to her and if he'd ever see her—or the rest of the world—again.

"He can't hear me. I have to get his attention," she muttered to Peregrine.

"How?"

"If I just put my head in—"

"It might pull you all the way through," he said, voicing her worry.

"I can get out again. I did it once."

"Will it last that long?"

She looked up at him. "What do you mean?"

He nodded at the door, his face pale. The edges of the

opening were wavering slightly—no, fading, like a wash of pigment in a watercolor blending into nothing. Evidently the magic that had built the portal was not stable. Why hadn't she thought about that before? Building a permanent, or even long-lasting, spell took time and effort, and the comte had set this spell while purportedly admiring the flower arrangements that morning. Furthermore, why would he have cared to make the portal a permanent one? He had no intention of using it again, once the duke had been caught.

"Then I have to try," she said. "Hold on tight."

"Sophie, I can't think the duke would want a young girl to endanger herself—"

"But I'm not just any young girl. I'm—"

Before she could say anything further, he lifted her hand and kissed it. "I know you aren't. That's why I don't want anything to happen to you," he whispered. "Very well, go. I've got you." He squeezed her hand.

Sophie tried not to think about the feeling of his lips on her hand and turned back to the door. Taking a deep breath, she thrust her face toward the portal.

A peculiar sensation, like angry bees crawling on her skin, nearly took her breath away. It was quickly replaced by a tugging sensation, as if the door was pulling at her. "Duke!" she shouted.

He looked up. "Good Lord! Lady Sophie! What are you doing here? How—"

"Got to—get you—" she managed to force out. It was almost as though the spell were trying to pull her face off.

He'd scrambled to his feet and took a step toward her. There was a strange expression on his face. "How? All I see is—well, your face, hanging in midair."

No wonder he looked so shocked, poor man. She was about to hold her hand out to him, then realized she didn't have one to give him. Her right hand, growing numb with cold, held the door spell open . . . and Peregrine held her other. Why hadn't she realized that she'd probably need two hands? Impatiently, she tried to tug it out of his grasp, but he only clutched it harder. Drat it, how could she make him understand she needed it, without telling him? She didn't dare turn back into the ballroom and tell him, lest the spell disintegrate so much that she couldn't reach through it again.

Very well. It was stupid and awkward and improper and thoroughly absurd, but she had no choice. She balanced on her good left leg and thrust her lame right leg, in its new built-up slipper, through the door and wiggled it. "Grab—it," she managed to say. "I—pull—you. Hold—tight."

He didn't hesitate but bent immediately and grasped her ankle with both hands. Sophie balanced a moment more in the doorway, gathering her muscles, then threw herself backward as hard as she could, back into Brussels.

And into Peregrine.

"Uhhf!" he grunted as she fell on him, knocking them both to the floor. It was the most beautiful sound she'd ever heard.

So were the other grunt and thud that followed as another body hit the floor quite nearby. She looked down and saw the Duke of Wellington, looking as dazed as he probably ever had, still clutching her ankle. Above him the portal into the comte's gray hell had vanished, only a wisp of cold breeze marking that it had even existed. In a second, it had blown itself out.

"Sophie, we have to stop falling on each other in ballrooms," Peregrine murmured, his voice cracking with suppressed emotion, into her ear. "People will begin to talk."

Chapter

21

Behind Sophie someone shouted, "The duke!" The cry was taken up around the room, and the crowd surged around them. Shouts of "He's back! He's safe!" filled the air. A few of the ladies burst into tears.

By the time Papa had helped her to her feet, the duke had risen as well. He ignored the shouted cries and questions and attempts by Captain Hill and his other aides to get his attention. Instead, he took both of Sophie's hands and held them tightly, looking down at her. "I must beg your pardon for being such a martinet in there, Lady Sophie."

She met his eyes and was glad that she could. "I'm grateful you were, sir. I'm not sure I could have done it without you."

"Oh, I expect you would have, given time."

She shivered, remembering the fraying edges of the spell. "I'm not sure how much time we had, really."

"Time or not, there's no way I could have done it myself. I

am at your service, madam." He let go of her hands and made her a deep bow.

"Sir!" Captain Hill looked as though he needed to sit down. "We didn't know—are you—"

The duke gave Sophie a quick, wry smile and turned to him. "I am quite well, thank you," he said, very loudly. The uproar lessened as those closest hushed their neighbors behind them.

"But what *happened*?" blurted out poor Captain Hill.

"I haven't the faintest idea," he said. "But as you can see, I am quite well."

"But—"

"You did it. I knew you would." Parthenope nudged past the captain. And then, for the first time since Sophie had known her, words seemed to fail Parthenope. She threw her arms around Sophie and burst into tears. Hester, who had been perched on her shoulder, flew into the air with a small squawk, then settled again when Parthenope drew back to find her handkerchief.

"Of course she did it," Papa said, his voice shaking. "Are you all right?"

"She's not *just* all right!" Parthenope blew her nose fiercely. "She's a hero—or a heroine, I suppose."

"Oh, really, Parthenope!" Sophie felt her cheeks redden. "Do I look like a hero?"

"Heroes are not always the biggest or the strongest, *petite*. They are just the ones who do what is most needed when necessary, without hesitating," Amélie said softly.

"I must concur," the duke said, nodding.

Sophie suddenly noticed that he was in his shirtsleeves

and remembered why. She started to take off the duke's coat and felt hands behind her easing it off her shoulders. Then Peregrine handed it to her, still smiling slightly, but with an expression in his eyes that made her feel slightly giddy. She passed the coat to the duke, who accepted it with a bow, then shrugged it on.

And then it was mass confusion again, with Aunt Molly and Amélie wanting to hug her, and the ball guests pressing toward them to exclaim, to ask questions, to touch her dress or the duke's arm.

Off to Sophie's left, a young woman's voice proclaimed, "Wait until my friends hear about this! They'll be positively green they weren't here."

"They will be no such thing, Miss Robbins," the duke said, frowning darkly at her. "Because you're not going to tell them."

She goggled at him. "Why, your grace—I didn't mean any harm—"

"No, I am sure you did not. But we are living in a war zone, ma'am, in case you had forgotten. I should not like the enemy to hear anything of tonight's events, even though it seems his ends were defeated and his agent caught. And so you will all do me the favor of not gossiping about what you may have seen or heard here tonight. You may say you had a pleasant evening. That is all. If I hear a breath of talk about this evening at the next ball or breakfast I attend, I will be most displeased."

A man smirked. "Worried that Bonaparte might go out and try to find himself another witch, eh?"

The duke's famously frosty gaze fell on him, and the smile vanished from the man's face. "Would you like it if he did, sir?"

"No—good Lord, no," the man mumbled, and did his best to melt away from the duke's notice. The duke paid him no further attention, but consulted his watch.

"My dear Lord Lansell, it is close enough to midnight that I think we all might use with a little refreshment," he said. "Might I suggest we all retire for supper and then come back for more dancing?"

Papa looked a little surprised, but immediately agreed. "An excellent idea, sir. Please, my friends, let us go down."

The duke waited with them while the guests began obediently to file toward the stairs. "I trust that will help keep tongues from wagging," he said in a low voice. "We can't have this all over Brussels by tomorrow morning. The emperor doesn't need to know that his plan failed—the less information he has, the better."

"Thank you. You are the only one who could have done it," Papa said, shaking his hand, then turned to Amélie and held out his arm. "Shall we, my dear?"

Amélie colored under his smile. "With pleasure."

To Sophie's delight, the duke turned to Aunt Molly. "Ma'am?" he said inquiringly. She broke into dimples and took his arm as well.

"Poor Aunt Molly," Sophie said quietly to Parthenope. "It will be hard for her. To have her lost lover return to her and then to have it all turn out to be a sham."

Parthenope looked pensive. "I expect we can keep her attention occupied tolerably well till we go home, where she'll have her garden again. And speaking of lost—"

"Not quite so quickly, if you please," said a cool voice.

Sophie turned. Norris Underwood stood there, eyes glittering unpleasantly above his customary smile, and she could feel tension rolling off him in a smoky wave.

"It had better be just a moment," Parthenope said crossly, "or there might not be any of Madame Mabuse's hazelnut meringues left by the time I get down there."

"Do not let me detain you, Lady Parthenope. My business is mostly with Lady Sophie. Though you too might find what I have to say of interest."

"What is this about, Underwood?" Peregrine asked, coming forward.

"Merely a gentlemanly agreement." He looked again at Sophie, and his smile vanished. "As much as our duke would like to fancy he can control what gets discussed tonight, I regret to say he's sadly mistaken as far as I am concerned. I have a simple proposition: You stop meddling with my courtship of Kitty Barker, and I won't make sure all of Brussels— and London too—learns about your interesting demonstrations this evening."

Before Sophie could say anything, Parthenope laughed. "What a gooserump you are, Underwood. *I'm* the one who made sure Kitty got to know the Richmonds, not Sophie."

He shrugged. "That doesn't alter the matter in the slightest. If you do not repair the damage you've caused me with her, I'll be delighted to drag your friend's name through every mud puddle I can find."

"Kitty is free to make her own—" Sophie began fiercely, at the same time that Peregrine said, "I'll call you out before I'll see you do such a thing, sir!" But a gentle hand fell on her arm.

"Did I hear my niece's name mentioned?" Mrs. Barker said, eyes wary but smiling pleasantly.

Mr. Underwood bowed. "In passing, ma'am. Are you going downstairs? I should be delighted to accompany you there in a moment or two, as soon as I have finished my business here. Will you excuse us?"

To Sophie's surprise, Mrs. Barker shook her head. "I think I should rather like to hear what is being said about Kitty . . . if I hadn't already guessed. Rest assured, Lady Sophie, that Kitty is quite safe from Mr. Underwood."

Norris Underwood flushed an unbecoming shade of crimson. "I beg your pardon, madam!"

"I expect you're here trying to blackmail Lady Sophie and Lady Parthenope into fixing your interest with Kitty, or you'll go gossipmongering. Don't do it, Mr. Underwood. It won't work. You'll never have Kitty. We know what you are."

He tried to speak, but nothing came out. His eyes had taken on a hint of hollowness, as if he were afraid, which he might well be, if the shop owners of Brussels had begun to call in their bills. Sophie found herself nearly sorry for him. Nearly.

"But you know, I have a bit of business I'd like to discuss with you myself." Mrs. Barker's face remained solemn, but a faint twinkle was visible in her eyes. "As I said, I know what you are. I also know that you're in line to be a baronet and that I'd rather fancy being called 'her ladyship.'"

Parthenope made a queer sound, which quickly turned into a cough. "Sorry," she said, pressing her handkerchief to her lips.

Mrs. Barker looked at her, and Sophie could have sworn she winked. "So what do you say, Mr. Underwood? I'm even more capable of buying myself a fine title than my niece is, you know. And I know what I'll be getting for my money, so there won't be any unpleasant nonsense. I expect we could come to a very comfortable arrangement, in time."

Sophie wished she had her fan to hide behind. Mr. Underwood was still flushed, but a calculating expression had come into his eyes.

Mrs. Barker saw it too, and nodded. She held out her arm and managed neatly to make it appear that he had offered his and she had taken it. "Thank you," she murmured. "I really could do with a cup of tea right now. Or maybe something stronger." Looking quite as if she was leaning on his arm, she led him toward the stairs, throwing a smile back at them over her shoulder.

Parthenope removed her handkerchief and gasped for breath. "Oh, my stars, I have never, in all my life, been so—so—"

"Vastly diverted?" Sophie wasn't sure whether to collapse in laughter or tears. Or both, perhaps.

Peregrine wasn't laughing. "Are you sure she understands what she's doing? She seems a sensible woman, but—"

"Mrs. Barker is a *very* sensible woman and understands quite well what kind of a bargain she's making," Parthenope told him. "Don't worry about her. She'll lead him a merry dance, and call the tune too." She dabbed at her eyes. "Now, speaking of which . . . will you excuse us a moment, Sophie?" She took Peregrine's arm and propelled him a short distance away.

Sophie watched as she drew him over to the fern-fronted corner where the musicians were set up. What was this all about? The room was emptying fast, thanks to the duke's pleasant but stern suggestion, and she suddenly realized just how tired she was. Couldn't they go downstairs too, so that she could sit down and have some tea as well—or as Mrs. Barker had suggested, something stronger.

But even better would be to slip away to her room and think about what had happened tonight—and not just the comte being Napoléon's man and her rescuing the duke. And then there was Peregrine. She could spend the whole evening thinking about him.

No—she didn't want to think about *what* had happened, but *how*. She took a breath and held her hand out toward one of the small chairs at the edge of the room. *Appropinquā mihi*, she said to it.

It skittered obediently across the floor, scraping slightly, and stopped in front of her.

She sank into it, and once again that evening wasn't sure whether to laugh or to cry. Was it truly back? Had rescuing the duke brought her magic back to her?

Or had it never left her—as the duke had suggested?

I won't let it go again. I won't forget, she told herself fiercely. No matter what happened, no matter how Aunt Isabel or anyone spoke of her, she was who she was: a cripple . . . and a witch. Being who and what she was had saved the Duke of Wellington. No one could take that away from her by whispering and tittering behind a fan.

The last guests were halfway down the stairs when Parthenope finally finished talking to Peregrine. They came back to Sophie, and Parthenope looked at her. "Did you get that chair over here the way I think you did?"

"Yes." And all at once Sophie knew that, given the choice between laughter and tears, she'd take laughter. "Shall we go down now? Sir, I hope you'll stay at least for a bite to eat—"

"Oh, he's staying all right. *Messieurs?*" Parthenope called, raising her voice and turning back to look at the musicians' alcove.

Most of the musicians had gone down to the kitchen for their own refreshments, but a couple of them were still there, conversing in low voices. Sophie hoped they too would take the duke's lecture to heart and not gossip about the evening's events. But on Parthenope's call, they stopped chatting. "*Oui, mademoiselle,*" one of them said, and picked up his violin.

"What is it? What are you doing?" Sophie asked. Parthenope had that particular gleam in her eye that she had come to mistrust.

"Just tying up all the loose ends. I'll see you downstairs in a little while." Parthenope almost skipped toward the stairs.

The musicians—two of the violinists and a flutist—had started to play softly as she fled—a waltz, but at a slower, gentler tempo. Sophie looked from Parthenope to the musicians, and a faint feeling of alarm pushed aside her weariness. It became much more than faint when Peregrine cleared his throat quietly.

"Lady Sophie, will you give me the honor of this dance?" he said, bowing to her.

No. Oh, no. Parthenope was going to *pay* for this. "But—I can't. You know I can't. Can't we just—"

"Well, strictly speaking, I can't either. I'm wearing boots, which makes dancing with any grace quite impossible. But I understand that you're wearing shoes that might make up for that a bit, and there's no one here to mind if we stumble and miss our steps." He held his hand out to her. "Sophie, please?"

How could she ignore the plea in his voice . . . and in his eyes? She gave him her hand and let him help her up. He put his hand on her waist, a little higher than usual, so that when she placed her hand on his shoulder, her right elbow was braced on his arm. He took her other hand in his and looked at her. "Ready?"

No. Never. She swallowed hard—how had her mouth gotten so dry?—and nodded. He began to move, very slowly at first and not to the music, in a simplified form of the slowest part of the German waltz. She gripped his hand hard and stared at his chin (dark with stubble—he had come straight from Ghent, hadn't he?), trying to keep her balance, trying to remember the steps, trying not to die on the spot. She was doing what she thought she'd never do again—she was *dancing*. She was out of time to the music and clumsy and awkward . . . and it was the most wonderful feeling in the world.

He didn't say a word for the first few minutes, apart from asking, "Are you tired?" after they'd made a couple of trips up and down the room.

"I . . . I'm not sure."

"Tell me if you are."

A moment later, when she could spare a particle of attention to something other than her feet and legs, she realized he was smiling. "What?" she whispered.

"Oh, nothing. . . . Well, not really nothing. I just realized I've won my wager with you."

That yanked her out of her daze. "What wager?"

"Don't you remember? It was at Mrs. Halliday's ball. I said that I should dance with you within a year."

"I—" For some reason, Sophie couldn't say anything more. Her throat seemed disinclined to help produce speech just then.

"So I've won. We didn't establish stakes, did we? Then I'll

name them now: that you'll listen to me. I have a great deal to say to you." He paused. "Or at least, I thought I did. I spent the boat ride to Ostend and the ride from Ghent composing a speech for you, but I'm afraid I can't remember one word of it. Oh, Sophie." His hand tightened on hers. "I was so worried about you here in Brussels with Mrs. Carswell—you don't know how often I nearly said to the devil with everything and crossed the Channel to rescue you . . . until I found out about the comte. Lord Palmerston was gracious enough to take my word that it was vital to England's security that I come over here—"

"To rescue me," she said.

"No," he said firmly. "Or maybe at first I planned to. But I discovered quickly enough what a misguided notion that was."

She risked a glance up at his face. He was looking down at her, eyes filled with awe. "Your magic," he said.

She looked away quickly, then lifted her chin and met his eyes once more. "Yes, my magic."

"It's . . . it's—"

"It's part of who I am. If it frightens you—if it's too—"

"It doesn't frighten me. Sophie, I can't even imagine what you're capable of—the wonders you can do." He shook his head and tried to smile, but his voice was shaky too when he spoke. "It's taken me a while, but I think I've finally come to understand that you're the last person in the world I need to protect. Cherish and honor and love with all my heart? Absolutely. Rescue or protect? Never."

Sophie felt a laugh tremble about her lips. "Parthenope always thought you were a fairly bright lad."

He stopped dancing, suddenly, so that she had to cling to him to steady herself. He took advantage of her moment of imbalance to draw her closer to him. "Impudent chit," he whispered, lips just brushing her ear. "Let's see how much sauce you care to dish out when we're married."

She rested her head against his shoulder and closed her eyes. All the tension and fear of the past hours drained away, leaving excitement and exultation in their wake . . . and something else.

"Quite a lot of sauce, I should think," she whispered back. "It's easy to be saucy when you're so happy."

Author's Note

Sophie's illness was polio. A small part of her is based on a lady I knew and loved as a child who'd had the same affliction, but who was not, as far as I know, a witch. She wore special shoes that helped her walk more normally, as did, by the way, Prince Talleyrand, the foreign minister to both Napoléon and Louis XVIII. Talleyrand was born with a clubfoot, but his lameness didn't keep him from being one of the shakers and movers of the era. Not all people with handicaps were so lucky. Outward disabilities like Sophie's were often assumed to be symptoms of inner defects, either mental or spiritual, or divine punishment for somehow being "bad." As much as I love history, there are parts of it I am glad no longer hold true.

Writing this book was like eating a *huge* box of candy, at least to this history geek. The second decade of the nineteenth century was an amazing time in London, in particular the years 1814 to 1815, which saw the two defeats of Napoléon (and the accompanying celebrations). These were the golden years for that London social institution Almack's, where a group of aristocratic ladies, including the fascinating Lady Jersey, decreed who was "in" and who wasn't. (I dream of writing a book about Lady Jersey and the Patronesses of Almack's someday!) Most of the places mentioned in this book were real, including Rotten Row and Carlton House, London home of the Prince Regent. The party at Carlton House, where Sophie and Peregrine quarreled, was based on an actual one, just as smaller details like Sophie's clothes and the customs of riding at five P.M. in Hyde Park and wearing black gloves when in mourning were part of life at the time. To prevent confusion, I have changed or blurred a few details as a compromise between historical correctness and ease of understanding for today's readers.

Brussels really was the party capital of Europe in spring 1815, as I have depicted it. English aristocrats swarmed over the Channel after Napoléon's first defeat in 1814, having been deprived of European travel (and shopping!) for so many years. Between them and the masses of officers sent over to engage in redefeating Napoléon (which they eventually did, at the Battle of Waterloo in June), life in Brussels was a constant succession of balls, concerts, dinners, picnics, breakfasts, routs, and card parties. Even on the eve of the first engagements of the Battle of Waterloo, Brussels partied, and many British officers fought and died still in their evening clothes. If you're interested in learning more about this time and place, I highly recommend Georgette Heyer's *An Infamous Army* (her account of the battle was studied by officers in training at Sandhurst, Britain's West Point) and Nick Foulkes's nonfictional but delightfully engaging *Dancing into Battle: A Social History of the Battle of Waterloo*.

Particular thanks are due, as always, to my agent, Emily Sylvan Kim, for her unflagging cheer and support, to senior editor Kate

Farrell at Henry Holt for her unerring and fabulous editing (thank you so much, Kate, for helping me get out of my own way), as well as to Sarah Dotts Barley and Rebecca Hahn. Profound thanks and my love to Elisabeth Lorin for correcting my execrable French (any infelicities or errors that remain are solely mine), for her gracious hospitality on visits to New York, and for being her warm, wonderful self. For community, camaraderie, fellowship, and information on parakeets I am indebted to the members of Verla Kay's Blueboards, where I spend far too much online time . . . but it's always time well spent. Thank you also to my dear friend, fellow history geek, and source of writerly support, Regina Scott, who has cohosted our teen history blog, Nineteenteen, since 2007 . . . and thank you to our readers for their continued interest, questions, and suggestions for book titles. And most of all, thank you to my beloved family for enduring my being such a bore about 1815 and for often even joining in my history geekiness.

Marissa Doyle